"Unputdownable"
(HIM magazine on DF

"A fine example of this
(Gay Times on FOR'

"A powerful futuris.
(Capital Gay on DEA

"...the MASTER of gay thrillers ... Me
name is a byword for thrilling gay adventure in
the past, present and future"
(Millivres on AQUAMARINE)

"This rip-roaring and colourful new gay thriller zooms along with a breathless enthusiasm that never flags"
(Time Out on ICE, WIND AND FIRE)

"Gripping"
(Scotsgay on STORM TIDE)

Also by MEL KEEGAN

THE DECEIVERS
GROUND ZERO
MORE THAN HUMAN
MINDSPACE
NOCTURNE
THE SWORDSMAN
DANGEROUS MOONLIGHT
TIGER, TIGER.
WINDRAGE
THE WINDS OF CHANCE
STORM TIDE
WHITE ROSE OF NIGHT
AN EAST WIND BLOWING
FORTUNES OF WAR
ICE, WIND AND FIRE

HELLGATE Series:
HELLGATE: The Rabelais Alliance
HELLGATE: Deep Sky
HELLGATE: Cry Liberty
HELLGATE: Probe
HELLGATE: Flashpoint
HELLGATE: Event Horizon

NARC Series:
DEATH'S HEAD (Complete & Unabridged)
EQUINOX (reissue)
SCORPIO
STOPOVER
APHELION

HOME FROM THE SEA

Mel Keegan

DreamCraft Multimedia, Australia

HOME FROM THE SEA

This edition published in June 2013 by DreamCraft Multimedia.

ISBN: 978-0-9872328-7-8

DreamCraft Multimedia
Box 270, Brighton 5048, South Australia

See MEL KEEGAN ONLINE for everything Keegan:
http://www.melkeegan.com

This edition is printed and bound in the United States

HOME FROM THE SEA

Chapter One

At four in the afternoon on an April day on which winter seemed to be making a determined effort to return, The Raven was quiet as a tomb. Jim Fairley stood behind the bar, rag in one hand, pewter tankard in the other, gazing through the little square window panes at an iron-gray horizon under a sky that promised no good to seamen by nightfall. A gale was coming up. After six years of watching the same sky through this very window, Jim could read it like a book. And sometimes six years seemed closer to sixty.

The wind was already starting to roar in the chimney, and he knew he should fetch in firewood, fill the water jugs from the big barrels under the eaves and put up the shutters. Gale or calm, The Raven would be crowded by seven, and between then and midnight he would be busy. It was not the only tavern on the road from Exmouth to Budleigh, but it was the best. Jim did not water the ale, he served full measure of rum, and he kept a table that was well respected.

The aromas of rabbit pie and salt beef, stewing apples and figgy duff had already begun to make the mouth water. Mrs. Clitheroe was back there in the kitchen, singing to herself, talking to the old black cat and the terrier that kept down the mice and rats. The old lady had no ear for a tune and was three-quarters deaf into the bargain, with a broad Lancashire accent and a girth to be measured in yards, but there was no better cook this side of Exeter itself, and Jim had long ago realized he was lucky to have her.

With a sigh, he set down the last of the tankards and poured a small rum for himself. The sound of cork squeaking out of bottle alerted old Fred Bailey to the possibility of a refill, and he raised his head from its pillow on his forearms, which rested on the scarred surface of the table in the chimney corner. He was the only customer at this time in the afternoon, and for every glass he paid for, he drank three. Jim gave him a wry look. Bailey replied with a gap-toothed grin and hunted through his pockets for a copper before he came swaggering up to the bar.

In his day he had been a sailor – a topman in the king's navy, if he was telling the truth, and Jim saw no reason to doubt him. He told stories to curdle the belly and set the hair on end, of storms at sea that almost swallowed warships, and the eerie calm in which the sea shone at midnight with its own light, while the voices of strange creatures sang out of the weird green twilight.

He was old now, stooped, with the reputation of a rummy, but on days like this one Jim actually envied him. At least Fred Bailey had something to remember. When he had a couple of sheets in the wind and drowsed by the hearth there, his mind would be miles and years away, reliving adventures Jim could only dream about, with the kind of mates Jim had never known, and probably never would. The Raven, he decided as he poured another small rum for Bailey, was hardly the most exciting place in the world.

Yet the tavern was his home, his business – his prison, if he wanted to be dismal about it. He knew he had nothing to complain about, and even if he had sobbed on the shoulders of the locals, they would only have scorned him. Jim Fairley was just 26. He owned The Raven right down to the last stick of firewood and keg of rum in the cellar. He had 60 silver shillings squirreled away in a leather sack under the bar, hidden beneath a broken stone known only to himself. And he had his life – and all four of his limbs, when he could so easily have been dead or crippled.

His left leg irked him but it was still attached in place, it was warm and it worked well enough to get him around, so long as he did not walk too far or too fast. Today it ached a little, reminding him keenly of London chimney smoke and the rumble of coach wheels ... of his father, and more pain than a lad of fifteen years should ever have had to learn about.

The day was long ago, but so sharp in his memory, it could still eclipse the present. For an instant Jim actually saw the street, felt the red-hot bar of pain, before he deliberately thrust the unwelcome scenes aside. He pushed the mug across the bar toward Bailey, and then toasted Fred in the dark rum. "Your health, Master Bailey."

"Aye, and yours, Master Fairley." Fred raised his mug and drank. "And you'll forgive me for mentionin' it, but you look peaky."

"I do?" Jim's brows rose, and he gave the leg a thump with one clenched fist. "It pains me sometimes."

"When it gets cold, and the rain comes in, and the wind." Bailey pressed one hand into the small of his back. "Don't I know about it? Don't us all!" He drank a little and considered Jim with a sobriety that was, in him, alarming. "You know what's wrong with you? Young feller like you. Oh, aye."

For one moment Jim almost choked on the mouthful of rum he had just taken, and he forced the muscles of his gullet to swallow smoothly. If old Fred had even the vaguest inkling of what was 'wrong' with him, then Jim was in dead trouble.

What was *wrong* with him?

He needed a good one. A good long one, with one of the handsome young seamen who tromped along the coast every week from Plymouth to Portsmouth, leaving one ship and going to another. He needed a tasty sailor of about his own age, who would take a single look at Jim and just *know*, the way like knew like ... a big, healthy lad who relished a bit of the other, a bit of rough instead of fluff, before he was on his way again and back at sea in a week, no one the wiser and both of them sated enough to hang onto sanity until the next time.

Seamen passed by every day and many stopped at The Raven. Jim was seldom short of company, and he knew he was choosy. He could have had the big Dutchman, three days ago – but the man's breath stank of pickled herrings. He could have gone with the blue eyed French sailor the day before – but he toyed with a knife and laughed at all the wrong remarks. He could have picked the young Scotsman with the fiery orange hair – but he was hairy as a bear. Not that there was anything particularly amiss with hairy men, Jim allowed, but his own preference was for something a little less shaggy, with a little tan on its hull, and –

"Your trouble," Fred Bailey was saying with keen insight, "is, you never get out. You never do ... stuff." He belched eloquently. "You never see nothin'. You never make the acquaintance of mates and enemies."

"I'm talking to you," Jim argued.

"I don't count. I'm a customer." Bailey frowned at him. "You want to watch out, Master Fairley. There's a nasty old biddy called Time, an' if you don't watch out for 'er, she'll catch you napping. You'll wake up one day an' you'll be an old rummy, like me – well past it. There ain't a lass in all of Devon an' Dorset that'll 'ave you, an' then what'll you do?"

Jim almost chuckled. Bailey did not know it, but there was already not a lass in Devon, Dorset, or any other county who would have him, because as soon as the doors were locked and the lamps were turned down, the truth would be out before the candles. Lasses asked for services Jim did not have to give, and twice he had blamed his apparent uselessness on his injury. The leg had been his salvation.

The truth was very different, but neither the Dorset girls nor Fred Bailey had any business knowing about it. Jim's left leg would be weak, frail, as long as he lived, but the right was strong enough to make up for it and what lay between was as virile as any man. More than some, Jim thought ruefully as he watched Bailey trying to nurse the rum in case there was no more where it came from, which could only mean his pockets were bare. Jim could either feed him rum or rabbit pie and stewed apples, and Fred knew it was food he would be getting, not grog.

"You," he said sagely, "need to get out." He gestured with the mug. "Out of this place. See the world, while you're …" another burp, more tenor, more resonant "…still young enough to do it."

The worst of it was, he was absolutely right and Jim could not argue a syllable of what he had said. The Raven *was* his prison. But it was safe, comfortable, lucrative; and it was all that remained of his father. Jim sighed, leaned both elbows on the bar and frowned out through the tiny glass panes at a sky that was darkening gradually with clouds driven in by a threatening wind.

He might have told Bailey that Arthur Fairley had invested every penny he had in the tavern; that he had come out from London hoping clean sea air would heal his lungs, which were rotten with the city smoke and stench. If Arthur had made the move five years sooner, the healing magic might have worked for him, but it was already too late when he bought The Raven. He was buried in the churchyard up at Budleigh, not very far from the previous owner.

"Aye, I know," Bailey sighed, as if he had heard every word Jim had not said. "Your da were a good man – 'e set you up, right enough, with this place … an' 'e done good by old Charlie Chegwidden, an' all."

"Charlie was an odd one," Jim mused. "I only knew him for two weeks, mind you. Hardly enough time to get to know him at all, before he gasped his last and Doctor Hardesty was pronouncing him dead as mutton."

"Charlie were all right. I knew his ma, before 'im. Thirty-odd year, she owned this place, afore it come to Charlie, an' then to you." Bailey drained the mug and set it down on the bar before Jim with a certain deliberation which hinted broadly. "Aye, nothin' wrong with old Charlie."

"No?" Jim stirred, and just as deliberately swept Bailey's mug up with his own, and plunged both into the pail of water to wash them. "Two whole weeks, after my father bought this place, he sits at the windows. Either here in the taproom or upstairs in his bedchamber. Just sits and looks out, staring at the sea, or at the path, like he's waiting for somebody or something. Never says a word. Never tells me what he's waiting for, or who. And then he falls on his face on the floor, right there, and I'm sending a lad to run for the doctor. It would have been quicker to send for the undertaker."

"Well, watchin' don't make a man queer," Bailey protested. "Charlie were a seaman, like me, 'sept 'e were in merchantmen an' me, I were king's navy, thirty long year. Could be, 'e were just watchin' the ocean, wantin' to go back to days that'll never come again." His voice was rich with nostalgia. "Last time Charlie shipped out, I were in port meself. Charlie went out on the *Rose of Gloucester*, out of Plymouth. By God, that ship were bloody notorious! But Charlie were lucky enough to be off 'er afore trouble struck. As I recall, 'is old ma took the coach down, an' kissed 'im goodbye on the dock, like she thought she'd never see 'im again."

For some moments Bailey was silent and Jim sorted through piles of ancient, dusty memories until he remembered Charlie Chegwidden's stories in useful detail. "She didn't," he said with a trace of wry humor.

"Didn't what?" Bailey yawned, issuing a draft of rum fumes.

"See him again." Jim stooped to retrieve the mugs and polishing rag. "The way Charlie told it, he wandered on home – oh, about eight years ago, would it be? – and his old ma was on her deathbed. She lived three weeks after he got back to The Raven, but she never woke up, never actually set eyes on him, before they took her up to the churchyard and did the necessary."

"Is that a fact, now?" Bailey seemed surprised. "Well, by God, I never knew that. I were at sea, meself, when the old lady passed away, an' only learned of it when I got me boots back on dry land an' came by for a pint. On 'er deathbed, you say?"

"That's how Charlie told it." Jim's hands could polish tankards all by themselves, they had been doing it so long. He was intent on the memories of Chegwidden – weatherworn and probably not nearly as old as he had seemed, sitting at the window on the seaward side of the hearth, gazing out, watching for something or someone who never arrived.

When he sold The Raven to Arthur Fairley, he had only one request, and it was not so strange. He was too sick and too tired to manage the tavern, but he would sell it for a low price, if the new owner would give him a clean bed and three squares a day, for as long as he still drew breath, and then see him decently buried at the end.

In fact, Jim's father knew nothing at all about running a tavern, and Charlie was invaluable in those two short weeks. He would not let the new owner be cheated on the price of ale and rum, and he convinced Mrs. Clitheroe to stay on and cook.

The churchyard in Budleigh was a busy place, Jim thought darkly. Old Nell Chegwidden was there, with Charlie right beside her; and Arthur Fairley lay on the low hillside under the big chestnut tree, where an empty space was reserved for his son.

And may it stay empty, Jim prayed fervently, for many years to come! He had even less desire to join his father than he had to linger in The Raven for the rest of his days, waiting for the big, handsome seamen to tromp up the path, buy a jar of rum, exchange knowing glances and winks with the proprietor, and follow him upstairs for an hour of –

"And another thing," Fred Bailey burped. "You need to get yourself a lass, afore it's too late. You know what folks in these parts sez about you."

"What do they say? That I'm a eunuch?" Jim guessed.

"Well, mebbe somethin' like that," Bailey muttered.

"And *mebbe* they'd be something like right." With a soft curse, Jim slapped his leg. "A lass, interested in the likes of me? It's already too late, Fred. It was too late for me when I was fifteen years old. Don't believe me? Go'n talk to Molly Hutchins. She'd be glad to tell you how much use I am in the dark."

The experience still stung. Four years ago, Molly had cornered him – a fresh, pretty girl of seventeen, looking for a likely husband. The scene ended in tears of disappointment and even a gentle kind of pity, when Molly convinced herself Jim was incapable due to old, old injuries. She mourned her own loss and his imagined plight for at least two days before she set her sights on a locksmith from Exmouth, and Jim was off the hook – chagrined, relieved, embarrassed, but at liberty.

The mournful look on Bailey's seamed, walnut-brown face almost made him regret telling the lie, but honesty might have been much worse. True enough, Bailey was an old seaman, but he had never looked at Jim and *known*. Not like the big Dutchman with the herring breath, whose hands were everywhere and who did not want to take no for an answer until Jim bit him hard enough to draw blood, and told him to bugger off, and not come back unless he had eaten nothing but rose petals, drunk nothing but spring water, for three days.

"Well, it's dead sorry I am about that, lad," Bailey said with all due sympathy. "So, you, uh, you 'ad a lass afore bein' fifteen?"

"No," Jim said darkly. There had been a few lads, he thought with acid humor, but no lasses. Not then, and not later. Of this he kept silent.

Bailey's eyes widened. "Then you're ..."

"A virgin?" Jim choked back a ribald snort. In fact, in a way it was perfectly true.

"Um ... aye." Bailey fidgeted in exquisite discomfort of his own making. "An' I'm right sorry about that, an' all. But it don't change the other."

"What other?" Jim was still thinking about the Dutchman, wondering what the odds were that he might be hunting for roses in April.

"You need to *git*. Out," Bailey told him. "An' aye, I know you buried your da a long time ago, an' I *know* this place is 'is legacy ... but yon door's goin' to start lookin' like a coffin lid if you don't get out an' feel the wind in your face, afore your bones start to rust up like mine." He shoved himself away from the bar and took a few unsteady steps toward that very door. "Gotta piss. Be back."

"Rabbit pie, and apples," Jim promised with a faint, indulgent smile as he watched Bailey make his way out and around in the direction of the stable and coach house, which were ten yards east of the tavern. The building stood a scant dozen yards above the beach, so close, gulls often clustered around the door to sun themselves and when the wind blew hard out of the south, the floor could be sandy.

Today the south wind whipped inside as Bailey opened the door, and it smelt of the sea, cool and clean on Jim's face. He breathed it in, savored it, and relished the idea that the same wind blew over the Canary Islands, the Azores, the Leeward Islands, Jamaica, Barbados.

The names were alchemy, sorcery, and Jim knew how right Fred Bailey was. He was 26, and for more than six of those years he had stood at this bar, polishing tankards, pouring ale and rum, counting coins, watching out for customs men from the Exeter and listening for rumors of smugglers on the coast who might be carrying brandy and treats from France –

Watching out for fine-looking seamen who enjoyed a good one … a good *long* one, with a jar of ale first and a sound sleep after, and not a word said to a soul.

This was what Jim needed most, he hold himself as he stacked the tankards in preparation for the evening trade. Mrs. Clitheroe was frying onions now, and Jim's belly growled. A voyage into exotic waters might have been grand; a roll in bed with a handsome lad would have been just as welcome, but first he needed to get to work. The firewood was unlikely to haul itself inside and he must make up the hearth, fill the water jugs and then batten down the shutters before the wind rose any further.

With a soft curse he came around the bar, strong on his right leg, weak on the left, which gave him a limp which had dogged him since he was not much more than a child. But he was lucky to be alive, and quite intelligent enough to know it. His gloves were stuffed into the pockets of the coat that hung with his hat on the peg by the window. He fetched them out, pulled them on and opened the door to the teasing, tormenting sea wind.

Chapter Two

The storm went through before dawn, leaving torn thatch, broken windows, a few trees down and a lot of seaweed dumped on the beach. The mountains of wrack would be stinking in a few days, if local farmers did not gather it up and dig it into the potato fields. Along with cow and horse dung it grew fine vegetables, and since learning how potatoes were grown, Jim had always found it easier to eat them when he knew they were raised on seaweed.

The Raven suffered no more damage than a shutter that came loose in the wind, and he was hammering up fresh timber, with a mouth still full of nails, when he heard footsteps behind him. They were coming up the path which stretched back to Plymouth in the west and wound on, following the line of the shore, till it reached Portsmouth in the east.

The footsteps stopped behind him and he said, muffled around the nails, "Just wait there, friend, I'll be done in a minute."

"Take your time, I'm in no hurry."

The voice was tenor and soft, the accent rich with the sounds of far off places. Jim felt a shiver race the length of his spine and hesitated in the act of striking the last half dozen nails. He twisted his head to look over his shoulder, but he was squinting directly into the morning sun and caught only an impression of a tall, rangy figure in a dark coat, a man with long hair, a hump on his shoulder and some kind of beast at his left side.

With an impatient grunt, he finished with the nails and threw down the hammer. "Done, thank God," he muttered as the stranger came on around to the door, beside which the shutter had broken lose near the end of the storm. The light was in his face now, and Jim found himself looking up a hand's span into wide, clear eyes, some shade between blue and violet and silver. They were framed by long hair the color of a hayfield in August, just before the last cut of the season was made; and the hump on the man's back turned into the round shape of the belly of the mandolin he carried on a strap across his chest. He was thirty at least, perhaps a few years more, if Jim was any judge – not so very much older than Jim himself – and when he smiled, he showed a full set of nice, white teeth.

The beast at his left side was a black spaniel who looked up at Jim as if she expected something of him. Jim dusted off his hands and offered the right to the stranger. "Now, you're not from these parts. I've never seen you on this path, and I've been here years. *You* ... I'd remember."

"Would you?" The man's shake was firm, dry. "And you're right, it has to be ten years since I was here, and you weren't at The Raven when I slept here for a night or three. I'm Toby Trelane." His eyes were almost mauve as he looked down at Jim across the little difference in their height.

And for just a moment Jim was so sure he saw the flicker of recognition, he caught his breath. Like usually knew like. Not always, but almost, and often enough for Jim's heart to skip in his chest and then race. He cleared his throat and held onto Toby Trelane's hand several seconds too long.

"Jim Fairley. What can I do for you?"

"You can tell me where to find the owner," Toby began.

Jim tapped his chest with one thumb. "You're looking at him."

"No, it's Charlie Chegwidden I need to see." Then Toby checked as he saw some shadow pass across Jim's face. "What?"

"The most you're going to see of Charlie is a headstone," Jim told him with a nod in the direction of the churchyard. "They planted him not much under six years ago. Goddamnit, did he owe you money?"

"Money?" Toby backed off a pace. His shoulders seemed to slump for a moment before he unslung the mandolin and leaned against the wall under the thatched eaves. "Not exactly. Not money, anyway, but ... well, damn. I'm not just too late, I'm too late by years."

And it was dire news, Jim saw. "He did owe you money, didn't he?" he guessed. "Or something as good as. You came here depending on what he had to give you?"

The remarkable eyes narrowed in the morning sun, and Toby breathed a long sigh. "Let's just say, life would have been a bloody sight easier if old Charlie'd been sitting on the bench there, smoking that poisonous pipe of his, like he always swore he'd be when we ... when I got back here."

"You took too long," Jim said thoughtfully. "Going by the stories he told, he arrived here about eight years ago, just in time to watch them bury his mother, and he ran The Raven till my father bought it from him."

Toby's brows rose, creasing his forehead. "He sold the tavern? You mean he – he sold it and walked away?" He seemed astonished, even appalled.

"Sold it," Jim affirmed, "but he didn't walk. He stayed right here till the day he died, which was about two weeks after me and my father took over." He frowned up at Toby. "You want to walk over to the churchyard? They buried him properly, with his name on a stone, and the parson said all the right words. Damn, he wasn't your kith and kin was he?"

But Toby made negative gestures. "No, he wasn't my uncle, if that's what you're thinking. But we were on the same vessel, and..."

And if anything Fred Bailey said had a grain of truth in it, shipmates were even closer than kin. Jim stooped for the hammer and leftover nails, and beckoned Toby toward the door. "Come and have a jar. You'll feel better with a rum inside you." It was close enough to luncheon for his own belly to be hoping for food, and as Toby and the spaniel stepped inside he asked, "You hungry? There's pie and pudding left from last night."

"Starving," Toby admitted as he retrieved the mandolin and set it down again carefully, just inside the door, where it would neither be sat on nor fallen over. "I've walked over from Exmouth, and I didn't get any breakfast! Can Bess have a dish of water?"

The spaniel wagged her tail as she heard her name, and Jim was seduced in an instant. "She can have a dish of ale, if she likes it."

"She likes it, but she gets drunk. Water'll do," Toby decided.

"And a slice of rabbit pie," Jim added. "And yourself –?"

"Pie sounds grand." Toby was swinging off his gray coat, and threw it onto a nearby chair. He glanced once around the tavern, and then back at Jim. "You haven't changed anything."

"What would I change, and why would I bother?" Jim stepped behind the bar and poured two mugs of brown ale before he went on into the kitchen to rummage for plates, bowls, spoons. He raised his voice so Toby would hear as he said, "My father changed nothing after Charlie departed, and the place reminds me of my old dad, so I keep it as it is."

"Then, your father's ...?" Toby was at the door, looking into the kitchen, which Mrs. Clitheroe had left clean and tiny enough to pass muster at a butler's inspection.

"My father's also in the churchyard, with Charlie and his ma." Jim thrust platters and dishes at Toby, and gestured at the tall pitcher of water.

He watched as Toby brimmed a dish for the spaniel. The man had fine, long-fingered hands and they were not battered, like those of a seaman, nor scarred like a soldier's hands, nor blue with gunpowder embedded under the skin, like the hands of a naval gunner. They were the hands of a musician, and Jim could easily imagine them playing another kind of music on his own skin.

The thought inspired a shiver and he stepped back out of the way as Toby set down the bowl. Bess lapped noisily, messily, and Toby scratched behind her ears. Jim felt a rush of heat in his cheeks, and covered the moment of vulnerability with activity. He pushed rabbit pie and plum pudding at Toby, and fetched his own, and Bess's.

The man had not been joking when he said he was starving. For some time Toby Trelane was so intent on the food, he did not even notice Jim's scrutiny, though Jim took him apart bone by bone, missing nothing from the windblown tangle of the hay-colored hair to the dull, scuffed leather of boots that had seen many a mile.

The dog was little less hungry, and Jim guessed Toby made sure Bess ate even when he was down on his luck himself. Without any doubt, he had arrived here expecting Charlie Chegwidden to have something for him, and Jim felt a pang of regret. Toby was almost certainly down to the last tuppence in his pockets, and he did not have the look of a seaman or a farmer, so work was not going to be so easy to find – at least, not in this area.

The thoughts preoccupied him and he did not notice the wide blue eyes on him until Toby demanded, "Did I sprout a wart on my nose?"

"No!" Jim chuckled and ate a little. "You said you've just come over from Exmouth. From a ship?"

"Yes." Toby took a drink. "It's the first time I've been back in the country for a long time."

"But you're not a sailor," Jim observed.

"I'm not?" The edge was off Toby's hunger now, and he divided his attention between Jim and the food. "Who says I'm not?"

"Your hands do." Jim gestured at them. "They're not the hands of a seaman – nor a fisherman, nor a farmer!"

"You're sharp." Toby gave him a rueful smile.

The kind of smile that filled a man's belly with butterflies. Jim was trying hard to see the signs, but this Toby Trelane was not so easy to read and for the moment he bided his time. Better to say nothing than to say the wrong thing. If Toby were the God bothering kind, he would march away in a righteous temper; and if he were furious enough, insulted enough, he might march right to the lieutenant at the local garrison, and Jim Fairley could be looking at the inside of a prison cell.

"So you're ... a scholar?" he guessed.

"Balladsinger." Toby gestured at the mandolin. "I can play a madrigal, sing a hundred shanties and love songs from France, Spain, Italy, and tell the brand of stories that'll earn me dinner. And a bed," he added with a note of wry humor. "You, uh, don't have a use for a balladsinger?"

"To entertain the kind of rummies who get falling-down drunk in here?" Jim was about to say his customers would not have known a sonnet from a psalm and Toby was wasting his time, but the morning light was just then gilding the man's face, shining on the big brass ring he wore in the lobe of his right ear, and he bit off the words. "You can try your luck, if you like," he offered. "I can't promise you a round of applause for your efforts, much less a shower of coins at your feet, but ..." He gestured at the corner between hearth and windows. "Pull up a stool, tell my old rummies a lively tale tonight, see what happens next."

What should happen next, he thought, was a rousing cheer for the traveling storyteller, a great deal of ale swilling, and then the customers would go reeling home while the proprietor and the balladsinger would climb the steep, creaking stairs up to the little room over the kitchen where Jim had a goose feather mattress, and –

"I'll do that," Toby was saying. "The worst I can do is get them so bored they shout at me to shut up!" He sopped up the last gravy with a wedge of pie crust. "So Charlie stayed here till he died?"

"He was sick when my dad and me got here," Jim told him. "Too sick to keep the tavern for his own, but smart enough to write his room and board into the bill of sale. He had a bedchamber upstairs, and he'd sit at the table there, by the window, and he'd ... watch."

"Watch what?" Toby wondered.

Jim's shoulders lifted in an eloquent shrug. "I used to wonder. I thought, maybe he was watching the sea. Or the path. Like he was waiting for something." Or *someone*. He lifted a brow at Toby. "You knew him well?"

"As well as a young man could get to know an old man, when they were on the same ship," Toby said doubtfully.

"But you're not a seaman," Jim protested.

"Not now." Toby made dismissive gestures. "I was only at sea for one voyage and it was ... quite a short one, as voyages go." He pinned on a smile and answered Jim's frown with a shrug. "It came to nothing. I might still have been at sea, but Dame Fortune had her own plans for me. So Charlie was sick?"

"Sick as a dog. Something to do with his guts, or maybe his heart, or perhaps both. We never knew. One day he just fell on his face, right there on the floor. I sent a boy to run, fast as he could, for John Hardesty, the doctor, but Charlie was stone-cold dead before the man got here and they buried him the next day."

"Ah." Toby had switched his attention to the figgy duff and the dollop of cold custard and was chewing slowly, thoughtfully, now his hunger was mostly appeased. He looked up at Jim with a speculative expression. "He, um, he had ... things?"

"You mean, possessions?" Jim's brows rose. "Everyone's got things."

"Then, if his old ma was already passed over," Toby mused, "what became of his possessions?"

It was an extremely good question, and Jim had no idea of the answer. "My father took care of all that. I never saw what happened to Charlie's stuff, but I don't remember it being sold and nobody ever beat down the door, demanding anything to settle debts. My father would have tossed out his things, if they were trash, or we could still be using them around the place, if they were any good." He sat back with the mug of rum and cocked his head curiously at Toby. "Charlie had something belonging to you." Not a question.

"You could say that."

"Something very valuable?"

But Toby only shrugged and looked away, which was as evasive a gesture as Jim had ever seen.

"Something secret, then?" he guessed.

"*Something*, at any rate." Toby spooned a large chunk of pudding into his mouth, and seemed to use it as an excuse not to talk.

"Well, I hate to disappoint you," Jim said honestly as he pushed up to his feet, "but if Charlie's stuff is still here, I have no idea what it'd be, or where. Would you recognize it, if you saw it?"

"Oh, yes." Toby's voice was dark, heavy. "Look, I'm sorry, Jim, it was just a bit of business between Charlie and me, and I daresay it died with him. I didn't mean to bring bad news to your door."

"You haven't." Jim had reached for the poker, which stood in the corner of the hearth with the set of fire irons, and was raking over the coals. They were smoldering low, in need of attention. "It's not your fault Charlie was sick. And I wish I could tell you I had a tavern crowd that liked a song and a story, but they're a boozy lot in here."

"But then again," Toby argued, "you've probably never had a proper balladsinger, have you?"

"Never *had* one of any description." Jim's eyes drifted over Toby's slender, rangy limbs. "Not yet, anyway."

"Then … I'll try my luck tonight." Toby finished the pudding in one bite and gathered up the dishes, and Bess's. "I'll wash these up, and I'll chop you some fresh firewood, and I can polish those windows."

"You don't have to," Jim began.

"Let me pay for luncheon before I do something honest to earn dinner," Toby said slowly.

And Jim could have sworn he was looking over the proprietor of The Raven from the buckle shoes to the brown britches and the pale green shirt which was open at Jim's throat, showing a generous expanse of his chest. Jim could not recall having been stripped naked by a man's eyes quite so comprehensively, and his throat squeezed.

But then Toby was moving, before Jim could make anything of the moment, and for the fifth time he smothered a curse. Toby Trelane was damnably difficult to read, and the price of making a mistake was dangerously high. It was one thing to daydream about a big, good-looking Dutchman, but quite another to breathe a word about such fancies to any man, unless you knew him better than you knew your own brother. Jim had a healthy fear of the magistrate – the bastinado, shackles and stocks and prison walls.

So he clenched his teeth and retreated behind the bar for the afternoon's ritual of polishing tankards while he waited for Mrs. Clitheroe to arrive and start the evening's pies and puddings. And he settled himself to watch Toby closely before he said a word or lifted a brow at him.

The woman arrived an hour later, already singing tunelessly as she bustled in from the tavern yard in the back. She thumped down a basket of meat and vegetables and shouted through in a voice made hoarse by thirty years of smoking tobacco and sipping gin. "'Tis only me, Master Jim!" And without waiting for an answer she began to murder an old Irish tune as she slammed salt pork and potatoes into the roasting pans and raked out the hearth.

The sound of an axe took Jim to the windows in the corner of the taproom. From there he could watch Toby work, and he whistled softly. The woodpile stood in the lee of the tavern, where the building kept out the wind and rain. It was a suntrap, and at eleven in the morning already warm enough for a man to work up an honest sweat. Toby had taken off the waistcoat and the patched cream linen shirt, and he knew how to swing an axe. He was facing Jim as he worked, keeping up a steady rhythm, and Jim watched for the pleasure of it until Mrs. Clitheroe bawled his name.

"Master Jim, these onions is all gone black-rotten in the sack 'ere. Will I go to market for fresh uns, or will thee?"

"I'll go," Jim offered, grateful for the opportunity to get out for a while. He made a grab for coat and hat, which hung on a peg to the right of the door, searched the pockets for coins, and found three pennies and a few assorted ha'pennies and farthings. More than enough for a sack of onions. "I'll be back in an hour, Mrs. Clitheroe."

"Take thy time," she shouted, "I's got plenty to do afore I gets to onions. Give old Joe me best."

She meant old Joe Flynn, the farmer from the high side of Littleham, who sold vegetables from a stall every afternoon. His wife was sick, his eight children were working the farm and the eldest sons, Christopher and William, were smuggling, running the gauntlet of the Revenue men two or three times a month. The Flynn boys would be lucky to see twenty years of age, but with work so scarce in the area and the only alternatives the army, the navy or, worse, a merchantman, their options were few.

Shrugging into the coat, which was new just last winter and the color of a red deer, Jim rounded the corner of the tavern. Toby was still working, while Bess sat panting in a patch of shade. Jim watched the axe swing for a few moments – watched the sun gleam on pale honey skin, and when Toby paused to take a breath he said,

"I have to walk over to Salterton market, if you want to stroll along."

Toby drew a sinewy forearm over his face and considered the suggestion before he shook his head. "I've just walked over from Exmouth, and I'd rather get through these jobs."

"Jobs you gave yourself," Jim observed. "I never asked you to cut wood, nor polish windows."

"No, but if your local drinkers are as tone-deaf and dense as you think they are, it's an honest way to earn a crust and a place to sleep," Toby said with dust-dry humor.

It was on the tip of Jim's tongue to tell him, there were other ways – easier and far more pleasurable – to secure dinner and a mattress, but he would not say it. Few men would be seduced by the suggestion of whoring for their supper; even fewer would take the remark as a jest.

"As you will," he told Toby. "Take your time. Grab yourself a mug of ale to wet your throat when you're done here. I'll be back in an hour, in any case." He looked over Toby's long, lean body, which did not seem to own an ounce of spare flesh. "They haven't been overfeeding you, have they? Watch yourself, if you stay here for long. Mrs. Clitheroe'll have you fattened up like a piglet."

"She likes her men round and plump?" Toby chuckled.

"I haven't asked. She's old enough to be my grandmother – and yours." Jim settled the tricorn on his head and gave the brim a tug as the breeze got under it. "Does Bess like a bone? I'll see what I can find."

"She'd be grateful," Toby guessed, and leaned the haft of the axe over his left shoulder to watch as Jim made his way up onto the path which took passing seamen from port to port.

Salterton and Budleigh nestled together, just west of the east end of the long, shallow bay. On a fine day it was a pleasant walk, and if Jim told the truth, he needed the exercise. People often watched how he favored the lame leg and assumed he needed to rest it. The opposite was true. The damned limb needed all the gentle exercise he could find for it; the more it got, the better it was, but the term 'better' was relative.

He limped. He had limped since he was a lad of fifteen, still four months shy of his sixteenth birthday. He would always limp, and that was the fact of the matter. Jim had accepted it and only noticed the gammy leg when other people, people whose opinion mattered to him, saw it. Today he noticed it keenly and one part of him wanted to try to stride out, hide the limp, while the more sensible part told him to walk the way he always did, be himself, and if Toby Trelane did not like it, then be damned to him.

Instead, he turned his face to the sun, took a lungful of the salt sea air and steeled himself against turning back to see if Toby was still watching him, and what look might be on his face. Some people wore expressions of pity or sympathy; others were scornful. Jim did not need the former, and the latter aroused his anger faster than a mug of ale tossed in his face.

What he wanted from Toby Trelane was just the simple acceptance of what he was, and who, and he was surprised to find a tightness in his chest, a certain flutter in his belly, as he wondered if he would get it.

The coastal path was overgrown on both sides, rank with sea grasses and wild barley which had escaped from fields belonging to farmers like Joe Flynn. It followed the line of the bay, with the rush of the sea on his right hand as he walked east, and the sound of birds, the distant bleating of sheep, the creak of a plow and the clop of heavy horses, at his left hand.

It seemed to Jim that he had lived his whole life in this one small place. Had it only be six years and eight months? He was nineteen when his father fled the city with lungs gone to ruin and a wife and two daughters in the ground. Two more daughters, both older than Jim, were still living in London, one married to a merchant, the other to a tanner. The last he had heard from them, he had half a dozen little nieces and nephews, and a standing invitation to come back to town and make his home with Janet or Kate, with their husbands' blessing –

Not, he thought, that they or their husbands had any inkling of where Jim's heart lay. He wondered how shocked they would be, if they knew he was a very long way indeed from being the eunuch they supposed; that the leg might be gammy but it was rarely painful, and he could give better than he got in one of those wrestling bouts that took place on a mattress by the light of a brass lamp … and the *last* thing he desired was a wife.

He could imagine the shock on Janet's and Kate's faces – and the horror, perhaps even anger, on their husbands'. Once they knew the truth, he would no longer be welcome in their homes even as a guest, and in London it was infinitely harder for a man to be discreet in his affairs, even if he could make the acquaintance of seamen who knew about these things, which was doubtful.

Here in the west, never out of sight and sound of the ocean, situated between Plymouth and Portsmouth with the sailor's path right at his door, life was a good deal easier. Safer. Jim was not about to move, even if there were times when he felt as if he was almost becoming part of the stone and thatch of The Raven.

With a chuckle, he mocked himself and quickened his pace. The sooner he shared the time of day with Joe Flynn – discussed the weather, inquired about the health of his wife, asked circuitously about the luck of Chris and Wills in the activities for which the Government would gladly have hanged them both – the sooner he could get back to watching Toby Trelane, and trying to fathom if the man would accept the offer of a bit of slap and tickle, or if he would flush crimson to the roots of his straw-colored hair and make a beeline for the nearest magistrate.

Not knowing was a nuisance. Trying to read Toby's signs was a sweet kind of torture, and Jim was going to enjoy it.

Chapter Three

The drinkers came in by twos and threes, after six o'clock when the day's work was done and the farms and forges closed down and shops ran up their shutters. The local men were an odd lot, Jim thought. Many were miserable, too poor, rightly, to be drinking here on a Wednesday night, but too morose not to. Times were hard, work was meager, and if a strong-looking male between fourteen and forty years of age did not keep his weather-eye open, the pressmen would be on him before he knew it.

Two of Jim's regular drinkers had been pressed, one for a whaler, one for a warship. Both had been away from home for seven years before their ships put back into Portsmouth and they were free to go. Israel Cooper and Billy Mulligan were smart enough not to get *too* drunk, the first night ashore. They could have been picked up again by the same pressmen, sent right back to the same ships. No few innkeepers in the ports had a standing arrangement with pressmen, to get the newly-released crews comprehensively drunk and then send a message regarding fresh meat ready for collection. Mulligan and Cooper made their way back to Exmouth and the villages strung out along the coast, and if one could get enough rum into them, they would tell the kind of stories that made a man's hackles stand on end.

Jim had heard them all, and had no desire to shiver through them again. Tonight, he was intent on the balladsinger. The windows shone; the firewood was stacked four feet high beside the hearth and the kindling basket was full. The brass fixings around the fireplace were so bright, Jim could have seen his face in them, and Mrs. Clitheroe swore the man was an angel because he had taken out the kitchen rubbish, cleaned down her table, filled up her water pitchers, brought in the wood to fire the kitchen hearth tomorrow, fed the cat and the terrier, and made her a cup of tea while she put her feet up, waiting for the pies to be done.

He was, Jim thought, the biggest bundle of contradictions wrapped up in a single package, that one could imagine. He knew seamen and ships, but he was not a sailor. He knew tools, but was not a laborer. He never spoke about women, and the wide blue eyes followed Jim from taproom to windows to kitchen and back, but the sparkle of recognition and invitation Jim was waiting for was still not quite there, as if Toby were waiting for *something*. Or hiding something.

Confounded, enchanted, captivated, Jim poured rum and ale and counted coins while he watched the locals come drifting in for grog or food or both. At seven, when more than a dozen punters were enjoying the fire, throwing darts at a painted wooden board or playing backgammon on the big oak table – made of timbers from the merchantman *Lady Grey*, which had gone down in this bay in the big storms a dozen years ago – Toby picked up his mandolin.

Eyes turned toward him. The locals might be rummies, but they knew a balladsinger when they saw one, and it was a long time since any of Toby's species had passed by. Most people were always in the market for a new song, a new story, or an old one told with relish. Toby gestured with the black enameled instrument and dropped a flourishing bow before them.

"Will you gentlemen hear a song?" he wondered. "A tale of love and anguish, perhaps? Or a grand story of blood and guts and a man's raw courage?"

It was Billy Mulligan who grunted, "Aye, so long as ye don't ask for more'n a ha'penny for yer time and trouble, cuz I's got three ha'pennies left in me pocket, and two of them's for rum, afore I has to git off home to a wife that wishes me six foot under and tells me so, three times every bloody day afore breakfast."

A laugh ran around the tavern, though Mulligan was not joking, and they all knew it. His wife was a shrew. Jim had met her several times. Edna Mulligan was one of those who curled her lip at Jim, fully believing him a eunuch; and if a man was no use between a woman's sheets, he was no use, period. He could only imagine Billy's troubles, if middle age and girth had begun to conspire against him.

"A ha'penny would be grand," Toby said affably, "especially if it were a ha'penny from each and every one of you in this house tonight."

And little Israel Cooper, with the broken nose and the bright brass hoop in his left ear, piped up from the backgammon board, "Not afore we've 'eard thy songs and tales! Tell us the same old rubbish, and thee'll get nuthin' from me, 'sept mebbe a swift kick up thy skinny arse."

"And rightly so." Toby dropped the lean buttocks onto the three-legged stool in the corner by the hearth, where it was warm and bright and they could all see him. "But I know a hundred stories you've never heard, and I know what songs they're singing this year in Spain and France ... and the ditties from Cork and Liverpool, too."

Again, the laugh, as he strummed a chord and began to pick a fine tune out of the strings. His speaking voice had a lilting quality which made Jim's skin prickle, and he knew even before Toby began to sing, he would be very good. The melody sounded Spanish but the words were English, and he wondered who had translated them.

It was a love song with an edge of tragedy, about a young man who ran away to sea before he could make a fool of himself over a local beauty. Three verses into it Jim began to notice, the lover left behind had not been named ... and no gender was ever mentioned in the lyric. The prickling sensation redoubled and he stood behind the bar, hands frozen in the chore of drying mugs as he listened to the tale, and felt curiously moved as it ended:

"The sea is my bastion, and I'm going home
"After too many years throughout which I did roam
"'Cross oceans and islands too strange to relate,
"Which have brought me at last to the seaman's bleak fate –
"For the storm is upon us; there's ice all around,
"And all the world shakes with the furious sound
"Of winds and white water; but I am at peace

"For I'm bound for the place where the silence has lease…
"Just one thing I ask for, before I go down:
"To send this last message; then, pleased, shall I drown.
"I left my old homeland, compelled by the need
"To leave you before I could sow ruin's seed.
"I ran from the town, leaving no faintest clue
"That I ran for the sake of a love I felt. *You*.
"For the love that I felt was my sin and my shame –
"There's no place for sinners, and you're not to blame.
"So the sea was my refuge, the ships and the mates…
"And now we'll go down, for our destiny waits,
"And the sea is my haven; my voice is the wind –
"The deeps are my homeland; and though I have sinned
"I bid you, remember the boy with red hair
"Who fled from the village, at harvest time there."

The song was bittersweet and lilting, and while he sang the tavern was so quiet, nobody even burped much less said a word to break the spell. A few clapped when he finished, and Toby dropped another bow but did not even pause to ask for a farthing before he struck up another song, this time ribald, cheeky.

"Come, cheer up, my lads, there's a hogshead of rum,
"Which we'll open tonight when the young ladies come –
"When the frills and the fancies are dropped on the floor,
"And we'll get so blind drunk, we'll forget what they're for!
"So cheer up, my hearties – we'll wait for them girls,
"Mine's the plump lass with the long golden curls …
"Or was she a redhead? I just can't recall –
"So I'll have one more rum, 'fore I skip, trip and fall,
"And I'll *try* to remember, tomorrow, with grace,
"Who I rolled in the sheets with … the name and the face.
"Now, I *think* 'twas a doxie. Fact is, I ain't sure!
"It's all the rum's fault, and there is but one cure –
"Put the cork to the hogshead and hammer it in!
"Don't drink till you're legless, nor indulge in no sin
"With no girl from no brothel who's ripe as no plum…
"So, how much'll you take for yon bottle of rum?"

He had them now, laughing and stamping in rhythm with a ditty they had never heard before. He was very good, Jim thought. Little wonder Toby called himself a balladsinger by trade, and could keep himself fed and bedded on the skills. The mandolin was old but polished, and the hands playing it seemed to move by themselves. It was effortless to him.

He sang again, the tale of a hunter who trailed a wolf across the mountains in winter after it took his baby son instead of a lamb; and then an Irish song about the anguish of being under the heel of the invader. He fell silent there, and took a mug of ale to wet his throat before he set the mandolin aside, leaned elbows on knees and looked from face to face. He held them in the palm of his hand now.

"Do you know the story," he asked them, "of Diego Monteras? Of the *treasure* of Diego Monteras?"

Like the rest of them, Jim had never even heard the name, much less the story. He had no doubt it was a complete fabrication, but he fetched himself a small rum, pulled a chair up on the side of the bar closest to the hearth and listened to Toby for the pleasure of just hearing his voice.

The ale was flowing nicely by now. The box of coins under the bar was healthily full. Jim was more than happy with the night's business, and if Toby had wanted Jim's own pillow for his head, he could have had it for the asking.

"It was in the days of Good Queen Bess," Toby was saying, "that a ship put out from the Port of London, bound for the islands and the strange seas of the Caribbean. She was an English galleon called the *Mary of Dee*, and she belonged to a gentleman adventurer by the name of Sir Geoffrey Gaunt. He was a God fearing man who loved his scriptures, and he probably should have been a priest.

"But he was the second-eldest son of the family of Sir James Gaunt … not the first son, who would inherit the title and fortune; not the youngest son, who would be sent into the priesthood. Just the second son, who would have to make his own way in the world. So Sir Geoffrey became an adventurer, and he earned his own knighthood when he made the Queen a great deal of money on a voyage to the Americas. He came home with a hold so full of gold, the ship staggered in the water –

"And he came home, also, with a story; and this story, he told to the Queen while they drank a little Madeira to celebrate his knighthood. In the ports of the Caribbean, where English ships skulked like thieves and traitors because the waters were Spanish and the air was sharp with the powder of Spanish cannons, the locals told a story about a man called Diego Monteras.

"Now, Sir Geoffrey was as skeptical as you or I. He was no man's fool, and smart enough for Queen Elizabeth to give him five thousand pounds right out of the treasury to mount an expedition. So Sir Geoffrey had to have heard this same story six or ten times, from the mouths of that many locals and natives, in just as many ports, before he started to believe there was more than a single grain of truth in the tale.

"You see, Diego Monteras was a Spanish traitor. And a heretic. And a blasphemer, a pirate, a thief, a scoundrel, and – if the stories were true – a sodomite. The love of his life was the last prince of one of the native tribes, a lad who'd have been royalty among his own people, if the Spaniards hadn't enslaved them all and killed most of them. This young man, who's gone down in history as Francisco, though that wouldn't have been the name he was born with, was the last scion of a house as old and as noble as the House of Tudor itself.

"It's said the Spaniards were working and torturing his people to death, but Francisco was protected as long as there were strong backs to save him. And when at last the chance came for him to escape, the men who had protected him sent him away in a little cockle shell of a boat, with the idea in mind that if his royal blood survived, their people could one day be reborn, and return to their lost greatness.

"It was a fine enough idea, but the pagan gods of sea and sky have always had their own plans, and a storm blew up out of nowhere. The boat was smashed to kindling by wind and water, and Francisco was almost dead when he was scooped up out of the waves by a crew of Spanish pirates ... heretics, traitors.

"The crew of the *Marianna* sailed out of a secret anchorage, under the command of a brilliant strategist and tactician who had been sentenced to death by the King of Spain, and by Holy Mother Church also. Capitan Monteras was judged guilty of the crime of being a sodomite in a land where the only love allowed is that of a man for a woman.

"Now, 'tis not for you and me to say what was right or wrong in Spain all those many years ago, but any honest priest, worth his salt, will tell you this: the matter is a private one which should be left alone, to be taken up between God and the accused upon Judgment Day. If there's a price to be paid, let the Almighty set the amount and let the sinner pay it willingly out of his own pocket, in whatever coin the Lord decrees to be right ... and then the two of them would call the debt settled and the go their separate ways in peace. Diego Monteras believed this.

"Pirate, heretic, sinner? Oh, yes, he was all of these things. But Monteras also believed strongly in God and Heaven and hell, Spaniard that he was, through to the marrow of his bones. And he believed that the men who'll be punished hardest and longest by the Almighty are those in the government, in the palace, and in the church.

"Condemned to a slow and terrible death by torture, Diego fled for his life. He took his ship out to sea in the dead of night, and into the teeth of wild weather. The *Marianna* never looked back. She packed forty guns. She was long and low in the water, one of those ships that were built after the painful lessons of the Spanish Armada were learned. She was fast, hard, and she preyed on Spanish merchantmen for more than a decade, seizing every manner of treasure, from gold and jewels to silks and jade, ivory and great art.

"All the treasure was equally divided among the crew, and Diego Monteras himself was already rich beyond a king's dream of avarice when young Francisco was scooped out of the boiling waters of the storm.

"Forget, if you prefer, the love which bloomed between them, for many of you might be discomfited to think long on this. You're not sailors, and have no feeling for the mateship that happens, six months at sea, far from home. So don't even give a thought to their private business ... but remember it for one moment, just long enough to know how and *why* young Francisco would give the treasures of his royal house to the man who saved him from the storm, and gave him a better home and life than he'd ever known.

"And here's the part of the story that caught the ears of Sir Geoffrey Gaunt ... and he told it to Queen Elizabeth, word for word, just as he'd learned it himself. They say he watched the Queen's green eyes fairly dance with the glee that comes from knowing there's another grand adventure out there, with blood and sweat and tears along the way and a pile of gold at the end of it!

"As you know, Francisco was the last of his royal house, and he had a secret, passed down to him from generations before. The secret of the treasure house of the god-kings and emperors of a heathen land which shone with gold and shimmered with jewels for centuries before the Spaniards arrived, dragged down the native princes and enslaved every last one of those people, to the last babe in arms.

"Now, you can imagine how Diego Monteras and the rogue crew of the *Marianna* were enchanted by this story of Francisco's, which he told to the bold and handsome young Capitan. And you know the

Marianna traveled far into verdant, perilous waters which had never even been sailed before, let alone charted. The wind fell dead away; the air was hot and heavy; the crew stood by the oars and rowed her up a wide, jungle-banked river which grew narrower and narrower with every mile they plied inland…

"Until they came to a hill, and at the bottom of the hill was a stone quay, ancient, half ruined, overgrown with vines – built in the time of Francisco's grandfather's grandfather. And at the top of the hill was a strange temple where the rocks were still stained brown with the ancient blood of human sacrifices made to the god of the sun.

"Oh yes, Francisco's people had been savage. As savage as folk who burn men and women at the stake and rend their bodies with tortures that would make your flesh crawl if I were to recount them to you. Don't be too quick to judge the ancient, heathen peoples of ages less wise, or less educated, than our own. Or, if you do judge the savages of bygone ages, judge also the Inquisition, and the offices of governments, even our own, that employed terrible brutalities … for much less worthwhile reasons.

"As Francisco had memorized the story as a young boy, the treasure house of his people was far in the earth, deep under the hill. He took Diego up the slope to the temple, and right there, behind the altar stone, was the hatchway that was promised in the legend –

"And *under* the hatchway, the long, steep stairway leading down and down, into darkness and cold, with the drip of water and the rank smell of moss and mold…

"A band from the *Marianna* followed the tunnels deeper and deeper into the earth, until even the most stalwart were ready to turn back in dread; and then, just as Diego himself was about to call enough and take his men back to the sun and the light – *then*, their torches picked up a glimmer, a reflection, a shine on the surface of solid gold.

"They had found it, the treasure of ages, passed down from vanished kings and emperors to a young man who had been made a slave by the same race that condemned Diego to torture and death for the sin of love.

"Four days, it took the crew of the *Marianna* to carry out the gold. Statues, idols, cups, necklaces, bracelets, crowns. They spilled their sweat willingly till the hold was full of the stuff, and then they hauled the ship around in mid-river, put the oars back in the water, and they sang as they pulled back toward the open sea.

"A week later they were safely back at their own secret anchorage, in a nook, a bay on the coast of South America which is so small, so insignificant, it barely shows up as a pimple on a map even today.

"Now, gold is very pretty and it has a nice shine, but Diego preferred jewels. He liked the sparkle of diamonds, emeralds, sapphires, rubies. He loved their color and their purity, and he had little use for metal, even a pretty metal like gold. So, over the space of years, he traded his share of the gold for this bauble and that bauble until he had no gold left of his own, and everything he possessed had been turned into the biggest, most perfect of the precious stones.

"He kept them in a brass-bound chest lined with scarlet velvet, and by night, by lamplight, he and Francisco would take them out and count them, play marbles with them, toy with them as if they were mere amusements. The two of them lived like kings themselves in their safe, secret anchorage while, one by one, the crew of the *Marianna* grew old, infirm, and many passed away peacefully of old age.

"In the end only a handful of old men were left, barely enough to crew the ship with a good wind in her sails, and nowhere near enough to stand by her oars if the wind fell. They all knew they were sorely close to the end of their time. They'd lived long, full, happy lives. They were content and they'd drawn their plans for what would become of the incredible riches they'd won, after they were gone.

"Every man on the *Marianna* had left family back in Spain. Now they were at the ends of their lives, and were in little danger, they wanted to pass on their treasures to their kin, to see future generations living well on their spoils.

"Each man wrote a letter to his family, and each buried his share of the bounty in a specific place which was marked on a piece torn out of a map. Then the letters and the tattered bits of the map were taken back to Spain and delivered by hand, by the very youngest of the crew – a mere lad of 50 years, called Felipe Chavez.

"At least a dozen of the letters were acted upon, and some of the richest Spanish houses today can trace their largesse back to them. But a few fortunes were never collected, and one letter was never delivered at all, because there was no one to receive it. Diego Monteras had left two brothers and an uncle, when he fled for his life. All had died childless, and although Chavez spent months hunting for any surviving members of the Monteras family, he found none.

"In a quandary he returned to the Caribbean, intending to ask his captain what should be done with his share, since there were no Monteras sons or daughters. To his great sadness, he learned that both Diego and Francisco had passed away, just a week apart, though whether there was a sickness or a storm, no one knows. They were buried together, and they lie close to one another even now, though their grave is unmarked and where it is, I cannot tell you.

"I *do* know the letter and the bit of map were passed from hand to hand, kept safe, secret … traded, lost, found, disbelieved, misunderstood … and the treasure of Diego Monteras was still out there, buried, waiting to be dug out of its hiding place by an adventurer who had the courage to believe in the story, and who could get his hands on the letter and map.

"This was the story Sir Geoffrey Gaunt heard over and over until even he, who was a born skeptic, believed it, and he began to listen out for tales not of the treasure, but of the *letter*, and that scrap torn out of a map. He crossed many a palm with silver; he plied many a man and woman with fine wine, and at last the trail took him to a hermitage, high on the cliffs above a bay known as Coffin Cove, because the waters were so full of sharks, any galley slave trying to escape by swimming ashore would be dead before he made it halfway.

"A friar lived at the hermitage … fat and old, and so bald, he had no reason to shave in his tonsure. He was Brother Alfredo, a keeper of books and records. He had thousands of them, rescued from ships and offices, stored in big wooden crates to keep the mice out of them.

"Did he have a letter? Sir Geoffrey asked. Did he have a bit ripped from an old chart of the coast of South America? Well, Brother Alfredo had a mind like a cote full of pigeons. Messy, like his house. He remembered the letter, and he tore the hermitage apart for two days to find the old, brown parchment. But in the end, when Sir Geoffrey had begun to think the whole affair was one enormous wild goose chase after all – oh, the monk found it. Sir Geoffrey had the letter and the map *in his hands*.

"The year had already begun to wind down. The winds were dead wrong for the undertaking of another quest. The Atlantic was about to grow stormy with winter, even if the crew were not anxious to get home, which they were … and back in London the Queen was probably twice as anxious to get a return on her investment! So Sir Geoffrey paid the monk in silver coin, took the letter and map, returned to his ship, and prayed to Saint Nicholas and Saint Christopher for a safe passage east.

"Luck was with him. His ship raced home before storm winds, and she docked on the Thames not six weeks after he'd paid the monk. The Queen was so delighted with the profits of this voyage, she knighted him at once. And it was then, as they drank a little Madeira to celebrate the day, when he told her the story of the treasure of Diego Monteras ... and word has it, he showed her the actual letter.

"The Queen read it. She read it again. She set it down and drank another cup of wine, and she looked up at Sir Geoffrey with the green eyes that had made the likes of Sir Francis Drake himself take a step back."

There, Toby fell silent, sealed his lips and surveyed his audience with a dark, self-satisfied smirk. Jim had hung on every word. The man was a master storyteller. Fred Bailey was the first one to demand to know what happened next – obviously the Queen backed Sir Geoffrey to return to South America on the spring winds and hunt for the treasure, but was it found? What became of Sir Geoffrey?

Several in the audience offered to buy Toby a rum, if a jar of ale would not keep him talking, but he held up both hands as if they had him at pistol point. "Not tonight! You want to know the rest? Come back tomorrow, and I'll be glad to tell you. For now? Haven't you seen the time? Get back to your homes, before your wives think you've been struck with death!"

They groaned, and a few fingers shook ruefully at him, but the ploy was an old one. He would get a second bite at this cherry, and perhaps a third, before they had plumbed his store of songs and tales. They might even come back a second time to hear them all again before they began to grow bored. Jim was impressed, not merely by the balladsinger's skill but also the haul of coins in the box under the bar.

The locals wandered out, some staggering and propping each other up, and trying to remember the words to The Hogshead. Jim wondered where Toby had learned it, and as the last of his customers drifted away into the night, he latched the door. He leaned on the old timbers and looked Toby Trelane up and down in the flickering light of the half dozen lamps.

"I'd tip my hat to you, if I was wearing it," he said honestly. "I didn't think you'd be able to seduce the rummy old bastards who drink here, but you had them wrapped around your little finger." He nodded at the bar, the coins. "You reckon you can you do it again tomorrow?"

"I don't know," Toby said honestly, "but I'm game to give it a try." He yawned deeply and knuckled his eyes. "Can I beg a blanket? I'll take the hearth corner, and be up and around before you in the morning."

"If that's what you want." Jim had more than half expected Toby to hold out his hand, look at him out of dark, bedroom eyes, but the man seemed genuinely exhausted. He was tired enough to want only to sleep tonight? It was a reasonable desire, even if Jim's own nerves were prickling with intrigue. "You can take any bedchamber, upstairs, if you prefer a mattress under your spine. There's no paying guests at the moment. You know this place well enough to know there's six bedchambers up there, and only me sleeping in one of them. I've got the warm one, right up against the chimney."

Now, Toby looked at him for a long moment in which Jim was so sure he was going to say *something*, he held his breath. But at length Toby said simply, "I'm beholden. I'll take Bess out for a breath of air, and then I'll lay my head down. Do you mind dogs in the bedchambers? She has better manners than most of the gentry."

"It's no problem to me." Jim turned away and grabbed a half dozen tankards, three handles in each fist, to cover the moment's awkwardness. "You can take Boxer out as well. He seems to have hit it off with your Bess. Lock up behind you when you step back in." The tavern's ratter was yawning at the kitchen door; his tail thumped as Jim spoke his name and glanced at him. "I suppose I'll see you in the morning."

"You will." Toby gave a low whistle to call both dogs, and lifted the latch. "Goodnight, Master Fairley."

"Sleep well, Master Trelane," Jim said with an acid-hot humor as he dumped the tankards, and he tackled the steep, creaking stairs without looking back.

The man was so hard to read, he could be dangerous. One moment, Jim was sure he had Toby pegged, and the next he was wondering. Mistakes would be so easy to make – too easy – and there was no way back from a blunder. One mistake was all it took to wreak ruin with a man's whole life.

With a sigh, he heeled off his shoes, tugged his shirt over his head, and sprawled out on the bed in the light of two tallow candles. The casement was open to the night air, and he glared at the stars framed in it.

"Who are you, Toby Trelane?" he wondered aloud. "Where are you from – and where the hell are you going?"

More importantly, what did he want? Jim's wilful memory dwelt on the lean, hard body he had seen chopping wood, the soft flaxen hair that stirred in the sea wind. His fingertips could literally feel that skin, and he could almost taste the man's lips. *Almost*.

Minutes later, he heard the quiet squeal of the door, the rattle of the sneck and then the solid thud of the bolt sliding home. Toby and the dogs were back in, the tavern was locked up, and Jim followed him up by the soft sound of feet on the stairs.

He took the room above the yard, and the door closed a moment later. The bed in there was too soft for Jim's liking. Put the weight of two men on it, and the mattress swayed and dipped. Then again, he admitted, if a man were sleeping alone, and all he was doing was *sleeping*, the mattress was soft enough to serve well enough.

Frustrated, annoyed, mystified, disgruntled, he turned over, punched the pillow and closed his eyes. Sleep was a long time coming and when it did settle over his mind, his dreams were full of an elusive lover who was always elsewhere, unavailable, unattainable, even though he smiled at Jim and winked in mocking invitation.

Chapter Four

The smell of kippers greeted him as he swung downstairs. He followed his nose to the kitchen to find Toby pushing a pair of the smoked fish around with a wooden spoon, in the black iron skillet where a little butter had begun to sizzle. Yesterday's bread stood on the table and the fat brown pot was brewing fresh tea.

He looked rested, Jim thought, while Jim himself felt barely half awake and annoyed. The kitchen door stood open; the dogs were lying across the threshold while the cat washed his face in the warm, smoky draft from the hearth. Toby wore a smile this morning. He was in the same britches and shirt, but his waistcoat was off and his hair was unbound, loose on his shoulders. He was so fair, it seemed he rarely needed to shave. No matter the hour, he looked good enough to eat alive, which only made Jim more annoyed.

"I was looking at your thatch," Toby said by way of greeting as he pushed the kippers off onto a pair of ivory-stained plates. "It's coming loose in a few places. You'll lose a lot of it in the next big wind ... I could fix it."

Jim answered with a grunt, and broke off a piece of bread.

"Look, if you don't want me to stay, I can move on this morning," Toby said with a faint but audible sigh.

"Did I say that?" Jim demanded.

"No." Toby slopped tea into two cups and spooned in a lot of sugar in lieu of milk, of which there was none. "But you look…"

"Do I?" Jim forced his mind back to reality and summoned a smile. "Don't take any notice to me. I think I got up on the wrong side of the bed." *Which was my usual side, since there was nobody in it to make me get up on the other bloody side!* He took a large mouthful of kipper and sopped up the salt-sweet juice. "Fix the roof if you feel compelled to, but you don't have to."

"I like to be busy." Toby gestured vaguely. "There's any number of jobs I can do around the place."

"You saying you want to stay on?" Jim took a long slurp of the tea, found it too hot and far too sweet. "I can't pay you much."

"I'd like to stay for a while," Toby said cautiously, "and you don't have to pay me at all."

"You're going to fix the thatch, and not hand me the bill?" Jim almost scoffed at the idea. "It'd cost me at least three shillings to get it fixed by the man who comes over from Exeter, and he'd drink a dozen pints of my best ale while he was at it."

"So the job ought to buy me dinner for a week or three," Toby said easily. "And then we'll see if your customers have had enough of me and my stories."

"They're good stories," Jim said almost reluctantly. "Good songs. It's always a pleasure to hear something new."

"It is." Toby sat back and studied him over the rim of his mug. "You, uh, you don't have a wife who's due back any moment? That is, I was listening to your customers. I couldn't help overhearing some of the things they were saying, and…"

Jim pushed away his plate with a sigh. "And they were muttering on about how I'm an odd fellow, all alone, and no use to a lass. About how I'm a *eunuch*," he said sourly.

"Well, not in those exact words," Toby said with astonishing gentleness, "but I suppose it's what they were saying. And I couldn't help noticing how you, uh, that is…"

"Have a gimpy leg." Jim frowned into his cup.

"You walk with a very slight limp," Toby amended. "I thought it made you a little mysterious. Interesting. I'd have thought the local lasses would be all over you, wanting to mother you."

"Smother me, maybe," Jim grumbled.

"Smother?" Toby's brows arched. "You're not really a – a eunuch?"

"No, I'm bloody not! But they like to think I am." Jim regarded him with a defiant glare, challenging him to make something of it.

"No offense intended," Toby assured him. "I was just curious, because you're alone. And it's so unusual to find a handsome young man alone."

"Is it?" Jim was about to tell him it was far from unusual, when the handsome young fellow was like *that*. When he was one of *those*. When his heart lay in places seldom mentioned in genteel company, and then only for a ribald joke. He wanted to snap the words at Toby, and only bit them off at the last moment because the confession could have been a close second cousin to suicide, if Toby were altogether the wrong man to hear any such admission.

Before he could speak, the balladsinger shushed him. "It's all right, Jim. It's nothing to do with me, if you don't want to run the gauntlet of women with a leg that won't serve you when you need it to. If you're not a eunuch, though ... well, there's still a lot to be grateful for, I should say."

And he pushed away from the table, taking the empty plates to the big brass bowl where Mrs. Clitheroe washed dishes. Jim watched him there, seeing the long lines of his back and legs, the strength in the sinewy forearms, the honey brown skin which looked soft as any girl's. He ached to just come right out and speak the truth, and he could not remember another time when reading a man's signs had been so damned difficult.

In the end he said nothing at all, but drifted out into the tavern yard and sat on a barrel there, stoking the long-stemmed pipe he rarely smoked. It was midmorning when he could be bothered to stir. He heard Toby up on the roof, singing softly to himself in French and Spanish, and he hopped down off the barrel when Mrs. Clitheroe appeared at the corner.

She wore a tight, worried face, and at once Jim knew something was badly wrong. He had been knocking out the pipe, and now set it aside and took the old woman's basket, which was heavy with vegetables.

"Edith, what's wrong? Are you sick?"

"Nay, Master Jim – not me. But ... I's sorry, mebbe I should've asked, but I put 'er in yon coach house, cuz it looks like rain."

"Who?" Jim wondered. The stable and coach house stood opposite the tavern yard, like the crossbar on a letter T. From the barrel by the kitchen door, he could not see the coach house's wide double doors.

"Just a gypsy lass," Mrs. Clitheroe said, flustered. "She come to me door afore first light, tryin' to sell me kerchiefs ... needin' a few pennies fer medicine. I could see what she wanted, sick as she is, poor bairn, an' I brung 'er 'ere. I couldn't send 'er away, could I?"

"A gypsy girl?" Jim echoed. "She's in the coach house now?"

"An' sick as a dog," Mrs. Clitheroe said distractedly. "Such a pretty little thing. I thought I'd give 'er a mug o' somethin' hot, an' see if I can find one of Joe Flynn's kids, send 'im to run into Exmouth fer the doctor."

"Do that." Jim gestured into the kitchen. "You get the kettle on the hob and I'll go and find one of Joe's kids. I know where they'll be at this time of the morning – and if they're not checking their snares in the hedgeback, I'll walk on up to the farmhouse."

He was moving as he spoke, and only turned back when a voice called down from above. "Something wrong, Jim? You and old Edith need a hand?" Toby shouted a moment before his face appeared over the line of the thatch.

"We might," Jim called up. "There's a young girl, sick, in the coach house. See what you can do to help the old lady while I find a lad to run for Doctor Hardesty. He's a good man – if he's at home, he'll come out."

He gave Toby a wave and swung away toward the stables. One of the coach house's doors was open, chocked with a brick to keep it from swinging shut, but he did not venture inside. If the girl was laid low with something catching, he had no desire to be one step closer, though he would hurry for Harry or Danny Flynn, whose young legs would make short work of the run to Exmouth.

The girl lay on a lap rug, curled on her side, and she was not moving. She looked like a bundle of old clothing dumped at the roadside, and Jim felt a pang of pity. He might have wondered if she had swooned, even expired, but he heard a low moaning.

"You hang on, love," he called quietly to her. "Mrs. Clitheroe's fetching you a mug of tea, and you'll have the doctor, soon as we can manage."

Did she hear him? Jim was not sure, and tarrying to repeat himself was the wrong thing to do. Instead, he pushed the lame leg as hard as he knew how on the path toward the hamlets of Budleigh and Salterton. And not for the first time he cursed himself, because running was entirely beyond him. What kind of useless leg of mutton was he, if a girl could die for want of a doctor because Jim Fairley could not run?

A very slight limp, Toby called it. He was being generous. Jim walked with one *hell* of a limp, and he knew it. He cursed himself mercilessly, all the way to the end of the lane leading up to the Flynn farm. If Toby Trelane had no interest in him on account of the gimpy leg, Jim was not about to blame him for the preference. Even if a colt like Toby liked bedding with men – and the signs were so confused, even now Jim was unsure – he was hardly likely to want damaged goods. This morning Jim accorded himself no skerrick of mercy.

The hedgeback where the Flynn kids trapped for rabbits was empty, and he turned into the lane. The sun was high and warm, and the air was sweet with flowers, light with scores of skylarks, as he left behind the coastal path. On another morning he would have called it a pleasant walk, but today he had no such charitable thoughts.

Twenty yards up the lane, he caught a glimpse of yellow and called ahead. "Mary, is that you? Little Mary Flynn, is your brother around?"

The girl was eight or nine, still at the tomboy stage where she would rather be trapping rabbits with her brothers than brushing her hair and learning to darn socks. She was on hands and knees under the hedge, dressed in gray skirts and a yellow apron, and she waved as she saw him coming. But it was her brother Danny, two years older, with bright orange hair and a face full of freckles, who answered.

His britches were patched at the knees, his shirt was ripped and his hands were dirty. Boys, Jim thought ruefully, would always be boys, no matter where they were. He had been a little ruffian himself at the same age, in London. He dug through his pocket for a bright penny and tossed it, spinning in the air, to Danny. The lad caught it deftly and viewed it with astonished eyes.

"A copper for you, lad, if you'll run an errand. You know where Doctor Hardesty lives?"

"So I should," Danny Flynn scoffed. "I run to fetch him for me Ma often enough. You sick, then?"

And, damnit, he was looking at Jim's left leg as he asked, which made Jim's hand itch to cuff him. "Not me, rascal. Tell the doctor there's a girl at The Raven and she looks so sick, if she was a dog, they'd have shot her already. Run, now, earn that copper, so you can spend it on any toffee you like, and rot your teeth without a qualm of guilt!"

The boy's cheeks pinked as if Jim had read his thoughts, and he took off fast. The little girl bobbed up to watch him go before she plopped back into the rank grasses, where she was chaining daisies and eating clover flowers. Jim watched her for some moments and then his eyes narrowed against the sun as he looked away into the distance, where the Flynn farmhouse was no more than a hundred yards up the lane. Her father would be selling vegetables at the market in Salterton.

"Will I walk you home?" he offered the child.

Her dark head shook indignantly. "If I goes home, I'll only 'ave to learn 'ow to read."

"Reading is a very good thing," he informed her. She made a face as if the idea stunk like fish stranded on the beach and three days rotten, and Jim laughed. "A dozen years from now, young lady, you'll probably change your mind, and *then* what will you do?"

A dozen years from now she would be a fishwife, he thought, with a babe in arms, a toddler at her feet and another on the way. She might look back longingly on the days when she could have learned to read and do sums, and become a pupil teacher instead. Or would she be wed to a lad she loved, body and soul, and be so happy, any human heart could only be envious?

With a sigh, Jim turned back toward the coastal path and headed for home at a slower pace, better suited to the leg. It ached when he overworked it, and he was rubbing it hard, pushing a clenched fist into the big muscles, when he limped back into the tavern yard.

In the same amount of time, Danny Flynn would probably have bolted into Hardesty's cottage, which was well to the east side of Exmouth, standing in a great garden of weedy herbs, where he grew a lot of the medicinals of his trade.

Coffee was on Jim's mind, and a slab of apple pie, and perhaps another shot at making heads or tails of Toby. He was headed for the kitchen, but voices from the coach house pulled him up short. It took him a moment to recognize Toby Trelane's voice, for the words were so strange, and then he was drawn to the door there like nails to a magnet.

Inside, Mrs. Clitheroe was standing by the lap rug with clenched hands while Toby knelt beside an odd little bundle of blankets, and the balladsinger's voice was soft, gentle, almost singsong. "*Réquiem ætérnam dona ei, Dómine. Et lux perpétua lúceat ei. Requiéscat in pace. Anima ejus, et ánimæ ómnium fidélium defunctórum, per misericórdiam Dei requiéscant in pace. Amen.*"

Surprise rendered Jim mute as he watched Toby fold the girl's small hands on her breast, close her eyes and kiss her forehead. She was dead? His throat caught, though he had never known her. "There was nothing you could do?" he asked quietly.

"Nothin'," Mrs. Clitheroe said sadly, "'cept say the right words, and it's just lucky young Master Trelane 'ere knows 'em, and sez 'em the right way."

"Lucky?" Toby echoed as he stood up. "Now, I'm not sure luck has anything to do with it." He angled a long, dark glance at Jim. "It's not a doctor she wants. Not any longer."

"It'll be Marcus Stiles, the undertaker, and a pauper's grave on the other side of the churchyard from my father and your mate Charlie, and Charlie's ma," Jim said soberly. "Damn, what a shame. Do you know who she was, Edith?"

But the old woman only shrugged, and dabbed her eyes with a kerchief. "She just come to me door, needin' pennies fer medicine. I don't even know 'er name." She rubbed her eyes, crossed herself, hugged herself. "I'll go fer Mr. Stiles, will I?"

"I think you'd better," Toby said thoughtfully. "And as for you, Jim Fairley, you'd best come inside, sit down and let me have a look at that leg of yours. You've given yourself all kinds of grief, haven't you?"

"It's fine," Jim lied.

"Tommyrot," Toby said tartly. "When Doctor Hardesty gets here, it's you he'll be looking at, I think."

"He's already looked – and there's nothing to be done," Jim said moodily, though he let Toby herd him out of the coach house and through the yard. "It aches if I punish it, and I just did – and all for what?"

"In a noble effort to save a young girl's life." Toby held open the door till Jim went ahead of him, with Bess on his heels. "Pull a stool up by the fire and let me see to you."

"I told you, there's nothing to be done," Jim argued, through he pulled the kitchen's three-legged stool into the warmth of the big cooking hearth and turned his leg so the heat could get to it.

As he settled, Toby was hunting through the many jars and canisters which lined the kitchen shelves, and he found what he wanted a moment later. It was lamp oil – whale oil, the finest thing for making clear, white light or treating rheumatics. It was best used hot. Jim had heard of men who were afflicted with the ill of the bones, and who immersed themselves in the bodies of freshly dead whales, the innards still hot with the life force of the leviathan, and they swore by the treatment. Jim could never have brought himself to do such a thing, but when Toby fetched the brown glass bottle of oil and stood waiting with an immovable look on his face, he hitched up his buttocks, dropped his britches around his knees and turned a little to let him get to the leg.

The scars were the size of the palm of his hand, old and white now. The pain came from inside, in the front and side of his thigh. When it afflicted him only rest and heat and a drop of the best Dutch laudanum, if he could get it, did him any good. Not that he was about to refuse Toby Trelane's hands on him, slick and shining with the whale oil which rapidly grew warm, and then hot, in front of the fire.

Toby threw down the kitchen rags and knelt on them, the better to work on the leg, and almost reluctantly Jim began to sigh. He closed his eyes, reveling in sheer relief, and his mind was floating when Toby said quietly,

"These are nasty scars, Jim, but they're only skin deep and they're old. There's nothing here to hurt you after all these years. What happened to your leg? Was it properly treated at the time? You said Doctor Hardesty's looked at it for you, more recently?"

With an enormous effort, Jim stirred and forced open his eyes. Toby's face was lit peach and cream by the fire, and his hair was like spun gold. In a moment of self-indulgent whimsy, Jim thought it might have been an angel kneeling there at his feet, and then he mocked himself for the foolish notion. He hunted for his voice, and for words.

"John Hardesty looked at it when me and my father took over The Raven. He used to come by three times a week to look at old Charlie Chegwidden, and he couldn't help but notice how I limp like the very devil. Lord knows, a blind man could see it. So I let him take a look, even though I knew there was nothing he could do for me."

"You knew?" Toby echoed, still massaging, fingers kneading carefully, gently.

"There's only one thing to be done about this," Jim began, and then stopped. "Actually, there's two, but the second one means cutting it off, and there's no cause for that."

"And the first thing?" Toby looked up at him, eyes deep and dark in the firelight.

Jim took a long breath. "It has to be cut wide open and probed, and about forty splinters of bone have to be plucked out of it, like pulling the spines out of a hedgehog skin." He shrugged. "I know how it would be done, and I'm not game for it. Not yet – not when all I have to do is respect the old injury and not overtax it. Cut it wide open, Toby, and I wouldn't walk for a month, even if the wound didn't turn green and stinking. Johnny Hardesty could be back in a week and cutting the bloody thing right off, if I was really out of luck!" He shook his head emphatically. "No. Not unless I get so crippled that it ends up being worth the risk, and then … maybe."

"I see." Toby's hands had always been gentle, and now they were more so. "How did it happen? You've been here at The Raven for several years?"

"Over six," Jim affirmed. "And I've limped since I was fifteen. I was run down by a coach in the street." He shrugged. "It'll happen, if you're stupid enough to run right out in front of a coachman when he has no chance of stopping four big horses."

"And one of the horses stepped on you," Toby guessed.

"I was lucky it was only one of them, and he only trod *once* on me!" Jim mocked himself with a humorless smile. "Oh, there was blood. They picked me up and took me to the nearest quack, who was a Welsh pox doctor, as luck would have it –"

"Luck?" Toby actually chuckled. And then, "Well, I suppose there's one thing a pox doctor knows a great deal about, and that's suppurating sores! I imagine he cleaned you up and bound the leg, cauterized it?"

"He did. And it healed, likely as not because I was so young." Jim gave the offending limb a glare. "A month later I got out of bed, put my weight on it and fainted dead on the floor. Six months later we knew, my father and me, I'd never walk right without a surgeon. So he brought one in to examine me." His face hardened as the ten year old memories scalded him raw.

"He hurt you," Toby said quietly.

"He ... hurt me." Jim looked into the fire. "He probed the wound with some kind of *thing*, and told us the bone had splintered and I was full of these hedgehog spines. They had to come out, if I was going to walk right again – but he couldn't guarantee not to do so much harm, he'd be taking the leg right off me, above the line of the old wound. So my father paid him at the door and told him we'd send for him when we were ready to have me butchered."

"And needless to say, you never sent for him." Toby's brows rose. "I can't say I blame you. But still ... you should be careful, Jim."

"You mean, don't hurt myself on account of a gypsy girl?"

"She wasn't a gypsy. She was Spanish," Toby said too quickly, and then seemed to stop himself and seal his lips.

But Jim had heard, and if he had been a cat his ears would have swiveled around. "You knew her."

"I'm afraid to say, I did." Toby's voice was heavy with regret. "Her name was Marguerite."

He would say no more but at once Jim sensed the restlessness in him and, sure enough, a moment later Toby took his hands away and stood. The leg was warm and relaxed now – rose red, and the skin had taken up the oil. Jim took his weight on his good leg, yanked up his britches buttoned them swiftly, all the while frowning at Toby.

"You're not going to tell me who she was, are you?"

The wide, bony shoulders lifted in an expressive shrug. "Just a girl."

"A Spanish girl."

"As I said."

"Your girl?" Jim asked as a curious thread of foreboding stitched through him. Damnit, had she been his wife –?

"Mine?" Now Toby chuckled once more. "Not mine! But yes, I knew her, and where she goes, trouble won't be far behind."

"She was a bad sort?" Jim hazarded as he fetched mugs and the thick, syrupy coffee left in the pan from breakfast. "A whore?"

"Just a trollop," Toby said with some generosity. "Not her fault, poor lass. When you come from the gutters of any city, orphaned at the age of twelve, it's often a good trick to avoid landing in some brothel or other. Marguerite stayed out of the whorehouses, but she was always traipsing after a man. If you know what I mean by *traipsing*."

"I can imagine." Jim thrust a mug of coffee at him. "So, what kind of trouble could she bring to The Raven?"

Toby's teeth worried at his lip for a moment. "It wouldn't come from Margie herself, so much as the company she keeps. Kept." He gestured vaguely with the mug, took a swig of the strong, sweet coffee and made a face. "Good Christ, you could dip sheep in this!" He reached for the blackened tea kettle, tipped half the coffee back into the pan and topped the remainder off with water.

"And I'm supposed to be on the lookout for trouble?" Jim demanded.

"Perhaps." Toby seemed genuinely uncertain, and met Jim's eyes levelly. "It's just luck I got here when I did."

A snort of mocking laughter ambushed Jim. "And you're going to save me from some fate worse than death, are you?"

The mockery was pointed, but he was not at all sure who was being mocked by it, Toby or himself. The balladsinger only chuckled. "Well, now ... I might be able to turn a foul wind into a fair sailing breeze."

"Meaning?" Jim dropped his voice as Toby stepped closer.

"Meaning, Margie adds up to trouble," Toby said thoughtfully, "but it doesn't have to involve you."

"But it involves you?" Jim's voice dropped again. "You're a puzzle, Toby Trelane."

Unexpectedly, the wide blue eyes glittered with amusement. "Now, why do you say that? Because I knew a poor Spanish girl who was so down on her luck, she was begging for pennies for medicine?"

"That, and ... the rest of you." Jim cocked his head at the man. "Balladsinger, traveler – not a sailor, but you often talk like one. You know the prayers for the dead, in the old language. You tell stories about men who love men. Who the hell are you? Where are you from?"

For a moment Toby seemed to hesitate and then he said, amused, "I was born in London, but my parents were from Tavistock. They're both dead now. I've a sister, but I wouldn't know how to find her. I grew up in Plymouth, went to school in Warminster. You could say I'm from lots of places, and call none of them home." His eyes danced as they studied Jim.

And for one moment Jim was so sure he saw invitation in them, he had lifted his right hand and placed it on Toby's chest before he was even aware of what he was doing. The gesture was done before he could stop himself, and in the next split second he actually waited for Toby to jump back and perhaps even lash out.

Instead, Toby's left hand covered Jim's, holding it there on his chest, and the moment stretched on and on, a year long, as Jim felt the old familiar jolt of excitement which always thrilled through him when like recognized like. Warmth flushed outward from his belly, reaching his cheeks as well as points much further south, and he watched Toby's lips curve into a smile.

Oh, yes, like knew like. The moment could have been a flash of summer lightning. Jim could almost taste Toby's kiss on his own mouth when footsteps raced up to the kitchen door, and it was Jim himself who jumped back with a scant second to spare before little Danny Flynn dove in.

Breathless, clutching a stitch in his side, he flopped down on the stool Jim had recently vacated. "I found the doctor," he panted. "Right behind us, 'e is – 'e were saddlin' up a nag when I left 'im, and 'e were comin' right 'ere, no stops."

"That's well run, Danny," Jim said ruefully, sharing a glance with Toby. "Now, you take a pastry and an apple, and then be off home. Mind you don't spend your largesse all at once!"

It would be toffee and liquorice, he guessed. Boys were always the same. Danny would spend his penny one farthing at a time and hide in the hedgeback to eat his sweets, where his many siblings would not see and want to share. The boy grabbed a wedge of pie and an old apple from the crate in the corner, and rushed out as fast as he had rushed in.

"He's a good lad," Toby observed.

"He is." Jim forgot the child at once, and was intent on Toby. "Well, now."

"Well, now, indeed," Toby agreed, and licked his lips, a tiny give-away gesture. "I *knew* I was right about you."

"But you never want to speak, not till you're sure," Jim added.

"Because the consequences can be dire," Toby finished, and shadows chased swiftly across his face before he could hide them.

Jim's humor sobered fast. "Damnit, you've been caught?"

"Me?" Toby's face shuttered. For several moments he did not speak, and when he did, it was in an odd tone. "It takes a terrible fool to have to learn by his own mistakes, Master Fairley. One learns not to be *quite* so stupid."

Which told Jim everything, and nothing. "A couple of lads were flogged for the sin of fornication just last year, at the assizes," he said bitterly. "You soon discover how to be careful."

"You do." Toby was listening. "I hear a horse."

"That would be John Hardesty, as good as his word." Jim set down his cup. "We've brought him out here on a wild goose chase. I'll go and tell him it's too late. You might have a word with Marcus Stiles, the undertaker, so at least they know what name to write in the parish record book. A name is better than nothing."

"Marguerite Fergo," Toby said sadly, "age 22, or 23, lately of the city of Corunna. May she rest in peace on this foreign shore."

"And what the hell was she doing here?" Jim wondered.

"A very good question," Toby whispered, but although the look on his face suggested he knew exactly what the girl had been doing on the Dorset coast, he was not about to breathe a word of it.

With a smothered curse Jim stepped out into the tavern yard, where the shadows were short and the full sun had warmed the bricks at the back of The Raven. He leaned his shoulders there, waiting to see Hardesty's tall chestnut horse as he came around from the path.

Moments later he called the man's name. "John! It was good of you to come, but I'm afraid we've only wasted your time today. The little waif died not long ago."

Hardesty was a big man, thick-set – fifty, with a face tanned brown as a walnut and deeply seamed. He had spent twenty years as an army surgeon, and had a piece shot out of his shoulder to show for some battle where he had actually grabbed up a musket and fought when the hospital was overrun. With a couple of brandies under his belt he liked to show off the scar, and would shrug out his waistcoat and shirt, displaying a torso only just beginning to run to flab. He wore a well-powdered gray wig which covered a scalp that had long ago shed most of its own hair; his coat was the color of a fox and his boots were thigh-high and polished till Jim thought he could have shaved in them.

"Wasted me time, have you?" Hardesty was hitching the gelding to one of the big iron rings set into the wall. He spoke with a Bristol accent, and gave Jim his hand. "She was just a young girl, so Joe Flynn's lad said."

"A Spanish girl, according to a guest of mine who recognized her, quite by chance," Jim said thoughtfully. "Mrs. Clitheroe said she was ill when she appeared out of the night, wanting pennies to go to the apothecary this morning. Alas, she didn't live long enough to make it."

"That's a shame, that is," Hardesty said with genuine regret. "Will I take a look at her?"

"It's a bit late for a doctor's attentions," Jim remonstrated.

"But we might want to be sure she didn't die of anything catching," Hardesty mused. "There was yellow fever on a ship that got in from points west, just three or four days ago."

"Yellow fever?" Jim echoed, and pointed Hardesty at the coach house. "She's in there, waiting for the undertaker."

He fell into step with the doctor but hung back at the door as Hardesty went inside. The girl lay under a coach rug, decently covered now. Leave it to Edith Clitheroe to think of the niceties.

"Is there anything you need?" Jim offered doubtfully.

Hardesty had stooped to lift down the rug and look at the girl's face, and he swore softly. "Poor little mite – so young and so pretty. And no, Jim, there's nothing I need. At first glance, I'll be buggered if I know what she died of, but it *wasn't* yellow jack. Be grateful for that much."

"Amen." Jim craned his neck but could see nothing.

"She's wearing an ugly big bruise," Hardesty mused a moment later. "Did you get a look at it?"

"I didn't get close enough to her," Jim admitted.

"Great black bruise on the side of her neck," the doctor told him as he set the blanket back into place. "She'd been roughed up, by the looks of her. A pound gets you a penny, she was injured in some bit of nasty business, and it just took a day or three to put her in the ground. There'll be a man behind this, you mark my words. Women are such fragile creatures. Lay a blow on them that a man might easily weather, and it'll be flowers in the churchyard come Sunday. Damnit, if she'd been alive, I'd have winkled the name out of her. I'd've been pleased to take it to the captain at the garrison, and get the man three months in Newgate Prison for beating her. Six months, if I could browbeat the judge into a moment's decency."

And now it would have been a rope around the neck of the same man, for the crime of murder, Jim thought, save that the girl had taken the secret to the grave with her. The bastard would never pay the price. He had caught one glimpse of Marguerite Fergo as Hardesty held up the blanket. She had been lovely, quite pretty enough to be caught in the snare of becoming the doxie of one man after another. It was a bad life, often filled with danger, and when a girl's looks faded with time, what would become of her? Jim sighed as Hardesty settled the rug and stepped back.

"Well, I'll tell Captain Dixon," he was saying. "I've got to go into Exmouth anyway, tomorrow, so it's no trouble to call in and see Roger. He has a horse he wants to show me … he knows I'm too soft hearted to let an old warhorse go to the knacker's yard for the sake of a few shillings and a feed in my paddocks."

"Sorry to have brought you out," Jim began.

But Hardesty would hear none of it. "It's a glorious April day, and a good stretch of the legs. Though, I wouldn't say no to a pint of ale and a piece of last night's treacle pudding, if you're offering."

Jim beckoned him toward the kitchen. "I'm offering! And thank you, John. It's good of you to be here for a young girl neither of us knew."

But Toby had known her, Jim mused, and the thought dogged him through luncheon and on into the afternoon, when Marcus Stiles arrived with his cart and a cheap pine box. Toby talked at length to the undertaker, telling all he knew of the girl, which was not really so much.

A plain wooden marker would stand in the churchyard. It would say, 'Marguerite Fergo of Corunna, age 23, died this 22nd day of April in the Year of Our Lord 1769.' Stiles was writing down everything Toby could tell him, and Vicar Morley would record every word faithfully in the parish register. The girl would be interred tomorrow or the next day, and in a week the incident would be forgotten.

Forgotten, Jim thought, by all but Toby Trelane. And Toby's face was dark as a thundercloud as he watched Stiles's vehicle rumble away. It was very obvious he knew a great deal more than he was saying, and a shiver assaulted Jim as he watched from the front windows of The Raven. The cart rattled off, drawn by a big black horse which walked patiently behind the undertaker, back towards Exmouth. Toby stood right in the middle of the path that followed the great sweep of the bay, watching Stiles's vehicle out of sight as if he expected to see *something*. Jim could not imagine what, and not knowing troubled him.

He listened with half an ear to Hardesty's chatter about a racehorse, foxhunting, a fighting cock that had won him the princely sum of two guineas, and the lord of the manor, whom he would not name, who went to France to buy brandy and came back with the worst case of clap Hardesty had ever seen, despite his twenty years of treating soldiers.

The gossip was interesting enough, but Jim could not concentrate on it, not when Toby was standing in the sun right outside the windows, with his hair shining like gold and every line in his lean young body calling to Jim with the allure of the forbidden, the delicious, the very fruit that had seduced Eve herself.

Chapter Five

The sky dimmed in the late afternoon, and the sea air grew chill an hour before rain began to pelt the thatch. Such weather in the evening was usually bad for business, and by five Jim had resigned himself to sharing a rum with Fred Bailey before he locked the doors early and took up the challenge of Toby Trelane.

But at six the laborers from the nearby farms began to duck in out of the drizzle, and by half after he was seeing faces from the villages within easy walking distance. A cauldron of stew was bubbling on the kitchen fire, full of pickled pork, onions and dumplings, and farthings began to rattle into the coin box. Jim lifted a brow at Toby as he poured a fifth mug of ale in three minutes, and Toby answered with a small, flourishing bow.

The locals were eager this evening. The same customers were back, and they had brought twenty more. On a night when Jim would usually have sat by his own hearth, watching the fire and listening to the wind in the chimney, the tavern was busy. At least for a while, the balladsinger was going to be good for business.

Tonight he sang a Spanish tune about a young girl whose lover went to war and had not yet returned, and perhaps never would, then launched into a ribald monolog concerning 'a farmer from Dorset who needed a corset, his back was all twisted and bent; along comes a lady who looks a touch shady, but has stays that'll lace 'round the gent. Then, right up from Dover a black Irish rover arrives with a nod and a wink; says, "What a surprise, you're a sight for sore eyes in pink corsets … might I buy you a drink?"'

The more the rum flowed, the better his audience liked the bawdy humor, and Jim wondered how many more of these songs Toby knew. But it was the end of the story of Diego Monteras they wanted to hear. Before he could sing again they sent him pie and ale, and had him retell the first half for benefit of those who had missed it. The food was soon dispatched, and Toby pulled up the stool as he launched into the end of the adventure.

With a familiar sense of amusement Jim settled to listen, and for half an hour Toby spoke of pirates and Spaniards, priests from hell and murderous angels, witches, ghosts, strange magic and hellhounds.

Sir Geoffrey Gaunt took the Queen's commission and returned to the Caribbean on the spring winds of the year following. He chased the treasure of Diego Monteras for three years – along the way, he found a haul of gold and diamonds that would have warmed the cockles of Queen Elizabeth's notoriously avaricious heart, but he never found the treasure which Monteras and Francisco had buried.

And in the final season before he called an end to the expedition and headed east, the letter and the fragment of map vanished. They were stolen, so went the story, and though Gaunt never knew for sure who had taken them, he suspected a merchant from Florence who had gone out to the Indies for exotic goods to please the rich Italian markets.

There, the story of the treasure of Diego Monteras reached its end, but Jim saw a wicked glitter in Toby's eyes and he could guess what was coming.

"It's still out there," he said to his rapt audience. "The most dazzling haul of gems, beyond anything the King of Spain himself could imagine, is still out there, waiting to be discovered by a lad – perhaps even one of you in this very tavern, tonight – who can hunt down the bit of map, make sense of its clues and follow it to a bay on the landward side of an island off the east coast of the Americas.

"Now, the Queen of England got a great shipload of gold, so she was happy. Sir Geoffrey was rich beyond anything he'd ever dreamed, so they were *both* happy. I've heard a reliable story that says a disreputable merchant from the wrong side of Florence coerced a money lender in Genoa for the largesse to buy three ships and outfit an expedition, the goal of which he never whispered to any soul aboard. The ships certainly anchored in friendly Spanish ports, where the merchant was made welcome, and then ..."

He shrugged expansively. "And then history loses sight of that little bit of map, and the treasure of Diego Monteras remains just where it was buried. Waiting," Toby added, looking from face to face, "for the right lad to find the clues and follow them to riches that could make any one of you a king."

The Raven was silent as the rummies savored the potential in the end of the story. Toby took a drink, strummed the mandolin, tuned a string or two, and glanced sidelong at Jim before he demanded of his audience, "So what'll you hear now? A love song, or something disgusting?"

Last night's customers shouted for The Hogshead, and Toby chuckled as if he had expected it. His fingers flew over the strings and he began, "Come, cheer up, my lads, there's a hogshead of rum –"

In a week they would know every word, Jim thought as he returned to the bar, but next they would want to know every word of the song about 'the farmer from Dorset, caught wearing the corset, the pink one with ribbons and bows; and the wild Irish rover who'd roll in the clover with anyone – yes, even *those*!'

Or, especially *those*? Jim wondered. The songs were wicked enough to get the local rummies laughing. If Toby knew enough of them, he could earn a decent living between Plymouth and Margate, wandering the coast, back and forth, always welcome whenever, wherever he arrived.

They crowd was starting to break up at nine, and he returned the mandolin to the corner by the hearth, with the stool and his coat. "Come back tomorrow," he called to the men who were leaving, "and I'll tell you the story of Dolly McGuire and the handsome young Vicar of Haughton Vale ... a haunted church with a graveyard that drove men mad, and a terrible secret it took a sweet young maiden to uncover – and how she went in a virgin, and came out ... well, come back tomorrow!"

They were hooked like so many trout, Jim knew. When the last of the locals had wandered home, leaving only two who were so drunk, they would snore in the back of the taproom they were thrown out at dawn, he raked through the coin box and dropped six bright halfpennies into Toby's hand.

"You don't have to pay me," Toby protested, "not when you're feeding me better than I've been fed in years, and I'm sleeping on a soft bed."

"You're due your share." Jim tipped the rest of the coins into a pouch, leaving sixpence in the box, in farthings and halfpennies, to make change tomorrow. "I'm doing business in the middle of the week that I'd have been delighted to do on Saturday. This crowd seems to love a bawdy song and a good story. You know a lot of them?"

"Scores of stories and hundreds of songs," Toby assured him. "I've been collecting them for years, since..."

He said no more, leaving Jim to guess – since he walked off the ship where he and Charlie Chegwidden had served for a short time? Or since he had lost the position that let him earn a living without battering his hands? Because the hands that had plied the mandolin were still fine, supple, slender, at an age when most men's had been turned to iron and leather by two decades of hard work. And Jim fiercely wanted those hands on him.

With the doors locked and the fire banked down to preserve the last embers till morning, he turned back toward Toby and waited. They were alone now – the drunks in the back were snoring, unconscious. There was only the wind in the chimney, the sizzle of the occasional drop of rain which made its way into the hearth. Bess lifted her head, looking drowsily at Toby, but she was curled up with Boxer while Toby –

The balladsinger was smiling, as enigmatic as ever, and for a moment Jim smothered a groan, fully expecting him to say something unfathomable and retire, as if he had forgotten the moment of recognition they had shared just before the Flynn boy ran in.

But Toby said nothing. His eyes smoldered on Jim, never leaving his face as he walked past him to the stairs, and up. He stopped on the third step and turned back. His left hand extended in the invitation Jim had been waiting for, longing for.

Jim's right fingers slipped into Toby's palm, found it warm, dry, firm, and then Toby's grip tightened on his hand and he went on up the stairs. At the top he hesitated, and Jim gestured toward his own room. He hardly knew his own voice as he said,

"The mattress is better on my bed. That is, it'll hold two … two tied in a knot, you understand … without flattening out like a girdle-cake."

"Then, your bed it is," Toby whispered, and let Jim lead him the other way, to the big room at the end, right over the bar, where the heat of the chimney made it warm as a lady's boudoir.

Two lamps fluttered to life, flames dancing in the draft from a shutter that could have fit better. The same draft raised a prickle of gooseflesh on Jim's skin as he turned to study Toby in the soft light. He was like pale gold, his eyes shadowed, and Jim fancied they were filled with mystery. There was much of the exotic about Toby, a quality that inspired Jim to discover his secrets if it took a dozen years. Or a lifetime.

"You're very beautiful, Master Fairley," Toby said softly.

"Me?" Jim was inclined to scoff. "I've got youth on my side – and all my teeth, which is only damn' good luck. But, you, now … you're not like the rest."

"The rest?" Toby took a step closer, close enough to draw a caress about Jim's face.

"The men you've meet on this coast, in this house." Jim closed his eyes to savor the feather-light sensation of the caress. "I've known a highwayman, and a young earl, and the bastard son of a duke, and a Dutch sailor. And you're not like any of them."

"I'm flattered." Toby's voice deepened, roughened, as he came closer still.

His arms slid around Jim almost experimentally and Jim lifted his head, hunting for the kiss he had been imagining since noon, when the Flynn boy beat him to it by no more than a minute.

It was light at first, as they both explored new territory, and Jim's heart jumped in his chest like a deer. Toby gave a groan, and his arms tightened around Jim. He leaned closer and his mouth was suddenly hard, his tongue flicking across Jim's teeth, and inside.

This was the kiss Jim had been trying to imagine. He clasped Toby in an embrace strong enough to test the man's ribs – found him slender as a lad, hard with solid, healthy muscles, supple as a dancer. His hands plucked at Toby's waistcoat, and the shirt beneath, while in the same moment Toby was tugging Jim's shirt loose as if he were desperate for the feel of skin on skin.

He heard a seam open as the linen pulled off over his head, and gave a breathless chuckle. "Where's your hurry? Take your time, Toby."

"Sorry. It's just … old habits," Toby said, as if speaking at all was nearly impossible.

"The habit of rushing?" Jim threw his shirt aside and watched as Toby dragged off his own. "You mean, rushing before you get caught?"

"Something like that." Toby was either intent on Jim's chest or reluctant to meet his eyes. Perhaps both. He splayed his fingers over Jim's breast, feeling the soft down in the hollow, thumbing the nipples.

It was Jim's turn to groan and he reached for Toby, hands clenching into lean young limbs, hunting for another kiss before he dropped the britches that had begun to bind him. And then he felt an odd coarseness he had not expected, and pulled his hand back. "Toby, what –?"

Toby's head was down, and he would not look up now. He just turned, put his back to Jim and the lamp, and let him see. Jim swore quietly, swallowing hard as anger rose, fast and hot.

The scars were old. The stripes were long healed but there were so many of them, and in such a pattern, he knew without asking, Toby had been flogged not once but several times. He had not seen his back earlier, when Toby was cutting firewood. Now he remembered the scene deliberately, he realized Toby had been careful to face him, keep his back out of sight, as if he thought he must guard the secret.

With a soft oath, Jim traced the lines of two, three of the longest scars. "Why? Because you – you like men? And you were caught?"

Even now, when the secret was out, he seemed reluctant to speak of it and chose his words with the utmost care. He turned around and put the scars out of sight by lying on them. Still in his britches, he sprawled across Jim's bed and looked up at him unblinkingly.

"I might have been caught, but the men who'd have been very happy to flog me never actually did catch me. I won myself these souvenirs by speaking out in the defense of others. It was a stupid thing to do, I suppose, but at the time it was a ... a matter of honor."

"Damn." Jim's erection had dwindled, and he sat on the bedside, stroking the shape of Toby's lean torso. "I know you don't want to talk about it."

"I don't want to talk at all." Toby's half closed eyes were intent on Jim's body, and his right hand crept into the warm folds at his groin. "I'm damaged goods, but if you still want me ..."

"You're very beautiful, Master Trelane," Jim growled, "and we're all of us damaged goods. What d'you call this?" He slapped his left thigh and then deliberately stood up, unbuttoned the britches and dropped them fast, along with his linen. With other men he had always dreaded this moment, because if one looked closely enough, his legs were obviously mismatched. The left was thinner than the right because the muscles were smaller, under the palm-sized scar he would carry for life. In a quick encounter he could often hide his legs in darkness or sheets, or contact too close for his partner to even see. But for the first time, with Toby, he realized he had no need to hide, and the realization was like the gift of liberty.

Toby saw everything. He saw the scar, the mismatched limbs and the hopeful erection which even now stood at half-mast. He saw it all, and he smiled. His hand extended for the second time, and Jim was glad to take the invitation.

He settled beside him, toying with the wide brass belt buckle, and then for the fun of teasing, ignored it and cupped his hand around the shape and bulk beneath the pale fawn britches. Toby was up and hard already. He gasped as Jim palmed him and pressed, and he did away with his own belt left-handed, flicked open the buttons and gave a curious wriggle.

Seduced, Jim delved inside, into warm linen and warmer flesh. He found a shaft as hard as a bar of iron wrapped delicately in satin, and curved his hand around it to measure its girth. Toby took a ragged breath and his hips lifted in a long, slow arch, sinuous as a snake.

He had a grace, even here, that Jim envied, and his hand began to move on the long, thick root of him while he watched Toby's face to see what he liked, and how he liked it. For some time Toby seemed content to be handled, and then he caught Jim's wrist to stop him and gave him a rueful look.

"One more minute, and it'll be over."

"I know," Jim said smugly. "I know what you need."

"But I don't want it to be over," Toby purred. "And I might be able to get by with your hand, but there's a lot more I'd *like*, if you were willing." He was catching his breath as Jim let him rest. "Have you done it often? Have you done it all?"

Oh, Jim knew what he meant, and while one part of him might have teased and pretended innocence, the rest of him was too eager. "Often enough," he confessed, "and yes, I've done it *all*, as you put it ... though not as often as you might think."

Toby relaxed visibly. "Ah."

"You didn't want an ignorant little virgin?" Jim actually chuckled as he caught Toby's britches in both hands and tugged them down and off.

"Not really." Toby propped himself on both elbows and watched as Jim clambered over him, swung astride him as if he were mounting a pony, and settled there. "It *can* be sweet, educating a virgin, but it's a weight of responsibility I don't relish. The loss of innocence shouldn't be taken lightly, and the education can be as bitter as sweet."

"Ouch," Jim observed. "Now, that was the voice of experience talking! You were ravished as a youth?"

"Good lord, no. But I've had a virgin or two," Toby said wryly, "and I suppose I'm too tender hearted to be cavalier about the deed. It's bloody hard work, getting it right, making it all sweet as flowers for them. And if you get it wrong, you're a monster." He shook his head with rueful humor. "Not tonight. Not here. I'm grateful for a man with some experience. A man," he added, hunting for a kiss, "who knows how to handle me, knows how it all works ... and what he wants."

"What *you* want," Jim added, breathing the words into Toby's mouth.

"What I might want," Toby murmured against his tongue, "if it were offered by a generous heart, with something like affection."

They were words Jim had never heard from a man, though he had been with many in the years since he awoke to his desires. The London docks were a rare education on long, chill autumn nights. Jim had lost count of the men he had known, some for a night, others for only an hour. Once, he had spent a whole week with a French lad who was waiting for a specific ship, but even then – affection? The word had never been thought, much less mentioned.

And all at once he realized Toby was right. It was affection Jim had been longing for. Not just the delicious frisson of skin on skin, the heavy beat of another heart against his own, the eruption of excitement, old fashioned lust and pleasure beyond price. These things were precious, but there was more, and Jim had never yet let himself think that far.

Toby was a few years older. He had four or five more years under his belt, and the wants and needs had begun to mellow. Jim leaned down, held his weight on his palms and looked into the remarkable eyes. "You're an odd one, Toby. Not like the rest."

"You've said that before. But do you cherish me for it, or scorn me?" Toby wondered.

"Scorn," Jim told him, "is the *last* thing I feel for you." And he put his head down to kiss as, slowly and deliberately, he settled on Toby, matched their bodies hip to hip, shoulder to shoulder, and began to hump in the ancient, exquisite rhythm.

Soon enough – and far sooner than Jim would have preferred – the leg began to spasm and a thin knife of pain lodged in the muscles. He knew when to stop, and looked down into Toby's face with a murmur of apology. Without a word, Toby's arms closed about him and Jim found himself rolled over, set down on the mattress with surprising gentleness, before the slow, humping rhythm began again.

Toby might have been lean but he had a strength like whipcord, and Jim envied his muscles as well as the legs that never seemed to tire. A fine sheen of sweat broke across Toby's skin. Jim's fingers slipped in it, across the scarred back, and Toby stilled. He lifted his head, eyes closed, and Jim felt a shiver course through him. It might have been the first time anyone had touched those scars with a caress, an expression of tenderness.

With a soft sound that might have been anguish the balladsinger moved down, and down again, and Jim held his breath, expecting the heat of his mouth, wanting it. Needing it. He gasped, swore, as Toby's lips discovered him, and his hands clenched into the sheet.

Oh, Toby Trelane was good at this. Jim could not remember another as skilled, nor as willing, and he reveled shamelessly in everything Toby gave him. At last the fair head lifted and Toby was on him again, hard, and heavy for one who was so slender. Those limbs possessed an astonishing strength, and Jim reveled in this too.

He was perilously close, and Toby knew it. He had wanted to taste Toby, feel the size and shape and heat on his tongue, but it seemed Toby was far too close to let him do it this time. Instead, he settled down and those strong hips kept the age-old rhythm as long as he could while Jim arched under him, thrust up against him, needing little more.

For a man whose songs could be ribald, he was strangely quiet as he came. Jim might have expected him to cry out, even to shout, but Toby made no sound at all. A moment later Jim followed him, holding onto the moment of pleasure, making it last as long as it would before reality encroached.

Rain pattered; one of the lamps stuttered in the draft from the shutter which had needed fixing for too long; far away, a dog was barking. The world righted and Jim opened his eyes to find himself looking into Toby's face. His cheeks wore a slight flush, the blue eyes were languorous, dark.

"Thank you," the balladsinger said, barely a murmur.

"You're thanking me?" Jim chuckled. "It takes two to dance this particular quadrille."

"And you dance it very well."

"So do you." Jim reached over the side of the bed for his shirt, which was bound for the laundry anyway, and used it to swab away the evidence. It was impossible to tell which seed was his own and which was Toby's, and the thought made him smile. He threw the shirt toward the door and reached for the counterpane. "I'd speculate you've had a great deal of practice."

"Some," Toby admitted. "And before you ask ... don't. Please."

"You're full of secrets." Jim frowned at him as he settled, head on the same pillow.

"I am indeed." Toby stretched his spine, flexed his hips and shoulders. "And you'll fare better for not knowing the reasons for them."

But Jim was far from certain. He was sure of only one thing, and the thought haunted him as he lay awake, long after Toby was asleep. He wanted Toby Trelane here for a long time. Wanted to wake up with this body beside him, see this face first thing in the morning and last thing at night. And the only doubt that bedeviled him was the question of whether the balladsinger would stay, or if he was the wandering type whose feet itched to move on, no matter how agreeable the place he found himself.

Chapter Six

Toby woke early, while dawn was still dim, and the first Jim knew was the kiss on the side of his neck, the whisper in his ear. "Stay where you are. I'll bring coffee, and a piece of Mrs. Clitheroe's apple pie, if you could eat it."

In fact, Jim discovered himself starving as soon as his eyes were open. With lazy appreciation he watched Toby gather up his clothes, and murmured in surprise as he saw a mark he had not seen in the lamplight. It was a brand, old and pale now, the kind of mark a horse would wear, high on his flank, where it had been invisible in the softer light. Toby had cracked the shutter and swung open a window for air, and just enough daylight made it into the room for Jim to see the brand.

"What's that?" He yawned, rubbed his face and peered at the mark until Toby pulled up his britches and set it out of sight. "Were you a prisoner?" It would explain so much.

"Of a kind," Toby said, as evasive as always. "You promised not to ask."

"No, I didn't," Jim retorted as he pushed himself up against the pillows and dragged the counterpane around himself for warmth. The hearths had been out for hours, the chimney stack was cold and the sea air was sharp with chill. "But I know how to respect a man's privacy," he added as Toby shrugged into shirt and waistcoat and swiped up his shoes and stockings. "Seriously, Toby … you've no need for secrets. Not after what we did last night."

"What we did wasn't much," Toby said chidingly, "and as I told you even then, you'll be better off not knowing any more about me than you already do!"

Jim was about to scoff and say he would be the judge of that himself, but Toby stepped out before he could speak. "Bugger," he said to the empty room. "I hate a mystery."

He heard the creak of the stairs and the rake of fire irons in the hearth directly below, and smiled. He knew exactly where Toby was, even before he heard him talking to the dogs. The front door opened, Boxer and Bess ran out; and then Toby was laughing, and Jim could not stay in bed any longer, no matter the offer of coffee.

Hastily dressed, still tucking in his shirt tails, he was at the bottom of the stairs when he heard Toby saying, "Zachariah Pickworth, you're green right up to the ears. If you're going to empty your belly, get *outside* before you do it!"

Zachariah was one of the pair of rummies who had been face-down and snoring in the back of the taproom last night. His mate, Henry Bincombe, was not even awake yet – and Toby was right. Zachariah was four shades of green, from pea to pond, wearing a cold sweat and a hangdog expression. He was a widower, so there was no harangue waiting for him at home, but last night's grog would have its way with him before he was fifty yards closer to the shack he called his 'doss.'

The rummy stumbled off into the morning while Toby was still attending to the hearth. He was on one knee before it, teasing sticks of kindling into the last embers, blowing on them to coax life into them. Jim dropped his hands onto the broad back, wanting just to *touch* for the simple pleasure of it, and Toby looked up at him with a faint, almost shy smile.

"Good morning," Jim said huskily.

"It *is* a fair morning," Toby agreed, "though the decent weather won't last long. The sky'll be dark by noon. If I was going to be on my way, this would be the moment, else Bess and I will get a good soaking before we find another roof."

"But you're not leaving," Jim said softly. "Are you?"

The fire had caught alight, and Toby stood. "If I'm welcome..."

"You know you are."

"I'll stay awhile." Toby gestured at the mandolin in the corner. "They seem to like my songs and stories."

"And they don't get the better part of you." Jim's palms settled on the planes of Toby's breast. "I do."

"You haven't had the *best* part," Toby ventured. "Not yet."

"All the more reason for you to stay." Jim looked him over in the morning light, seeing the faint blond stubble on his cheeks, the tousle of his hair, and the inexplicable little quirk in his brows. "What?"

"Nothing," Toby said evasively.

"Fibbing's a sin," Jim informed him.

For some reason, the observation made Toby laugh aloud but he said only, "I promised you coffee and pie."

"Go on, then." Jim gestured him to the kitchen. "I'll get this fire going properly. Mrs. Clitheroe won't get in for hours yet, and you won't see a customer before noon. We have the place to ourselves."

"Except for Henry Bincombe." Toby gestured at the heap in the corner. "Ye gods, he drank his fill last night!"

"Henry always does." Jim watched Toby make his way back to the kitchen. "He inherited a hundred guineas when some old uncle died, and he's drinking it all away."

"Which is good for Master Fairley's business," Toby called through from the kitchen hearth, where he was raking over the coals now, breathing life into still glowing embers.

"But not as good as the balladsinger's going to be," Jim called back. "I've never seen such a crowd at midweek! If you know enough songs and stories to bring them back on Saturday night –"

"I know a lot more than that," Toby promised. "I told you, I've been collecting them for years."

"Since you lost your situation," Jim guessed. The fire was strengthening and the kindling was dry enough to crackle right into flames. Satisfied, he stood and worked the leg to and fro to limber it.

Toby's voice surprised him, so close, he could hear the breath carrying the words. "What situation would that be?"

"Oh, the employment that let you get to thirty years of age and more, and still have hands like these." Jim reached for them, picked them up and turned them over. "These aren't a laborer's hands. I *know* laborers' hands."

"I'm a balladsinger," Toby said pointedly.

"You weren't when you were fifteen or twenty." Jim pressed a kiss into the right palm. "Not before you had a grand stock-in-trade of songs and stories, and it takes years to find them, learn them. So ... you had a patron, did you?" He wound both arms over Toby's shoulders. "You've no need to guard your secrets so jealously. I won't tell."

"A patron." Toby seemed to mull over the wording. "I suppose you could use the term." His eyes were bright with rueful, self-mocking humor. "But it's not what you're thinking."

"And what am I thinking?" Jim wound his fingers into the soft fair hair, teasing it at Toby's nape.

"You're thinking," Toby speculated, "I followed my nose to Italy, where I was seduced by a count and sat on silk cushions till my arse grew calluses, playing the mandolin and warming the count's sheets by night, like as not."

Jim laughed delightedly. "It would've been the sweet life. True?"

"Oh, absolutely," Toby said in fatuous tones. "I still have the calluses on my backside from all those cushions. You didn't notice them?"

"I never got close enough to your bare arse to make its acquaintance," Jim told him. "I'll pay closer attention tonight." His fingers spanned Toby's skull, massaging gently, which made him groan in simple pleasure. The fingertips slipped down, and down again, and inside his shirt collar. And there they paused, for Jim felt another roughness, a scar he thought at first was part of the flogging – but scourgers had a code, he knew. They would 'flog a man fair,' never laying the whip on his kidneys or his neck, and this scar was at Toby's nape. "What...?"

"Just a mark." Toby shrugged. "You know by now, I'm covered in them."

"Another scar." Jim fingered it, and swore softly. "Exactly where a chain would lie, if you wore one."

"A chain?" Toby's eyes darkened by shades and he bent his head, laid his mouth on Jim's to silence him.

The kiss was hard, searching, and again Jim took everything Toby would give him. Men seldom kissed. All those sailors he had known, from the westcountry back to the docks of London itself, wanted to wrestle in the dark, grapple with young limbs, get on top and push and shove. Tenderness and familiarity were the least of it. It had been *fucking* – Jim entertained no doubts about what it was, what he had done, and had done to him. Affection had nothing to do with it.

This – this was a world different, as Toby kissed him long, deep and hard, until he must have known every part of Jim's mouth as well as he knew his own. At last he lifted his head away, drew back. His lips were swollen. His Adam's apple bobbed as he swallowed and said in a rough voice, "Coffee."

With that he vanished back into the kitchen, and it was several moments before Jim remembered the mark on his neck. It felt like exactly the kind of gall a man would develop when he wore a chain around his neck; the kind of chain, Jim thought, on which a big, heavy cross would hang. The kind of thing a priest or monk would wear.

Fascination prickled through him and he followed Toby into the kitchen, watched him spooning coarse coffee grounds and sugar into a pan of boiling water. His eyes were drawn to the slender musician's hands which had never done enough hard labor to show the wear and tear, and a dozen questions hovered on his tongue, demanding to be asked. He hunted for the right words as Toby slopped the coffee into a pair of battered mugs, but they were elusive as foxes in the snow and in the end he said thickly,

"You're a puzzle, Master Trelane."

"I am indeed." Toby offered him a mug.

Jim took it. "You're not going to tell me, are you?"

The fair head shook slowly. "They're my secrets. I've the right to own them, and keep them."

"Even though you're sleeping in my bed?"

"Even though. Just as you've the right to secrets of your own." He laid a finger on Jim's mouth. "Don't ask, for I won't tell."

"Damn." Jim's lips parted, and he sucked the tip of the finger for a moment. "I've no right to press you, I suppose."

"No right at all." But Toby was smiling again.

"And if I do, you'll leave."

"I ... might. And I don't want to. Not yet." He glanced around the kitchen and out into the taproom before he nodded in the direction of the bedroom, above. "I like all this. I'd be happy to stay here for a very long time, if only..."

"If only I keep my nose out of your business and let you be," Jim finished. He muttered a curse, fended Toby off and tried the coffee. "You brew a good mug."

"There's an art to coffee," Toby informed him. "There's also some pickled pork left over. I'll fry it for breakfast, if you like, and then get busy with the thatch. Have you looked at the sky? I want to get finished before *that* gets here!" He gestured at the open kitchen door, where the sky was a pale, uncertain shade and a few dirty gray clouds had begun to stream.

In fact, Jim had not even looked at the sky since last evening. Toby's remark sent him to The Raven's front door, where he had a view across the sands and the bay beyond, and he swore again as he saw the horizon – or *failed* to see it. A sea mist had come up overnight and the sky was ripped by a wind, high up. Another storm was coming in on the coattails of the first. Any sailor could see it coming, and Toby had recognized the signs at a glance.

"Sweet Jesus," he muttered, "it's the mother of the bastard that came scampering through the other night."

"I watched the first one from a stable door in Exmouth," Toby called from the kitchen. "The taverner wouldn't let Bess come inside, and sure to God, I wasn't going to leave her, or any dog, out alone in it. Thunder and lightning frighten them."

And he cared enough about a dumb creature to spend the night in the stable. Jim felt a little catch in his throat, and for several moments watched Toby Trelane rummaging among Mrs. Clitheroe's pans till he found what he wanted. Damaged goods, was he? Flogged to tatters not once but several times; wearing a brand on his flank such as horses and slaves wore, and a gall on his nape which could only have been left by the kind of heavy chain worn by monks and priests –

Had he been transported? Jim ached to ask. Had Toby been convicted of a crime and sentenced to years, or even life, in the Carolinas? Had he escaped and made his way home? But Jim knew better than to ask, for Toby's secrets seemed to pain him. The more daylight they were exposed to, the more they hurt – and with a start Jim realized that of all the things in the world he wanted, hurting Toby was the last of them.

So he clamped down on the wicked curiosity, ate the fried pork and eggs he was handed, and before eight o'clock chimed the two of them were working hard enough to raise a sweat.

It felt to Jim as if they were racing the clock. Every time he looked over his shoulder, the sky had darkened by another shade. They never saw the sun that day, and he counted more than thirty assorted ships and smaller vessels, all bolting for Exmouth, Falmouth, Portsmouth, ahead of the weather. They wanted to be unloaded, with the cargo under lock and key, and then be out again, well beyond the twenty fathom line and with a sea anchor set, before the storm hit. Jim had never been to sea, but he had spent long enough with sailors to know their wisdom.

The thatch was the hardest job, and because he could not manage ladders and roofing with any safety, Toby was on his own to finish what he had started in half the time he had reckoned on. The late morning was muggy with air so laden with moisture, sweat refused to dry. Jim threw off his shirt when he picked up the axe and set about cutting a pile of fuel and kindling for the kitchen. Toby had cut enough for the taproom hearth, but from long experience Jim knew how much fuel the kitchen would use.

He glared at the sky, wondering for the tenth time if the storm would go through in a night or if it would linger for a week-long downpour, till the lowlands turned into lakes and he was sweeping water out of the tavern. It had happened twice before and the locals only shrugged, as if it was to be expected.

"I'll cut the wood," Toby's voice said from the roof, as Jim began.

"You keep on with what you're doing," Jim told him tersely. "I'd rather swing an axe than climb around up there!"

"You'll make your leg ache," Toby warned.

"So you can rub it for me." Jim took a loose grip on the handle and sent the steel biting into the wood with vengeful force. He paused to look up and saw Toby outlined against the sky. "You know what you're doing?"

"I've never thatched a roof, but I watched the thatchers do it." Toby chuckled. "You're afraid we're going to leak like a sieve?"

"Afraid you're going to fall and break your neck," Jim corrected. "Then again, you look like you've been climbing around like a bloody monkey in the rigging, setting sails, half your life."

"Do I?" Toby had shifted the hammer into his left hand and was counting hoops and nails. "I'll be done in a few hours. We have that long."

He had dodged the issue neatly, leaving Jim with a rueful curse as he returned his attention to the wood.

They ate cheese, onions and yesterday's bread a little after noon, when Mrs. Clitheroe arrived late, full of apologies and explanations.

Her grandson had come to her cottage with warnings of bad weather. She lived near the bottom of a slope, and often flooded in heavy rains. "Now 'e wants to cart me off to Exmouth," she grumbled, thumping onions and potatoes onto the table.

"Kind of him to offer," Toby observed.

"'Sept I don't want to go," she said tartly. "I does nothin' but fight wi' yon stupid little cow of a wife of 'is. It's like they always sez – two women under the same roof, an' one of 'em a fool!"

"So stay here." Jim gestured at the ceiling with his mug. "There's only Toby and me in the house, and bedchambers going begging."

"Oh, I'll sleep in me own kitchen, down 'ere," the old woman began.

"You'll have a proper bedchamber," Jim corrected. "If the rains come for days, we'll be flooded as well. You remember two years ago, and the year before? Take a room upstairs, and be dry."

"Up them stairs, wi' these legs?" She gave him a mocking look. "Aye, when the rain gets up to yon doorstep, thee can carry me up."

"We can indeed," Toby told her. He lifted a teasing brow at Jim. "A pair of strong, healthy lads like us? No problem. Eh, Jim?"

"No problem," Jim said, deadpan. "But if we don't want to be setting out every pot and pan we own to catch the rain, we'd best get busy. Eh, Toby?"

With a flourish, Toby set aside his mug and plate. "Your pardon, madam," he told Mrs. Clitheroe with exaggerated gallantry, "I regret, I have to go and nail a roof."

She was still cackling when he had shinned up the ladder and returned to the thatch. Jim grabbed a tankard of ale and headed back to the task of carrying the split wood into the coach house, where it was stacked against the wall, furthest from the door. He could not step into the building without thinking of the Gypsy girl – Spanish girl, he reminded himself. Margie Fergo, lately of Corunna.

He stood in the place where she had ended her life, and sighed. How delicate and temporary life was; and how uncertain. From the coach house he could see the roof, catch a glimpse of Toby, and the future seemed to dance ahead of him like the will-o'the-wisp, half-seen, elusive, filled with promise and danger in equal measure.

The hoarse cries of gulls destroyed his reverie and he shook himself hard. The birds were heading for land, which boded ill. A glance at the horizon showed great slashes of rain, purple clouds against an indigo sky, and as he frowned at them a gust of oddly warm, wet air fell in his face. It would soon be stingingly cold, and rain was not far behind.

He set to work with a will and was filling the water casks from a pair of pails when Toby stepped into the kitchen. "I put the ladders back where I found them, tied down behind the stable." He plunged his hands into the washing water and dried them on the yard of sackcloth by the big brass dish. "What now, Jim? There's at least one shutter I *do* know of that needs fixing."

It was the shutter in Jim's bedroom, and mention of it brought a rush of heat to his face. Mrs. Clitheroe was oblivious, but he felt the flush in his cheeks and covered it by giving Toby a wink. "Check them all, while you're at it, and make sure they're locked down tight. Then, if you can manage it, you could run up to the market in Budleigh – you know it? – and get us half a gallon of milk and a pound or two of salt butter. God knows when we'll get any more." He nodded toward the bar. "Take sixpence out of the coin box and fetch some apples and cheese as well, if you can find any. I'd go myself, but –" He slapped the leg that infuriated him more today than usual. "I'll be far too slow, and unless I miss my guess, you'll be coming home in the rain even if you run!"

It was only later when he realized what he had said. *Coming home*. As if Toby Trelane belonged here now. Part of Jim ached to believe it was true, but he mocked himself for the whimsy. Toby was still a stranger. One tumble on the sheets did not make him a lifelong mate, though Jim knew he could feel himself falling hard.

"Fool," he told himself mercilessly as he hurried back to work. "You're a bloody halfwit, Jim Fairley, and if you're not careful you'll be learning it the hard way!"

Load by load, he brought the flotsam and jetsam of the spring season inside and stacked it beside the big wooden trapdoor to the cellar. The mountain of oddments had become daunting by the time the smell of stewing beef and onions issued from the cauldron on the hob, and Toby materialized at his side.

"We're all secure upstairs," he reported. "I begged a bag of rags from Mrs. Clitheroe and hammered them into a couple of casement frames, like caulking. I think we'll survive." He was looking at the trapdoor. "Can you manage here? I mean … damn, you *know* what I mean."

He meant, could Jim make it up and down steps that were as steep as ship stairs, twenty times, or thirty, to get this pile of gear stowed, and do it by the light of a single lantern.

"I'll manage," Jim muttered, furious with himself for the frailty of the limb – and for the vulnerability of his emotions, which was worse.

Toby's hand was light on his shoulder. "You'll sit down by the kitchen hearth and have a mug of something, and wait for me to get back from market. Sixpence from the coin box, you said?" Jim nodded. Toby hesitated. "With the weather like this, you'll get no business for the next day or three."

"All the more reason to get in some milk and butter." Jim gave him a push. "We've got plenty of lamp oil, and Edith says we can make do with what salt and flour and sugar we have. Go on, Toby, while you can. They'll be closing down the stalls and running for home in another half hour."

"Then I'll be quick." Toby drank a cup of water to the bottom and shrugged into the coat he had left on the chair in the corner. "Bess? Come on, girl, you fancy a run? What about you, Boxer? Come on!" He gave Jim a crooked grin and left the tavern via the bar, where he stooped to pull out the coin box and count out an assortment of farthings and ha'pennies.

The door had banged behind him and the dogs when Mrs. Clitheroe looked up from the pastry she was abusing with a rolling pin so old, the wood was nearer black than brown. "Now, 'e's a right good lad, is that un."

"Yes." Jim poured himself a mug of tea. "Yes, he is. And he's so full of secrets, you don't know what to make of him half the time!"

"Master Trelane?" She cackled again, like a broody hen. "I'd say 'e's been 'round the block a few times, is all. Thee's never been the places Toby Trelane's been, nor done the things 'e's done. None o' that makes the lad wicked, mind."

"Just makes me sheltered as a hapless little virgin girl," Jim observed with dry humor, and held up a hand to forestall her apologies. "No, don't say a word. You're far from wrong. Fred Bailey was saying the same thing – I need to get out, he said. Get out and do things, before I'm too old."

"An' old Fred'd be right," she said shrewdly. "Stuck in 'ere all day with the likes of Fred an' me…? Make thee old before thy time, it will. Still, Master Trelane's 'ere now."

"To stay?" Jim had sat on the stool at the hearth, and looked up at the old woman quizzically.

"To stay for long enough." She threw her considerable weight against the dough, rolling it out for the usual pies and pasties, though Jim doubted there would be any drinkers in the house tonight.

"Long enough for what?" He chuckled.

Mrs. Clitheroe looked at him cannily. "I dunno," she said at last. "But yon lad's good fer thee – 'e's a breath of fresh salt air in this musty old place. What, you didn't smell it?"

In fact Jim did, but he said nothing and finished his tea in silence, content to watch as she cut out the rounds for the pies, stacked them, and threw raisins into the leftover pastry pieces. His leg ached, if he bothered to notice it. He preferred to ignore it until it pained him too badly, and then reach for the rum in preference to the Dutch laudanum, since the rum did not knock him flat on his back and leave him dizzy.

The backdoor into the tavern yard was open, and he heard the rain begin. The sound of big, fat drops falling onto wet flagstones was exactly like the crackle of bacon sizzling in a skillet, and his nostrils flared as he smelt the rain too. It was sharp with the tang of the beach, and when a swirl of cold air wafted into the kitchen, he smelt the ocean there also – the scent of ships and harbors, ports that were the starting points for places unknown, and the mysterious lands known only as points on maps, with names like Barbados and Hispaniola, Java and Borneo.

With a shiver he went to the door, about to close it against the cold, rising wind and the steel-gray daylight, when he saw Toby come loping back into the yard with the dogs at his heels. His hair was plastered flat to his head; over his shoulder was a sack, tied down tight to his back, and he ran with his hands thrust deep into coat pockets, the collar pulled up about his ears.

The easy loping gait made Jim as envious as admiring. Toby was in fine condition – not even breathing hard as he came to a halt in the shelter of the eaves, where he slipped the sack off his shoulder. "Everything you wanted, and a couple of treats. They were almost giving away the milk and butter, to get rid of it before the storm. They don't know when they'll have a chance to sell it again – and sure to God, the cow won't stop making the stuff!"

They were inside as he spoke, and Jim secured the door behind him. The kitchen was dim, lit only by a half dozen lanterns. Toby took off coat and boots, and set them close to the fire to dry as Jim opened up the sack. Milk, in brown glass jars with the corks waxed into place; butter and cheese wrapped up in scraps of oilskin and tied with string; eight big red apples; and a bag that might have been a tobacco poke, but was stuffed with mint humbugs the size of a child's thumb.

Surprised, delighted, Jim chuckled. "We'll reward ourselves for hard work, will we?" He gave the mountain of gear a look of resignation. "Maybe after we've shifted *that*."

"Into the cellar." Toby was intent on the trapdoor, which was nestled into the back corner of the kitchen between the back door and the hearth. His brows knitted into a faint frown. "Well, now."

"Well ...?" Jim prompted.

But Toby shrugged away the question and grabbed a spare lantern from the shelf at left of the door. "Soonest started, soonest done, and I've worked up an appetite today." He stooped to light a taper at the hearth and took a deep breath over the cauldron of simmering beef and onions. "I won't be singing and storytelling tonight, but I'd say I've already earned my supper. Yes?"

"Supper, and a lot more," Jim decided, mindful of Mrs. Clitheroe.

The remark brought a sparkle to Toby's eyes as he lit the lantern. "Then, let's get this lot shifted, and we'll settle down and watch the storm come in. There were fishermen at the market – did you want fish? I don't care for it, myself, except for kippers – and they were saying the storm'll land on these shores around dusk. They were seeing lightning over the horizon before noon, and decided to head in early."

The lantern was burning brightly, and Jim beckoned him to the trapdoor. "Give me a hand with this. It's heavy."

The timbers were old, salvaged from a ship sunk on the coast about the time The Raven was built, a hundred years before. Two strong backs lifted it easily enough. Jim looked up into Toby's face, about to say he would go down first with the light, since he knew the steps, which were steep and inclined to be slick with moss. The look in Toby's eyes banished the words, and Jim hesitated. Toby had the lantern in his left hand, the better to balance his weight against the wall with his right, and he was already going down.

He *knew* these stairs – it was obvious he knew the cellar as well as he knew the rest of the tavern. But as a guest in the house of Charlie Chegwidden's old mother, who had owned The Raven outright since she was widowed, he should never have been shown this part of the building, and Jim was surprised. Disquieted.

Without comment he followed Toby down, watched him light a second lantern at the bottom of the steps. There, he took a lamp in each hand and turned around, peering into the coagulated, tar-thick shadows as if –

As if he was searching for something. Jim came down to the bottom stair and hovered there, intent on him for some moments before he found his voice. He said quietly,

"If you tell me what you're hunting for, I'll help you look."

Toby gave a small start and turned toward him with an almost sheepish expression. "I'm being a boor. I apologize."

"Don't apologize. Explain." Jim frowned around at the familiar cellar with its storage barrels, crates and cases. Sugar, flour, salt, tea and coffee were kept on the shelves in one corner; the kegs of rum and barrels of ale were stored, stacked one atop another, in the opposite corner, and between the two were crates of nails, coiled rope, assorted tools, discarded kitchen pots and rags, all manner of flotsam set down here against the day it was needed, now long forgotten and decaying.

"You're still looking for something of Charlie's, aren't you?" Jim wondered, more a statement than a question. "The same thing you expected to get when you arrived here, not knowing he was dead, rest his soul."

"Rest his poor soul," Toby echoed philosophically. He shrugged. "Forgive me, but you know I am." He hesitated and wore an apologetic look as he confessed, "I had a good look around upstairs while I was fixing the shutters. I even had a quick look around in the loft, while I was working on the thatch, in case…" He breathed a gusty sigh. "Sorry. I just thought, maybe Charlie might have hidden some of his things away where you and your father didn't find them, and –"

"And you might get what you came here looking for, after all," Jim finished. "You didn't find anything, then?"

The fair head shook, and Toby gestured with the lantern in his right hand. "I'm not seeing it here, either."

"What's it look like?"

"It doesn't matter, Jim. Honestly."

"I told you, I'll help you look. Whatever it is you're searching for, I probably don't even know I've got it, so – take it, and good health to you." Jim swiped the lantern out of Toby's left hand and played it around the cellar, casting evil shadows into the corners where moss grew, blue-green and malodorous. All he saw was the same old barrels, kegs, crates, cases.

"It doesn't matter." Toby was heading back up as he spoke. "There's a lot to move – stay where you are, and I'll pass the smaller things down to you. You know where you want to stash all this rubble?"

"Rubble?" Jim echoed.

"*Stuff*, then." Toby was back in the kitchen, and peered down at him, face lit weirdly from below. "Ready for the small pieces?"

It took less time than Jim had imagined to move the mountain of *rubble*, and he gave some thought to the sheer convenience of having a second pair of strong hands at the tavern. Toby would be useful.

If he stayed; and all at once Jim was uncertain. Toby was here *looking* for something, and if he found it – and even if he didn't – what was there at The Raven to keep him here? He sighed as he finished stacking the oddments to make most of them accessible, even while he knew he would not need anything here for six months, by which time it would be forgotten.

He was done when heard Toby's voice from up above, sharp with concern: "Whoa! It's all right, Bess ... come here, girl. It's fine. It's nothing."

The leg was acid-hot, as if with a knife wound, as Jim climbed back up. He heard the second roll of thunder, startlingly close at hand. The first had been muffled by the cellar, but Bess was shivering by the hearth and Boxer was wide-eyed, poised on his toes as if he would run at any moment, though there was nowhere to run to. Without being asked, Toby lent his hands to get the trapdoor back into place. It landed with a solid *thud* of ancient timber on older stone, and Jim blew out both lanterns. They sat smoking on the shelf while he came to the fire to warm his hands, and he and Toby listened to the wind. It had begun to howl softly in the chimney now, like a tormented soul trying to escape some hell.

"It's gunner be bad," Mrs. Clitheroe said sagely. "It's gunner be bad as the big un when I were a slip of a lass, an' four big ships was sunk between 'ere an' Portsmouth. Me uncle were on one of 'em, an' 'is wife come to live wi' us after, cuz the old bugger were a swine fer drink an' left 'er wi' nuthin' when the sea took 'im."

"Damn." Jim felt a shiver, right to the bone. He lifted a brow at Toby, who nodded.

"I've seen a few bastard storms, and this one's got the makings of a demon." He was moving as he spoke, heading for the tavern's front door, which he opened a mere crack to step outside.

Even that small gap let the wind whip in and Jim was quick to haul the wood back into place. They stood under the thatched eaves, watching surf crash onto the beach under a sky streaked with great arcs of lightning. The horizon was invisible in a blue-gray haze of rain, but Jim saw the whitecaps of waves, twice the height of a tall man, and the sea was gray and seething as molten lead.

A demon, Toby had said. The term was apt. The rain stung Jim's face and he was wet to the skin in the few moments they watched the sea and sky, trying to read nature's intent. No one was on the coastal path and no ships were in sight. They should be well out by now, with sea anchors set and a light crew of experienced hands aboard, secured to ride it out.

Lightning sheeted out the sky and the thunder boomed a scant second later, making Jim duck while his heart leapt into his throat. Toby's hand on his arm drew him back to the door. They wrestled it open and shut, and dropped the bar across it. Jim only used the bar when a sea wind came screaming in, strong enough to test the bolt. In all his years at The Raven this was only the fifth time he had slammed that bar into place, and with the shutters hammered down, the tavern was effectively locked against the world.

"Dam*nation*," Toby whispered, hugging himself. "I'm soaked to the bone. Will I get the big fire going out here in the taproom, or will we stay in the kitchen?"

"I'm for staying in the kitchen," Jim decided. "It's smaller – easier to heat and light." He plucked at his shirt and made a face. "I'm as wet as you are. You got dry clothes?"

But Toby made negative noises. "Only stockings and linen. I don't have much, as you well know."

He only seemed to own what he could carry, and he had come looking for Charlie Chegwidden, expecting his fortunes to change. Jim sighed. "My things ought to fit you. You're thinner than I am, but I never wore my clothes tight. You're taller than I am, but – the same."

"You're going to give me your castoffs?" Toby asked in a tone of such bitterness, Jim shot a startled look at him.

"I'm going to lend you some clothes before you catch your death of cold and die at my feet," he said sharply. "If you're even half as good at the balladsinger's trade as you say you are, you'll earn nice money here and in a week you can bugger off to Exmouth and buy whatever you like."

Toby had the grace to duck his head with a sheepish smile. "Sorry. I'm a little out of practice at being sociable."

"So I notice." Jim marched past him, to the kitchen door. "Edith, we're going up to get dry. How long till supper?"

"It'll be a good 'alf an hour," she told him over her shoulder as she slid a black iron tray of pasties onto the big hob to bake. "Take thy time, thee's got plenty of it."

So Jim headed for the dark well of the stairs without a glance back at Toby, only knowing the man was following by the footfalls a few paces behind him. He lit a brace of candles on the chest of drawers on the landing, and used one to light four more on the table at his bedside. The room was dim, chill, almost dank. Though the shutters were secured, a draft was getting in somewhere, cold on his cheek and making the candles stutter as he set them down.

He kept his clothes in two brassbound trunks by the foot of the bed. A seaman had left the chests here for safekeeping and never returned, nor even sent a message. More than three years after the man vanished, Jim baled up his belongings and pushed the bundle into a corner in the loft, in case he ever reappeared, but the trunks were useful. He humped them into his own room, where they remained.

He threw them both open and stood back. "Pick what you like," he invited Toby, bluff with a moment's embarrassment. "It's all the same to me."

"Is it?" Toby lifted out a handful of shirts and held them to his face. "Your things. They smell like you."

"The smell of me didn't bother you last night," Jim began, on the point of taking umbrage before he saw the soft smile on Toby's face. "Oh."

"They smell of … *you*," Toby repeated. "Jim Fairley, you're just as out of practice at being sociable as I am."

"I reckon I am, at that." Jim raked all ten fingertips through his damp hair. "I've known a few men, it's true. Well, more than a few! But none for more than a week, a lot for less than a day and some for less than an hour."

"I know how it is." Toby had dropped the wet clothes fast and reached out now, offering his hand.

Jim took it. The fingers were cold, wet. "For godsakes get into dry things! My mother used to say a man caught sickness in his lungs and his bones, running around in wet clothes. One day the ailment makes away with us all – it's the way your old mate Charlie died, as far as John Hardesty knew."

The mention of Chegwidden darkened Toby's mobile face, and he turned his attention to the clothes. A shirt, a pair of britches; the stockings and linen he had dumped at the foot of the bed – some of the few items he owned, carried in the capacious inside pockets of his coat.

He was thin, hard, pale in the candlelight, and shivering slightly. On a whim, Jim snatched up a blanket and wrapped it around him, and Toby held it there as he sorted linen from britches. "If you don't mind, I'll dry off a little before I put on your clothes, or they'll be almost as wet as mine."

"Don't get dressed on my account." Jim managed a creditable chuckle. "You're a pleasure to look at, in the state the gods created you."

"Skinny and covered in scars," Toby said disdainfully.

"Maybe you are." Jim only shrugged. "Maybe that's what I like."

The remark won him a chuckle. "You're a rare one," Toby informed him, studying him, head on one side.

Something in the dark eyes made Jim's pulse quicken. Without waiting to be invited, he took Toby by the shoulders and pressed him back, down, onto the bed. He sprawled here, all wiry limbs and fair skin, and Jim took the time to look long and hard at him, before he went down beside him and began to touch. A thousand caresses began at his face and breast and ended at the nest between the lean thighs; and there, Jim put his head down and began to work, while his own body throbbed eagerly to life.

He took his pay in groans and heavy breaths. Toby never seemed to make much noise, no matter how excited he became, but when the blood must have been like liquid fire in his veins, he whimpered. Jim heard all this, and slowed his fingers and tongue even while he relished the salt-sweet taste of Toby, and the heat and bulk in his mouth. He knew Toby was close and pushed him on now, urged and encouraged, before he held his breath and drank down the rush of blood-hot seed.

The whimpers abated, and for a moment he thought Toby wanted to rest. Jim waited there, grateful for the respite himself as he felt the tense shaft begin to relax against his lips. But what Toby wanted was very different. Astonishingly strong hands took him by the shoulders, brought him around and dumped him down, and before Jim could even curse Toby had him bare from breast to hips. Long arms went around him, lifted him into the right place, and then Toby moved against him and the straw colored hair was tickling Jim's belly.

It had been too long, Jim thought with some tiny corner of his mind that was still thinking while he and Toby moved together. It had been much too long, and life had a way of racing by, never to be recovered. Was The Raven his prison as well as his home, as Fred Bailey maintained? For a moment, as Toby's mouth, his tongue, brought Jim to a crest of ecstasy and excitement he had seldom had the time or liberty to court, he thought it might be.

The rattle of the shutter before the gale, the battering of rain lashing sideways off the sea, welcomed him back to reality. Thunder growled; the sea roared in counterpoint. Toby lifted his head and looked along at Jim with dark eyes and a wistful smile.

"You're a rare one indeed," he said thickly, as if his lips were still reluctant.

"I could say the same." Jim sat up, reached for Toby's head and kissed him hard. "Do you taste yourself on my tongue?"

"As much as you taste yourself on mine." Toby stretched his shoulders and plucked at the blanket. "Damn, do you feel that? It's getting colder."

"And I'm hungry," Jim added. "You want to eat?"

"We just did." Toby licked his lips.

"Yes, well you'll forgive me if I saved a corner for pie and ale!" Jim swung his legs off the bed and deliberately refused to notice the pain in the left. "Get dressed – I'll take your clothes down to the kitchen, put 'em over a chair in front of the fire."

"You're too good to me," Toby accused as he pulled an old shirt of Jim's over his head. It fit him as well as it fit Jim, and looked fine on him.

"Maybe I am." At the door, hands full of wet britches and linen, Jim paused. "Maybe I like to be. I'm allowed." He studied Toby for a moment longer, and stepped out.

Chapter Seven

Jim woke with a start and for a moment wondered where he was. His back ached, his head was thick as honey and he smelt pickled pork frying –

The kitchen. The three of them had opted to pull the big chairs out of the taproom, stoke the hearth and open a bottle of rum. The old lady soon went to sleep, snoring softly with Boxer and Bess at her feet on the new rag rug, while Toby and Jim passed the bottle back and forth, listened to the storm and made desultory conversation about government, ships, battles long ago and, as the rum had its way with them, old lovers.

It must have been after midnight when Jim slept at last, in the corner chair, and he knew a moment after he woke, what had jerked him out of his dreams. The dogs were gone, though Mrs. Clitheroe was still snoring quietly in the chair opposite, and the tavern's front door had just opened. The noise that had hauled Jim out of a confused dream about being locked in the hold of a ship with the water rising about his knees, was the thud as Toby set down the big timber locking bar.

With an ear cocked to the weather, Jim heard no thunder. For the moment the wind was silent in the chimney and he heard no lash of rain at the shutters. Rubbing his eyes, yawning, he followed the waft of fresh air. He smelt the sea, heard the roar of the waves before he stepped into the shaft of silver-blue daylight falling in through the open door. The morning was bitterly cold, but if the sky could be trusted, it was after nine already.

Little wonder his back ached and his neck suffered a powerful crick. He was rubbing both as he came out into the daylight, nostrils flaring on the scents of beach and ocean. His eyes protested the light but he saw Toby at once, and permitted himself the rare pleasure of just looking at him while the man had no idea he was being watched.

He was standing in the middle of the path, and for some moments Jim thought he was waiting for the dogs. Then he saw the truth, and his brow creased in a frown. Toby was looking out for something or someone. With his eyes, he was searching as far as he could see in both directions on the path before he looked out to sea, and Jim would have sworn he was hunting through the man-sized waves. He could only be looking for a boat.

The sky was low, dim, some shade between blue and purple, and though the rain had eased for an hour, more was on the way. The lowlands would be quagmire already and by evening, Jim knew from old experience, the flooding would be up to the doorsills of the poor people's houses. The air was chill, heavy with humidity, but Toby stood out there for a long time, getting damp, growing cold enough to hug his arms about himself – *watching*.

At last he turned back to the tavern, and Jim stepped inside a moment before he would be seen. He retreated to the bar, where a single lantern burned, and made a show of counting bottles as Toby stepped back inside. On the threshold, he whistled for the dogs. They hurried in as they saw the door about to close, and the taproom plunged back into semi-darkness.

"Cold out." Jim did not look up from the shelf under the scarred timbers of the bar.

"It's bloody freezing out," Toby corrected. "But the dogs needed to go about their business. You and Edith were still asleep – I tried not to wake you, but Bess insisted. *Out*, she said, or it'll be puddles, or worse, and Boxer didn't have an argument to make against the proposition."

Despite himself, Jim had to chuckle. Toby was certainly being evasive but he did it with enormous grace and charm. "You put a slab of pork on the hob before you stepped out. It'll be sizzling by now. Breakfast?"

"Too late for breakfast, too early for lunch." Toby rubbed his hands together. "It'll be raining again in an hour, and I think it'll rain all day. Have you ever flooded here – the tavern itself?"

"Twice." Jim abandoned the bottles and picked up the lantern. "There's a beck that runs down to the sea not thirty yards east of the stableyard. It'll hold a lot of water, but if there's enough rain on the higher ground, up there by Squire Lawson's place, we'll be bailing ourselves out."

"So, two days of rain, three, before we fetch out the buckets?" Toby wondered shrewdly.

"Three." Jim frowned at him. "Two storms in three days … it'll take *one* more day of the kind of rain that got Noah rummaging for hammers and nails, then you'll be helping me hump the firewood and food upstairs, and the grog." He was back in the kitchen, following his nose to the sizzling slab of pork.

"The cellar floods?" Toby was a pace behind him.

"It would, if I didn't seal the cracks down with mortar." Jim lifted the skillet over onto the table, set it down on a patch already burned black by hot iron. "It's a trick I learned when I was a lad, back in London. You lift the trapdoor, throw an oilskin over it, close it again so the rag-ends hang down below, like caulking, I suppose. Then you trowel mortar in all around. You could hammer in some oakum, but the stuff stinks like – well, like tar, because that's what it is! It's fine in the bilges of a ship, but you don't want it in the house, much less in the kitchen. The mortar's good enough to keep the water out of the cellar, else you'll be bailing it out by the bucketful, and the whole place stinks to high heaven with mildew for a year after."

"Like the stink of bilges. I know it well." Toby was hunting for clean crockery as the old lady woke. "Pork and eggs for breakfast, Edith?"

"Nay, lad, not yet. Least, not fer me. But I's gunner make a pan o' coffee." She hauled her bulk out of the chair and pressed both hands to her spine. "It's not rumblin' an' flashin'. We's dry upstairs, then?"

"For the moment." Jim examined the edge of the carving knife, and set about the pork while Toby cracked half a dozen eggs into the grease that had cooked out of it. He watched Toby without comment, wondering if he would answer an honest question, and then thought better of it. A devious question, perhaps. "Not many people around this morning?"

"I'm sorry?" Toby gathered the eggshells and crushed them between his palms.

"When you stepped out with the dogs." Jim's eyes were on the meat, in the interests of his fingers. "You didn't see many people on the path."

"No one at all," Toby said in an odd tone of voice – taut; filled with unspoken meaning.

Jim took the tone as his cue and angled a glance at him. "What, you were expecting someone, on a morning like this? Who'd be mad enough to run out in the lull between deluges?"

For a moment Toby hesitated, and then dropped the eggshells into the sack under the table where Mrs. Clitheroe dumped her debris. "I can't imagine," he said, much too cheerfully.

Oh, yes he could! Jim bit his tongue to choke back any comment, and slid three thick slices of meat off the broad blade of the knife, onto a plate. "There, get that into you. I swear, if you get any skinnier –"

His voice dropped to a murmur as he took the plate. "I thought you said you liked a man skinny and covered in scars."

"I didn't say I don't," Jim countered. "Grab those eggs before they burn!" He glanced at the old woman, who was singing tunelessly to herself as she simmered an iron pan of coffee on the small hob, on the other side of the wide fireplace. He was silent as he watched Toby scoop up three fried eggs with the big wooden spoon and slap them onto his plate.

He pinched salt from the silver bowl and dusted them down, and held out a hand for Jim's plate. "Mother Nature's going to keep the roads clear for a while." He slid Jim's eggs beside the pork. "Which means I won't be singing for my supper."

"There's ... other ways to earn your supper," Jim whispered.

A lovely blush warmed Toby's cheeks. One side of his mouth curved into a smile but he said, "Well, now, I'm not a whore."

"And I wouldn't ask you to be." Jim salted his eggs. "You've already mended the thatch, secured the place for the storm, cut wood and helped me hump a ton of *lumber* into the cellar. Good enough, I should say."

"I ... oh." Toby chuckled. "I'm sorry."

"You're touchy on the subject," Jim observed.

"I suppose I am." Toby was already eating.

"Voice of experience?" Jim hazarded as he thrust a fork into the meat and only then realized how hungry he was.

But Toby was not about to answer, and took the offer of a mug of thick, black coffee as a diversion.

Jim let him be, but an hour later the balladsinger was back out on the coastal path, eyes roving in every direction, and if Jim troubled to notice, he felt the prickle of the hackles beginning to stand up on the back of his neck.

Soon enough, rain drove Toby back inside. He was restless now – throwing darts, pacing the tavern until Jim pulled out the box of dominoes and scattered them over the table where Fred Bailey and Billy Mulligan had sat drinking the first time Toby sang The Hogshead.

"Do you play?" he asked as he sorted the dominoes.

"Doesn't everyone?" Toby pulled up a chair. "The stakes? I've no money, mind you! But I can pay in chores … if I lose."

"I smell a challenge." Jim chuckled. "What'll you take … if I lose? Money?"

"Oh, no." Toby dropped into the chair opposite. "Not money."

"You *need* money."

"Perhaps. But not as much as I *want* something quite different." He lifted a brow at Jim. "We understand each other?"

A pulse hammered in Jim's throat as he dealt the dominoes. "I believe we do. That'll be the stakes, then, will it?"

Toby's blue eyes were shades darker, and at last he relented with a wide, genuine smile which softened the lean contours of his face, stripped years from his age. "Only if you want to play this game, Jim. Only if you don't mind losing, just as I don't mind for a moment. So long," he added quietly, "as I was losing to you."

The pulse in Jim's throat beat harder, faster. "Oh, I can't say that I mind at all, Master Trelane."

"Then, I'll fetch us a little rum," Toby suggested, "and we'll play."

Win or lose, it was almost all the same to Jim. *Almost*. But there was enough of the hunter about him even now – lame leg and all – to make him relish the fantasy of Toby under him, heaving and gasping as he was plundered like any fair maiden of legend. He mocked his own fancies and studied the other man's face over the hand of old, smooth-worn dominoes. Half-lit in the glow of three lanterns, he was equal parts angel and imp and Jim wanted him fiercely.

They played for hours, winning and losing by turns while the afternoon wore away. Rain hammered relentlessly at the shutters and then eased in the early evening, and Toby slipped away from the table with a soft word to Bess and an apologetic look at Jim.

"I'd best let the dogs out while there's a chance to do their business without coming back like drowned rats. Bess hasn't had a proper bath in a long time – get her wet, and she's going to reek, bless her."

"Boxer'll smell just as strong. You've no rush," Jim told him. "I'm going to go up and drag a razor over my face." He waggled a brow at Toby. "I do believe I'm winning this game, and I don't want to take the cheeks off you when I collect what you owe me." He raked his fingernails through his two-day stubble.

The remark made Toby laugh quietly. "You only *think* you're winning, Master Fairley! Still, by all means shave ... you're prettiest when you're a peach."

He was gone on those words, leaving Jim blinking after him. A peach? Jim had never thought of himself as pretty in any sense of the word, but if Toby was persuaded in that direction he saw no reason to argue. Chuckling, he tackled the stairs to his bedchamber, mindful of the leg that was still protesting the cellar steps.

Two big ship nails pried out of the shutter outside the casement, and he opened one side a crack to let in enough daylight to risk pulling a blade across his throat. He was still using his father's shaving knives, excellent blades ground almost hollow through so many years of use. The soap was indulgently fine, made of whale oil and the whitest ash, and smelling of wild mint.

Whistling absently, he lit a candle to warm water in the tin mug, and was entertaining idle fantasies about a future at The Raven that included Toby Trelane when he heard the slop and splash of footsteps on the path. Still working the soap in the mug, steadily beating it to froth, he went to the window, wondering who in his right mind would be out on a day like this.

A man was coming, as he would have expected – it was not a woman's dainty tread. He was in a shabby brown coat, battered hat, muddy boots, hands thrust into his pockets, butting his way into the wind from the direction of Exmouth. The coat was dry, Jim saw at once, so he could have come no further than The Cattlemarket, at Foxholes Hill. The taverner there – big Artie Polgreen himself – watered the liquor, rarely changed the sheets and employed the poxiest whores in the westcountry, but the house had its regular customers. Jim did not recognize the newcomer, and had not expected to. Most men who walked this path were strangers, seamen on their way from one port, one ship, to another.

But Toby knew him.

For the second time that afternoon Jim's hackles began to rise as he heard Toby's voice call from the door right below this casement, "I've been expecting you."

The man came to a halt ten paces away and lifted his head. The tricorn perched forward on that head, crammed down to keep it on against the wind, prevented Jim from seeing his face, but he was looking Toby in the eye as he said,

"I bloody knew you'd get here first, Trelane. Quick as a ferret as usual. You always were."

"I just didn't sit about with a bunch of well-poxed whores, getting blind drunk," Toby retorted.

"Better than the rest of us, ain't you?" the man sneered.

"More sober, perhaps," Toby said quietly. "You're not welcome here, Bellowes. They'll have buried poor Marguerite by now."

"Dead?" Bellowes had a rum-rough voice, like gravel on a shovel. "You've seen her?"

"She was running." There was a sharp edge of anger in Toby's voice. Jim had never heard it before, and he hung on every word as Toby said, "It was just pure luck, happenstance, that she came to the doorstep of the old lady who cooks here, begging for a copper or two to buy medicine in the morning. She made it here, and she died."

Bellowes spat into the mud at his feet. "She were sick."

"And you beat her," Toby added scathingly. "It takes a fine, fine man to take his fist to a woman. What, you beat her till she picked up her skirts and ran, on a night that was cold, wet, filthy?"

"She's dead? Then she's dead, and there's the end of it," Bellows snarled. "Let it be, Trelane. She's not why I'm here. You fuckin' *know* why I'm here."

"Oh, I know," Toby said almost too softly for Jim to hear. "And you're too late, Barney. We all are."

The man missed a beat. "Chegwidden's gone? He's swindled the lot of us, and buggered off?"

"He's as dead as poor Margie," Toby informed him, "and he's been dead for years. The house belongs to Jim Fairley now, and his father before him. You don't believe me? Walk on up to the churchyard, read the headstones. It's no secret that Jim and his father came out here, bought the place from old Charlie and gave him a good home, a little care and comfort, while he sweated through the last few weeks of his life."

"Well ... shite." Bellowes snatched off his hat and dragged both hands over his face, which was sheened with oily sweat. He glared at Toby, and from above Jim saw a shining bald head and gray-brown hair caught back at his nape with a green riband. "So Charlie's gone to hell ahead of the rest of us. It don't change one damn' thing, Trelane."

"It does," Toby said quietly, "when I tell you there's nothing here."

"Nothin'?" Bellowes echoed. "What in the name o' Christ are you sayin', Trelane?"

And he barged toward Toby, in through the open door, out of Jim's sight and hearing. Jim's heart beat a tattoo on his ribs, and his palms prickled with sweat as he set down the shaving mug. What he needed was the blunderbuss, but it was under the bar with the bags of shot and powder. He had no weapons upstairs, and the whole length of the taproom separated bar from staircase.

He heard voices but could not make out the words as he slipped out and along the passageway. He pressed against the wall at the top of the doglegged stairs, out of sight around the corner, and went down one at a time, hoping the voices would become more distinct. Most of what he could pick out were curses as this Barney Bellowes character grew angrier and began to snarl at Toby.

It was getting ugly faster than Jim could slither stealthily downstairs, and he heard the high, sharp notes in Toby's voice before he began to make out words. So Toby Trelane was no angel – and Jim had suspected as much for some time, since no angel ever had so many secrets, and was so vigilant about protecting them. But Jim had taken an instinctual dislike to Bellowes, and if he was going to take sides on gut feeling alone, he would stand by Toby every time.

"For the love of God," Toby began, sharp with alarm.

"Don't you bloody quote God at me," Bellowes roared. "I don't trust you, Trelane. I *never* trusted you. Time an' again, I told Nathaniel to get *shot* of you. You'd've been fish food, if it were up to me."

"Then I'm grateful it wasn't. And if you'll just put the pistol away and talk for one minute –"

Pistol? Jim froze, two steps short of the corner where he would be plainly visible from the taproom. He swallowed hard on his heart, which seemed to be beating in his throat, and took a deep breath.

"Shut your yap," Bellowes growled. "Twice I've told you, Trelane, and I ain't got no breath to keep repeatin' meself all night. You come clean, you hand it over, and you keep a head on your shoulders."

"Barney, there's nothing to hand over," Toby said in desperate tones. "I've searched this house from loft to cellar! I've been in every inch of it and there's nothing. *Nothing*."

The mystery was like splinters of glass under Jim's skin. He had always abhorred a mystery, and this one was maddening because he had come to care for Toby. Healthy lust was only a part of what he felt. It was sheer dread that gripped him by the throat as he inched nearer to the corner, listening to the sound of shoe leather on the floor as Toby moved – dread that there would be a vast emptiness where Toby had been, and the world would be colder, darker, at least in the corner where Jim lived.

"Like I'm goin' to believe one word outta your trap?" Bellowes was sneering. "Stay right where you bloody are, Trelane! You get on your knees, you put your hands on your head and you start talkin' truth before I beat it out of you!"

"Like you beat Marguerite?" Toby said bitterly.

"Forget the doxie! And stay where you are! I swear –"

Whatever Bellowes was about to swear, Jim never knew. He heard the slap of footsteps on stone, the rasp of a chair being shoved out of the way, a smothered curse, and then a pistol shot, deafening in the confines of the taproom. Toby grunted, not a cry of pain but the solid "*ungh*" of a man who had been punched, the air knocked out of his lungs. Jim's heart seemed to stand still and then raced, and he thrust himself away from the wall now, in the half minute of safety before Bellowes could reload. Who was it who said, the only good thing about a pistol was that it had one shot, and until it was reloaded it was just a club; and as clubs go, it was puny.

Sure enough, as Jim moved out onto the lower flight of stairs Bellowes was digging through the pockets of the threadbare brown coat, scrambling for powder and shot. Jim's eyes were wide, searching for Toby, and he swore as he saw him. He was bent back over a chair, struggling for balance while scarlet blossomed around his right arm. Blood soaked the shirt sleeve while Jim watched, but Bellowes had shot wide and Toby was more furious than hurt.

His teeth were bare in a wolf-like grimace as he shoved himself upright, kicked away the chair and seemed to ignore the wound. Bellowes was struggling with the leather pouch, spilling gunpowder over his boots as Toby launched himself – younger, taller, stronger, infinitely angrier. With his left hand, he batted the pistol and powder bag right out of Bellowes's grip. Bellowes was still grabbing for them when Toby clenched the same left fist and hammered an immense roundhouse into the side of the man's head.

The blow sent him sprawling. He was so far off balance, he dove over the table behind him and kept falling, into the cold, unlit hearth at the far end of the taproom, where kindling and fire irons were kept. The second hearth was only lit in the very dead of winter, with snow up to the windowsills. In April it was clean and polished. Bellowes went into it, face-first and cursing.

Jim was intent on the fire irons, fully expecting Bellowes to roll over, snatch up the nearest poker and come after Toby with it. He did not even feel the leg as he propelled himself toward the bar, and under it, both hands seizing the blunderbuss. The gape-muzzled boat gun was always kept loaded. If Toby had only known this he would have gone for it at once, but Jim had never had cause to mention it.

Waiting to hear the clatter of the pokers, curses and threats from Bellowes, he swung back toward the hearth at the far end of the taproom, and it was Jim himself who swore.

Bellowes had not moved. Toby was beside him where he lay, half in the hearth, half out, and Jim watched him give Bellowes a shove with one foot, and another, harder.

"I think you can put the naval gun away, Jim," he said softly.

"He's knocked himself senseless?" Jim wondered, shifting his grip on the blunderbuss. He felt the leg keenly now as he paced the length of the taproom, and around the table that had sent Bellowes sprawling.

"He's broken his ugly, stupid neck," Toby whispered. "Well, there's a wise old saying. As ye sow, so shall ye reap." He looked up at Jim, eyes wide and dark, and dropped carefully to his knees beside the body.

And then he was murmuring, and Jim had heard these words before from his lips. *"Réquiem æternam dona ei, Dómine. Et lux perpétua lúceat ei. Requiéscat in pace. Anima ejus, et ánimæ ómnium fidélium defunctórum, per misericórdiam Dei requiéscant in pace. Amen."*

"Amen," Jim echoed. He had set the blunderbuss on the table, and blinked down at Bellowes with ice cold curiosity. "What *is* that recitation?"

"A prayer for the dead." Toby stood and hissed through his teeth as he became aware of the wound.

"The old language," Jim observed.

"Latin." Toby closed his eyes. "It's still spoken today, by a few of us."

"Lawyers and priests." Jim looked away from the body, with its neck twisted at a crazy, horrible angle. "You're not a lawyer."

"No." Toby's eyes were shades darker. "I'm not. And I'm bleeding like the proverbial stuck pig. You'll have to help me, Jim."

Reality snapped back into focus like a physical blow, and Jim took a deep, hard breath to the bottom of his lungs. "Sit," he told Toby.

He grabbed up the blunderbuss and thrust it back under the bar. Before he went in search of a yard of ragging to bind the wound, he threw the bolt to lock the tavern's front door. They were lucky. The weather had kept drinkers away, and even as he locked up, he heard the rain coming back in, spattering in the puddles outside and drumming on the shutters. The only people who knew Barney Bellowes had arrived here were himself, Toby, and Edith Clitheroe, who stood in the kitchen doorway, wringing her hands and looking from Jim to Toby and back with big, startled eyes.

Chapter Eight

The trapdoor slammed down into place, and Jim dusted his hands as he and Toby stood back. Mrs. Clitheroe was stoic, brewing tea, slicing apple pasties and hard old cheese, and by now a little of the color had returned to Toby's face. For some minutes he had been waxen, sweated, as Jim tore the sleeve out of the ruined shirt and examined the wound. He clenched his teeth as it was doused with strong rum, before Jim bound it tightly with strips cut from an old bed sheet. It was the best cure anyone knew for flesh wounds – and thank the gods, Barney Bellowes's aim had been as atrocious as his temper.

The body was still cooling, wrapped in two well-worn sacks, tied with a dozen yards of line and dumped down at the bottom of the steps. It lay in the cellar, out of sight but weighing heavily on Jim's mind. "That's two dead bodies on my property in three days," he said darkly as he scraped a chair up to the table and took a mug from the old lady. "In the six *years* I've been here, the only other dead body I've ever seen belonged to Charlie Chegwidden, who died of old age and infirmity ... and all three of the departed are connected to you, Toby." He looked up at the balladsinger, brows arched, took in the shuttered face, the downcast eyes. "I think," he said softly, "it's high time you told me the truth. All of it."

"Yes." Toby sank into the chair opposite, took a mug of tea and held it between his palms. "Yes, I rather think it is, before..." He looked away.

The wound was hurting him quite badly but Jim had seen at once, Toby Trelane was far more accustomed to pain than any man should be. He was simply ignoring it. The shirt sleeve was pinned back up at the shoulder; the bloodstain was drying out to a dark, rust-brown color.

"Yes, I owe you the truth," he whispered, "before anything else happens here. Lord knows, I knew I should have told you before, but I couldn't bring myself to speak." He looked up at Jim, and away again. "I'm not proud of the things I've done. Had to do. Been compelled to do, and subjected to. Not that I'm trying to tell you I was a victim. I walked into it with my eyes wide open, and when it went wrong I was stuck tight as if my boots were a foot deep in stinking mud."

The sound Jim heard in his voice was sincerity, and a muscle inside him relaxed. Since Bellowes's arrival he had half feared Toby was some sort of charlatan, a charming swindler and convincing liar. But whatever else was going on, he was sure by now that Toby was none of those things. He settled to listen with an open mind.

"You heard what Barney said?" The blue eyes were wide on Jim. "I was the first to get back here because I'm the one who *didn't* sit in a pox shop, drinking myself legless. I left them all drunk as lords, and walked over here. I was looking for Charlie Chegwidden, as you've always known. He was ..." Toby shrugged. "Charlie was the trustee of the group, all of us who survived to the end, and who started out on a merchantman called *The Rose of Gloucester*. You must have heard of it."

The name was familiar. Jim searched through his memory while Toby waited, and at last he ventured, "If I'm remembering right, there was a mutiny aboard. The story made it back to the towns along the coast here because she shipped out of Plymouth and a few of the lads were local. I remember, just a few days ago Fred Bailey said Charlie'd shipped out on her, but he was off her before *trouble* struck. Right?"

"Yes ... and no. Charlie was aboard in the trouble." Toby shrugged expressively. "They ... we mutinied because any number of the crew were being abused. There were floggings too often, and much too brutal. The captain was a God fearing man by the name of Jeremiah Graves." Shadows gathered like crows in his face. "Two weeks out, Graves hanged a lad for having relations with another boy – and getting caught. A month later, it was another death aboard when a man died under the whip. His crime was to speak his mind to an officer about the treatment of his fellows. A few weeks later, the captain hanged another young boy for being in love with his friend ... and he flogged the ship's priest for trying to counsel him to leave such matters to the Almighty." Toby's voice was rough as crushed silk as he spoke these last words.

"Jesus," Jim whispered. "You?"

The fair head nodded. "Of course it was. But you already guessed this, didn't you?" He sighed heavily. "I never had very much faith, Jim. I'd seen too much as a youth, growing up in rough places. Whatever I had, I lost on that voyage when I watched the suffering of my companions. I heard the prayers of innocents go ignored, as if the Lord didn't care a fig about his children. They tell us never a sparrow shall fall without the eyes of the Almighty upon it, and yet innocents pray for respite and justice, and get nothing." Toby seemed to clench his teeth to stop the flow of indignation, and began again in a quiet tone. "I protested three times. I was flogged to ribbons, you've seen the scars. Touched them. When the mutineers rose up, obviously I went with them!"

"I'd be shocked if you hadn't," Jim said evenly. "They killed the crew, and that damned captain?"

"No. A few were killed in the fighting, and the bodies thrown to the sharks. We put most of them, captain and all, ashore in the Azores with enough supplies to last them until another ship came along and took them off." Toby looked into his cup as if it were a crystal ball. "We knew we couldn't go right back to England without being arrested and hung. To go anywhere else, we needed enough money to pay fat bribes, stay in the shadows, till we were forgotten. New names, new trades ... the Carolinas, perhaps, or the Indies. So we went hunting."

"Hunting?" Jim echoed, warming to the story.

A glitter was back in Toby's eyes now. "Treasure."

Jim groaned. "You can't be serious! Treasure hunting?"

For the first time in so long Toby laughed, but it was a painful sound. "Not at once, but eventually, after we – well, we came by a map. Or, a piece of a map, and as it happens one of our number had spent fifteen years in the navy, looking over the shoulder of a navigator. Harry Price was killed not long after, but he could read charts in his sleep.

"We took our bit of map to Lisbon, in Portugal. Paid a handsome fee to a chartmaker, and our navigator spent two afternoons going over the best maps in the world, matching what we had, until he found it."

"A bit of a map?" Jim demanded. "You were mad enough to take on the Americas, the Caribbean, on the strength of a little piece of a chart?"

"There was a lot more to it than that," Toby protested. "No one was especially mad, though we were all desperate enough to be rash. You see, we heard the story in Kingston, Jamaica, of a great treasure ... months before this, in the wake of the mutiny we'd picked up a cargo. All perfectly legitimate, contracted for in Caracas and delivered properly to market. We got paid," he added, "honest pay for honest work, which you don't often expect from a crew of mutineers!

"The news about the mutiny hadn't yet reached Jamaica. We knew we were running in front of it, safe enough to go ashore, drink in their taverns, spin yarns with the locals. And there was a story we heard from a blind old woman who was said to have been a great beauty in her day, and now tells tales, minds children...

"It all began a long time ago, back in the great days when Spain was shipping gold out of the Americas faster than the natives could dig it out of the ground, and enslaving the Indians, working them to death by droves, to do the labor. It seems one of the natives they enslaved was a prince by birth, the last scion of a royal house with a lineage going back further than Henry Tudor himself. The tribe protected him even in captivity – or especially then. They thought, if he could escape, maybe their people could be reborn someday through his royal blood. In those days kings were seen as gods too, you know.

"So this Indian prince was jealously protected until they could arrange for his escape, and it was just damned bad luck when a storm came up, swamped the little boat he was trying to sail away from Spanish territory. He was clinging to the wreckage when the lookout aboard a pirate vessel saw him, and they pulled him aboard.

"He must have been a beautiful young man, because the captain of the pirate galley took a shine to him. Fell head over heels for him, in fact. They couldn't even pronounce his real name, so they called him –"

"Fernando." Jim swallowed hard. "I know. I was listening. I heard the whole story, the Treasure of Diego Monteras."

Toby produced a faint, lopsided smile. "Well, then, there's no point in me telling it again, is there?"

Jim was gaping. He knew he was sitting there with his mouth hanging open as if in an attempt to catch flies. "You mean, it's true?"

"Every word of it." Toby drained his mug to the leaves and set it down. "It's not just a good story, Jim. And incidentally, it *is* a good yarn. It's bought my supper many times over. People love hearing it because there's magic in it. But the best magic is, it's true. The bit of map and the letter came into the possession of the old woman in Jamaica. She was charged with keeping it safe by her grandson, who'd won it playing pitch and toss, but he never came back to collect it. He was killed in a battle with pirates and she kept the map, the letter, because she knew she was losing her sight and she realized how valuable they were. Nathaniel Burke – he liked to call himself our leader, and most of us found it easier to agree than argue – Nathaniel paid her a trifling sum for it, though the purse was more than she actually needed. Enough for her to live out the rest of her life with a maid to take care of her, food on the table, and a cottage above the beach."

He sat back and regarded Jim levelly, soberly. "So there we were, Jim, in Kingston, with a ship – *The Rose of Gloucester* – that was sturdy enough for those waters, and a crew that had nothing to lose, and a bit of a map. We headed first to Portugal, as I told you before. Not England. We picked up a cargo in Barbados to pay our way, and the voyage east was easy enough. In Lisbon, our navigator made the match between that fragment from Diego Monteras's chart and a very good new map from a master chartmaker."

"And ..." Words almost failed Jim. "You outfitted an expedition."

"We picked up another cargo in Lisbon, bound for the port of Sao Luis. Again, legitimate work." Toby was immersed in the memories now. "The pay wasn't good, but it was enough to get us back to South America, which was at least in the right part of the world and comfortably far from waters where English warships are common. It was summer when we offloaded the cargo, and the *Rose* sailed north. Believe me, we knew *exactly* where we were going."

"Jesus, Mary and Joseph," Jim breathed. "You found it."

"We ... found it." Toby took a long deep breath. "An iron-bound chest of gems, about so big." He sketched it in the air. "Like a mid-size brandy keg. It was Diego Monteras's own share of the wealth, and enough to make a king green with envy. Diamonds, emeralds, rubies, pearls, tiny items of exquisite beauty and utterly beyond price." Toby tipped back his head and closed his eyes. "God! We thought we were free. We thought we had the rest of our lives to live and love and grow old in peace. Charlie and I got very drunk in celebration, and the next morning Nathaniel turned the *Rose* around and headed us back to civilization, to take on water and fresh food for the voyage home."

His face darkened there. Jim was hanging on every syllable now. "A bastard storm came up out of the Atlantic," Toby said quietly. "It was black as a funeral shroud, and a hundred miles across. We couldn't make any of the Portuguese anchorages and we were running short of everything, including the time to make attempt a safe passage east before the fair season closed down.

"We ran ahead of monstrous winds, just two sails up and praying for calm waters. We got them, limped into the lee of an island without any name, and set about making repairs. We were a mess of broken rigging and smashed yards, we could go no further." His face looked bruised now. "The devil sent the bill. He always does. And we paid up in spades.

"We were jumped by a ship of His Majesty's navy, and thank gods she was just a tiddler, a sloop of war carrying 20 guns and a crew of 50 men at most. They knew the *Rose* on sight, since we were bloody notorious as a mutineer crew that was still at large. They came up on us in the half-light before dawn when our lookouts were dead asleep, damn them, and boarded us.

"It was only sheer luck that the king's men didn't find the treasure – they weren't looking for it, and Nathaniel had just enough warning to get it hidden. Less than an hour later, we were named as mutineers and sentenced to hang right there on our own deck. We weren't even to be shipped back to England in chains to stand trial." The blue eyes closed.

"You fought," Jim whispered.

"We fought. Of course we fought! Cornered animals always will." Toby took a long deep breath and got a grip on himself and the raw memories. "Nathaniel was armed – he always is. He had a couple of pistols that were always kept loaded, and still are. We used to tell him, one day he'd shoot off his own cod, since he kept a brace of loaded pistols stuck in his belt! But that day we were damned glad he had them. He's a good shot, far better than Barney ever was. Barney's ... well, he *was* cockeyed. He couldn't see straight, much less shoot straight."

The memories had a grip on Toby now. He was back there, miles and years away, living it all again. "So Nathaniel puts one shot right through the forehead of the white-wigged lieutenant in command of this tiddler of a naval vessel, and the other smack in the throat of his second in command, almost takes his head right off at the shoulders. Hell breaks loose. Every man on both crews is suddenly diving for muskets, pistols, swords, tools, anything we can get our hands on."

For a moment he was silent, and his voice was hoarse as he said bitterly, "The decks really did run scarlet. A number of us were killed outright, more died later from their wounds. But we accounted for the naval crew right down to the last jack tar, may God forgive us, which I doubt he will. It was a matter of survival and liberty ... and even a whipped dog will turn and fight at the end, supposing it's the death of him." He shivered visibly. "The deck of the *Rose* was a battleground, as if we'd fought a small war, which we won. There's a place in hell set aside for the winners of battles, Jim, and I fully expect to roast there for a very long time indeed. Not," he added pointedly, "that I'll be alone on the spit.

"We had only barely enough hands left alive and strong enough to crew the *Rose*, get her out of there. Some of the men were for seizing the naval sloop, but the rest of us pointed out the wisdom of scuttling her. She was far too recognizable – she'd get us killed before we were out of waters where we could expect to run into English ships.

"So the stores of the little warship were transferred to the *Rose*, guns, powder, shot and all, and then we took the sloop herself out into deep water and opened the seacocks. She was gone in a few minutes, and her crew with her, God rest them. They were good lads, following orders, and we ... we were fighting for our very lives. We either died fighting or we died hanging by our necks from every yardarm on our own ship – what choice did they give us?

"Hours later, we slithered away under cover of darkness and turned south, to the comparative safety of Portuguese waters. The question was," he said philosophically, "what to do next?"

Jim steepled his fingers on the table and studied them. "You could have stayed in the Americas. Those Portuguese harbors would have sheltered you."

"True. And a few of us made that argument." Toby sighed heavily. "But we're Englishmen, and several of us are sinners, like so many men." He lifted a brow at Jim, knowing Jim would know what he meant. He was not about to come right out and say it, since Mrs. Clitheroe was listening. "Few of us spoke the language, and fewer yet could stomach the food. Many wanted to go home, and I can't say I blame them. With money in their pockets, it was Bristol and Liverpool and Southampton they wanted, not Caracas and Paramaribo and Fortaleza." His brows rose, creasing his forehead. "So we sat down around the captain's table, drank a great deal of rum, argued a lot, fought a little, and came to a decision.

"We'd split up and head in eight different directions. The navy was looking for the ship, the crew as a whole, not a bunch of individuals, you see. One by one, we'd be safe. The *Rose*'s records were destroyed, of course. But we rightly feared we'd be recognized if we stuck together. A hundred people watched the *Rose* victualing and taking on crew back in Plymouth. Put a bunch of us together in one place – oh, yes, we'd soon be spotted, arrested. Hung.

"We left the *Rose* beached about a mile up an inlet, where the river's tidal. I daresay she's still there – rank-rotten, of course, since the weather soon takes a ship apart, the moment she's neglected. Or perhaps a crew found her, floated her off, and she's plying the Caribbean under a different flag, perhaps even a pirate flag. I hope she is. I came to be fond of her, and she was always a good ship, no matter the cruelty that took place on her and the meanness of her first captain.

"From Sao Luis we traveled east on different ships, all merchantmen. For myself, I was on a Spanish vessel, *La Dama de las Flores*. I worked my passage with every manner of task that can fall to a deckhand. Thank heavens I knew my way around a ship by that time! After the battle, with so few of us left, we all did everything on the *Rose* just to stay alive. If you didn't possess a skill, you learned it fast." He gave Jim a faint smile. "You said I had the look of a monkey who's been used to scampering about in the rigging, setting lines. I've done that – aye, and in a storm!

"The *Dama* took me to Corunna, and from there I wandered. Just wandered wherever my feet would take me, and earned my living where I could, and *if* I could. I did many a job ... came to speak Spanish fluently in a few months. Wandered up into France and back south again. Became a balladsinger quite by chance, when I had a bit of luck in a seamen's tavern, singing Spanish versions of English shanties, which they thought was hilarious.

"The rest of us had headed to other ports – France, Flanders, Denmark, Ireland. I never knew where the others were. We agreed on only one thing: we'd come back here to The Raven at this very time, give or take a day or three, as the winds blow. The 20th day of April, 1769. And we swore we wouldn't turn up here one day ahead of the date."

"But why here?" Jim demanded. "I mean, I'm extremely glad you *did* walk up my path! But why?"

"Charlie Chegwidden," Toby told him promptly. "His mother owned this tavern, and when she died it was to come to him. We all knew this. He was the only one of us with a proper place to go back to, a place to call home … and he was the only one of us that the whole group trusted. The rest of them?" He shook his head slowly. "They couldn't be relied on not to break up the treasure of Diego Monteras, bauble by bauble, drink half of it away and disappear with the other half. Charlie was a simple man. A good man. And," he added thoughtfully, "he looked as healthy as a horse when we parted company.

"Captain Graves's papers were tossed into the sea. With my own eyes I watched them float away in tatters, and the crew of the naval sloop had all perished. There was no actual written record that Charlie was ever on the *Rose,* much less still aboard at the time of the mutiny. Somebody might have seen him sign on in Plymouth and happened to know him by name, but we reckoned it was far from likely. He had no business in Plymouth, no kin there. We all believed he was safe enough to be coming home. Now you tell me, our own Fred Bailey saw him that day, and remembers." Toby shrugged philosophically. "It looked like a fair wager, and we took it. I believe we had luck on our side yet again! Fred might have his suspicions to this day, but he's never said a word, and why would he, him being a friend of both Charlie and his old mother." He frowned at Jim now. "How did Charlie die?"

Jim sat back, looking along at Mrs. Clitheroe, who had heard every word. She was sitting in the chair by the hearth, the black cat asleep in her lap, both dogs at her feet. Her eyes were shrewd as those of a hawk as she surveyed the two young men. She had been cooking here since Charlie's mother owned the tavern – she knew everything about The Raven's business. Jim's only secrets were much more personal.

"He was ill when me and my father got off the coach and started looking around for lodgings and a livelihood. We talked to the parson, and Vicar Morley told us to come right here. Seems old Charlie had let it be known he wanted to sell on account of his health. But he didn't want to leave, he was absolutely decided about it. He wasn't about to take one step away from The Raven, as long as he lived. And he held to the promise, Toby. He kept his word till the last. He was protecting the chest, wasn't he? And that's what you came here looking for."

"Heaven help me, it was." Toby sat back and knuckled his eyes, pulled his fingers through his hair, worked his neck too and fro. The arm was paining him, and Jim came around the table to examine it. Toby watched with heavy eyes as he unpinned the sleeve, untied the bandage, and peered at the wound. "I thought, if I could just take a few of the baubles, not even a handful, I'd be away and gone before Nathaniel and Barney and the rest sobered up and appeared along the path. A *few* of the baubles, Jim, and a man could live well, lifelong, if he was careful in his spending. I wasn't greedy, and as sure as all hell, I didn't want to look into the faces of Barney and Nathaniel and that crew ever again." He shrugged. "I never had luck. I don't know why I should be surprised Charlie died, but I knew the others wouldn't be more than a day or three behind me. I spotted Barney and Nathaniel on the street in Exmouth – Marguerite was traipsing about after Barney. Seems she'd attached herself to him eight or ten months ago. Well, he kept her out of a brothel for the last of her days, which is something to be grateful for. Bless her poor heart, she had the same lousy luck as myself."

"You?" Jim made negative noises. "Your luck changed the day you walked up the path, looking for Charlie Chegwidden, and found Jim Fairley instead." He studied Toby closely. "You don't have to worry about the bold Barney Bellowes any longer. How many others were in Exmouth? How many are we expecting?"

For a moment Toby continued to frown at him. "You'll throw in with me?"

"For a chance at a share in the prize, and for the sake of mateship?" Jim demanded. "You and me?" He dropped his voice, well under the old lady's range of hearing. "If you know what I mean by *you and me*."

"Oh, I know what you mean!" Toby permitted a low chuckle. "When we went our separate ways there were just eight of us left of the original company from the *Rose*, counting me and Charlie. Now, Charlie's long gone and Barney's stone cold in the cellar, which leaves five of them, and myself. I saw Nathaniel and Joe in Exmouth. That's Nathaniel Burke and Joe Pledge. Eli Hobbs and Rufus Bigelow and Willie Tuttle are still out there, headed for Exmouth and then here. I'm just lucky Nathaniel and the others stayed in Exmouth long enough to drink themselves legless and get good and poxed! Barney just sobered up first and risked the weather to get here. And you have to admit, Jim, the prize is worth getting wet and cold."

"The prize." Jim was on his feet now, pacing between the table and the hearth. "The trouble is, I've never seen any such chest. There's nothing on this entire property that looks or smells vaguely like it."

"The real trouble is," Toby corrected, "Nathaniel and the rest of them won't believe a word we say. They're going to say I came here, found the chest, took it out of here and hid it, with or without your knowledge."

"And me?" Jim was conscious of a pulse hammering in his throat. "They're going to take one look at you and me and – you know."

"They'll assume we're partnered up to swindle them." Toby pushed up to his feet. "I'm so sorry, Jim. I've put you in terrible danger."

"Damn." Jim closed his eyes for a moment, feeling the thin edge of old fashioned panic hovering in his nerve endings, and then he rubbed his face hard, forcing himself to think. "It's too late for them to get here tonight, I'd say. For a start, there's more heavy weather on its way – do you hear the wind and rain? If they haven't shown up already today, they're not going to."

"The weather might win us an extra day," Toby hazarded. "But the only way for you to be safe is for me to go."

"That's not going to stop Burke and Pledge and the crew walking right up to my door!"

"True. But you can always say you never saw me, nor Barney." Toby's shoulders lifted in a faint shrug. "The only people who know Bellowes was here are in this room. You can be sure Nathaniel and the rest will search this house from cellar to rafters, so we'll need to get the body out of there."

Jim was two steps ahead of him. "Dealing with Bellowes is simple enough. As soon as it's dark, we'll drag him out to my boat – she's just a rowboat, on the beach not fifty yards from here. We'll carry him out just far enough to float, and let the tide take him. The fish'll have him halfway bare to the bone before the weather breaks, and by then Burke and his crew will have finished here, and gone. If his remains wash up, he'll be buried as a 'stranger taken by the sea,' and there's the end of it."

"Then, I'll be gone in the morning," Toby said softly, "and when they turn up at your door, Jim … for godsakes let them do what they want, smash what they want. They'll be in a fine fury when they find nothing here, but since you're living the life of a simple innkeeper, it's obvious you never found anything Charlie hid. If you'd found it, you'd have bought yourself a title and be living up in London! Now, Charlie's buried in the Budleigh churchyard so, sure as hell, he didn't make off with it. It's a mystery, it'll always be a mystery. They can take the puzzle away with them. And then," he added darkly, "you and I might discover just what old Charlie did with that chest!"

"And where will you be?" Jim asked quietly. "What's to say the likes of Burke and Pledge won't put a pistol ball in me, the way

Bellowes took a shot at you? I want you here, Toby. Maybe not in plain view of the bastards, so I can tell them I never even heard of you, and be believed. But I want you close enough to hear a good, loud shout … two pistols and the boat gun, loaded and ready. All right?"

"All right," Toby agreed. "I'm so sorry, Jim."

"Don't be." Jim gestured at the building around them. "This whole scheme was already underway when my father bought The Raven. It's not your fault any more than it's mine. But I'll tell you this: I can't go up against a man like this Nathaniel Burke. I've never fought, never pulled a pistol on a man." He slapped the aching leg. "This is Jim Fairley we're talking about. It was home in London first and then stuck here all my life. You could say I've been mollycoddled in the shelter of being lame since I was too young to know what fighting was about."

Toby breathed a long sigh and beckoned Jim out of the kitchen – out of sight of the old lady. In the darkness and privacy of the taproom, he took Jim in an embrace and held him tight. "I'm not going to walk out on you, if this is what you're thinking."

"I didn't say you were," Jim began, and then could not speak, for Toby's lips hunted for his mouth and silenced him efficiently.

"Try giving them what they want," Toby suggested huskily, a long time later. "If they want to ransack the whole tavern, just stand back and let them do it. You know, we both know, Charlie hid the chest here somewhere. We just need to find it."

Jim took a long, calming breath. "I'll put my hands up and back off."

"If you get the chance, you get the hell right out," Toby growled. "If they try to run you off, just go, Jim, and stay away long enough for them to be done and leave."

"But what if they find the chest?" Jim's tonguetip moistened his lips. "Think about it, Toby. They come here, they tear this place apart and they find it. You and I come out of it with nothing."

"Nothing but the gift of our lives," Toby argued. He cocked his head at Jim, looking curiously at him in the soft light spilling out of the kitchen. "Now, what are you thinking?"

In fact, Jim's mind was racing. "I'm thinking," he said slowly, "what we need to do is find the chest before they do." His brows popped up at Toby in challenge. "There's leverage for you."

The suggestion inspired a groan. The blue eyes closed for a moment before Toby regarded him with rueful amusement. "There's more than a touch of the pirate in you, isn't there?"

"There might be," Jim admitted. "But the first thing on my mind is staying alive. All the jewels in the world won't do us any good if we're dead and buried! And speaking of dead ... I want to haul Barney Bellowes out of here. My flesh is crawling, every time I remember there's a body lying festering in my cellar."

Toby listened to the wind and rain. "It's not a good evening to be out."

"It's the best," Jim argued. "In this weather, nobody's going to see us taking the boat out. And look at the time. The tide's turning right about now." He rubbed his palms together. "How's that arm of yours?"

"Sore, but it's only a flesh wound. I've had far worse, as well you know." Toby beckoned him to the door and opened it, admitting a blast of ice-cold air and stinging rain. "It's dark enough, if you're determined to do this."

"I'm bloody bound and determined," Jim told him. "There's no way in hell I'm going to sleep tonight with a dead body under the trapdoor!" He did not have to feign a shudder. "Do you know where the oilskins are kept?"

"In the back room, the one with the big wardrobe ... I'm afraid I searched the wardrobe. Looking for, well, you know." Toby leaned heavily on the door to shut it against the wind. "I'll go up and get them, will I?"

"Do that." Jim watched him fetch a lantern from the bar and head back into the kitchen for a moment to light it at the hearth.

Even Mrs. Clitheroe was not so deaf that she had not heard at least some of what was said, and she was hovering with a face full of questions. Jim waited till Toby had vanished up the stairs in a maelstrom of macabre shadows, and then he pitched his voice so she could hear him clearly.

"We're in a lot of trouble, Edith."

"Bad men on their way 'ere," she said with surprising calm. "Aye, I 'eard enough. One of 'em dead already, down below – an' well deserved. Master Trelane's lucky to be breathin' tonight."

"And we have to get rid of the body," Jim told her. "It can't be the doctor and undertaker in the morning, or we're done for, Toby and me." He paused, looking down into the shrewd old eyes. "I can't explain, not here and now, but when it's all over I'd be glad to make you a mug of coffee and tell you every last morsel I know." He paused long enough to lick his lips. "Do you trust me?"

"Oh, aye," she said with grim determination. "I dunno the 'alf of what's goin' on tonight, but I know it's nuthin' good, God 'elp us all. If thee *does* know what's goin' on, well – thass good enough fer me."

"All right." Jim gave her a grim smile. "Then you keep the dogs out of the way and get some hot food going. "Toby and me –? We're going to send Master Bellowes back to the sea, right where he came from. And I'm afraid we're going to get ourselves half drowned while we're at it."

She puffed out her cheeks. "Thee'll be takin' out yon boat."

"We will. And we'll be feeding the crabs this time, instead of catching them!"

"Feedin' 'em wi' that bugger down below." She had such a murderous look on her face, for a moment Jim was sure she was about to spit in the direction of the trapdoor. "It'll be fish stew, wi' 'ot bread an' pickles." She was on her way to the hearth to set up a pot, and turned back with as impish a grin as an old woman could conjure. "Mind, I don't think I'll be eatin' much fish in these next few weeks … not fish that were caught off the shore 'ere. Not after what them fish've been eatin'."

Jim would not have believed he could find a laugh, but he did. "Just you be sure to say nothing of this, Edith. Ever – to anyone. It could be the death of all three of us, if you do. And a nice purse for you, if you keep silent. Yes?"

"Oh, aye," she said darkly, glaring at the trapdoor. "I know the likes of that un down there. The world's full of bad uns, Master Fairley. I'll be buggered if I know what the Almighty were thinkin' when 'e made 'em, but when they get sent down to the burnin' place – good riddance to 'em, an' it ain't no sin to send the buggers there."

She was still speaking when Toby reappeared with his arms filled with the oilskins. She never saw him cross himself, but she heard him say, "Amen. And yes, Edith, I'll say a prayer for him, as I did for the girl."

Edith Clitheroe snorted. "I'll say it fer thee. 'Our Father, please send this un straight down wi' a message tied to 'im: 'Burn to a crisp on both sides, basted in lamp oil, turnin' often.' Amen."

The prayer made Toby laugh aloud when Jim would never have believed it possible tonight. Still chuckling, he beckoned Toby to the trapdoor. "We've nasty work to do. Soonest started, soonest finished."

The work was more heavy than nasty, at least as far as the door into the stableyard, and from there on, more wet and cold. Barney Bellowes was not merely dead, he was already growing stiff with what John

Hardesty called *rigor mortis*, and not much harder to carry than a log of firewood weighing the same as a man. They had tied him up in old sacking as soon as they had him in the cellar, and Jim was glad he did not have to look into the dead face.

He took the feet while Toby climbed backwards up the stairs with great care. Edith shut the door to keep the dogs in the taproom, and Jim and Toby shrugged swiftly into the oilskins. The old woman pulled open the backdoor, propped it, and Toby held up a hand to stop Jim.

"Let me take a look around, make sure we have the place to ourselves."

"Quickly," Jim agreed.

He was gone no longer than a minute, and when he stuck his head back into the kitchen the rain was sluicing off the oilskin cape in torrents. "Nobody," he reported, blinking water out of his eyes. "It's filthy out here – I doubt there's another human soul abroad in ten miles."

"Which suits us." Jim had stooped to take the feet again, and as they manhandled the dead weight through the door he called back to the woman, "We'll not be long. Brew up, Edith."

With that they were out, struggling against the wind and rain – as Toby had said, they might have been the only human souls left alive in the world. Around the corner of the tavern, they butted directly into the wind. Jim thought he could have leaned on it, and swore fluently as they labored across the path and into the coarse bushes beyond which was a mess of storm-driven sand and kelp. Wind and rain stung the eyes while the ears filled with the roar of gale and sea.

His boat was kept in good repair, beached high on the sands, above the tidal zone, keel to the sky and the oars stored beneath. They dumped Bellowes for long enough to flip the little craft over, and Toby shoved the oars into the locks. The body seemed to be getting heavier by the moment, and they were both cursing as they got it into the well of the boat.

Cold as the night was, sweat prickled Jim's ribs as they hauled the boat through the mounds of wrack and into the breakers. Then the water stole the breath right out of his lungs as it broke around his knees and thighs, and he clambered over the side as soon as it was afloat. Toby stayed longer in the freezing wash, shoving the craft until he was sure the outgoing tide had it.

The waves were violent, smashing on the shore and almost swamping the boat at once. Toby was bailing as hard and as fast as he could, the moment he was aboard, and only the fact the tide was going out made it possible for them to get the craft into the water at all.

In moments they were far enough from shore for Jim's heart to be in his mouth, and he knew they did not dare go much further. They had to get back in against this very tide, and even with Bellowes's weight out of the boat, it would be far from easy. The same forces that helped them get out far enough to push the body over and be sure it would be a mile offshore by morning, turned against them as soon as Bellowes hit the water. Without needing a word spoken, Toby took one of the oars, Jim the other, and they pulled as if their lives depended on it while the water around their feet grew deeper with frightening speed.

They were dangerously close to swamping in the brutal thrash of the sea, and Jim was keenly aware that they could die within shouting distance of the tavern. Never in his life had he done such work. He had never believed himself strong enough, and was sure it was sheer desperation and the blazing desire to survive that kept him pulling with all his weight while his body screamed. He heard Toby grunting in pain and gave a thought to the wound before he thanked whatever sailor's gods might be watching that Toby was so strong.

It seemed a year since they heaved Bellowes over before Jim felt the rasp of pebbles under the keel and threw down the oars. He and Toby were over the side at once – smashed under a wave higher than Jim was tall. They fought for breath, coughing on salt water as it receded, and threw their backs into the work of hauling the boat back up through the wrack.

Every muscle Jim possessed was trembling with fatigue, cold and pain when they flopped the boat back over and thrust the oars underneath. Still, Toby insisted Jim stay in the concealment of the bushes just above the beach while he made sure they were alone. Jim stood with his raw palms on his knees, cursing his leg and listening to the rasp of his breathing.

"All clear," Toby shouted over the wind, and grabbed him by the arm to get him moving. "Are you all right?"

"I will be," Jim panted. "Damnit, Trelane, you're trouble to me!"

And he caught one glimpse of a rare, mirthless grin as Toby steered him in the direction of the stableyard, and shelter.

Chapter Nine

The wound was bleeding badly. Toby looked pale and his lips compressed in pain as Jim took off the old bandage and swore over the damage they had done. The ruined shirt lay on the floor at their feet, and Jim tried not to look at the scars on his back. He fetched the rum bottle and doused the gash again, making Toby hiss through his teeth. Then, a thick pad of clean rags and several yards ripped from an old skirt, tied on so tightly, he knew the hand and arm would soon be numb.

"Can you stand this?" he asked as he finished the knots.

"It's nothing," Toby said gruffly.

"Like bastard bloody hell is it nothing," Jim argued. "Your hand's going to be blue in half an hour! But by then the bleeding will've stopped." He stepped back, gathering rum, rags and shirt. "Tell me when you can't stand it anymore, and I'll loosen it."

"Not till the blood stops." Toby made a grab for the rum and took a large swig before he let Jim take it back. "I've seen wounds before. Too many of them, and a lot worse. This one? It's a scratch."

"You know best." Jim sighed, and paused long enough to draw a light caress around Toby's cold face while Mrs. Clitheroe's back was turned. Just then she was ladling stew into two deep bowls, and saw nothing as Jim leaned down and kissed Toby's forehead, where the fair hair still hung in wet ringlets. "Stay where you are. I'll go up and get us some dry clothes. You want a job to do? Get rid of the old shirt. Burn it. Leave nothing to give anybody the hint of an idea there was ever violence in this house."

"And I'll hide Barney's pistol," Toby said grimly as he hauled himself to his feet. The offending weapon lay on the chair by the table. One handed, he wrapped it in a clean swatch of the ragging Jim had used to bind his wound, and without a word he thrust it into the bottom of the barley bin on the pantry shelves by the hearth. He buried it deep under the pile of grain and replaced the top. "There. Even Nathaniel won't be looking for the treasure of Diego Monteras in the bottom of the barley bin," he said wryly. "In his mind, it's a chest he's looking for, much bigger than this bin. Good enough?"

"Good enough." Jim swiped up a cold lantern, lit it from one of those on the back of the table, and swore as he stepped away from the hearth. He was sodden and cold enough to make his teeth chatter. The wind was howling around the tavern, tearing at the shutters, making them bang and singing in the chimneys with a demonic voice, but the thunder had spent itself now. One more day of this deluge and they would be flooding, and like anyone along the coast, they could only hope for blue skies and a glimpse of the sun.

In the dim privacy of his own bedchamber Jim peeled out of the sodden clothes and took a moment to scrub himself with an old blanket, so hard, it might have taken off his skin. Dry but far from warm, he shoved his legs into fresh linen and britches and rummaged for shirt, waistcoat, and the same again for Toby. The leg nagged at him, the pain steady, persistent, acid hot and stubbornly defying him to ignore it.

Hunger rumbled in his belly as he made his way back down. The lantern cast wicked shadows, and the hearth where Bellowes had died might have been a gaping mouth. Jim took a moment to pick up the fire irons, set them back into place and even checked the floor for any dusting of ash which had been disturbed. By the time he was done, no clue remained to suggest the scene.

The stew smelt divine. His mouth watered as he returned to the kitchen, where Toby was already eating. In the dim light he was pale as a ghost, not quite shivering. The bandage was blood-soaked, though not as badly as Jim had feared. By morning it should be dry and, with luck, unnoticeable under a shirt.

As Toby sopped up the last liquid, Jim handed him the clothes. "Get warm, for godsakes! And then ..." He lifted a brow at the man.

He was on his feet a moment later, using the high back of a chair for privacy as he stripped to the skin while Mrs. Clitheroe was either oblivious or politely pretending to be. "And then...?"

Jim was already eating before be pulled a chair up to the table. "I'd be surprised if you were in any mood for sleeping! It's a filthy night, and that wound'll be paining you ... and Bellowes has to be on your mind."

"And Nathaniel, and the rest of them." Toby buttoned the front of a pair of britches that were a little too loose. He gave Jim a hard look.

"The pair of us ought to just *go*. If we're not here when the bastards arrive –"

"If we're not here," Jim said quietly, "they'll tear this place to pieces, drink every drop of grog in the house, and if they don't actually find the prize, they'll come looking for us. Six years, Toby, and I've never even seen a hint of it. Say Nathaniel's crew tears The Raven apart and finds nothing. They'll assume we got out in the night with the goods, and ran. If they catch up with us – and they will! – they'll beat the pair of us to blood or to death, trying to winkle words out of us that neither of us has to give."

"Yes." Toby looked away. "Jim, is there anyone you can turn to for help? You know the local vicar, and the doctor. If you went to them, first thing in the morning, and asked for a couple of dragoons ...?"

"I can do that," Jim said slowly. "But if I were this Nathaniel Burke of yours, and I saw Jim Fairley under guard – well, now. I'd know several things, wouldn't I? I'd know Master Jim knew *all* about the treasure, which probably means one Toby Trelane crossed his path recently, or Master Bellowes, or both. If I couldn't find Trelane and Bellowes, I'd soon be asking myself what this cove, Fairley, had done with them. Maybe he shot the pair of them. Maybe they're buried under the flagstones back in his tavern yard ... or did he feed 'em to the crabs out in the bay? Maybe this Fairley shot them because he *did* find the prize and intends to keep it! Or did Charlie Chegwidden give up the secret on his deathbed? Either way, it would seem this Fairley has no intentions of sharing – he knows Nathaniel's crew is back, he's called in dragoons to guard him." He lifted a brow at Toby. "If you were Nathaniel, what would you do?"

He was dressed now, crouched by the hearth and holding both hands to the fire. "I'd either wait – weeks, if it took so long – till the dragoons just went away again, as they eventually must. Or, if I was impatient, I'd waste a couple of pistol balls on them. Then I'd come for Master Fairley." He looked up at Jim, eyed wide and dark. "I'd know for a fact, Trelane and Bellowes walked the path across from Exmouth and vanished. I'd soon find out Charlie died a long, long time ago, and since Toby and Barney were wiped off the face of the Devon ... well, this Fairley *cove* must be a dangerous bastard. Handy enough to kill a nasty piece of work like Barney and rotten enough to cut down a nice lad like Toby; and all for what? A king's ransom in precious stones. Why else would a man murder?" He straightened and thrust both hands into the pockets of the britches.

He was deliberately ignoring the wound, Jim knew from the faint pinch in his features as he moved it. Toby was far from a stranger to pain. He knew how to disregard it when the need arose. "A guard of dragoons might delay the day, but in the end Nathaniel Burke would come for me, armed to the gills, ready to tear me apart along with the tavern," Jim finished bleakly.

"He would. Damn, I'm so sorry, Jim. I've just brought death to your house. I never intended to – it wasn't supposed to be like this." He pulled his shoulders square. "Look, I can make my way back to Exmouth at first light. Head them off, if they're on their way here – tell them about Charlie, for a start. I can tell how Barney pulled a pistol on me. The wound proves it! Then I can also tell them *I* killed the bugger, borrowed your boat without you knowing a thing about it, and dumped his body on the tide."

Jim nodded slowly. "But Nathaniel and his people will still be heading here. You'll be with them, and you'll have to pretend you don't know me from Adam. They'll expect you to help them tear the house to pieces."

"I can do that. It's only a sticks and stones, Jim. You can always rebuild a house. Or I can volunteer to hold a pistol on you while they do it," Toby suggested. "At least *I'm* not likely to actually shoot you! Then – let them rip the place to pieces, if you like. Lord knows, maybe they'll actually find the prize and just bugger off with it, and leave us in peace."

It was possible. Jim mulled over the proposition for some time, while Toby stared unblinkingly into the fire. At last he asked almost soundlessly, "Could you let them do that?"

"What – find the prize and walk away from here, leaving wreckage and ruin behind them?" He dropped his buttocks onto the chair by Jim's, a few feet closer by the hearth. The firelight gilded his face and his hair had begun to dry almost curly. "I'm still a balladsinger and this is still your tavern. We can repair what they broke, and we'd have our lives. The future." He dropped his voice to a faint whisper. "Each other."

He was right, and Jim gave an expressive groan. "Damnation! You know, for one moment I was sure I could smell a fortune. I could almost *feel* those baubles among my fingers." He mocked himself with a grin, and gave Toby his hand. Toby took it lightly, squeezed it. "All right. When you've got enough daylight, start back. You're sure they won't take the price out of your hide, for Bellowes's death?"

"They might." Toby's face shuttered. "Nathaniel might. But

Barney's been a hardcase every day since he signed on the *Rose*. Nathaniel used to tell him, one day it'd be the end of him." He glanced down at the wound. "He almost killed me, what chance did I have?"

"Almost killed you for what?" Jim's brows arched. "Nathaniel will be asking the same question."

"For things that were done and said between us a long, long time ago." Toby seemed to wrestle with himself, and Jim knew much remained unsaid. "He used to tell me, a sodomite priest belonged in hell with a spit shoved through him from his arse to his gullet, turning on that spit over a slow fire for the rest of eternity." The blue eyes were haunted as he looked up at Jim. "It wouldn't take much to make Barney pull a pistol on me. I just got the better of him at last. Even if Nathaniel took it out of my hide, as you said, he'd also reckon it was overdue and Barney had it coming."

The reasoning was sound. Jim looked up at the clock on the mantel over the fireplace. "We won't see them before afternoon tomorrow, not in this weather. Which gives us half a chance, if you're game."

"Game?" Toby echoed. "For what?"

"For tearing the house apart just a *little* more gently," Jim told him. "If Charlie hid the prize somewhere on this property before my dad and me got here, he certainly never touched it again. He died two weeks after he signed the bill of sale, and it's a safe bet this chest of yours is still here. Where else would he put it?"

"Where else indeed?" Toby was on his feet now, obviously thinking hard.

"Did he own any other property, besides The Raven?" Jim wondered.

But Toby made negative noises. "The fact is his mother, Helen – Nell, to those who knew her well – owned The Raven outright, after the death of his father when Charlie was quite young. He always said he chafed at being tied to a woman's apron strings, so he went to sea in his teens, to make his own way in the world. He was still shipping out when Nell was very old. A man gets to love the sea and goes back to her, the way he'd return to a lover. It was only providence that brought him to *The Rose of Gloucester* the day that swine of a captain was signing on a crew for the run to the Azores, the Caribbean, the Carolinas and back. No, Jim … The Raven was all Charlie owned. So, if he still had the chest, it's here somewhere."

"Oh, he had it." Jim stood in the middle of the kitchen, turning around and around, using his eyes to *look* at the place for the first time in years. "In the weeks before he died, he'd sit at the window either in the taproom or in his bedchamber, watching, always watching – now I know he was watching out for any one of you to come walking up that path."

"We all swore we wouldn't come back a day ahead of the date we set," Toby reminded.

"I haven't forgotten," Jim mused. "But a man like Bellowes could easily have come back a year early, or five years, and stolen the prize from Charlie either by force or trickery. I think Charlie believed one of them would. He was … vigilant. That's the word. Even when he was green to the ears with the ailment that put him in the ground he was *vigilant*, as if he half expected someone like Bellowes to creep up on him and hold a pistol to his head, for the secret of where he'd hidden the prize. I never knew if Charlie kept a pistol on him, but from what I know now, I'd have to guess he had two or three stashed, loaded, against the chances of a swindle."

The argument was compelling, and Toby accepted every word. "All right, so we assume the treasure of Diego Monteras is still here. The only other piece of turf Charlie could lay claim to was his mother's grave, and he wouldn't have buried it there. Not when Nathaniel would have defiled the grave to recover it. One thing Charlie always did was lift a mug to his old ma when a new bottle was opened. She raised him alone, when his father died. He had no siblings, just two little brothers who died as babes."

"So it's here. *Somewhere.*" Jim looked down into Mrs. Clitheroe's face, wondering how much of this she was hearing. She was listening intently and Jim ventured, "You knew Charlie well, Edith, didn't you?"

"Better than 'is ma even knew 'im." She had the cat on her lap, and a cup of ale in both gnarled hands. "I can tell thee many a truth 'bout Charlie Chegwidden that Nell never dreamed of."

"But you never knew he was hiding a chest of … valuables."

"I knew 'e were 'idin' *somethin'*, but a man's got a right to 'ave 'is share o' secrets. S'not fer the likes o' me to ask." She petted the cat absently, thinking back across the years. "An' 'e were fond of 'is guns. That much were no secret! As I recall 'e 'ad *three* bloody great boat guns, always loaded, one under the bar, like Master Fairley 'isself … one in the pantry, and t'other up in 'is bedchamber. An' 'e were always watchin', like thee, Master Trelane. An' now," she added darkly, "we know why."

"We do." Jim gave Toby a deeply speculative look. "I'd start in his bedchamber."

"I looked," Toby began. "Chests and trunks –"

"Hearthstones, floorboards, loose plaster on the walls, or new plaster that looks like it was added just in the last eight years." Jim managed a creditable chuckle. "I'll wager you didn't have time to look at those!"

Toby echoed the rueful humor. "I didn't. And we ought to be looking at *every* hearthstone, every floorboard, every flake of plaster in the house."

"The good news is, we have all night." Jim cocked an ear to the rain. "Even Barney Bellowes waited for the sky to clear before he came here. If he'd been a day earlier –"

"You could be dead already," Toby finished. "Lucky for the pair of us, he was blind drunk in Exmouth. Drunk enough to take his fist to a poor young girl. I'd walked away from them before it happened. Barney liked to swing a kick at Bess, if she got too close. I've smashed a bottle over his head before now, for similar malice." He mocked himself with a crooked grin. "What kind of a priest would you call me?"

"A bloody good one." Jim did not even have to think about it.

But Toby's head was shaking. "A priest ought to have some skerrick of faith. I've none. Or, none left. I never had much to begin with, and what I owned was soon knocked out of me aboard *The Rose of Gloucester*." He rubbed the back of his neck where he still wore the gall, a constant reminder that the weight of a cross had rested there for many years. "Put it out of your mind, Jim. I surely have. I'll pick up that particular gauntlet when I'm called to be judged – and by damn, the only authority I'll be judged by is the Almighty. If he wants to burn me for being exactly as he made me, and loving just as he designed me to love … well, it's his prerogative, I suppose. But it doesn't reflect very well on him, does it?"

The words framed everything Jim had always half-felt, half-known, without ever being able to think the matter through to its bitter end. Toby had trodden this path a long time ago, and gone on. For a moment Jim dwelt on what he had seen and suffered, and then consigned the past to another day when he could brood on it at length – or when Toby would speak of it.

For the moment, time was wasting and he felt the prickle of excitement. Like most boys, he had grown up on stories of pirates and treasure and exotic islands where palm trees nodded in the heavy, humid air and a king's ransom lay buried under golden sand. As a man, he had listened to the tales of men like Charlie and Fred Bailey, stories of the brutality of the navy, the hardships and danger of life on the whalers in oceans filled with ice and ripped by massive storms. With the gammy leg, Jim had resigned himself to living in his imagination, with daydreams fed and colored by the stories of men like Chegwidden and Bailey – and Toby Trelane. What he could never have imagined was that the thrill would walk up to his own door –

Or that a violent death would be stalking him as surely as Toby. His skin prickled again as he took a lantern in each hand and headed up the stairs with Toby on his heels, carrying two more. A great gust, no less than gale force, broadsided The Raven just as they came up onto the landing, and Jim ducked involuntarily.

Toby whistled. "Listen to her blow. You want to be in the rigging in this weather, Jim, fighting with a bunch of tangled rope that's so slick with rain, you can't get a grip on it, while the ship leans over and almost puts her gunwales underwater, smacking into every wave like a diving porpoise, and the wind seems to grab hold of you with fingers like ice and tries to tear you away into a sky that's all silver with mist and wild water."

"Christ." Jim took a breath, held it, let it out slowly. The pulse in his throat was hard and fast. "You've done that." Not a question. "Fred Bailey tells those same stories, and ..." He looked down at his leg. "Maybe I'm lucky to be too lame for the navy to take an interest in me."

"I'm not sure I'd call it luck," Toby mused, "but any luck you had changed when I showed my face here. Did it change for the better? Now, there's another question!"

He was right, but Jim felt the thrill now, the challenge, and he was not about to run up any surrender flag without a fight. He led Toby to the bedchamber where Charlie had slept, and they lit a dozen smoky tallow candles to augment the lanterns.

First, the rugs came up. The mattress was lifted, shaken, probed, opened in long slits on the bottom, and Toby thrust his arm, elbow-deep, into the straw stuffing. A shake of his head, and they upturned the table at the bedside, and then the trunks under the window. Nothing.

They held the lanterns to the walls, peering at the plaster, knocking on it, finding loose pieces and pulling them carefully out. Nothing was hidden in the walls, and the remaining plaster was probably older than Jim. They puzzled the plaster bits back into the holes and turned their attention to the floor.

The bed squealed as it was shoved into a corner, and now Toby stamped on the floorboards, hunting for loose ones. Most were tight, but two moved a fraction, enough to make them suspicious. Jim fetched the smallest of the fire irons and forced it into the gaps between the slack boards and their snug neighbors. They lifted out cleanly, and in a wash of lantern light he and Toby peered into the space beneath.

Nothing. Jim swore and sat down on the bedside, watching as Toby dismissed the floor from his attention and began to examine the fireplace. The musician's hands tried every stone, every brick, jiggling and pulling until he found three loose enough to be interesting. He glanced at Jim, beckoned with a nod of his head, and together they wrestled the bricks out.

Again, lantern light probed into the dark places, but they were empty and Jim muttered blistering curses. The bricks jiggled back into place and Toby stood, hands on hips, glaring at the room. "I'd have been prepared to swear we'd find it in here."

So would Jim, but his mind had raced on. "It could be in any chamber, under any floor, in any wall. Hand it to Charlie – he made a bloody good job of this! If he'd been able to read and write he might have left a letter, not to be opened till one of you returned."

"But Charlie never learned how to read," Toby said with wry amusement, "and the treasure of Diego Monteras is not the kind of secret you'd ever share, to have someone else write it for you." He huffed a sigh. "We have a long night ahead of us, I think. Could he have buried the chest somewhere else, not on your property but very close to it?"

The question was shrewd and Jim gave it full consideration. "No," he said at last. "Right in front, it's beach and tidal. Nothing stays buried. The sea washes anything right out. To the east, it's the beck, and inclined to flood every two or three years. Anything you bury there will be washed out of the ground. To the north it's heathland and paddocks, and it floods when the beck washes over. To the west it's fields belonging to Squire Lawson. Half the time they're under the plow. He grows barley to feed his cattle through the winter." His brows rose and he scratched his chin thoughtfully. "Mind you, Charlie grew up in this area. He'd have known there's old mine workings not far from here. They're still taking tin and copper out of the ground but a lot of the mines are dead, abandoned." Then he dismissed his own idea. "No, the mines are dangerous and anybody born on this coast, like Charlie, knows it. The roofs come down, the pits are flooded with rainwater ... and there's always gypsies on those heaths. You go lumbering in with a heavy load and an hour later ride away without it – anything you left behind wouldn't say hidden for long. Charlie'd know this as well as I do. Damn!"

"Patience, Jim." Toby's hands fell on Jim's shoulders. "Two of us and all night to search, and we know what we're searching for. The odds are with us." He leaned in and down the little that separated them in height, and laid a kiss on Jim's mouth.

Jim's arms went around his waist and for some time they were silent, content to eat each other alive. "What wouldn't I give," Jim said with unrepentant humor when they parted, "for a soft bed and an hour to beguile away with you, and nothing to do in the morning but sleep it off."

"You make it sound very tempting," Toby admitted. "But an hour could be the difference between having the treasure of Diego Monteras in the palm of your hand, and looking down the business end of a pistol and begging Nathaniel Burke not to shoot the pair of us in the head."

"We work," Jim said with grim conviction. "Work now, hump later."

"Win through tonight," Toby agreed, "and we've months and years, a lifetime, to learn each other's secrets."

"A lifetime." Jim smiled, and it was not a sham. "I like the sound of that." He pecked Toby's cheek with a kiss and stepped out of his embrace. "So we work."

Each bedchamber consumed an hour, and there were six of them including Jim's own and the one they had already searched. Mattresses, floorboards, plaster, bricking in the hearth – nothing was overlooked and they were tired, filthy, hungry, when they returned to the kitchen.

The backdoor stood open and steel blue light streamed in. Dawn was not far away. Mrs. Clitheroe was absent – she would have gone out to the privy, Jim guessed – and the dogs were nosing around the stableyard, about their business. He put a pan of water on the hob for coffee and gave Toby a dark look.

"We're running out of time," Toby said quietly. "We need to look behind the hearth stones in both the fireplaces in the taproom ... God! How strange, and how fitting, if Barney broke his stupid neck right on top of the prize!"

"And we should check the walls in the taproom, and then in the kitchen here, and then every floorboard in the kitchen before we get into the cellar. Not to mention the stable and the coach house."

"Not enough time," Toby repeated, and gave Jim a faint, tired smile. "It was worth every moment we spent, and at least we can be sure about the taproom before I have to go." He gave Jim his hand. "You know Burke and Pledge and the others will be here, if not today, then tomorrow."

"Oh, I know." Jim held Toby's hand tightly for a moment. "But I'll feel a thousand times safer with *you* holding the pistol on me!" He hesitated, and then framed what was on his mind with great care. "Are you sure you can you do it, Toby? Be sure. Can you let them tear this place to pieces find the prize, then stand back and watch them walk away with everything?"

"I can." Toby had obviously thought it through. "Right from the beginning, I knew I'd have to fight Nathaniel and Barney for any share, much less a fair share. They'd find some way to short change me. When the gemstones are on the table, Jim, and hellfire starts to twinkle in men's eyes, the pistols will be out. There'll be blood, trust me, before the prize is divvied up, because it *won't* be an even share-out. Two words in the wrong direction and I could be buried in your churchyard right beside Marguerite. Could I stand well back, let them toss me some scrap so they can mock me before they walk away?" He lifted his chin. "I can – because when they're quite finished mocking me with scraps, they'll not be back. And I ... I think I've found somewhere to belong." He frowned deeply at Jim. "If you'll have me."

"Have you?" Jim echoed. "You mean, to have and to hold, sickness and health, till death us do part and all the old twaddle?"

"Twaddle?" Toby chuckled richly. "Hardly twaddle. I used to speak those words."

"You've married people?" Jim was surprised, and knew he should not have been. The idea was as strange as it was charming.

"Not lately." Toby spooned coffee and treacle into the boiling water and lifted it off the hob. "I told you, put it out of your mind. I have. Whatever I was, I'm not the same man now. All I want is peace, rest, honest work, and someone to be with in the dark."

The sentiment touched Jim profoundly. He took a mug from Toby and caught his hand again. "You're welcome here. More than welcome. I've waited half my life for you."

"You're saying I was late?" Good humor made Toby's eyes lighter, brighter. "I got here as soon as I could. The date was set many years ago." He lifted Jim's hand to his lips, kissed the knuckles in a curiously chivalrous gesture. "Let's finish searching the tavern itself, at least, before I have to go. There's time, if we get a move on."

The coffee was strong enough to wake the dead. Jim almost gagged on it and then choked it down, for he needed the heat and the odd jolt in the limbs and mind he always felt after he drank the brew. Some men swore it would sober them up after a binge on rum and ale; smugglers swore it would propel them through a night of high seas and icy rain, playing hide and seek with the excise men. All Jim needed was the strength and resolve to get back on the aching leg and finish what they had started, before daylight began to brighten in earnest.

Chapter Ten

Nothing. And if he was honest with himself, Jim knew he had expected nothing, because the taproom was so familiar to him. If there had been a loose stone in the wall, or a false back on the shelves under the bar, or a stone in either of the fireplaces that was less than snug, he would have known about it.

As delicious as it would have been to find Charlie's secret and Diego Monteras's legacy under the hearthstones where Barney Bellowes had snapped his own neck like a carrot, the fireplace was empty. As they worked over it, testing every brick, they both heard a profound silence in the chimney. As they sat back on their knees – dirty, tired, frustrated, anxious – Toby said softly,

"The wind's dropped. The storm's passed us by, Jim, and it's an hour since dawn." He pushed up to his feet and inspected his filthy hands. "If I'm going, I've got to go now or this whole scheme is for nought."

"I know." Jim stood with difficulty, favoring the leg. He would be aching the rest of the day and like as not tomorrow, after the night's unaccustomed work.

What he needed was a shot of the best Dutch laudanum, and he knew he would be taking it the moment Toby had gone. He used the laudanum as infrequently as may be, because John Hardesty had warned him, the stuff was worse than grog for making a man come to need it for its own sake. But Hardesty had long trusted Jim, and never hesitated to provide the laudanum; and Jim usually kept a bottle in the house.

He rubbed the leg slowly, heavily, aware of Toby's eyes on him.

"Yes, I'm not the best. I won't try to dupe you! But it was worth it. We've learned a lot. We know – absolute fact! – where the prize *isn't*. I'd like to see Burke and his crew start in the taproom and the upstairs, and get tired and angry."

"The angrier they get, the more violent they'll be," Toby said doubtfully. "After I've gone, you keep searching. Treat the kitchen to the same kind of rape and pillage we've given the rest of the place. Have Edith douse the fire in the cooking hearth. Now I come to think of it, I can't imagine a better place to hide a fortune than right underneath a blazing fire that's never allowed to go out."

"I could wish we'd thought of that first." Jim moved restlessly to and fro to ease the leg. "You'll want to wash, and then … damnit, Toby, be careful. You've said a few things tonight that make me think you're not much safer in Nathaniel's company than I would be."

"I'm always careful." Toby's face was filled with regret. "I'm still alive. And as for you, Jim Fairley –" He reached out as if to touch Jim's face, then saw the dirt on his fingers and thought better of it. "Don't set up your lip to Nathaniel, not even for a moment. Don't make clever remarks. Play the part of the coward, put up your hands and even blubber, if you can manage it! Do that, and Nathaniel will utterly scorn you. When I offer to hold a pistol on you, he'll turn his back on us both. No harm'll come to you."

"He won't assume I found the prize long ago?" Jim speculated as they stepped back into the kitchen.

Toby took the big basin to the barrel and filled it. As he rolled up his sleeves and plunged his arms into the cold water he looked around at the kitchen and, by extension, the tavern. "You wouldn't be here, still, if you possessed a king's ransom. You'd have a big house up on the moors, and servants to run about after you while you drank smuggled French brandy and went up to Bath to take the cure, see if the 'waters' would soak the pain out of your leg." He glanced along at Mrs. Clitheroe, who was feeding the cat with herring tails, rewarding him for the three mice which had been laid out for her perusal that morning. Dropping his voice, Toby said very softly, "You can still have those things, Jim. Keep on searching, every minute, and if you find the prize – you get out and you run, and keep on running."

A lump had formed in Jim's throat. "And you?"

"I'll help Nathaniel and Joe rip this place timber from timber, and when we find nothing, and they start to guess you did and made off with it, well …" He gave the old woman a glance. "Edith and I can point them in the wrong direction. They'll be hunting you in Liverpool and Glasgow while you've actually sat your arse aboard a ship bound for the Carolinas. And don't," he said darkly, "*don't* come back, Jim. Ever."

"But …" Jim swallowed the lump in his throat. "Not without you. I'll get on a ship, sure enough. But not until you're right there, one step behind me, and Bess with you as we walk aboard."

"Damnit, Jim!" Toby's voice rose a little in frustration. "Don't let them get their hands on you. Just – don't."

"I could tell you the same," Jim growled. "In fact, I *am* telling you." He watched Toby close his eyes for a moment as if in despair, and pressed on regardless. "If I find anything, I'll run. I'll borrow a horse from John Hardesty. He's got three or four out to grass. He won't miss one, and he'll do me the favor, especially if I tell him I'm being chased like a fox."

"Just don't tell him why," Toby said quickly. "Tell him anything, but not the truth!"

"Credit me with a grain of sense," Jim remonstrated. "I'll tell him a story. Heaven knows what – I'll think it through on the road! And I'll make my way to Southampton. I know a few taverns just this side of the port. I'll take a room there, and I'll bloody *wait*, Toby. I'll wait six months, if that's how long it takes you to drag your boots to Southampton and ask around, and find me. Then … yes, a ship. The Carolinas or Kingston, Jamaica. I don't care where." He paused for breath and looked into Toby's wide, bright eyes. "Together. All right?"

The blue eyes were *too* bright. Sure enough, tears spilled though Toby wore a smile. "All right. Now, for the love of God keep your wits about you. And before you say it – I'm on my mettle, Jim, like a bantam cock with its spurs on, just about to be tossed into the pit to fight for its life."

The analogy was stingingly sharp and Jim winced. He followed Toby back to the taproom, where his coat was hanging, and the mandolin. Bess lingered in the kitchen with Boxer, and twice Toby called her before she came to him.

"She doesn't want to go," Jim whispered.

"Nor do I." Toby slipped the strap of the mandolin over his head so the instrument lay on his shoulder, giving the oddly humpbacked appearance Jim had glimpsed from the tail of his eye, the first time he saw Toby. "I … heaven help me, but I do believe I love you, Jim." His smile was crooked and self-mocking, as if he thought he should apologize for the emotion.

"Likewise," Jim said gruffly. He glanced over his shoulder, but the old woman was busy and he took the moment of privacy to seize Toby by both shoulders and kiss him soundly. "I think you'll be back sooner than you know, and then … like the fiddlers say, we'll play it by ear."

He gave Toby a push before he could haul the man into an embrace that would be their undoing, and lifted up the bar to open the door. It was heavy enough to task his shoulders, but a rush of anger made it seem much lighter this morning.

The sky was thickly overcast, but the wind had stopped. The air was dank, cold, and as he stepped outside he heard the gurgle of running water. For a moment he thought it was the flow from the eaves trough into the rain barrels, and then he *knew* that sound.

The beck was up over its banks, as it had been two years before. The coastal path was not just glistening wet. As they strode out into the middle of it, they found the water over ankle deep, and not thirty yards east, where it banked down, the path was gone, replaced by a slate gray lake, its surface wind-rippled and full of sunken debris. Jim saw broken fence posts, uprooted saplings, a wagon wheel bobbing in mid-water. The way back to Exmouth was not merely impassable, it was treacherous with hidden pitfalls. He knew the path well enough to know the way on east to Kersbrook and, far beyond, Sidmouth, would be even worse.

"Well now," Toby said with an acid kind of humor, "so much for all our noble sentiments and terms of endearment! We're *stuck*, the both of us, well and truly!"

"I'd say the word is *besieged*," Jim suggested. "But look on the bright side. If we can't get out, Burke and his crew can't get in."

They were standing almost up to mid-calf in cold water while Bess ran back and forth at the edge of the lake, yipping forlornly. Toby looked from horizon to horizon. "Much more rain, and the tavern itself will be under. There'll be knee-deep water in your stableyard in two hours' time, if the level in the beck doesn't go down. Have you seen it like this before, and had it fall?"

"Twice, last year." Jim was intent on the sky. "So long as the rain stops right now the beck won't get any worse, but *look* at that." He was glaring at a bank of clouds the color of a funeral shroud.

"There's no wind, mind you," Toby mused. "There's enough rain in those clouds to drown us all, but it's not coming this way. Not yet, at least." He gave Jim a taut look. "It buys us some more time."

The thrill prickled through Jim's whole body again. "Come on, then. While we can. I want to start in the stable and coach house."

"Not the kitchen?" Toby was behind him, feet sloshing noisily through the water.

"If the stable and coach house are going to be three feet underwater by tonight," Jim said bleakly, "we won't be able to search them at all. The yard runs down a slight bank – you didn't notice? The whole tavern is built up, three feet or so higher than the rest of the property."

"I noticed." Toby unslung the mandolin and stopped on the threshold to heel off his sodden boots. "Whoever had the inspiration to build the tavern higher – cheers to him!"

"Not inspiration. Convenience." Also barefoot by now, Jim gathered up his shoes and stockings in both hands and padded inside. "The Raven was built right on top of the ruin of an inn that stood here before. The cellar's far older than the rest of the house. The old inn burned down about a hundred years ago, so Charlie told me, and at the time they just pushed the rubble flat, packed it down and built *this* house right on top. The pile of old brickwork puts us three feet higher – thank God for small mercies. "

Toby had wrung out his stockings and draped them over the back of a chair. He hung his coat back where it had begun and put the mandolin under the bar, along with the blunderbuss. He shoved his feet back into the wet, disgusting boots, and made a face. "When we find the prize, the first thing I'm going to buy is a spare pair of boots, so I don't have to wear wet ones. Stables?"

"Stables," Jim agreed. "I can't offer you my shoes, because you have bigger feet. Anything I own would cripple you. But I do know a cobbler in Exmouth who makes boots to fit, if you come back tomorrow for them. They're expensive – I could never afford them."

"Till now." Toby was on the threshold. "I'm going around the outside, else I'll leave puddles everywhere I step."

"One minute, and I'll be with you," Jim promised, already headed for his bedchamber, and the first pair of boots he could find.

The stable would hold eight horses, and dry feed was stored in nets and barrels opposite the stalls. Jim did not keep a horse of his own – he had no use for one – but passing gentry often broke their journey here, especially in winter when night fell much earlier and the weather could be dire. The Raven had a reputation for clean beds, good food, unwatered ale, and a certain discretion on the part of the taverner. If a man wanted to bring a paramour here, no questions were asked.

With the stable empty and blue daylight streaming in through the open doors, the job of checking every square yard of floor and walls was as simple as it was ravenous for time. At last, agile as a monkey, Toby shinned up into the loft and poked into every corner while Jim watched and hoped. His face looked down from the shadows and he called,

"Nothing here but a century's worth of dust and some drowsy spiders. Charlie!" He addressed the thin air, as if Chegwidden's ghost might be there. "Charlie, what did you do with it, damnit? What *could* you do with a chest the size of a keg of brandy?"

"You could break it down … in which case you could hide the contents in a dozen places, or a hundred," Jim reasoned slowly.

"Christ, if he did that, we'll never find it." Toby slid back down the ladder and dropped the last few feet to the floor. He stood for a moment with both hands over his face, and then shook his head emphatically. "No, the Charlie Chegwidden I knew was a simple soul. The idea of splitting it up into twenty places, or fifty, wouldn't have entered his head. He was the kind of man who'd just dig a hole and bury what he wanted to hide. And it's here *somewhere,* Jim. We just haven't found it yet."

"Dig a hole," Jim echoed, leaning on the door jamb and looking out into the stableyard. A light drizzle had begun to fall, leaving the flagstones slick and shining. "He wouldn't risk sharing the secret with anyone else."

"Right." Toby joined him there, standing behind him with his chin on Jim's shoulder. "Whatever he was going to do, it had to be done with one pair of hands – and from what you've told me, his mother was on her deathbed at the time he arrived home, so the tavern would be full of friends and well wishers. Whatever Charlie did, it was so silent, so cautious, nobody ever knew he'd done it."

"So," Jim reasoned, leaning back into Toby's warmth and his hands, which were idly charting his torso as if the territory were exotic, "one thing he *didn't* do was tear up any of these flagstones in the yard. They're too big, too heavy, and they've been in place so long, if you disturbed one, the mess would be obvious. Everyone in the tavern would want to know what he was doing, digging up the stableyard. Edith would remember."

"And the floor in the stable here is just mortar," Toby added as Jim turned into his arms. "Very old mortar."

"Which hasn't been broken with an axe." Jim's arms slid up around Toby's neck, and he sighed. "Coach house, kitchen, cellar. That's all we've got left."

Toby feathered a kiss across his lips. "I'm hungry. I'll get us some food, if you want to start in the coach house. You know it better than I ever will."

The coach house was smaller than the stable, with room for two modest vehicles, though Jim rarely had to accommodate even one. He used it as a storehouse more often than not, and today he swore as he stepped into its gloom. It was a chaos of crates, trunks and barrels, some of them so old, they had been gathering cobwebs since Nell Chegwidden's day, and all of them in plain sight, which was his guarantee they contained nothing more valuable than nails or pickled onions gone black with age.

Up above were rafters; the floor beneath his feet was mortar and the walls were plain, unplastered stone. Fists on hips, Jim gave it all a bleak look and was still swearing when Toby followed him in. He had brought cheese, bread, salt beef, prunes and a pint of ale, and they ate mechanically while sizing up the job.

"There's a full day's work in here," Jim said through a mouthful of food.

"More like two days," Toby hazarded. "The best we can do is try to think like a simple soul, and get done what we can."

Jim took a swig from the dark glass bottle. The ale was flat and strong. "You took a look at the water level, out towards the beck?"

"I did." Toby took the bottle from him and also drank. "She's still rising, but not as fast. I give us till late tonight at this rate, and then the whole yard, stable and coach house with it, will be under." He craned back his neck and peered into the rafters. "Not even Charlie would be simple enough to shove the prize into a crate or a keg and just leave it where you can see it from the door! But, I'm thinking … how about *under* one of the big trunks back there?"

"Or would he have packed the prize into a smaller bag," Jim mused, "and buried it inside an ocean of rank pickled onions?" He made a face. "There's a pry-bar here somewhere."

"You'll take the onions? Damn! Then, I'll take the rafters," Toby offered. "You don't want to be up there, Jim." He had seen the ladder leaning against the wall in the back.

The work was as filthy as before, and much more aromatic. One barrel was half full of pickled walnuts that had fermented long ago and reeked to high heaven. The onions looked like hundred year old eggs floating in a lake of tar, and Jim wrapped his nose and mouth in a scarf as he probed to the bottom, raking around in search of a bag, a box, anything.

"Nothing," he told Toby as the other man shinned back down the ladder. "Give me a hand with these barrels – the stink would make a pig lose his dinner! Damnation, I've *got* to get rid of these."

"They must have been here since Nell Chegwidden owned the place … and they were a good bet." Toby sneezed repeatedly on the dust he had raised in the rafters. His clothes and hair wore a fine film of it, and he brushed himself down as he surveyed onions, walnuts, forgotten potatoes that had turned into wizened clusters of black roots.

One barrel held contents so rotten as to be utterly unidentifiable. The crates contained a rare assortment of nails, broken china, little glass window squares, oakum, discarded tools, oddments of clothing set aside to be ripped for rags. Jim vaguely remembered sweeping the clutter together and stowing it, in the weeks after Charlie passed away. One by one trunks, crates and barrels were resealed, and he glanced up into the dimness high overhead. "No sign, I suppose, that Charlie was every up there?"

"No sign," Toby said dryly, "that anything human has *ever* been up there! There's twenty years of pigeon dung on everything, and you can't see through the dust on the cobwebs. I startled a dozen wicked-looking spiders, to get into the corners."

"Shite." Jim sighed in annoyance. "*Under* the barrels, then?"

"Under." Toby was frowning at the floor and seeing exactly what Jim saw – a lot of very coarse mortar which had been laid down before either of them was born, and had not been disturbed since. "If Charlie was able to get a pick through this floor," Toby said resignedly, "he'd have to park something big, heavy, dirty, stinking, on top of it, to cover up the work. He'd be thinking, nobody's going to be interested in pickled walnuts and rusted nails." He pushed up his sleeves. "How's the leg? Can you help me manhandle them aside?"

The leg was aching, and Jim knew better than Toby would ever guess how close to the end of his endurance he was. He had done more work in the last day than he had done in months, and he knew he would pay the price for it. The thought of a generous swig of laudanum had begun to taunt him, but he took a deep breath, physically shoved the pain aside. "I can help," he said quietly, "but this is the last for me, today and maybe tomorrow. I'm sorry."

"Don't be." Toby took a grip on one edge of the first barrel, tipped it toward him and began to roll it sideways to expose the floor underneath. "You think I can't see you limping on that leg – and you think I don't care? You do me ill, Jim, if you believe I'll watch you in pain and not fret."

It was so long since anyone had cared, Jim was almost discomfited. He felt a flush of embarrassment as he shouldered in beside Toby and worked with him to move the entire load. Every time they shifted a barrel or crate, they peered at the same old mortar; and when they moved the last one it was Toby's turn to whisper fluent curses.

"Not the floor, then. Damnit, Charlie, you old rascal! You left me a good one to solve, didn't you?" He glanced sidelong at Jim, and dropped both long arms around him. "You need to take the weight off the leg."

It was true, and Jim did not argue. He took the dusty kiss Toby was offering, and dropped his buttocks onto a leather-bound trunk which creaked beneath his weight. "Loose bricking in some part of the walls?"

"Possibly. Probably." Toby flexed his back and shoulders, which were obviously aching. "We're not going to find it, Jim, not in here, not in the time we have left. Can you hear *that*?"

Now he mentioned it, Jim was absently aware of the gurgle of running water, and he hoisted himself back to his feet with an oath. Toby was at the door, where a sheet of water, inches deep now, rippled on the stones flagging the yard; and beyond the yard, the water stretched on toward the beach. The coarse bushes marking the head of the dunes and following the path seemed to be standing in a lake that moved perceptibly with the waves breaking seventy yards further out.

To Jim's shrewd eye, the tavern had just less than three feet of vertical space left before they would be getting their feet wet indoors. He had always known a moment must come when their priorities changed, and this was it.

"It's time we got the tavern secured," he said bitterly. "We need to get food and firewood and rugs up off the floor, get the good furniture upstairs. Can you handle it? I'm going to trowel a pail of mortar around the trapdoor to the cellar, while I've still got the chance."

"Old fashioned oilskins and mortar," Toby remembered. "I saw the gear not ten minutes ago. Now, where was it?"

Four sacks of mortar were stacked behind the ladder, and a roll of cracked old oilskins, tied with frayed rope, lay with them. They had been used before, for just this purpose. While Toby carried them back to the kitchen, Jim hunted for the broad pail and the big trowel he used to mix the mortar. He found them soon enough, but even then he realized they had probably left it too late to save the cellar. Even with the fire blazing in the kitchen, the mortar would take six or eight hours to dry. They were cutting it too fine, and they both knew it.

"Last chance to get out and go home, Edith," Toby told the old woman as they let the dogs out for a constitutional.

The front door of The Raven stood wide open to a strange view – as if the sea washed almost up to the door, with just a scant few yards of gravel and pebbles between the granite step and the lap of the water.

"I can get you out to Budleigh," Jim suggested, "if you want to stay at the church. It's set too high to flood ... though the graveyard surely will."

She gave an animated shudder. "When I were a lass, it rained ten days one March, put the whole churchyard underwater. The boxes washed right outta the ground. Any poor sod who'd been buried in the last ten month were floatin' away, an' 'alf the 'eadstones sagged after that, so they looked drunk as a gaggle o' lords."

"So, you don't want to go to the church," Jim concluded.

"An' me cottage'll be up to its windersills," she said disgustedly. "It goes under even afore yon path does."

"What about going to your grandson's house?" Jim was watching the dogs paw at the water. Bess took a lap at it and whined. It was likely closer to salt than fresh, and fifty privies would have overflowed into it, back up the course of the beck. "I can see the boat – you see her there, Toby? She's still upside down, and she's hung herself in the bushes, but we can flop her over between us."

"Flop 'er over an' go *where*?" Mrs. Clitheroe demanded. "Thee thinks Exmouth's gunna be any better? Me grandson'll be bailing out 'is parlor, an' that stupid cow of a wife of 'is, she'll be weeping an' wailing, some bilge water about the end o' the world. Nay, lad. I'll say where I be."

She made an excellent point, and Toby gave Jim an almost amused look. "I think we'll be settling in for the duration. A day or three till the beck stops running, then it'll be all hands on deck with every mop and broom you possess."

"We've done it before," Jim admitted, resigned to repeating a process that would be just a little less tedious with Toby in residence. "I want to get a lot of firewood upstairs – and food. You can always put a pan on the hob in any of the bedchambers. Keep a decent fire going, wait it out. It'll take as long as it takes." He turned his back to the odd view of a world comprised almost entirely of water, and was already deciding which furniture to move, and which of the firewood Toby had cut just days before was the driest and best. "If you want to get a start, I'll mix enough mortar to secure the cellar. There's enough life left in this leg of mine to help you get the good chairs upstairs. Take any bedchamber you prefer, Edith, and … now, what's got into *them*?"

He was talking about the dogs, whose yapping was swiftly turning into loud, angry barking, and he turned back from his survey of the tavern to see what they were up to. He saw Toby's face first. It had set into a mask as hard and as dark as quarried slate.

The blue eyes flickered in Jim's direction and then returned to the west, and the water. The pink tip of Toby's tongue ran once around his lips to moisten them, and he said softly,

"We just ran out of time, Jim. And out of luck."

Chapter Eleven

A boat was sliding in from the sea. It looked like a whaler's longboat, Jim thought, and the two men at the oars were skilled. The sea was calmer than it had been in days, and the run of the tide did not seem to trouble them much as they brought the craft in. It grounded out when its keel hit the path, and one of them hopped over the side. His boots were rolled right up to the thighs to keep out the water as he forced his way through, cutting the shortest line for the tavern door. Wisely, Mrs. Clitheroe beat a swift retreat. Jim heard the squeal of a hinge as the kitchen door closed halfway over.

"Nathaniel Burke," Toby said very softly. "He always fancied himself the skipper of our company. Don't misjudge the other bastard, Jim, but of the two Burke is the dangerous one, because he's intelligent."

"And the other?" Jim asked in the same undertone.

"Joseph Pledge. Joe to his friends and enemies alike. Keep a wide berth between the two of you … he likes to hurt. To Joe pain is hilariously funny, so long as it's someone else's agony." He whistled softly to Bess. "Come here, girl. Stay close, now." He gave Jim a sidelong glance. "He'll hurt any of us, if he can, and the dogs are fair game."

"Boxer – here, lad." Jim slapped his thigh to bring the ratter to him, and watched Pledge disentangle himself from the oars and step over into the cold swirl of the water.

Of the pair, Nathaniel Burke was also the more physically imposing. He was a tall man and big through the shoulders, with white scars on his face, neck and hands, visible from a good distance away. His expression seemed to be set in a permanent grimace, as if he had worn the look for so long, it has set in place. He was not a young man, Jim saw; ten years older than Toby at least, and he wore his years with less grace than Toby. In his day he must have been passable handsome, but now the stubble clinging to his cheeks was white, the bags under his eyes were the size of a seaman's chest and his nose had been broken, set off-center, so it angled toward his right cheek. His clothes were well worn but just as well repaired; his tricorn was black, set at a rakish angle at odds with the slope of his nose.

With their weight out of it the boat floated off once more, and Burke and Pledge dragged it up to the gravel and pebbles marking the edge of The Raven's old foundations. If the tavern had not been built on the leveled ruins of a previous building, it would have been flooded already, and Jim knew how lucky they were. Biding his time, keeping silent, he studied the strangers.

Joe Pledge was short, as rotund as he was muscular, oily, with yellow teeth which were bared in a grimace of effort as the keel scraped up onto the pebbles and refused to be moved any further. Under a battered tricorn, his brown hair hung in greasy ringlets about a face as square-jawed as a prize fighter; his skin was sallow, where Burke wore a mahogany tan, and as his coat shifted with effort Jim saw the butts of a pair of pistols in his belt. Like Burke, he was not dressed well, and he had none of Burke's sense of style. The tricorn was crammed down over his eyes, the coat flapping, the waistcoat unbuttoned, the shirt beneath stained by pickles and the same tobacco juice that had yellowed his teeth. Jim took in all of this with one glance which lingered on the pistols.

Another pair of almost identical pistols rode Burke's own broad belt, and Jim remembered what Toby had said – they would be loaded, even if Pledge's were not. The coat pockets of both men bulged. He knew the look of shot and powder bags when he saw them.

"There should be three more of the bastards," Toby said softly as the boat grounded out the second time, and without waiting for Burke or Pledge to speak he pinned on a smile and called, "You took your time getting here, Nathaniel! I thought you'd never show your face! Where's Eli and Willie?" And to Jim, so softly that his voice would not carry, "Eli Hobbs and Willie Tuttle. They drifted into Exmouth the evening before I walked out. The last one, Rufus Bigelow, hadn't arrived when I left."

Coughing heavily after the exertion of pulling up the boat, Burke spat into the water and pulled the back of his hand over his mouth. His voice was deep, rum-rough, with the accent of Bristol. "They's back in the drinkin' house, still gettin' 'emselves proper soused and bedded. They'll be along in a day or three, when this shite weather lets up." He glared at the sky as if he had a private, personal grudge against it. "So, Toby. They told us back in Exmouth ... we're just a mite late to drink Charlie's health in rum. He's dead and gone these last six years or so, and The Raven belongs to another young lad. Nice lad, they said, but gammy-legged. And the whores whereabouts say he's a eunuch. *This* un. You been here all along, Toby?"

"Been here," Toby said in a light tone of voice. "Sang for my supper a couple of times, cut some wood, helped get her battened down for the storm."

"Sang fer yer supper?" Pledge echoed, and barked a laugh. "Yer didn't fuck fer it? Now, there's a turn up fer the books." His accent was London, not quite Cockney but close. He peered at Jim now, brows knitted over dark brown eyes. "This un's pretty. Yer didn't try yer luck?"

Heat bloomed in Jim's face, and when he looked back at Toby he saw the pink rising in his cheeks. It might have been humiliation or anger, Jim could not guess, since Toby's expression was carefully shuttered.

"Yes, well I might have tried it on," he growled, "but Master Fairley doesn't have a share in such sin and infamy, and I was gentleman enough to let it rest with innuendo."

"Gentleman? You?" Pledge roared with laughter and jabbed Burke with his elbow. "And 'e's usin' them big words again."

"Him that speaks Latin like he was born to it," Burke mused, as if it represented a serious flaw in Toby's character. He thrust both hands into the deep pockets of the blue coat, deliberately shifting it to show the pistols. "You look well fed, well slept."

"I did my work." Toby's eyes dropped; his lips pressed tight. "Master Fairley runs an honest house. You work, you get fed and a place to sleep. And there were plenty of jobs, with the storms."

"Aye, maybe so." Burke's dark eyes moved on to Jim now, and Jim met them with the faintest flinch, held them with difficulty. Burke and Pledge should be complete strangers to him – he must not let them realize Toby had described them, much less warned against them. Burke continued to flay him alive with his eyes, but he spoke to Toby. "Where's Barney?"

"Flat on his face, drunk, the last time I saw him," Toby said promptly.

"What, 'ere?" Pledge demanded.

"No." Toby gestured into the west. "The Cattlemarket. Artie Polgreen's house, back yonder, closer to Exmouth."

"Barney left bloody Exmouth a couple of days after you, Trelane." Burke hawked and spat. "He was headed right here."

"He didn't get here." Toby shrugged offhandly. "He probably got waylaid. This isn't the only tavern on the coast, and some of the others have the kind of doxies he fancies. You know." He cupped both hands, a foot in front of his chest. "He's back there somewhere, getting himself thoroughly poxed and waiting for the water to go down. You want me to take the boat, go and scare him up? I walked past two other inns on my way here. I know where they are."

For a long moment Jim was sure Burke was about to tell him to go, and he held his breath. Being alone in The Raven with these two was far from desirable. Burke was still scrutinizing him, deliberately rude. At last the big man growled, "Leave him be. If Barney wants to be absent when the spoils get divvied up, and if he comes up a handful or two short for his bone-bloody-idleness, so be it." His brows rose. "To business, lad." He was intent on Toby. "Let's be having it. You've been here long enough."

Now, Toby cleared his throat. "I haven't found it yet." He shot a glance sidelong at Jim. "I've been trying not to let Master Fairley know I've been looking, but I've searched the upstairs, the stable, the coach house. Even the taproom, when he was asleep. Nothing yet. Charlie made a damned good job of hiding it – and be glad he did, Nathaniel. If he'd made it easy, Jim or his father would have stumbled over it. It's been a long time."

Jim knew he ought to be saying *something*, and he summoned a chuckle. "I have no idea what you're all talking about, but I do know this. It's cold out here, and it's starting to rain again. Will you come inside, have pie and ale, and tell me what in hell you want? God knows, if you tell me what it is, I might be able to help you!"

Fat chance of Burke and Pledge telling him, he knew, but it was a sound gambit, typical of the publican who had dealt with every kind of man across the years. He called the terrier with him and retreated to the kitchen with a leisurely pace, exaggerating the limp. The more lame Burke and Pledge believed him, the greater advantage he would have, if a moment came when he needed it. He called the dogs with him, held a finger to his lips to silence the old woman, and listened.

The two men stamped inside and the door slammed. Burke's voice was sharp with anger. "You think I's going to believe a word of this bilge? You bugger off and *get it*, Trelane, right bloody now. You drag it out here, quick sharp, or I's likely to lay another set of stripes across your back, like all the ones you earned before. Whose brand are you wearin' on your arse?"

"Yours," Toby said hoarsely, in an odd voice Jim had not heard before. "It's been so many years, Nathaniel –"

"Not so many that I's forgot," Burke snapped, "and nor am I likely to. You just remember whose brand you're wearing. You drag out the swag, drag it out quick enough, and I'll forget you tried to gull me."

"I didn't – I'm not trying to swindle you," Toby protested. "I've turned this place inside out and shaken it, I just haven't found it yet. Now you're finally here, you can help. You think a place this size can be searched, rafters to cellar, in a few days with one pair of hands, in this weather, while trying not to be seen?"

Burke hesitated, and it was Pledge who said sourly, "The lad makes a point. I wouldn't like to be 'anded the job, wiv me life dependin' on it."

"A very good point indeed." Burke admitted slowly, musingly. "Master Fairley, I'll thank you to come back out here."

The pulses were hammering in Jim's temples as he stuck his head out of the kitchen. "I'm slicing a rabbit pie. You don't want food?"

And then his mouth dried as Burke calmly lifted the pistol from the right side of his belt, pulled back the hammer, and drew aim dead center on Jim's forehead.

"I'll ask you again," he said to Toby. "Drag out the swag. Drag it out now, lad, or it'll be a pistol ball for Master Fairley and a cane across your back till you can't stand."

"Sweet Jesus." Toby dropped to his knees at Burke's feet. "Flog me to death, Nathaniel – I can't give you what I haven't got. I've searched – go up and look at the mattresses! Every one of them's ripped open on the bottom. For godsakes, don't murder on my account. Like Barney always says, I'm going to hell, nothing's surer – there's enough on my slate to burn me for a decade. Don't make it a century, not with the blood of an innocent. I don't want that on my hands."

It seemed to Jim the tableau froze and time stopped dead. The clock on the mantel might have stopped ticking, for all he was aware of it. Pledge was leering at Toby, expecting Burke to pull the trigger; Toby was hunched, head down, poised on his knees. There was no way for Jim or Toby himself to get to Burke before Burke made the shot, or before Pledge pulled one of his own pistols. Burke had the habit of keeping his weapons loaded at all times, but when Joe Pledge was walking into a scene like this, Jim had to believe his were loaded too.

He found his voice with an effort of will and slowly, slowly raised his hands. "I don't know what you want," he rasped, not recognizing his own voice, "but if you're desperate to search the house – get on with it. I've lived here a long time. Tell me what you're looking for. I can tell you where it might be. Then take it, whatever it is, and go. Just go away. Stay away. All right?"

"Nathaniel, please." Toby did not lift his head. "I remember the day you branded your mark into my hide, and I was glad of it. I've never had reason to dupe you, I don't have a reason now. A handful of baubles is all I ask, and my freedom. A handful, and I can live well for the rest of my life – I don't ask much. I found a place in Spain, I'll be going back there. Just help me search, take what you want, and let me go. Let Master Fairley go – he's done nothing, Nathaniel. Killing him would be murder. You want the stain of it on your soul?"

"Shut up, Trelane. You sound like a priest again, and you got no right. Not with an arse that's been ridden like yours." Burke spat in Toby's direction, but the hammer dropped softly on the pistol and the weapon slid back into his belt. "Well, now, Master Fairley. It seems I believe you."

Jim summoned his voice and found a croak. "Damned good thing you do, because it's the truth. You've got me flummoxed, Captain, and I hate a mystery."

"Captain?" Burke echoed.

"You look like the skipper of a rough, disorderly crew." Jim lowered his hands slowly. He gestured at the door, and beyond. "The longboat. I thought you'd just come ashore. You've a ship in the bay, have you?"

For a moment Burke seemed apprehensive and then his face creased into a grimace which was probably supposed to be a smile, displaying long, tobacco stained teeth. He laughed with the sound of congested lungs. "One thing at a time, young Fairley, and all in its right order. You didn't notice this bugger ferretin' about in your nooks and crannies, countin' your cobwebs?"

"No," Jim lied. "I've been too busy. The first storm did a lot of damage, I had windows to fix, and a door –"

"Aye, all right." Burke turned his back on Jim, intent on Toby now. "Get your feet under you. When I want you on your knees, I'll tell you."

"Nathaniel." Toby stood with a grace and ease the other two might have envied, and Jim held his breath.

"Show me," Burke invited. "Show me what you've searched, and how. Make me believe you, like I believe that gimpy-legged eunuch over there, who's white with dread and likely peein' his britches."

Given the chance to divert attention from Jim, Toby seized it. "I started upstairs. After the first storm, I mended the thatch – searched the loft while I was up there. There's a trapdoor in the ceiling. Come up, and I'd be glad to show you."

"Nathaniel," Pledge growled warningly, hanging back.

"Speak your mind." Burke crossed both arms over a chest like a barrel.

His left arm did not work quite like the right, Jim noticed, as if an old wound bedeviled the shoulder, but those arms were thick as the limbs of a young tree. Wrestle with him, let him get a rival into a bearhug, and the result would be broken bones, suffocation. Jim saw all this and noted it down while he forced himself to listen to Pledge.

The London accent was thick enough to be sliced with a bread-knife. "Yer gunna believe 'im?" Pledge demanded. "Yer put yer mark on him, yer mark of *ownership*. Yer think 'e's not gunna grab the first chance 'e can get to wriggle out like the worm 'e is?"

"You don't believe him," Burke observed with curious amusement.

"No, I bloody don't," Pledge said hotly. "What I believe is, 'e found the swag yesterday, the day before mebbe, 'e took it out and Master bloody eunuch Fairley didn't see nuthin', and if this little shite of a parson can give us the slip and take the lot, 'e'll do it, and laugh."

"I's sure he would," Burke agreed, "but he ain't going to get the chance, Joe. Calm yourself. We'll search this place, rafters to cellar. If I has to, I'll put a torch to it, burn it down and go through the rubble one shovelful at a time. If Toby's tellin' the truth, we'll find the swag sooner or later. If he's lyin', and I'll grant you, he probably is, we'll find nothin'." He smiled at Toby almost benignly. His right hand reached out, tangled in Toby's hair, tousled it gently. "And *then* I'll have the truth out of him, the way you saw me have the truth out of the Spanish lad, that time in the Azores."

Pledge was chortling now. "And the Portuguee, in Barbados." He doubled up in glee and slapped his thigh. "Damn, d'yer remember 'ow 'is eyes bugged 'alfway outta 'is 'ead when yer shoved a belayin' pin right up 'im, and branded 'is tits wiv a pair of doubloons straight outta the brazier? Ha!"

"Then, there'll be plenty for you to enjoy," Burke said, still fingering Toby's hair in a mockery of tenderness, "unless the lad's tellin' the truth. In which case, you'll be too busy countin' your share of the swag to care what happens to this un."

The Adam's apple bobbed twice, three times, in Toby's throat. "Honestly, Nathaniel – I've searched. It's *got* to be here. You'll find it, and when you do – all I'm asking is a handful of *little* ones, and you let me go. You won't see me again. You always said I'd earned it. Freedom."

"Aye, maybe you has." Burke withdrew his hand. "We'll see. Right now, you can earn your ticket of leave with the truth. If you's bein' honest with me, we'll find where old Charlie hid the swag. If you's not..." The tricorned head cocked at Toby. "I wouldn't be you, lad, if you's lyin' to me. You know me. I'll winkle the truth out of you. You want to walk away from here? You play nice."

"I want to walk away." Toby's head bowed. "I'm telling you God's honest truth –"

"Don't you *dare* quote God at us!" Pledge roared. "One more word about God outta them filthy lips, and I'll hammer you right through the deck!"

"Joe, now, be calm before you hurt yourself," Burke said with infuriating good humor. "You don't lay a hand on Toby. Not even a finger. Not while he's wearin' my brand, and I's tellin' you not to. You want him, you ask *nice*, and you give back what you borrowed in the same condition you borrowed it. You know how it goes ... it's been a long time, but you ain't forgot."

"I ain't forgot." Pledge was seething, and gave Toby a glare that would have felled an oak. "But don't bloody dare quote God at me, or when the time comes to 'ave the truth outta yer filthy 'ide, I'll ask Nathan, all *nice* like, fer the pleasure o' doin' you meself."

Burke gave that congested laugh and slapped Toby's backside. "And there's a treat I'd be happy to grant. So, lad. Time you were showin' me, eh?" He turned back to Jim now. "And you, Master Fairley, lay on this food and drink you promised. You can't get away from here. The water's up to your doorsill, you can't row the longboat single handed ... and I saw the old woman back there in the kitchen. Your grandmother, is she? You vanish on me, Fairley, and I'll put a bullet in her, somewhere it'll take her three days to die in the kind of agony you wouldn't wish on your worst enemy, you bein' the nice lad you are."

"I might," Jim breathed, "wish it on you, Captain ... but I take your meaning. I have no foggiest notion what you're talking about, but if you want to search the house, go ahead. Start with the loft and work down, and if you want to burn the place and sift over the rubble, at least have the decency to let me and Edith and the dogs step outside before you set it alight."

The remark made Burke laugh aloud. "Maybe I won't have to. Maybe," he added, shoving Toby in the direction of the stairs, "we'll just find old Charlie's hidin' place, and be on our way."

The sense of impotence was overpowering. Jim stood in the kitchen doorway, watching as Burke and Pledge followed Toby up, and his head reeled with everything he had seen and heard. The threat to Edith Clitheroe was very genuine, and only the deafness of old age prevented her hearing it for herself. Jim did not repeat it.

And he realized Toby could only have told him a fraction of the story of what had happened in the time between the mutiny on *The Rose of Gloucester* and the day the eight survivors went in eight directions, to stay ahead of the law. The details – personal, painful, shaming – he had kept to himself, and now those old secrets were flaying him alive.

"Does thee know these buggers?" Edith tugged at his sleeve. "Who in 'ell is the one wi' the pot belly an' the ringlets an' the wicked temper?"

"I only know what Toby's told me," he said as softly as he could and still be heard. "They're the last survivors of a mutineer crew he sailed with." He looked down at her, saw the clench of her face. "Charlie hid something belonging to them. They're here to take it, and if they don't get it..."

"They'll kill us all," she finished.

"Edith, don't be panicking," he began.

"I'm not bloody panickin'," she growled, "an' I's seen enough. The big bastard 'ad Master Trelane down on 'is knees, an' I don't need to see no more. They's like to murder us, thee knows it, well as I do. If we let 'em."

The same thought was scudding through Jim's mind, and he studied Edith with a frown. "Will you trust me?" he asked, not for the first time.

Her eyes narrowed. "Aye, I'd trust thee – sooner than that fool of a grandson o' mine!"

"All right, then." Jim dropped a hand on her shoulder and steered her back to the table where her best work was done. "You just stay well away from them, and do exactly what I tell you. Promise me this, now."

Chapter Twelve

The sounds of industry took Jim upstairs and he stood, tight-lipped, watching as Joseph Pledge tore the mattress off the last bed and strewed its stuffing across the floor. Every other bedchamber in the house was a similar shambles, including Jim's own, where everything he possessed was cast about like so much rubbish. Burke and Pledge would turn to the stones in the fireplaces next, before they took an iron and began to pry up the loose floorboards. Everything Jim and Toby had done with care, leaving the tavern habitable, was being redone with the violence of frustration, as if only reducing the house to a dismembered chaos would appease the aggravation of finding Chegwidden long dead and the prize out of reach.

Without a word, Jim watched Pledge shove the bed across the floor in the last room and attack the boards with the narrowest of the fire irons. Toby stood back, let him assault the timbers, and met Jim's eyes with a tight look. His own eyes were wide, dark, filled with dread and warning. *Don't provoke them – let them wreak their havoc, it's only timber and linen and straw, it'll mend!*

Jim heard the words as clearly as if Toby had spoken them, and he backed off, sealed his lips, merely watched as if the process interested him. Nathaniel Burke wore a face as black as a thundercloud, but he had his temper on a tight rein. He was by far the more dangerous of the two, Jim realized. Pledge might be deliberately cruel and stupid as a brute, but he could be goaded, forced into risks that would be his undoing. Burke had the cooler head – the brain of a snake and a deep streak of malice which might outdo Pledge's.

"I told you, Nathaniel," Toby said as they exhausted the possibilities of the upstairs. "I've already done all this, and found nothing."

"So you say." Burke had taken off his hat, bundled it into his pocket. His hair was sparse, salt-and-pepper, and the lantern light gleamed on his pale, bare scalp. "And you'd like me to believe you."

"I'd like you to recognize the truth when you hear it." Toby sighed and leaned both shoulders against the wall. "You think I *want* to come under your hand again? As if I have some secret craving to be whipped till I faint? You have me confused with the wrong man."

"Has I, now?" Burke leaned on the wall beside him, with one fingertip idly tracing the lines of Toby's nose, lips and jaw. "Seems to me you took a lot and came up smilin'."

"I took it like a man and wouldn't let the bastards reduce me to blubbering and begging," Toby corrected acidly. "Smiling? Not me, Nathaniel. You could be thinking of your little French molly. What was his name?"

"Ah." Burke chuckled deep in his throat. "Jean Pierre. You remember Jean Pierre, Joe?"

"I recall 'is mouth, and 'is arse," Pledge said gruffly, panting as he finished with the floor. "Nothing 'ere. No *fuckin'* thing." His eyes were blazing on Toby. "I'd 'ave yer nailed to a wall an' screamin' yer god-damn' lungs out, if it was up to me. Be bloody glad yer wearin' 'is mark."

"I am," Toby said quietly, looking into Jim's face. "A thousand times, I had cause to be very glad indeed I wore his brand." His brows quirked at Jim. "Does it seem strange, Master Fairley, for a man to be grateful to be branded, carrying the mark of another man's ownership?"

"It does," Jim admitted. "But if it meant being the plaything of one man rather than the amusement of a dozen, I daresay I'd take the brand. It was like that for you, I suppose."

The blue eyes were full of gratitude. "It was. I survived … and as much as you've likely already come to despise Nathaniel, there's a truth you won't get past. He's the reason I survived."

"He branded you in an act of charity?" Jim asked scornfully.

The question inspired Burke to a belly-laugh. "Charity? Ye gods, what nunnery d'you live in?"

"I don't live in a nunnery at all." Jim met Burke glare for glare now. "So you're one of *those*."

"One of what?" Burke's laughter was gone.

And Toby's face was sharp with warning: *Careful!*

"One of those," Jim said, almost without inflection, "who prey on folk less powerful than themselves … one with an eye for the pretty, the lovesome. One who'll take what he wants, when he wants it. You fancied a pretty thing to beguile away the night? What, there were no women on hand? Or was this one –" nodding at Toby "– simply prettier and more lovesome than the girls, and you thought you'd take him for your bitch instead."

Burke's lips pursed as he studied Jim thoughtfully. "You're a deal more savvy than you look. As a eunuch, you'd likely know all about being a man's molly."

The words were far truer than Jim liked to admit, but there was danger in admitting it. "I don't know anything about it at all," he said in level tones, "and I'm not a eunuch. I'm lame. There's a difference."

"Thass not what them lasses back in Exmouth sez," Pledge jeered.

"Well, they're wrong, aren't they?" Jim kept his voice quiet and never took his eyes from Burke, trying to read his expression every moment. "Maybe I just don't have a use for the kind of doxies you meet in ale houses. Maybe ..." He looked along at Toby. "Maybe I have a taste for sweeter flesh, and I know real beauty when I see it. In a woman," he added quickly, lest Burke know where his heart lay. "And I've run a sailors' tavern for years, quite long enough to know all about matelots and punks, mollies and bitches." He shrugged. "Six months at sea, well out of sight of a petticoat, and I can imagine how a lovely face and a smooth, slender body would start to look irresistible."

"There's a lot of truth in what you say, Master Fairley," Burke mused. "And this un here, this Toby Trelane, till lately a priest – did you know that? – this un was so pretty, eight and ten years ago, he should never've been at sea. I often wondered what witlessness put his stupid arse on a ship."

To Jim's surprise, Toby managed a shaky laugh. "I saw a notice posted, the requirement for a man of the cloth on a merchantman whose captain was a churchgoer and intended his crew to follow his example. The notice also asked for a doctor, a navigator and a topman. I walked through a door and talked to the owner – not the captain."

"And signed your damn' fool life away," Burke finished. He looked sidelong at Jim. "As the lad told it to me, he was runnin' away from a scandal in Norwich. He'd been caught with the handsome young verger, the pair of 'em clasped tight in a carnal embrace." His lip curled as he looked at Toby. "So the lad runs as far as he can, and as fast, and finds hisself in Portsmouth ... and glory be! *The Rose of Gloucester*'s takin' on crew, and Captain James Graves wants a preacher as well as a sawbones. *Graves*." He spat on the floor at Jim's feet. "I bloody knew I should never've signed on with a skipper with a name so filled with evil."

"And yer'd know all about evil," Pledge muttered, finished with the hearthstones. Little piles of broken plaster lay around the walls, and he kicked them away as he came back around the broken bed frame.

"So, yer gunna winkle the truth outta this git, Nathaniel?"

"Or are you going to take a look at the taproom, the kitchen, the stable, the coach house." Toby pushed away from the wall. "Sweet Christ, Nathaniel, I don't want to die under torture – and I will, because you're trying to torture words out of me that I just don't have to give. I can't tell you what I don't know, no matter what you do to me."

Every word was painfully true, and Burke could see it as clearly as could Jim. Pledge was vengeful out of frustration and spite, but Burke's clearer mind was already working, churning on schemes and plans. "Aye, all right, lad." He slung an arm over Toby's shoulders. "I's not sayin' I don't believe you. Like as not, we'll find the prize buried under one of the old privy sites! That'd be old Charlie's amusement, that would. Soon as the waters go down, you'll be diggin' 'em up. Master Fairley'll tell us where they be. You'll stink fit to frighten off a herd of swine, but you'll walk away, and with your skin intact, if you're a good lad."

At the last remark, Toby sucked in a breath. "Nathaniel, it's been a long time."

"And you're nowhere near as pretty as you were, years ago," Burke agreed, "but you're still pretty *enough*, and you still wear my mark, and the only woman in this house is Fairley's old witch of a grandmother. Aye, you'll do."

Toby looked away. "Tonight, then."

"For old times." Burke tousled his hair. "And to *remind* you whose mark you wear, so tomorrow you'll go on bein' a good lad."

Jim's mouth was dry as dust as he watched Toby nod, tight lipped, pale. "All right," Toby said tautly. "But not *him*. Not Joe. I've done nothing to make you give me to Joe Pledge."

"Nothin' at all," Burke agreed. "All the more reason to be good." He grinned brashly at Jim. "Does it shock you, Master Fairley? A whole company of filthy sinners under your roof, and one of 'em a priest."

"I'm not shocked at all." Jim heard the razor's edge in his voice and smothered it fast. "I've known too many sailors. The only thing that concerns me is Trelane's welfare. He's been working here for a few days, and I've come to call him my friend."

"Oh, I'll not hurt him." Burke's right hand was charting the form of Toby's backside. "Well, not much. Way back at the start, he didn't need me to teach him the ropes and separate the virgin from his sweet dreams of romance. Did you, *Father* Trelane?"

"No." Toby's eyes were downcast. "What he told you ... it's all true, Jim. I did run from Norwich, on a coaster under cargo. I probably wasn't even a priest any longer, not in the letter of the law, by the time I signed aboard the *Rose*. I was running days ahead of the news. Before it reached Portsmouth, well, we'd shipped out. On that score at least, I was safe." He took a long, deep breath and summoned a smile. "If we survive to remember this, one day I'll tell you the rest of the story."

"Fair enough." Jim rubbed his hands together and surveyed Burke and Pledge darkly. "You said you wanted food. It was on the table a long time ago. Pie and ale, and all the rum you can drink, if you want it. In case you're wondering – and you bloody-well ought to be! – the water's just starting to wash under the doors. I don't care what you take or what you break, so long as you harm no one under my roof. Leave the old lady alone. You hear me, Burke?"

"So the eunuch has fangs!" Burke's arm was still over Toby's shoulders, steering him out of the bedchamber and back to the stairs. "You'd be wise not to threaten me, innkeeper."

"I'm not threatening." Jim was a pace ahead of them, and turned back. "I'm trying to strike a deal." He had Burke's attention now, while Pledge fidgeted and grimaced in the rear. "I'm still young enough that I'd like to hang onto my life for as long as I can – young enough," he added darkly, "to still care whether I live or die, and how. As for the old woman … I promised my poor dead mother I'd take care of her mother, and I'll not go back on a promise if I can help it."

"Very noble of you. Now get down them stairs and bring out the food." Burke shoved Toby ahead of him.

"And the rum," Pledge added.

"Not rum." Burke's voice was sharp. "Not one drop o' rum, Joe – keep a clear head, goddamn you. You want the little molly to give us the slip?"

"Oh, I know what I wants 'im to gimme," Pledge muttered, and then raised his voice. "Ale then. I'll take a jar or three of ale to wash the sea outta me throat."

"You'll take *two*, and not one drop more." Burke swung on him. "Three, and you'll be stupider than usual. Do like I's tellin' you, Joe, and you keep both your eyes on the bitch. It'll be my pleasure to hump him good and hard, for old times' sake … but I'll not be trustin' him. Not till the prize is *here*." He made a fist, clenching it so tight, the muscles of his forearm trembled.

The sense of it impressed Pledge. He gave a yellow-toothed grin and went on down the stairs ahead of Jim. Burke had Toby by a handful of his hair, and pulled him closer. Jim's own fists clenched, his fingers itched to make a grab for one of the pistols, but he took his cue from Toby. The blue eyes were half closed, his face was impassive, his whole body relaxed, just rolling with Burke for all the world like a boat without a rudder.

"Now, you listen to me," Burke was saying, and Jim forced himself to pay attention through a haze of rage such as he had never known before. "You belonged to me once, Toby lad. Fact is, you still do. I never gave you no ticket o' leave. You owe me, Trelane. You's alive today because you came under my hand, my protection. You swindle me, and there's no place on God's green earth you can hide. I'll find you, and when I do, you'll spend a year beggin' for death before I make you the gift of it. You understand me?"

"I understand you," Toby whispered. "I always did, Nathaniel. I never said I didn't owe you a debt, and you should know me better than to think I'd try a swindle. I might not be a priest, but I'm an honest man."

"All right, then." Unexpectedly, Burke let him go, gave him a push. "Get downstairs and get some food into you. By damn, you're a skinny bag o' bones. But you'll be workin' like the bloody slave you are tomorrow – you'll be takin' this place apart, brick from brick, if need be. So get some food in your belly."

With a dark glance at Jim, Toby headed down in Pledge's wake. At the head of the stairs Jim came eye to eye with Burke, and choked off a tirade. At last he said tautly, "You own him?"

"I won him." Burke was intent on Jim, gauging, judging. "I won the pretty little thing on the turn of a single card. Ten minutes later, I burned my mark into the cheek of his arse and dared any other man to lay a finger on him without my say-so. And I never said so. You can believe me when I tell you, he was pretty enough to drive the wits clean out of a man's head, at that age."

"He still is," Jim said quietly. "In a different way, perhaps, but the beauty's still there." He tilted his head at Burke. "Your protection saved his hide, and I'm grateful for that. It's one favor I owe you, Captain. The only one."

For a moment Burke blinked at him. "Damnation, you're sweet on him yourself."

"He's my friend," Jim rasped.

"Aye, mateship's how it starts." Burke looked Jim up and down with fresh eyes. "Six months out o' port, it turns into more and there ain't no goin' back. Not when you's had a taste of the other." He accorded Jim a rare, genuine grin. "Take care, innkeeper. Make sure you don't get that taste, or you'll be hellbound with the rest of us."

With that he was gone, leaving Jim to take the stairs more slowly, exaggerating the limp at every step. He came down into the light of a half dozen lanterns set up in the taproom, and as his feet hit the floor he swore. The water was an inch deep – it would already be trickling into the cellar, though at this rate it would take a long time to fill the space below. It was too late to get the mortar down now – not that Burke would let it be done, since the cellar must be torn apart along with the rest of the house.

And in fact Jim suspected the cellar was the only hiding place left. The walls of the coach house were too thin to offer a cranny the size Chegwidden would have needed. Unless he had broken the prize down into a hundred tiny parcels, which Toby swore would not have occurred to such a simple man, the treasure of Diego Monteras was not in the coach house.

It was also not in the tavern, Jim mused, unless Charlie had hidden it in the kitchen hearth, right under the fire which was never supposed to go out. He angled a glance in through the half-open kitchen door, watching Edith working around that same hearth. She had been cooking here since Nell Chegwidden was struck down by sickness which killed her within a year, around the same time as Charlie arrived home for the last time. If the hearth had ever deliberately been doused, she would know.

At the bar end of the taproom, one table was set up with pies and pickled pork, cabbage and cheese, old apples and ale. Pledge was already eating; Burke was still loading up his plate. Toby had just poured himself a mug of the dark ale when Jim called, "Toby, give me a hand for a minute. You can eat soon enough."

The call seemed to come as a relief. Toby was grateful to get out of the reach and earshot of Burke and Pledge, and he joined Jim in the kitchen door, rolling up his sleeves, ready to work. Burke's eyes were on him every second, and on Jim, and Jim said loudly enough to be heard, "We need to get a good wedge of the kitchen firewood up off the floor before the water rises, or we'll be eating cold food." He gave Burke a grim look. "No need to help, Captain, but you'd best let us get it done while we can."

Burke waved them away with one hand, and drew a pistol with the other. "Mind your manners, the both of you. You's got nowhere to run, and I'll put a pistol ball in the first one who steps outta line."

"I believe you," Jim breathed. "And even so, this firewood's got to be moved. Toby?"

The kitchen door swung wide open, affording Burke an uninterrupted view of the hearth area, where Edith had retired to her chair with the dogs. Of the cat, there was no sign. Toby wore a doubtful expression, but the more Burke could see, the better Jim liked it. He beckoned Toby to the job and began clearing the mantel and the small table. "Stack as much as we can in here and on the bar." His voice dropped to a murmur. "The fire's going to be out in another hour –"

"And you know the cellar's starting to flood." Toby was already hefting split wood.

"What chance," Jim wondered softly, "the prize is under the hearth? Who'd ever think to search *under* the kitchen fire?"

"A good chance." Toby stooped for another load. "Even money, Jim. It's either under the hearth or in the cellar." He looked over his shoulder at Burke. "Please God, we can find it."

"Please God," Jim echoed. "You can still say those words after … everything."

Color flushed in Toby's cheeks. "You know most of it now. All the things I'd never have told you, and hoped you'd never find out."

"About how you're his property." Jim heaved an armful of wood onto the mantel and paused to frown at Toby. "And you really are."

"Was," Toby corrected. "Nathaniel might say he never gave me any notice of freedom, but it's been a long, long time since the survivors of the *Rose* went their separate ways. I'll carry his mark to the grave, but I swear to you, Jim, I've done honest work since I walked away from that company. I was allowed to walk away because we were hunted men. Put me and Nathaniel together in the same place and we'd have been fifty times more recognizable in a crowd than we were alone."

"You came back," Jim said pointedly. "The time and the place were set. Right here, and right now. And here you are."

"Looking for Charlie," Toby whispered. "Two days ahead of the others, and hoping to take a handful of the prize and vanish into the mist before they caught up with me." He stooped for more wood. "You know what I hoped for."

"And you found me instead." Jim divided his attention between Toby and the table where Burke and Pledge were stuffing their faces and drinking noisily. "Damnit, Toby, you should have told me!"

"That I left the priesthood in disgrace, went to sea to evade the church authorities and served my penance as a whore?" The fair head shook. "You knew I made an enemy of the legal captain, took part in a mutiny and was on the run for my crimes. It was enough. The rest..." He thumped a load of wood down onto the table. "Leave me a shred of dignity. You didn't need to know any more."

"Damaged goods," Jim said softly. "That's what you called yourself."

"And I am. I never denied it. But I'm not a whore now – I was what they made me, and what I had to be, to survive."

"I'm very glad you did survive." Jim went back for more wood. The mantel was stacked now, and the table. They would be loading up the bar soon, and anything they said would be overheard. "I'm glad you found your way to my door, and as for the rest ..." He looked away, at Burke and Pledge. "It's not over yet."

With the table stacked, they trooped back and forth from the kitchen woodpile to the bar, two loads, three, four, while Jim worked up a sweat and the leg began to hurt as if a knife were thrust in among the muscles. He had bent to pick up another load when he heard the sound he had been waiting for.

A soft thump; heavy breathing; a groan of protest, the scrape of a chair leg and then a heavier, splashing *thud*. Toby spun, and Jim viewed the scene with smug satisfaction. Pledge was the one asleep on the table, snoring. Burke had held out a fraction longer, had half-drawn a pistol, pushed back his chair and then dropped to the floor, where he lay in the water, nose and mouth bubbling.

"What in hell –?" Toby demanded, as breathless as if he had run a mile.

"Dutch laudanum." Jim slapped his leg. "I keep a bottle in the house. I told you, I use a few drops of it when the pain gets beyond bearing. Two or three drops, and I'm dozy. Six drops, and I'll be dead asleep. Like them."

"In the food?" Toby splashed across to the table, and as Jim watched he retrieved every pistol, every knife he could find.

"In the ale," Jim corrected. "I told Edith to count nine drops into each mug and twenty more into the pitcher ... and I told her to add salt, a lot of salt, to the pies and cabbage. The pickled pork is salt itself. Oh, they'd drink as soon as they started eating."

Four pistols and seven assorted knives stacked on the bar beside the wood, and Toby pulled both hands across his face. "That's why you didn't let me drink."

"If I had, you'd be face down with them." Jim dusted off his hands.

"How long?" Toby wondered. "Till they wake?"

"If it were me, four or six hours," Jim mused. "Burke's a lot bigger, so he'll wake sooner, but I've the remedy for that. Edith?"

She stood, scattering the cat, and produced a brown glass bottle from the pocket of her voluminous green skirt. This she gave to Jim, and he and Toby rolled Burke onto his back. Jim forced open the man's mouth and ignored the reek of his breath as he placed four heavy drops directly onto the back of his tongue.

"He'll not wake for six or eight hours," he said darkly as he straightened. "Pledge might start to wake sooner. Toby?"

Again, the open mouth, and three fat drops fell on the back of Pledge's tongue. Even Toby was satisfied, and Jim watched him relax visibly. "Damnit, Jim, I'm beholden." He gave Burke a solid kick. "For old times, he said. As if I'd want to be reminded."

"Forget it, if you can," Jim said softly.

The blue eyes were wide. "Can you?"

"I can try." Jim passed the bottle back to Mrs. Clitheroe and beckoned both of them into the kitchen. "We've got a few options, now." He pulled a chair up to the hearth, where the fire was still burning in the black iron basket which sat a hand's span above the bricks, and barely three inches out of the water sluicing across the kitchen floor. Edith returned to her chair and Toby perched on the three-legged stool. He lifted Bess up onto his knee to get her out of the water. Jim tucked Boxer under his arm and wondered where the cat could be, until he saw a sinuous shape move, black in the shadows on the shelf among the canisters of tea, sugar, oats.

"Options," Toby said thoughtfully.

"A few." From somewhere Jim found a faint, wry smile. "They can die, Toby. They can feed the fish, the same way Barney Bellowes did."

Toby's eyes closed. "Could you do it?"

"Kill them?" Jim pulled a tub chair closer to the warmth, settled and balanced the terrier on his lap.

"Murder," Toby corrected. His brows quirked. "We have the better of them. The advantage is in our hands. Kill them, and it'll be murder in cold blood."

"No court in this land'd convict thee," Edith said tartly. She had cupped a hand behind her ear to catch every word.

"True," Toby agreed. "And we can surely kill them, Jim – it's all too easy. But think, before you do." He held up his palms. "There's no blood on these hands, not yet. I've never killed. I've done a lot … been *made* to do a lot … that I'm not proud of, but I've never killed a man and I don't intend to, if I can help it. There's one stain I don't want on my poor soul."

"You still believe any of the old Bible twaddle?" Jim was astonished.

"I don't honestly know," Toby admitted. "But I'll tell you this. When Judgment Day rolls around, as you can be sure it will, I'll be able to stand up in front of the Judge and say honestly, I never took a human life, much less murdered." He shrugged eloquently. "It's important to me, Jim. I'm going to burn, no doubt about it … but I don't think I'll burn for very long. Not compared with the likes of Nathaniel and Joe. The goblins'll grant me manumission from Purgatory a hundred years ahead of them. It matters."

In fact, it did. Jim thought back to his father, who was so fond of the Psalms, always in church on Sunday, careful not to blaspheme, just as careful to contribute to the poor fund. Arthur Fairley would have agreed with Toby without hesitation, and as for Jim – he was far from sure it could all be dismissed as 'Bible twaddle.' At least *something* inside that thick, mystifying, confusing book might be true. And if it were true, the lighter the burden of sin one carried with him to Judgment Day, the better.

"Damnit," he muttered, "you're not going to make it easy!"

"Nothing ever is." Toby was stroking Bess, and intent on Jim. "We have options other than murder."

"Two that I can see," Jim said slowly. "One, we take their longboat and leave. We just go, and don't come back."

Toby nodded slowly. "I thought about leaving. The trouble is, if we vanish, they'll wake up sure we had the prize all along, and we took it with us. You heard Nathaniel. We'll be hunted, and eventually we'll be found. We're easy enough to recognize in a crowd."

"Especially me, with this leg." Jim breathed a long sigh. "Then, we find the prize, don't we?" He looked from Toby to Edith and back. "The last option we have is for us to find the prize before we let the buggers wake up."

"Yes." Toby licked his lips and sat forward, betraying his eagerness. "We take a small share, and we leave the rest. Trust me, Jim, we can be rich as lords on a *very* small share, and we can be gone before they're clear headed enough to see what's on the table in front of them."

One brow raised at Toby and Jim asked, "Burke wouldn't hunt us down, to recover what we'd taken?"

"Not if we took less than what would be my share anyway." Toby smiled, lopsided and engaging. "He has his own odd code, and he keeps to it. I was there, I shared the same risks, did the same work. He put his mark on me and I did my duty by him, never shirked in what he asked of me." Color rose in his face as he confessed this much, but he lifted his chin. "I'm due a share."

"As a slave?" Jim asked uncertainly.

"A *small* share," Toby allowed, "along with my freedom. I'll also leave them a letter – Nathaniel can read, after a fashion. I'll tell them Barney's dead, and how, so there's one less way the prize has to be split. There's more for everyone with Barney out of the way, and even Charlie, rest his soul." His face shadowed again. "And that's another thing. There's two more of Nathaniel's crew back in Exmouth that I know of, and a third who should have arrived by now. If we want to walk away from this as free men and not have to spend the rest of our lives looking back, we need to settle with Eli Hobbs, Willie Tuttle and Rufus Bigelow at the same time. Have it done, finished."

"Well ... shite." Jim passed a hand before his eyes. "You're not asking for much, Toby."

"I know." Toby stood and let Bess have the stool, where she perched looking down at the water. "But I also know these men. If we split the prize with Nathaniel and Joe, and cut out the other three, it'll be Eli and Willie right behind us, and I'm not too sure about Rufus, either. He was always the best of the bunch – which isn't saying much. They're perfectly capable of murdering all of us, Nathaniel and Joe as well, to get what they call their fair share." He gestured west. "Eli and Willie are at a tavern not far on this side of Exmouth. The Cattlemarket."

"I know it."

"And I'd give you good odds, Rufus will've joined them by now."

Jim was silent for some moments. "You want to bring them here."

"*After* we find the prize." Toby was looking into the fireplace even then. "We find it first. There's a tradition among thieves and pirates. Division of the spoils. In the company I knew, the captain took half. The first mate took a quarter of what was left. Then the remainder was split up according to shares. Gunners got three shares apiece; ordinary men got one. Slaves due their freedom, a half share and a ticket of leave." He looked away. "Slaves not due their freedom got nothing but the gift of life and the chance to live another day."

"And if we can get the five of them here," Jim said slowly, "they'll hold to this?"

"They will. I'd swear to it. I know them." Toby took a kick at the water and muttered an oath. "If we're going to do this, Jim, it has to be soon. It'll be hard enough to search the fireplace already, and in a few hours we'll be wading up to our knees in the cellar. The longer we talk, the harder it's going to be."

"And our lives depend on it," Jim finished.

"Yes." Toby's face darkened. "I'm rather afraid they do." He paused, and his voice was plaintive. "Please, Jim."

For better or worse, the decision lay in Jim's hands, the first time he had ever carried such a burden of responsibility. He might have struggled with it, but Toby knew these men too well and he was right. "Then, we'd better find it," he said tersely, "because we'll never convince Burke and the others we don't have it. We might as well put ourselves out of our misery, if Charlie Chegwidden's outsmarted us."

"He hasn't – not yet," Toby whispered. "He was shrewd enough to keep the secret safe for six *years* after they put him in a hole in the ground, but I knew Charlie. He wouldn't try to swindle Nathaniel – and not because he had any affection for him!"

"It was all about sheer bloody fear?" Jim guessed, with a glance into the taproom.

"Let's say, he had a healthy dread of Nathaniel." Toby had picked up the small brass bucket in which the cinders and ash were carried away from the hearth, and was bailing water into the fire basket to put out the coals. "I wouldn't care to have Nathaniel Burke hunting me!"

Jim hauled himself up onto the aching leg and gave Boxer the chair. "Edith, I've a job for you. Those swine will be starting to think about waking up in six or eight hours. Make note of the time, and with an hour to spare, pry open their nasty mouths and give them four more drops apiece, right on the back of the tongue. You can do this?"

She made a face. "I've dosed enough bairns in me time … not that any of 'em 'ad rotten teeth."

"Careful with the laudanum," Jim warned. "Too much, and you can kill them – and you heard what Toby said. You don't want murder on your conscience any more than we do."

She waved him off as she heaved herself out of the chair. "I'll get up there an' get a fire goin' in the big bedroom, an' all."

"It's a mess up there," Toby warned. "Do what you can, Edith. When we've found what we're looking for, I'll come up and help."

"When," Jim echoed. "*When* we've found it."

"*When.*" Toby had the fire out now, in a mass of hissing coals and gray smoke. He straightened, one hand in the curve of his back, and gave Jim a rare smile. "I've got to believe it's here."

So did Jim. As Edith stepped out he caught Toby's head in both hands and held him to a kiss that left them both breathless. His lips felt bruised as he stepped back and said, "All right. Now we find it."

Chapter Thirteen

The water was cold enough to make Jim's finger joints ache, and filthy enough for him to lose sight of his hands two inches below the surface. He and Toby had slung every lantern they possessed from the mantel, filling the fireplace with light. The fire basket stood out in the kitchen now, still hot enough to cast grudging warmth though it was cooling rapidly, and the sweat of effort continued to prickle along Jim's ribs after the sheer effort of clearing out of the hearth – water, cinders, soot, ash, the debris of recent fires – while the water washed everything right back in. The fire basket might never have been moved since it was set in place when The Raven was rebuilt on the ruins of the old inn.

Toby was pale, grim, tight lipped as he leaned on a pry bar, trying every stone in the hearth in turn. He was working fast, in the scant moments after Jim took the big yard broom and sent a dirty tidal wave sweeping out into the kitchen. For two seconds at most, as every wave went out, they saw the bricks of the hearth itself. Toby would pinpoint a new crevice between them, jam in the pry bar and throw all his strength against it.

Nothing was moving, while the sweat rolled off the pair of them, no matter the aching cold of the water. At last Toby surrendered and took a moment to catch his breath. He leaned both hands on his knees, chest heaving.

"There is no way between heaven and hell old Charlie was up to this," he panted. "Not single handed. And there was *no one* he'd share the secret with – not even Nell, if she'd be awake when he came home, which she wasn't, may she rest in peace."

"The prize isn't in the hearth floor, then," Jim agreed bleakly. "Well, damn. That was the best idea yet. You want to try the fire back?"

"We have to try everything." Toby straightened his spine with an obvious effort. "And we don't have much time."

He was looking at the far corner of the kitchen, where the trapdoor was under several inches of water by now. As soon as they lifted it, the cellar would start to flood fast. If Charlie had buried the prize in the floor, they were not likely to find it before the cellar was bailed out by a bucket-line of hired laborers. Men like Burke and Pledge were too impatient and much too angry to wait so long, and Jim's skin prickled as he grasped the danger.

Toby had turned his attention to the stones at the back of the hearth, and Jim dropped a hand on his arm. "Leave them. They'll be above water for hours yet. It's the cellar floor that scares me spitless."

"You're right." Toby pulled both hands over his face and grabbed a lantern in each fist. His eyes were dark, hollow, as he gave Jim a hard look. "You be bloody careful on those steps. They were slick even before they were wet. They'll be lethal now – if you're not sure, stay up here and let me do this."

The thought was kindly meant but Jim would have none of it. "And how many years have I been climbing those steps in all weathers? They get slick as glass, winter and summer alike, soon as it rains. There's always mold in there – even when the cellar's dry, you can still smell it."

"All right." Toby paused to take a gulp of coffee. Both mugs had gone cold on the corner of the table while they worked. He took two lanterns in each hand and splashed through the water to the trapdoor with Jim on his heels. They set a half dozen lanterns on the pantry shelf, perched in front of flour and rice, barley and oats, and Toby lifted a brow at him. "You're sure?"

"Dead sure." With a soft curse, Jim thrust both hands into the water, hunting for the big iron rings to lift the trap.

They were cold and the trapdoor was so heavy, under the weight of water, he and Toby strained and swore as they wrestled it up. It dropped back with a splash, and the kitchen seemed to drain itself into a pit as black as the gateway to hell.

Cautious as a lame old wolf, Toby took a pair of lanterns and looked in, and down. "Let me go first."

He was by far the more nimble, and Jim was not about to argue. If Toby had the strength and agility to scramble around in the rigging of a ship that was rolling, pitching in a storm, he was capable of negotiating a flight of mold-slick steps in semi-darkness and moving water.

With great care he found the top step, and the second, and felt his way down, balanced like an acrobat. Still, halfway between trapdoor and floor he missed his footing and went down on his right hip, hard enough to make him shout with pain, shock, anger. He would wear a bruise for a month, Jim knew, but Toby was up a moment later and hanging lanterns from the hooks set into the old timber beams so close over his head, he almost had to duck. With the lights in place he came halfway back up, and on one knee Jim leaned down to pass him the rest of the lanterns, save one. Jim clutched the last in his left hand as he made his own way down, right hand clawing at the wall as if he might find purchase there.

Everything was wet. His feet slithered on the blue-black slime which grew on the steps as soon as the rains came. Twice he felt the sickening dread, sure he was going to fall. Toby was right below, ready to make a grab for him, but only Jim knew how much a fall could hurt him. It could cripple him, as the hedgehog spines of bone that quilled his leg moved, shifted – it could send him to the surgeon right here, right now, to have the leg opened and probed, or else sawn off not much under the hip –

And then, how fondly would Master Trelane think of him? Jim wondered as he caught himself on the thin edge of the fall. How greatly would Toby desire a man whose leg had been taken off as the price of his life? The same uncertainty might have been in Toby's head, for as Jim made it down within reach the balladsinger's hands were there at once, steadying, buttressing. He stepped right into an embrace tight enough to knock the air out of his lungs.

"Easy, easy. Goddamnit," Toby whispered against his ear, still punishing him with the embrace. "If we get out of this, Jim, I'm going to coddle you till you're sick and tired of me … and then I'll just coddle you some more."

It would make a nice change, Jim thought, pushing his face into the bony angle of Toby's shoulder. There had been far too little coddling in his life, and none at all since his father died. He soaked up Toby's body heat as long as he dared, and then fended him off with a sound of reluctant humor.

"I'm not done for yet. And we've got more work ahead of us than I like to think about."

Even then Toby was watching the amount of water trickling down the steps from the kitchen, where it was still coming in under the house's outside doors. "Two hours," he judged, "and we'll be ankle deep, and after that we won't find any damn' thing on the floor, or under it."

"Shrewd guess?" Jim stepped back and cast about for inspiration.

"It's like watching a ship's hold flood, when you've opened up a seam." Toby dragged a handful of hair out of his face and thrust it behind his ear. "You watch for a few minutes, get an idea of how fast she's flooding, so you know how long you have to fix her up or get her offloaded and let her go."

"You've watched a ship trying to sink itself," Jim observed. Toby answered with a mute nod. "Two hours, then." Jim took a kick at the water, to judge how deep it was already. "Same as we did in the hearth? There's brooms down here, and irons."

"Same again," Toby agreed grimly. "You want to sweep while I lean on the bar, or try your hand with the iron?"

Jim's whole body was hurting, head to foot. He had never done this kind of work, nor kept up the pace for so long. He doubted it would make any difference which job he took. "You're handy with the iron," he growled, snatching up a big, battered yard broom.

The worst of the job was moving the piles of *stuff* which had been stashed down here over so many years, he had no idea what most of it was. In minutes they had exhausted the possibilities of any open area of floor, and the real work began – humping crates, trunks, kegs and barrels to lay bare parts of the floor which human eyes had not seen in years.

"You piled all this lumber here?" Toby asked, panting under the weight of a keg of nails.

"Some," Jim told him. "Some of this stuff was here when we bought the place. I remember my father telling Charlie, 'Don't you start thinking I'm going to count the sundries in the cellar and pay for 'em one at a time!' A lot of this gear must've belonged to Nell Chegwidden." He hoisted up a crate, felt the pull in his shoulders and arms, and splashed across to the new pile taking shape on the area of floor they had searched first. "I never bothered to open most of these, never even thought about them."

"You had no cause to," Toby reasoned, panting under the weight of another load. "What was Charlie to you? A crusty old salt, telling strange stories and staring out of those windows at the path, or the bay."

"Waiting for you," Jim added.

"Or for whichever of us made it back here first." Toby wiped the back of his forearm across his sweated face, leaving a streak of dirt there. "It could have been Eli or Willie or Rufus, any of us, who got here first. We scattered on the wind, and eight years was a lifetime."

For Jim the same eight years had been just as interminable, for different reasons. A lame leg, the confines of home, and always the sea, the horizon, mocking him with the promise of adventure he would never share. He watched Toby for a moment, working with strength and energy Jim could only envy, driven by a desire to stay alive a little longer. Perhaps to take that handful of gems and live long enough to enjoy them.

"Jim?" Toby stopped long enough to angle a concerned look at him. "You're in pain." Not a question.

"Of course I bloody am," Jim said brusquely.

"Go up and rest," Toby began.

"Sod that." Jim stooped for another load. "Like the saying goes, you're a long time dead … I'll rest then."

The remark won him a husky chuckle before Toby applied himself to the work as if defying it to beat him. But the water was soon noticeably, measurably higher, and Jim watched it gloomily. They would never be done with the entire floor before they must turn their attention to the walls, which invited an element of luck into the scheme.

He had always hated anything that pivoted on luck. Jim Fairley was not a gambling man. If he had been, he would have hesitated to wager a shilling on their chances of beating Charlie Chegwidden at the years-old game of hide and seek.

And he would have been wrong. The water was lapping ankle deep, and Toby had abandoned the floor moments before with a passionate curse. Jim awarded himself one minute of rest and perched on a barrel, rubbing his leg against the ache, the cold, the fatigue. His eyes had almost fallen out of focus as he concentrated on the leg, let his own body overwhelm him for this moment. And it was then – when he *stopped* looking – that he saw it.

Tired eyes and mind snapped back into focus as if a dragoon had pulled back the hammer on a loaded musket. "Toby."

Something sharp, dark and acid in his tone made Toby spin toward him, poised in mid-water with a keg in his hands.

They had shifted enough of the cellar's final stack to make the wall behind it visible for the first time. There, no more than a foot above the lap of the black, filthy water, was a picture – a cameo image painted on an oval of bone or ivory half the breadth of Jim's palm.

He hopped down off the barrel with a grunt, and stooped toward it. The picture was well painted, if quickly, a likeness good enough to jog a man's memory, make a face from yesteryear come alive once more. The cameo hung on what was left of a red satin ribbon, from the long, rusted spike of a ship nail driven into the space between two stones, where the earth and mortar had been dug out.

He plucked it off the nail and turned it to the light – a woman's face, and young when the tiny portrait was done. She was a redhead with pale skin and a heart shaped face; and beneath the likeness were the initials 'H.C.'

"Helen Chegwidden," Toby whispered, "everyone called her Nell for short. I've *seen* this, Jim, many times. Charlie used to carry it with him. I think he loved his mother more than any other woman who ever crossed his path. He used to say, 'She's the gold you can't spend, the diamond you can't wear, the treasure you hunt the world for and find back at home."

"Damn." Jim swallowed hard on a dry throat. "Charlie couldn't read or write, you said?"

"No." Toby was intent on the face in the cameo. "Did he mark the hiding place with this? Did he leave it for someone who'd know it, if they saw it?"

"Like you." Jim's heart beat faster. "How many in your company did he share the cameo with? Not Burke and Pledge, surely? They'd have mocked him, spat on it out of scorn."

"He used to show it to me and Rufus," Toby remembered. "Me, because I'd been a priest, he knew I understood a man's love and respect for the woman who birthed and raised him. Rufus, because he was another one raised by his ma, after his da passed on and left a woman and eight children to fend for themselves."

"Then, Charlie *knew* you'd recognize this," Jim said slowly, "and Rufus would know it. The others wouldn't have seen it, much less remember … 'the treasure you hunt the world for, and find back at home.'" His brows arched at Toby, and he slapped the cameo into his outstretched hand. "Charlie's talking to you. You can't hear him? He couldn't write, he knew he was dying and he didn't dare share the secret. He's *talking* to you, Toby."

And even now, even here, Toby crossed himself and shivered as if the old man's voice had indeed whispered in his ear, across the years. The blue eyes were wide, pale in the light of four lanterns all burning the purest whale oil, as he handed back the precious little picture, retrieved the pry bar and went down on one knee in the water.

"You see the place." Jim's right fingers dove into the space where earth and mortar had been dug out.

"I've got it. Stand back, now."

The tip of the bar slid in and he worked it this way and that, pulling, pushing, using every ounce of his weight to shift a stone that had not moved in eight years. Jim held his breath, longing to help and suspecting he would only get in the way. He felt none of his aches and fatigue now. A pulse hammered in his ears as he knelt to see what Toby was doing, and he murmured as the stone gave at last.

It moved a bare half inch, and then another, and another. Toby transferred the bar to the other side and weighed on it again, moving it back and forth now, keeping it moving until he and Jim could get their fingertips to it. Jim thrust the cameo into his pocket, dried his hands on his shirt and got a grip on the protruding edge of the stone. He gave Toby a look. "On three."

They heaved together, every bit of strength and weight they possessed, and stone scraped on stone, coming loose, and looser. A second heave, a third, and it was halfway out. A fourth, and it passed the tipping point. Toby barked a warning for Jim to watch out for his feet, a scant second before the stone hit the water.

They grabbed for the lanterns, angled them so the pure white light streamed into the hole, illuminating a cavity in the tavern's ancient foundations. Jim whispered as he saw not one fist-sized leather sack, but at least half a dozen. "He broke it up," he guessed, "to be able to get it through into the stash."

"The chest wouldn't have fit … these bags are old powder pokes," Toby said softly. "Here." He handed Jim his lantern and reached in. "One. Two. Three." He set them down on the barrel where Jim had been sitting moments before, and went back for more. "Four. Five."

"How many would you be expecting?" Jim hardly knew the sound of his own voice.

"It's been a long time – memory plays tricks," Toby warned. "Six. Seven." Then he was feeling around, searching blindly, out of the reach of the light. "Eight. Nine … and that's the lot. Nothing else here."

Nine battered leather gunpowder sacks, the kind used by musketmen and about half the size of a man's deep coat pocket, were arranged on the barrelhead. As Jim watched, Toby drew the leather thong on the first one. He held his breath as the poke opened, part of him expecting even now to see black powder or lead shot –

But no, the inside of the old leather sparkled, scintillated, as if starlight had been caught in the bag and was trying to escape. Jim's mouth fell open. He felt a sudden dizziness, an overwhelming weakness in the vicinity of his knees, and he set down the lanterns and made a grab for Toby.

They were both wet and filthy, beyond tired and hungry, as they hugged, kissed with a fury that left the iron tang of blood in Jim's mouth. "Christ," he murmured when Toby let him breathe again, "we did it. We're in with a chance, Toby – in with a chance to walk away from this!"

"Oh, we'll walk away, I guarantee it." Toby was beginning to sober, visibly becoming aware of the cold, the sodden clothes, the fatigue. "This?" He picked up the open poke, trickled a few gems into his palm and held them to the light. Red, blue, green – rubies, sapphires, emeralds, sparkling as brightly as the last day they had glittered in the hands of Diego Monteras and the love of his life, the Indian prince the Spaniards called Fernando. "This is the price of our freedom, Jim, and our future. All we have to do now is play out the hand we were dealt ... we hold all the trumps."

Jim glanced up into the square of light from the kitchen. "Burke and Pledge?"

"And the rest of the company. Eli Hobbs and Rufus Bigelow and Willie Tuttle. No loose ends left to fray out and catch our feet in a year from now, or ten years." He dribbled the jewels back into the pouch and touched Jim's face with cold fingertips. "I *want* those years, Jim. I want them with you, if you'll have me."

"If?" Jim echoed. "Don't be so daft, Toby. If I could have got my hands on the blunderbuss, Nathaniel Burke and the bold Joseph Pledge would be dead already. I couldn't stand Burke's hands on you, and every word out of Pledge's mouth was like rat poison."

"They were mostly true," Toby said quietly. "I was grateful to wear Nathaniel's brand. I did earn it, exactly as you imagine I did. And as for being a priest ... well, that was over a week before I signed on the *Rose*. If Captain Graves had known who he was signing aboard – *what* he was signing on – I do believe he'd have burned me himself instead of waiting for the devil to do it."

Jim cocked his head at the man, watching him gather up the nine pokes and thrust them into an old turnip sack, the better to carry them up. "You believe any of that bilge water?"

"Do I believe in the scriptures?" Toby's head shook slowly. "I've seen too much, and suffered too much, to believe any of it word for word any longer. But I do believe there's *something* out there. Is it God?" He shrugged eloquently. "God or gods, angels or the powers of the cosmos. Perhaps a spirit like Vesta, who was the goddess of hearth and home to the Romans ... in the end, what's it matter, so long as there's *something* more than flesh and bones, pain and mortality. Something to come after the pathetic charade of this life," he added darkly as he tied off the sack. "Jim? Go up ahead of me, now – and you be bloody careful on those steps!"

"As if I'm going to fall and break my neck now you've got the treasure of Diego Monteras over your shoulder," Jim scoffed, and headed for the stairs with the brightest of the lanterns in his right hand.

A pace behind him, Toby snuffed the rest one by one, gathered them up, and was close enough to Jim to touch him, every step of the climb back to the kitchen.

Chapter Fourteen

It seemed the stars had been plucked out of the sky and cast into the big earthenware bowl in which bread dough was punched as it rose. Every manner of gemstone Jim knew and some he did not winked in the lights of the four lanterns hung from the beams over the table, and in that moment neither he nor Toby felt the cold of wet clothes, the protests of tired, sore muscles.

Snoring issued rudely from the taproom, and when he lifted a brow at Edith she made a disgusted face. "Aye, they's asleep, right where they fell. Their 'eads is propped on logs outta yon woodpile, else they'd 'ave drowned an hour back." She rumbled a wicked chuckle. "Does thee want me to roll 'em over? They'll not be wakin' up again, not if I just rolls 'em over an' lets yon water get at 'em."

"No, just keep them asleep," Toby said quickly. "You know how."

"Aye, that I do." Mrs. Clitheroe nodded in the direction of the stairs. "I got a fire goin' in the big bedchamber. Go up'n get dry, afore thee catches thy death, the pair o' thee. I'm comin' up meself, soon as I get some food together. Take the skillet up wi' thee, Master Trelane. It's a deal too 'eavy fer me."

"I'll do that," Toby promised.

"The dogs," Jim wondered.

"Upstairs, outta the water," she told him. "Bessie's a right mess, long coated like she is. Boxer'll do, but 'e were shiverin' wi' cold, such a little mite as 'im."

"I'll dry them," Toby swore, but his eyes were still on the gems.

So were Jim's, and he was casting about, looking for something to hold the mass of them. The water was well above his ankles now. He was conscious of pushing his way through it as he made his way across the kitchen and lifted the oat bin down from the pantry shelf. By April it was getting along towards empty, and waiting to be topped off when the harvest came in, in July or August. He tipped the remains of the grain into a spare basin and moments later watched as Toby scooped up great handfuls of the gems, dumped them into the bin and folded the nine old pouches on top of them, like packing to hold them safe.

They filled it almost to the top, and with every bauble inside he and Jim stood looking in with a sense of disbelief. "There's enough to ransom a king," Jim whispered.

"Or buy the lives of two like us," Toby said softly. "This needs to be somewhere safe … and I know the place. Jam the stopper in tight, and come on." He seized a lantern and took the stairs two at a time, leaving Jim behind, wrestling with the bin and cursing the leg.

But Jim thought he could guess where Toby was going. At the head of the stairs he turned right, leaving a trail of wet footprints to the end of the passage. Right above was the little trapdoor into the loft, and against a near wall, a tub chair which would bear the weight of a man standing on the seat.

The trapdoor squealed, timber on timber, as it opened. Jim had the bin under his arm, and had only to hand it up to him, watch him stash it to the left of the hatch where an assortment of tools was kept, for running repairs on the thatch.

"Done." Toby coughed and managed a chuckle. "I did a good job on the roof – it's dry enough up here to be dusty." The big, strong hands dragged the trapdoor back into place. It settled with a solid *slam* before he hopped down off the chair. He had set his lantern on the little sideboard where linen, candles and strewing herbs were kept for the bedchambers. The light cast odd shadows around his face as he turned back to Jim, and caught Jim in both arms. "We're almost done. We can *do* this."

He was cold, almost to the point of trembling, and Jim held on tight to him. "You're bloody freezing!"

"I'm wet and tired … and angry," Toby said against Jim's hair.

"And scared," Jim added.

"Not now. But I was, before you put the bastards down." Toby leaned back, and his features thinned with dread. "You have no idea what Nathaniel would have done to me."

"Yes, I have." Jim took Toby's angular face in both hands, brushed his mouth with both thumbs. "I know exactly what Burke had in mind, and it made me so angry I could have choked the breath out of him with my own hands. We can," he said thoughtfully, "do as Edith suggested. Roll them over and let the water have its way with them."

Toby's eyes closed for a moment. "Murder," he whispered. "And even so, if it ended with Nathaniel and Joe, I suppose I *might* ... but it doesn't end with them, Jim – the other three are out there, and they're not fools. They'd know we made off with Nathaniel and Joe."

"And they'd know why." Jim took a deep breath, held it, exhaled it as a long sigh. "You said something about them being at The Cattlemarket."

"Hobbs and Tuttle where there, and drunk as a couple of lords, when I passed by the place and stopped just long enough for a jar of ale. Rufus must have arrived by now, unless this evil weather's kept him in some port in Holland or France." Toby hugged both arms around his own chest as the cold set in, in earnest. "I'll go back there in the morning."

"We," Jim corrected. "We'll go as soon as there's enough light to get through. At this moment all I want is warmth, a little rum, a lot of food. A soft bed," he added with a groan, "if we can stuff enough straw back into a mattress to make a comfortable place to doss down. Damnit, Toby, the buggers made a mess."

"We knew they would," Toby said bleakly as he followed the flickering light of a fire, which issued from the big bedchamber.

Mrs. Clitheroe had been in here. A broom still leaned against the wall by the door – she had swept the confusion of straw, rags and plaster dust into a pile in the corner and set a fire in the hearth. A pan of water was on the hob, for tea. The dogs had curled together by the fire, wearing a pair of bewildered faces, and Jim was not surprised to see the big black kitchen cat sitting up on top of the wardrobe, surveying the scene with wide green eyes.

"I'll fetch up the skillet, and the food," Toby offered. "See what you can do with the mattress, eh, Jim?"

"And I'll organize the small room for Edith," Jim added. "It's tucked in right by the kitchen chimney, so it'll still be warm ... Toby, take a look at Burke and Pledge as you go by. Make sure they're still *well* asleep."

The balladsinger's lean face set into lines like carved granite. "I'll do better than that. I'll truss the pair of them like hogs for the butcher. If they wake during the night, the worst they'll be able to do is whine and cuss." He paused, halfway out of the room, with haunted eyes. "Don't give the bastards a thought before morning. I'm afraid I learned more than I ever cared to about binding a man, Jim. Trust me – they won't get loose."

And Jim believed him. He peeled out of his boots and britches and wrapped a blanket around his hips as he padded away to the chaos of his own bedchamber. Everything he possessed had been torn out of trunks and drawers and thrown aside like so much rubbish. He swore lividly as he hunted for enough clothes to get himself and Toby decent and warm.

Voices on the stairs announced Toby, and he was talking over his shoulder to Edith as they climbed. The old woman made long, hard work of the stairs – her legs could sometimes be even more of a challenge than Jim's left. She reached the top puffing and oathing, just as Jim opened up the small room. "Food, Edith," he told her, "while I organize sleeping space for you."

"Oh, to set this old spine to a mattress," she crooned, as if it were a mortal sin.

"Pork and onions, bread and cheese." Toby hefted the bag he had carried up along with the biggest of the skillets. He dropped his voice. "Take this from me, Jim. I'll go and *see* to them." His brows quirked at Jim, and Jim took bag and pan with a mute nod.

The small bedchamber was less disordered, only because there had been a lot less in it to begin with. A box of kindling and split wood stood by the hearth, and he knelt carefully to coax a fire to life before retrieving the broom and sweeping rubble dust and mattress stuffing right out through the door. The mattress itself was half empty, and he systematically pushed straw back through the ripped hole until it was taut enough to do service.

On a whim, just as his nose began to catch the aroma of frying meat, he cracked open the casement, pushed back the shutter and looked out over the ocean. Sandy Bay stretched east and west, and for the first time in days the horizon was clear. A vast swath of the sky was cloudless, filled with stars, and the westering half moon rode like a carriage lamp, ringed around by the chestnut colored flares of scudding clouds.

After so many years of watching the sky and sea, Jim foresaw a calm morning. No more rain for a few days at least – a chance for the beck to drop back within its own banks, so they could open up the doors at front and back of the tavern and sweep out the water. The cellar was another matter, and for just one moment Jim considered the unpleasant task of bailing it out. Then the memory of the king's ransom hidden in the loft mocked him, and he growled a laugh.

He would never lean on another broom, he thought, nor stuff another mattress. And if he ever ate salt pork and kippers again after this night, it would be for the sake of nostalgia. It would be venison, partridge and salmon after this, he told himself as he added fuel to the fire and hunted up enough blankets for Edith to spend a comfortable night.

They all needed rest. While the old woman tended the food in the big bedchamber, Jim went carefully down and called through the dank taproom, "You need a hand there, Toby?"

"No, I'm just finishing." Toby straightened, stepped back and held the lantern to display his handiwork. "They're not moving, Jim, not so much as a muscle, until we give them permission to twitch."

The way he had tied them was studied, Jim thought. He had used the kitchen rope, a thin, fine line used for everything from tying sacks to securing the load on a barrow. Burke and Pledge lay in water, spines bent like a couple of bows, hands and feet secured together, and the line passed over each gullet. They would only punish themselves if they tried to struggle. Both heads remained propped on the split logs, or they would have drowned already.

"They can't get the tip of any finger to so much as an inch of rope," Toby said darkly. Vengefully. "They'd be there till the breath failed in their lungs, if we chose to walk away from them. Good enough?"

He was splashing back through six inches of water on the taproom floor as he spoke, and stopped at the bottom of the stairs, two steps below Jim. "Good enough," Jim decided. "They'll keep, Toby. He laid one hand on Toby's shoulder. "I took a look out … the sky's clearing. We've seen the worst of the flooding; it should be going down again now."

"Thank God," Toby breathed.

"You can still say that?" Jim pressed against the wall, giving him enough space to squeeze by.

"Figure of speech. Perhaps thank some goddess who's been watching over me since the night Nathaniel put his brand on me."

"One day," Jim said darkly, "you'll tell me the whole story."

"Only," Toby murmured, "if I'm too drunk to have enough sense not to speak of things that'd be better forgotten." He leaned both palms on the wall, on either side of Jim, and kissed him soundly. "Thank you."

"For what?" Jim's voice was husky.

"For trusting me." Toby ducked his head for a moment. "After the things you saw and heard, when Nathaniel got here –"

"After those things, it's a bloody miracle Burke and Pledge are still alive," Jim rasped. "I never suspected myself of being a selfish, jealous sod, but I think I could learn to be, in matters concerning yourself." Toby looked sidelong at him, taken aback. "I won't share," Jim elaborated, "any more than Nathaniel Burke would share." His voice gentled. "But it'll be my great pleasure to spoil you, the way a man spoils the one he loves most in the world."

"No marks and collars and chains, then." Toby was only teasing, and his eyes were bright.

"Not unless the collars are studded with jewels." Jim rose to the teasing. "And the chains are gold, and holding pendants of emeralds and sapphires which match your eyes. And as for marks ... any mark I leave on you will be from some frantic embrace, and it might last long enough for me to see a hint of it, the next time we lie down together."

To his intense gratification a blush rose in Toby's face. "Well now, that would be entirely different."

And Mrs. Clitheroe chose that moment to lean out of the room above and yell, "Grub's on, if any bugger's 'ungry enough to eat it!"

Hunger was the wrong word. Jim was ravenous, and Toby looked just as famished as the slabs of pork and fried brown onions slithered onto a couple of plates. Toby tore into the food as if he had not eaten in a month, while Edith poured half coffee, half rum. She took a mug for herself, and a piece of bread stuffed with meat and onions. She was in the leather chair by the fireplace while Jim perched on the three-legged stool and Toby sprawled on the floorboards, letting the dogs creep close and feeding them while he continued to eat as if he had never seen food for an eon.

Food and warmth went a long way to reviving Jim. The strength of youth was still his greatest ally, as old Fred Bailey had told him many times. The leg throbbed but it was not weak, and the rum settled it, soothed it, until he turned the old blind eye and deaf ear to it. He knew Toby was watching him, but Toby of all people knew how to ignore what could not be cured.

He looked down into the wide, dark eyes, gave Toby a smile and was gratified when it was returned. The food filled the void within, though Jim would have been lying if he said he tasted it. In the chair opposite, Edith was starting to drift into semi-sleep. She must be exhausted, Jim realized. She might not be his grandmother, as Burke had assumed, but she was quite old enough to be, and she had been awake and on her feet for far too long.

"Edith, get you to bed," Toby said quietly, one hand on her knee to shake her out of a doze.

"I 'as to keep watch on them villains," she said tiredly.

"No, you don't. I tied them so tight, their hands'll be blue," Toby assured her. "If we start hearing bellowing and cussing from below, one of us will go down and dose the pair of them with enough laudanum to put them out for another six hours. You can forget about them till you've had some sleep." He smiled into her craggy brown face. "You can keep watch on them in the morning while Jim and I … get this sorted out." He looked over at Jim now, face softening. "I promise you, Edith. By sundown tomorrow you'll rest easy."

"And there's a warm bed waiting for you." Jim jerked a thumb over his shoulder, in the direction of the small room. "The fire's on, there's a pile of blankets. What else will you need?"

"The privy," she muttered as she hoisted herself out of the chair, "but I'll make do wi' a chamber pot, an' chuck it out the winder, come mornin'." She cackled with exhausted humor, and clapped Jim's shoulder on her way by. "God love thee. God love thee both. I seen the treasure with these old eyes!" At the door she paused, face shrewd indeed. "It'll be a big secret, then, will it? I won't be tellin' that silly young swine of a grandson o' mine?"

"Not yet," Jim agreed. "A fat purse of gold coins for you, Edith – but keep the secret until Toby and I decide it's to be told."

"Aye. An' if it's to stay a secret, lifelong?" Edith hazarded.

"Then it stays a secret, doesn't it?" Toby got to his feet and dusted down his britches. "That fat purse of yours can be topped up three or four times, to keep you in your leisure in a cottage at the top of the hill which never floods, with a young maid to do your bidding and take care of you in your old age. Yes?"

Again, she cackled. "Oh, aye. I knows 'ow to keep a secret, an' the better the secret, the easier it is to keep."

She was gone with those words. Six short steps, and the door opposite opened, clicked shut. The big room's door remained open.

Bess and Boxer and the cat had the run of the upstairs. While Jim watched, Toby set down the basin from the washstand and half-filled it from the pan on the hob. The water was too hot for the animals, but it would soon cool. The dogs had eaten, and Jim took a moment to shred a piece of leftover pork and put it up on top of the wardrobe. The tomcat would eat when he deigned to.

The bed looked like forbidden luxury. He sank down on the side of it and felt the mattress give more than it should have under his weight. The split in the bottom would have to be stitched up. But not tonight. With a groan, Jim threw off his waistcoat and tugged loose his shirt. He knuckled his eyes and when he opened them again he saw only Toby, who stood just out of reach, side-lit by the firelight, haunted, lovely.

Without a sound, Toby Trelane stripped to the skin and draped the britches and stockings over the chairs, where they would be almost dry by morning. And then he turned deliberately to display the mark, the brand on his flank. For the first time Jim was invited to look closely, and he studied it for some moments.

The brand was a capital B with wings sweeping out and up from the upright stroke. Nathaniel Burke's mark. He would endorse documents with this sigil; he might have signed aboard the *Rose of Gloucester* with it. Jim leaned over and with one fingertip traced the outline of the wings. The brand was a decade old now and starting to blur just a little, but it would never fade entirely. Like the scars on his back, Toby would wear it to the grave.

He was looking down, watching, waiting for Jim to say something, and Jim searched for the right words. "I can't erase this," he said at last. "And I don't think it ought to be erased. It's part of who you are. It was the price of your life, so you told me."

"It was." Toby sighed heavily and turned toward Jim, head bowed. "The crew of the *Rose* weren't angels. There was an element of scum among them, and when the mutiny cut them loose to run wild they got the bit between their teeth and – ran. They stood together just enough to keep the *Rose* viable. Nathaniel likes to call himself the captain because it was he who had the strength – the power of personality, the ruthlessness and readiness to kill. It was enough to hold the crew together, and make the *Rose* an attractive proposition for others who joined us in the ports between Caracas and Jamaica."

"And you?" Jim wondered, loath to pry and yet greedy to know the details. "You could have jumped ship, turned your back on them and found another way."

"I intended to." Toby sat on the side of the mattress beside him. Their double weight made it sag again. "I just left it too late. I wanted to jump ship in an English-speaking port, because at the time I didn't have more than a few words of Portuguese and Spanish combined. I've a good ear, but we were never in one place long enough for me to learn, and then ..." He looked away. "Nathaniel took on the survivors of a crew that'd been whittled to nothing by a storm and sickness aboard. Their ship was rotten at the waterline, leaking like a hulk. She went down while we watched, off the coast of South America, and our crew was suddenly a dozen hands stronger, with another man aboard who'd called himself a captain."

"There was blood," Jim guessed.

"Oh, there was blood." Toby's head tipped back. He worked his neck to and fro, where the muscles were stiff. "Four days after the new crew came aboard the *Rose*, a Liverpool character called Ephraim Buckley made his move, a bid to seize command. He tried to pull a pistol on Nathaniel." The shadows of memory wreathed Toby's face, finding every bone and hollow. "You might have noticed, Nathaniel's left arm doesn't work quite the way it should."

"I noticed. Shot?" Jim was not surprised.

"The pistol ball buried itself right in the bone," Toby said grimly. "It's still in there, causes him a lot of pain he'll never admit to. Rufus and I held him down and tried to get it out ... we cut and cut till we thought we'd kill him, but we couldn't get to it, and all the while he was screaming his head off, with vast amounts of rum in his belly and none of it dulling the pain enough to ..." He shuddered visibly. "In the end all we could do was close the wound over and cauterize it with a smoking iron. We didn't have a surgeon aboard, but Rufus had tended to sheep and I'd stood by the dead and dying often enough, me being a priest in my wasted youth. Neither of us was squeamish."

"Damn." Jim swallowed hard. His throat was dry as dust. "And where was Ephraim Buckley of Liverpool while this was going on? Dead?"

"Dying." Toby blinked several times, as if banishing the ghosts. "Nathaniel was already down on the deck when he put a pistol ball into Buckley's gut, and Joe Pledge had the man in irons before he knew what was happening. Buckley lived the day out – long enough for us to cut into Nathaniel and almost kill him without even getting to the ball. Joe swore he'd hang, draw and quarter Buckley, if Nathaniel died ... and you can be sure he meant to do it. Then Nathaniel woke, dragged himself to his feet. He came up on deck, looking closer to corpse than living man. He had Buckley bound to a hatch, naked, and the crew of the *Rose* took turns with a navy cat, cutting him to pieces, head to foot, back and front, till there wasn't much left that you'd recognize as ever having been a man."

He was shivering with the memory, and without thinking Jim turned to him, both arms going around him. "Ghosts," he said. "They're just ghosts. They're out, now, in the light. Ghosts can't stand the light – just let them go, and they'll not be back."

"Let them go," Toby echoed, leaning heavily on him. "Let them go." He seemed to catch himself, shake himself, and his voice firmed. "You can take me if you want. Fuck me. Nathaniel surely intended to – it was what he wanted of me, most often, back in the days when we were hunting for the treasure of Diego Monteras." He blinked at Jim, eyes wide and sane in the firelight. "Take what you want from me. It's yours to claim."

The offer was raw. For the life of him, Jim did not know if it had been made out of love, desire, guilt or duty. Roughly tender, he pulled Toby closer and pressed a kiss to his forehead. "Don't be so daft. When and even *if* I do that to you, Master Trelane, it'll be because you're wanting me to do it so much, you can't speak for trembling with need. And if I do it, it'll be because I want it for *us*, for your pleasure as well as mine." His arms tightened for a moment, enough to inspire a grunt from Toby. "As for Captain Burke ... well, now, he's hogtied and lying in the cold water, out of his head on Dutch laudanum. I'd say his pigeons are coming home to roost by the flock."

"You don't scorn me." Toby seemed puzzled.

"Scorn you? For heaven's sake, why should I?" Jim was surprised.

"I'm dishonored," Toby said simply. "And the worst thing is, I did most of it to myself. I *was* a priest. I *did* shag my handsome young verger. Even on Sundays ... it was far from the first time, when we were caught! I *did* run away, and sign aboard the *Rose* under false pretences, with credentials that would have been rescinded." His voice dropped. "I stayed too long on the *Rose,* was caught between the scum of one crew and the bastards of another, and I *was* glad to drop my britches and ask Nathaniel to put his brand on me as if I were a heifer on the way to market."

The rasp of his voice made Jim shiver. "You survived, and any debt you ever owed to Nathaniel Burke – and I don't believe you did! – was repaid long ago, likely a dozen times over. You were a free man when the survivors of the *Rose* split up. You're a free man today. And," he added, "if we can just negotiate the morrow, you'll be a rich man as well as a free one!" He took hold of Toby with two fists buried in his hair, making him look up, turn his face toward a kiss. "What is it you're looking for, Toby? Absolution?" Toby's eyes clouded. "I'm not a priest," Jim said hoarsely. "I can't give you absolution. All I can give you is love."

"Love," Toby echoed, as if it were a word of high magic. The blue eyes closed. "I've heard it said love is the only real absolution under heaven."

"Is it?" Jim heard a chuckle in his own throat. "If it is, then consider yourself absolved." He tugged Toby back and down, onto the bed. "Consider yourself loved."

He put his head down, silencing Toby with his mouth, while his hands feathered over him from brow to knees and back again, dwelling across his chest, where his nipples rucked like pebbles, and between his legs, where the root of him rose, hard, proud, seeking. A groan issued from Toby's throat and he spread those legs, lifted his knees into his belly, offering everything that he was.

But Jim shushed him, whispered to him to be calm. "Another day," he said against Toby's ear. "Now's not the time, not when the pair of us need to be fighting fit tomorrow. I need you strong and quick, not hopping about, raw and aching, because you thought you owed me some bloody debt of duty!"

For the first time in so long, Toby smiled. "It's yours to take, Jim, any day you think is the right day."

"Only because we both want it," Jim said gruffly. "And then you can roll me over in the clover, tickle me pink and till my field. I like it no less than you do ... always supposing," he added thoughtfully, "you *do* like it. Or did the bold Nathaniel teach you to hate it, and despise yourself for surrendering to it?"

Toby caught him, pulled him over and down, until Jim was pillowed on him. Under the weight, his voice was breathless. "He taught me to hate it when it's not done with love. Taught me the difference between love, lust and the *shite* one endures to survive." He looked up, bright eyed. "You want a lesson in this part of life? Talk to almost any woman, Jim, and certainly those who work in any whorehouse! You think the deed is any different, any more dire, because it's a man on his hands and knees, just waiting for it to be over?"

"Shush," Jim told him, and kissed him to silence. "You think too much."

"Make me stop," Toby whispered.

It was a challenge Jim was pleased to take up. He knew Toby's body by now, its scars, its tender places, where to touch him to make him gasp, where to stroke to bring him up hard and urgent.

There was so much he wanted from Toby – so much he could have taken from him now, tonight, while Toby was so vulnerable, he would not have protested. But the last thing Jim wanted was to take advantage, and he made it as simple as their first time had been.

Did Toby know what he was doing? The balladsinger's face was soft with some melange of affection, exhaustion, even relief. If he had been thrown down and hard ridden, he would have accepted it as his due, but to be caressed, kissed, cherished, touched his heart rather than his body; and Jim was sure it was love he felt rather than old fashioned lust, when at last he let Toby carry his weight and began to hump against the soft-hard pillow of his belly.

He could have been buried in Toby to the hips, and they both knew it. Instead, he lay between the long blond legs, looking down into Toby's face, sharing kisses that searched and nipped and teased. Time for the rest later, he thought, when the shadow of Nathaniel Burke had gone and taken the ghosts with it. Years lay ahead of them, and they would be good years, filled with every sensual indulgence.

For tonight it was enough to rub and hump, moving together in a rhythm that was oddly like a dance. Close to the end, Toby's hands burrowed between them, found them both and dealt them the same knowing caresses while Jim laid claim to his mouth, plundered him till Toby could have been in no doubt as to where he belonged now, and to whom.

Jim had never known the luxury of having a lover, a partner who would be there in the morning, and every morning. He had never realized he had a possessive, jealous streak inside him. But he put his own mark on Toby now – a sweet, stinging bite brand on his shoulder – and he did not like to think back on how satisfying it would have been for him to show Burke and Pledge the business end of the blunderbuss.

As always Toby was silent in his coming, but Jim permitted himself a cry. He smothered it in Toby's hair while he hung onto every last instant of pleasure, savoring the release as a man will when pleasure has always been elusive. Beneath him Toby's body calmed, his breathing stilled little by little until at last he was at rest.

He was soon asleep, too exhausted to fight his eyes open a moment longer. Jim was no less weary. He fumbled for a kerchief to clean them, reached over and snuffed all but the smallest of the lanterns. Then he closed eyes that were hot, sore, gritty, and permitted himself the luxury of sleep.

Chapter Fifteen

Roars of rage, distant yet obnoxious, roused Jim from a dream about white sands and green water, nodding palms and blue-eyed sirens who splashed in the warm shallows –

"He's awake," Toby's voice said from the companionable darkness at his shoulder. "Christ, did we sleep too long?"

The fire had gone out hours before, but the dogs were still curled up by the hearth. Both were awake and staring at the bed. Full daylight streamed in through the cracks around the shutter, and Jim did not think it was much before dawn proper.

He sat up with an oath, dragged both hands across his face and swung his legs out of bed. His body was stiff, throbbing, but he knew movement was the best thing to limber him up. He caught his britches up from the hearthside, shoved his legs into them, and padded to the casement.

The sun was not yet up but the sky was clear. No clouds sullied it, as far as the horizon, and he said over his shoulder, "I was right. We've seen the last of the rain. The beck'll fall back to normal by tonight."

Again, the enraged, bull-like roaring from downstairs, and now Toby slithered out of the bed. "We've a lot to do today."

"And it starts with *him*." Jim felt his face set into grim lines as he picked up his shirt and waistcoat, and shrugged into both. "That's Burke, not Pledge … and I've heard about all I care to."

"I'll give Edith a knock, get that laudanum of yours," Toby said quietly.

She was already in the passage when Jim swung open the door. The dogs ran out, but only as far as the top of the stairs, and Mrs. Clitheroe held out the brown glass bottle without being asked for it. "I fell asleep," she said, still slurring a little. "I should've been dosin' 'em an hour ago."

"Well, now," Jim said, lifting a brow at Toby, "why don't we give

Nathaniel a dose of what's good for him? Because if he doesn't shut up, I'm going to wrap the skillet around his nasty neck, and that *can't* be good for a man."

Toby's mouth twisted into a crooked grin. "Of the two, I'd prefer the skillet, but ... perhaps not today."

They took the stairs carefully, heading down into near pitch darkness in which Burke and Pledge were pinpointed by the noise Burke was making. The single lantern left burning on the bar had died long before and the shutters were still locked in place. For some moments Jim waited for his eyes to grow accustomed to the gloom, and when he could pick out vague outlines, he beckoned Toby.

They made their way around behind Burke, ignoring the roared threats and promises of tortures Jim was sure were not even physically possible. With both hands Toby captured the man's head, pinched his nose shut and forced open his jaws. Jim opened the bottle, held it in place – how many drops of the precious laudanum went into Burke's throat, he was not quite sure, and nor did he care. The man was big enough to sleep them off. In moments he lapsed back into porcine snores and they turned their attention to Joseph Pledge, who was still far from consciousness. He knew nothing as the bitter drops fell onto the back of his tongue.

Satisfied, Jim thrust the laudanum into his pocket and beckoned Toby to help with the bar locking the door. The hinges squealed with rust; they needed oil, a job for which Jim made yet another mental note, but the dawn sky was clear, cloudless. The first inch of sun was above the horizon now, and the world –

The whole world seemed to be water, calm, gray-green, sullen. The illusion would soon pass, Jim knew. Twice in six years the beck had spilled up over its banks, but a day, two, without rain and they would see the flagstones in the stableyard again. The tavern would clean up, as it always did.

The longboat sill lay a dozen yards from the door with its nose up on the pebbles, and Jim frowned at it. "It's going to take two to row that thing."

"Good thing there's two of us," Toby observed. One long arm rested over Jim's shoulders but his eyes were on the sea, gauging the run of the tide, and he smiled thinly. "We've got the current with us, on the way east. Mind you, it'll be a hard slog on the way back."

"On the way back," Jim argued, "there'll be four or five of us. What, the likes of Hobbes and Bigelow don't know how to row a boat?"

The remark inspired a quiet laugh. "Give them a good enough reason, they'll row."

"The treasure," Jim said dryly, "of Diego Monteras."

"Treasure," Toby breathed, "would be the best reason any of our venal company could imagine." He leaned over and dropped a kiss on the side of Jim's neck. "I meant what I said last night. What I have to give is yours for the taking."

"I could say the same," Jim said easily. "Breakfast? I don't know about you, but I want some food in the belly before I put one foot in any boat!"

"And a pistol in each pocket." All trace of humor fled from Toby's face, leaving his eyes oddly pale in the morning light. "And plenty of spare powder and shot."

"Oh, yes." Jim stepped back into the tavern, where the water was down to just below ankle deep and so filthy, he could barely see his shoes through it. "Call the dogs downstairs while I go back up and get the fire going."

Like the rest of the house, the kitchen was still inches underwater. The swirl there was filthy with the cinders and ash from the gutted hearth, and Jim noticed a definite reek of mildew this morning. He muttered the kind of language that would have earned him a boxing for his ears when he was a boy. Local laborers would be scrubbing with salt and vinegar for days, in every crevice, to get the mildew out – and much of the stink was coming up from the cellar. A bucket-line would be working there through an entire day to bail it out, before braziers would burn for days more, to get it dry enough to even start the salt and vinegar scrub –

And there Jim stopped himself, wondering why he was fretting about the day to day business of a sailors' alehouse.

Even if he and Toby took only a small handful of the prize – so little, the likes of Burke might never guess it was gone – they were rich men, and the largesse would last long if it was wisely spent. They could hand the job of cleaning up to a foreman and spend a month in France. They could sell the place and buy a whole new tavern, somewhere less prone to the constant risk of high water from a beck that never stayed inside its own banks after three days of rain. They could outfit a ship, chase the horizon to places Jim had always dreamed about but never actually thought to see with his own eyes.

Such thoughts consumed him as he reset the fire. He was in the kitchen, hunting for kippers, eggs, bread that was not too green around the edges, when he heard a voice he recognized in the yard right outside the backdoor.

"Ho there, Master Fairley, are you well? I knew you'd be flooded again, Jim – is there anything you need?"

It was John Hardesty – and Jim kicked himself. He should have known the doctor would come over as soon as the rain stopped. Hardesty was much more than a good doctor; he was a decent man, with the welfare of patients in mind. Jim's heart was in his mouth as he splashed to the door, but before he could drag it open he heard Edith Clitheroe calling down from a casement above.

"G'mornin', Doctor," she shouted. "We's all alive, if that's what 'as thee wonderin'! We's upstairs, well outta yon flood."

Jim threw his weight against the door to force it through the water, and pasted a smile onto his face. "John! It's good to see you, and it was kind of you to come by. I'd offer you coffee if I had it, but the fires are out ... will you take a jar of ale instead?"

A small rowing boat was bobbing in just enough water to float it off, a few yards from the three-foot pad on which the tavern had been rebuilt when the old ruins were flattened. A brawny young man sat at the oars and Hardesty was in the front, the big brown leather medical bags around his knees. He was not in oilskins this morning, and his shirt was open in the heavy, humid air. His oarsman was slick with sweat, eyes narrowed against the first bright light they had seen in days.

"Another time, Jim," Hardesty called. "I'd love to be sociable, but there's a dozen more houses to visit before I turn this cockleshell for home ... damn these rains. Are you managing?"

"More or less," Jim told him cautiously. "The bloody cellar's flooded again. It'll be a shite of a job to get it dry, as usual, and it's already stinking." He paused, slapping his left leg. "I worked too hard, getting us battened down, and I'm afraid I used a lot of the laudanum, John. Too much, actually ... I slept like the dead! Any chance you can let me have another bottle?"

"Will tomorrow do?" Hardesty frowned at his bags. "Promise me you'll be cautious with the stuff – it can be death of you, faster than the leg, if you're foolish with it."

"As well I know," Jim said grimly, at that moment thinking of Burke and Pledge. "You can trust me, John. These last days have been the worst I've known since I was a lad, and ... here I am, to tell you about it."

"Well said," Hardesty approved. "I'll come back in the morning, then. Christ alone knows what I'm going to find in the cottages up yonder. I've seen broken bones and gashes that've already gone green as pond scum, just between here and home! Idiots have been wading in thigh-deep water, stepping on poisonous old lumber. I'll be sawing legs off, if me best poultices don't work."

"What, more 'weeds' from your garden?" In fact, Jim knew the good of herbs and was joking, not mocking.

"Weeds, indeed," Hardesty scoffed, but he was chuckling. "I'll get back to you as soon as I can, Jim. If you find yourself in strife, send a lad to run and get me."

"Tomorrow or the next day will be fine," Jim judged. "The water'll be dropping today. I could come over to your place tomorrow night, if you'll be there."

Hardesty waved. "I'll be there. No one in the house needs a doctor, then?" He craned his neck back to look up at the casement. "And you, Edith – you're well?"

"Oh, aye," she said dismissively. "The worst thing's them damn' stairs, wi' these bloody knees o' mine, but I'm up 'ere now."

"We got the food and firewood and lamp oil up, before the water got to it," Jim added. "We'll manage nicely, John – but I'm grateful for your concern. That's a favor I owe you."

Hardesty waved off the gratitude. "I'll see you for dinner tomorrow, if you can make it through." Then, to the boatman, "Go on, Freddie, let's see some muscles. We've a mile to go yet, before it's cakes and ale!"

The boat turned slightly and pulled out, right through the stableyard and past the coach house, which was as bizarre a sight as Jim could imagine. He waved, lingering on the backdoor step until Hardesty was out of sight, and only then permitted himself the luxury of breathing properly.

"You don't trust him?" Toby's voice asked from the other end of the kitchen.

"In fact, I do," Jim said with wry humor, "which is the whole problem. John's as law abiding a man as Nathaniel Burke *isn't*. If he knew there'd been death and mayhem in this house, he'd make tracks for the garrison, report the whole business to Captain Dixon, and we'd have dragoons up to the rafters before luncheon. Burke and Pledge would be in the bailey before they woke up – which would suit me just fine. But I'll give you short odds, the others, this Willie Tuttle and Eli Hobbs, would soon get wind of it. They'd go to ground before Dixon could get the irons on them, wouldn't they?"

"They'd be gone like rats," Toby said quietly. "Like the vermin they are."

"And when the coast was clear, we'd have to go through this whole business again. Give it a week or a month and they'd be here, as nasty as Burke and Pledge, and likely just as hard to deal with." Jim shook his head, a sharp negative. "I want it done *now,* Toby. I want it over and finished, so we can get on and do ... whatever it is we're going to do with one small handful of those baubles."

"That's about the size and shape of it." Toby rubbed his face hard. "Time's wasting, Jim."

"We eat, then we're on our way," Jim said with bleak determination. "Kippers and eggs?"

They sizzled on the skillet in the big bedchamber. The two dogs were hungry, intent on the pan, nostrils flaring, and after Jim served himself and Toby he scraped a pile of the hash onto a spare platter. The tomcat remained on top of the wardrobe but he was sitting up this morning, grooming himself with a skilled pink tongue. The shutters were open, and a fresh sea wind filled the room as the sun climbed swiftly

Any other day Jim would have called it a lovely morning, but he saw none of its beauty today. The food tasted like straw and he forced it down, eyes on Toby, whose face was tight, clenched. Jim lifted a brow in question and he said,

"Pistols, powder and shot."

"I've a pistol and a boat gun of my own," Jim mused, "and Burke and Pledge came in armed with two pistols apiece. Scum like them take care of their weapons before they look to the comfort of their women, so I'd be glad to take theirs, unless these old friends of yours at The Cattlemarket would recognize them."

But Toby made negative noises. "A pistol's a pistol. Nathaniel was always well armed, but there's nothing special about the cannons he's carrying now. Leave the boat gun, Jim. It's too visible. If Eli and Willie got one glimpse of it, they'd be likely to shoot you down before they bothered to inquire about your business."

"Time." Jim stood and dusted off his hands.

"Time," Toby agreed. He looked up, saw Mrs. Clitheroe in the doorway and forced a smile. "Edith, will you do me a favor? Catch Bess and hold onto her. She's going to want to come with me, but I'd prefer to have her out of harm's way."

"Aye, I will." She faltered. "But, thee's comin' back 'ere after, isn't thee?"

"We *are*," Jim said loudly, emphatically. "We'll be back before dusk at the very latest, and probably a lot sooner … and we won't be alone. I'll leave the laudanum on the bar, and you keep dosing Burke and Pledge every three or four hours till mid-afternoon. Keep an eye open for the boat. When you see it, get back upstairs, quick as you can, and stay well out of the way. Don't even let them see you."

"I can do that," she said darkly. "Bess? Come on 'ere, Bessielove, come wi' me and I'll feed thee some cheese. Thee likes cheese. Come on, Boxer – cheese fer thee an'all."

Both dogs took the lure, and the door to the small room clicked shut behind them. With a grim glance, Jim and Toby headed downstairs, and Jim came to rest in the middle of the taproom. Burke and Pledge were still snoring, still trussed. Toby frowned over them as he collected his coat from the rack by the open door.

"These bastards are going to have heads like merry hell itself when they wake," Jim said, amused. "I did this once, myself – only once, mind you. Took the medicine, and again, and yet again, to stay away from the pain, the time I took a fall off a horse. Two whole days, I was away with the pixies. Didn't know a thing about the world. When I woke, all I wanted was for somebody to find the common mercy to put a pistol ball in my skull, put me out of my misery!" He fetched the bottle from his pocket, pulled the stopper and pinched Burke's nose. The man's mouth fell open and several drops dribbled onto his tongue. Jim performed the same service for Pledge, and left the bottle on the bar as he had promised.

Not quite on a whim, he reached under the bar for a bottle of rum. Toby was shrugging into his coat, and watched without comment as Jim liberally doused both Burke and Pledge, even filled their mouths with the spirit. Now, they would never convince even their oldest friend that they had not drunk themselves legless on purloined grog and passed out. The pain of overindulgence in laudanum would be scorned as a hard-earned hangover.

"They're well out of it," Jim judged. "You have your knife there?"

Toby drew the skinning knife from the inside pocket of his coat, stooped over the prisoners and cut the intricate knots out of the ropes. As they fell loose, Jim gathered up the oddments of line and stowed them under the bar. He fetched back three empty rum bottles and a fourth half-full, and set them on the table, right beside the sprawled bodies.

"Wicked," Toby observed. "When Eli and Willie clap eyes on these two, they'll be too full of scorn to be spare Nathaniel a civil word."

"Which," Jim said grimly, "is the plan. Pistols and shot, now."

Burke's and Pledge's weapons still lay on the bar and Jim watched, impressed, as Toby checked all four over from lock to barrel. He had handled weapons often enough to have more familiarity with them than Jim had ever possessed – and since Toby had run with Burke's crew, the aplomb was hardly surprising. Jim's eyes remained on the men as he fetched his coat, thrust his arms into it, but Burke and Pledge were too deeply unconscious to even twitch.

One pistol went into each coat pocket; powder poke in the left pocket, spare shot in the right. Satisfied, he took his hat from the rack and stepped out into the bright light of an April morning which would have been lovely, if not for the murky brown lake lapping right under the tavern walls.

The longboat was old, patched, but with the weight of two men in it, it was not taking water. Jim was satisfied, and slid in at the right-side oar as Toby took the left. His hands curved around the wood and he thanked his father's saints that he had done this work often. Almost every day, he would row out into Sandy Bay to put a line in the water for dinner and pull up his crab pots. He had the muscles for the job and, more importantly, the calluses.

It might have been much longer since Toby had rowed a boat any great distance, but he had worked hard for years. His hands were as tough as Jim's, and his body was far stronger. Jim always favored the leg, nursed it, thought of what he was about to do, before he began. Toby was still young enough to have no care about his limbs, and did not hesitate to throw his full weight against the oars.

The hardest pull was to get the boat out over the submerged path, where barely a hand's span separated keel from gravel. Moments later the current took hold of it like a great hand pulling the little craft along. Jim rested on the oars, feeling the boat run by itself. He knew the whole bay as well as anyone who lived in the few miles east of Exmouth, and he gave Toby a humorless grin.

Now, they only pulled to speed the boat, and watched the shoreline pass by – the little headland, the slow, gentle rise of the land up slopes checkerboarded by tiny fields green with the spring barley. Little towns were strung out along the coast; the lower-lying settlements were still as flooded as The Raven, and looked forlorn.

The Cattlemarket was east of Exmouth, in the hamlet of Foxholes Hill. A dozen cottages, a forge, a schoolhouse, a barn, stood just high enough on the slope to be above the new shoreline. This part of the coast was also draining faster, Jim saw. It was only a matter of a few miles from home, but the lie of the land here was different and the floodwater had already begun to recede. Foxholes Hill would be dry days before Budleigh.

"There it is." He pointed out a gray-shingled roof, set a little apart from the rest of the hamlet. "You know it well?"

"Alas, I do. It's a bawdy house," Toby said ruefully. "I don't think there's a sailor in these parts who doesn't know it – Hobbs and Tuttle knew it well enough to head straight there. They've a fancy for the kind of doxies you find in such houses."

"And you don't?" Jim leaned heavily on the right oar, to turn the boat.

"I've a taste ... for the *other*, as you're very much aware." Toby lifted his oar out of the water to make it easier for Jim to turn the little craft, then dipped the blade back in and began to pull with him, in the same easy rhythm. "The kind of pleasures you and I enjoy aren't likely to be found in any of these houses, no matter how bawdy they are! Well," he added, "not till you get into places much wilder than anything you find on these gentle shores. There's a rogue harbor called Tortuga ... lawless, godless, no place for delicate flowers, but I'll admit – it has a few of its own delights, if you know where to look for them."

Jim did not doubt a word of it. He wanted the stories of *The Rose of Gloucester*, but it would be years before Toby spoke openly of those days, if he ever did. For the moment Jim did not ask, but pulled hard to bring the boat in against the current. Sweat prickled his face and torso as he felt the keel rasp onto gravel, and Toby hopped over the side.

They were close to the path above the beach, Jim guessed. With the water levels falling rapidly here, the boat would be safe right where it had grounded out. The oars rattled in the well and he stepped over, up to his knees in murk and swirl as he got his bearings.

A finger of smoke angled up from the chimney of The Cattlemarket. The white-walled, gray-shingled building was a little larger than The Raven, and Jim knew it was many times busier. It was also infamous as a disorderly house, and when the lads from the garrison were not carousing here, they were raiding the place in search of smuggled grog and dissolute women performing heinous acts that were, so the local parson preached, 'an abomination to God and Man.'

But at ten in the morning on the day after the rains stopped, the house was quite orderly. There was nothing particularly bawdy about it and certainly nothing heinous going on. The only women Jim saw were less dissolute than simply hungover. Two were headed out to a clothesline, lugging a wicker basket of laundry between them. Another was emptying pisspots into the privy, a few yards from the rear corner of The Cattlemarket, showing that management and staff had the gentility not to just tip them out of the windows. Jim was impressed.

Red eyes greeted him and Toby as they stepped up to the threshold. He thought he knew the face of the girl in frills and flounces, sitting in a tub chair at the door. He had seen her at the shops in Exmouth. This morning she was smoking a pipe and holding her head as if her skull was parting company from her shoulders.

Certainly, she knew Jim. "Master Fairley, what in the world can we do for the likes of you?" she demanded, as if the volume of her own voice hurt. She meant, what was a eunuch doing, visiting a notorious brothel in broad daylight? Then her eyes passed on to Toby and she smiled. "Ullo, love, you decided to come back, did you? Told you, you'd get only the best 'ere, not up the road at yon ale'ouse. The Raven ain't got no girls, just an old crone who does the cookin', like I warned you."

"Yes, well, perhaps I enjoyed the ale there, and the cooking," Toby said, amused. He accorded Jim a wink and asked, "How's your head, Rosie? You look like you could use a tincture."

"I could, an' all," she admitted, bloodshot eyes closing. She took a few puffs of tobacco smoke. "You'd be lookin' for them mates o' yours."

Jim and Toby shared a swift glance and Toby said in careful, level tones, "I am, as it happens. Where would I find them?"

She gestured over her shoulder. "They was upstairs, in wi' Peggy and Marie ... prob'ly still there." She coughed on the smoke and winced, holding her head between her hands. "Gawd, 'ow much rum did I gargle last night? I should 'ave me bloody brains looked at."

"Go and have a nice lie down, sleep it off." Toby patted her shoulder as he stepped by, in through the tavern's low doorway, a pace ahead of Jim.

Dim light, the smells of hearth smoke and frying kippers, perfume half-masking the earthier scents of unwashed bodies and distant chamber pots, greeted them. Jim took a moment for his eyes to get used to the light before he glanced around a house he had seen once or twice, albeit years before. Nothing had changed. The floor still needed sweeping, the tables could have used a lick of beeswax, the innkeeper was still portly, ruddy-faced, wearing a ridiculous bag wig which was slithering back from his shining bald forehead. He was in a vast leather chair by the hearth, and looked up from a half-doze as the door closed behind Jim and Toby.

"Well, now, Artie Polgreen, you're looking a mite healthier," Toby said with congeniality Jim knew was sham.

"You mean, I haven't died yet," Polgreen said acidly. He tugged the wig back into place with a vengeful jerk.

"I thought you might, the morning I walked by your door and stopped long enough for a jar of ale," Toby admitted.

"I had a drop of two of bad grog, is all." Polgreen made a face and smoothed the ruffles of a shirt stretched taut over his belly. "What brings you back, Trelane?" Small brown eyes nested in fat and creases transferred to Jim. "What brings *him* with you?"

The question was pointed, and Jim had been expecting it. He was the local competition, at least as far as drinking men were concerned. "Me? I'm on my way to Exmouth – which, this morning, means rowing a bloody boat. Toby's been at The Raven for a few days –"

"Singing for his supper, no doubt." Polgreen peered down his nose at Toby. "Too good for the likes of The Cattlemarket, ain't you, Trelane?"

"I had business elsewhere," Toby said evasively. "I still do. I'm just looking for Eli and Willie. Point me at them, and I'll soon be back on my way. I'll even take Master Fairley with me, since you don't seem to want him inside your establishment."

Polgreen rearranged his immense limbs in the chair and stretched, yawned. "Ain't no place for eunuchs in a brothel … well, not unless it's one of *those* houses," he added thoughtfully, studying Jim rudely. "I don't keep no molly house."

Anger surged like the tide and settled just as fast. Jim forced a chuckle. "You've been listening to too many rumors, Artie. I'm not a eunuch, I'm just lame in one leg."

The man was frowning at Jim's legs; or perhaps a tiny tad higher. "That ain't what our Esme says."

"Your Esme," Jim informed him, "has never been closer to me than the other side of a bar. She's a gossip, as well as a trollop, with a tongue like vinegar. If she was selling horse racing tips, she'd have been shown the business end of the bastinado before now."

"Aye, maybe so, maybe so," Polgreen allowed. He sniffed disdainfully and nodded at the stairs. "Hobbs and Tuttle are still up there. They might be awake by now … Peggy and Marie came down an hour ago."

"I'll go and wake them." Toby took a step toward the stairs, and paused. "Did Rufus Bigelow ever show his face here?"

Polgreen roared a laugh. "It'd be a sight to take seven years off your life, if he did!" He peered at Toby. "He's dead."

Jim shot a quick glance at Toby, saw a shade of his color fade away. "Dead? Since when? What do you know, Artie?"

The big man pushed forward in the chair, resting both elbows on his knees, which made breathing difficult. He sounded winded as he said, "Soon as your Willie and Eli sobered up a bit, they were asking after him. They paid me a coin to send a lad into Exmouth, talking to people on the docks, looking for Bigelow." He pulled a kerchief from the pocket of his waistcoat and mopped his face. "Word is, he took a knife in the guts over a game of cards, three, maybe four years ago. In Kingston. As in, Jamaica."

"Well … damn," Toby breathed. "Rufus was the only decent one among the whole company."

"Other than you, you mean," Polgreen scoffed. "Not decent enough to play fair at cards, it seems. Or," he added scornfully, "too cack-handed to get away with it." He settled back into the chair, laced his fingers on his vast middle, and closed his eyes, though his voice was a roar. "Polly! Where's that tea, girl? Am I going to fall dead of old age before I get it?"

Without another word, Toby beckoned Jim to the stairs, and they went up quietly. The Cattlemarket was almost empty at this hour of the morning. The doors to the bedchambers stood open, and the windows were also open to the sea wind, blowing out the thick, heavy aromas of human bodies, stale grog and forgotten food. Every room they passed was empty.

At the chimney end of the house, one door remained closed. Toby stopped there, and the blue eyes were on Jim as he applied his knuckles. A series of sharp raps solicited an answering groan from inside, and he knocked again, louder. A man's voice, dense with the sound of Glasgow, growled,

"If thass Peggy wi' the coffee, come on in, lass. If it's any bugger else – get ye gone, an' stay gone."

Undaunted, Toby pushed open the door and stepped inside. A pace on his heels, Jim took in the dim room with one glance while the smell assaulted his nose. Without asking for permission, he threw open the windows. One bed stood against the back wall; the hearth was cold, the counterpane so rumpled, it was difficult to tell a second body was in the bed, turned upside down so its feet were tucked under the pillow.

The roar of protest as sunlight lanced into the room made Jim chuckle, and Toby said, "The one with the red eyes and the screwed-up little monkey face is Eli Hobbs, who looks like he hasn't seen the sun in days. The pair of feet you're almost seeing can only belong to William Tuttle, since Rufus seems to have died, rest his soul."

"Rufus – what?" Hobbs was sitting up, scrubbing his face, and it did bear an uncanny resemblance to a monkey, Jim thought. He was tanned dark brown, with shaggy hair and small, gappy yellow teeth – a short man, wiry, who looked as if he would be nimble enough to be a topman when he was sufficiently sober to climb a ladder, let alone a ship's rigging.

"Rufus Bigelow," Toby said sadly. "That fat fool, Artie Polgreen, told me he's dead. You paid him a penny to send a lad to ask after him, in Exmouth? There's the news the boy brought back."

"I paid the fat-arsed halfwit tuppence," Hobbs corrected, "an' aye, thass the news. Yer old mate's gone tae hell ahead of ye, Trelane."

"Well, it means one less man to divvy the spoils among, doesn't it?" Toby said with mock cheer. "I should think you're glad to know Rufus isn't coming back. And I *assume* you're actually still hoping to get a share."

Hobbs was scratching his face, hacking mucus out of his lungs, and Jim looked away as he spat onto the floorboards. "Whatcha rambling on about now, ye silly wee dobber?" He threw back the counterpane, revealing a thin, hard, naked body on the mattress beside him. "*William*!" he bellowed, and landed an open-handed blow on one small buttock, hard enough to leave his palm print there and draw a roar from Tuttle. "Wake up, ye bastard bampot! Move yer bloody arse."

The blow had shocked Tuttle awake. He rolled over, clutching at his head, and Jim saw a flushed face, eyes that seemed to be glued shut, copper-bright hair curling around a thin neck, wiry muscles and pale, freckled skin. "Eli, in the name of sweet Jesus bloody *Christ*, will yer shut yer yap?" The accent was Manchester, if Jim was any judge. "Wot's *wrong* with you, man?"

"I need tae pish, I wanna bevvy afore a die o' thirst, an' – where's me claes?"

"His what?" Jim wondered.

"His clothes," Toby translated, already casting about the room. "Your *claes* are right where you threw them, you *diddy*. Here's your *breeks*, and your boots, and the rest you'll have to sort out from Willie's *claes*." He dumped a pair of britches and a pair of scuffed boots on the end of the bed, and stood back. "And if you've any desire for a share in the prize, you'd best get your feet under you before the goddess of good fortune passes you by." He glanced at Jim as he spoke.

And Jim waited for the gist of what Toby had said to seep through into some part of Hobbs's brain, and Tuttle's, that could still think. He counted to four before Hobbs's eyes widened. He made a grab for the pale brown britches and struggled his legs into them before he stood up.

"Ye mean, auld Charlie were fair and true? He done like he said he would, an' the prize is safe?"

"The prize is safe," Toby told him. "But *auld* Charlie's as dead as Rufus, and he's been dead a great deal longer. Get your *breeks* on, both of you. We've got a boat, you can help row it back down to The Raven."

But Hobbs was intent on Jim now, and the little monkey face was clenched with suspicion. "Aye, and who might this un be?"

"Jim Fairley," Jim told him. "I own The Raven … and it seems I've been guarding your prize since Charlie Chegwidden passed away."

"Is that right, now?" Hobbs was up, stamping his feet in his boots, which made the hungover Tuttle wince. He snatched up a shirt and dropped it on over his head, glaring at Jim all the while. "Ye'll be wantin' a share o' the prize, nae doubt – and ye'll be sore disappointed. Ye'll nae get Charlie's share, if thass what yer thinkin'."

"That," Toby said loudly, "is for Nathaniel to decide."

Hobbs turned the glare on him now. "Nathaniel bloody Burke don't gimme orders, nae on dry land, nae wi' the prize safe in hand." He clenched his fists, as if he had the treasure of Diego Monteras between his fingers already.

On the bed, Willie Tuttle was awake, aware, sitting up and hanging on every syllable, and his mouth clenched at the mention of Burke. Jim's hackles prickled as he saw the fury, the hate. No love was lost between these men. Like Burke and Pledge, Hobbs and Tuttle were together out of necessity – and because they did not trust one another long enough for them to take their eyes off each other.

"Yes, well, get out to the boat," Toby suggested, withdrawing to the door, "and take it up with Nathaniel."

Tuttle was scrambling for his clothes and looking greener around the gills every moment. "He sent you here, did he? And like the good little dog, you did just like you were told."

"Let me say, I know better than to enrage the man," Toby allowed, "which is something you'd do well to learn, Willie."

"I ain't afraid of him." Tuttle reeled to his feet, propped up against the headboard. "Two wrong words to me, and Nathaniel can have a pistol ball right between his bloody beady little eyes, and welcome to it."

"And very welcome to it indeed," Toby said softly as he stepped out and closed the door behind Jim. He pressed his face into his hands for a moment, took a deep breath, and when he looked up at Jim again his eyes were sparkling. "There you have them. Eli and Willie, the Scotsman and the Mancunian, in all their glory … and if you're wondering whether Nathaniel and Joe distrust this pair of scallywags, you're right."

"They hate each other's guts," Jim observed, amused, scandalized.

"They certainly do." Toby went ahead of him, down the stairs. "And I, for one, am going to stand well back and let them fight it out for themselves. I know Nathaniel will make sure I get a small share – those are the rules. Nathaniel made them and he must be *seen* to enforce them, if he has any desire to hold onto command. You've seen the prize now, Jim. You know well enough, a small share will be grand, if it makes the bastards go away and leave us be, not just today but forever."

At the bottom of the stairs they stopped to watch the women and Artie Polgreen, who was snoring in his chair, a half-full mug of strong, dark tea balanced precariously on his belly. His wig had slipped sideways over his ear now. Jim nodded good morning to Esme, who had gossiped about him, and Polly and Lizzie, who had been hanging out laundry, and Marie, who had been emptying chamber pots. They all knew him; a couple of them smiled at him, though he perceived an aspect of pity in their faces. Esme studied him as if he were an insect and Jim dropped a low, sweeping bow before her, making her pout.

Then he and Toby were out again, blinking in the strong sunlight and glad to waft the stench of Polgreen's establishment out of their heads. Gulls were scavenging along the shoreline; a ketch was butting its way west, low in the water and hunting for any breeze in the light air. The longboat was already three feet above the high water line.

"I apologize for the rest of the company," Toby said ruefully as he and Jim climbed back into the boat to sit, waiting for Hobbs and Tuttle. "They're unpleasant characters even when they're sober and not hungover, and you're not exactly seeing them at their best."

"There's going to be trouble." Jim parked his buttocks on the seat, laced his fingers and studied his palms. "We left Burke and Pledge flat out and stinking of rum. Would that be normal – would Eli and Willie expect it of them?"

Toby seemed resigned. "Perhaps. I don't honestly care, Jim. Let them fight it out like a pack of mongrel dogs squabbling over a bone. At the end of the day I'll take what's always been mine, and we'll do very nicely."

"And if Nathaniel Burke doesn't live to see the end of it?" Jim wondered shrewdly. Toby turned to face him now. Jim gestured back in the direction of The Cattlemarket. "Hobbs and Tuttle hate him. Given the chance, or the reason, they'd be glad to kill him."

A grimness settled on Toby's face, an expression Jim had never seen there before. "Well now," he said softly, "that would be a terrible thing, wouldn't it? I'd cry myself to sleep for a week over it."

"Damnit, Toby," Jim began and then stopped, swiped off his hat and rubbed his scalp, hard enough to almost bruise. His voice was a rasp as he looked back into Toby's face. "Is this some kind of game you're playing?"

For a moment Toby did not answer, and then the fair head shook and he looked away, out to sea, where the ketch had changed tack. "A game? No. I just want to finish out today as a free man, and if I have a few coins in my pocket, so much the better." He chanced a sidelong glance at Jim. "Eight years, I've thought on this, tried to reason a way around these men, but they are who they are, Jim, and *what* they are. And I'll tell you this much. I'm not about to get between them and try making the peace. Any one of the four would be happy to put a pistol ball in me … and what's it matter to you and me if they're at each other's throats like starving hounds?"

What indeed, Jim thought hotly as they waited for Hobbs and Tuttle. His mind was on Burke and Pledge, stinking of rum, snoring like pigs on the taproom floor. And on the bin Toby had stowed up in the loft. He squeezed shut his eyes, forced his heart to be calm and his mind to be clear as they waited.

Twenty minutes went by before The Cattlemarket's door slammed open and Eli Hobbs came barreling out. He was sober now, and with a pint of coffee inside him he was spoiling for a fight. Tuttle was right behind him, looking ashen and drained, as if he had spent most of the time heaving up his belly – but he appeared no less belligerent than Hobbs as he stomped toward the longboat. Jim and Toby stepped over the side, and without being asked, Hobbs and Tuttle helped to shove the craft down toward the water.

Chapter Sixteen

Even on the shoreline around The Raven, the water was receding visibly. Jim saw sodden hummocks and woebegone bushes where that morning there had been only a lake. In another day it would be all mud, filth, debris and hard work. The old cellar under The Raven would be noxious already, with mildew and the blue mold which infested the walls at the first sign of dampness.

The longboat grounded out on sand, thirty yards from the front door, and Jim jumped over into shin-deep water filled with brown, tangled weed. The whole beach would be aromatic until local farmers gathered the kelp to feed the fields. Since the sky was clear now, a regiment of women and children would be out by twilight, packing the kelp into big wicker baskets.

All this was second nature to one who had lived on this shore for years. Jim might have mentioned it to Toby, for the sake of making conversation, but the look on Toby's face was too dark, too preoccupied, as he watched Hobbs and Tuttle hop out of the boat and march away without a backward glance.

They headed directly for the tavern's front door, and Jim whistled softly as he watched them barge right inside. Edith Clitheroe should be well out of their way, with Bess and Boxer at her heels. Jim thrust both hands into his pockets, wriggled his toes in disgustingly wet boots, and lifted a brow at Toby.

With a wicked, mirthless grin Toby beckoned him up to the tavern. They stood at the open door, watching, listening, as Eli Hobbs threw open a window for light and swung a series of savage kicks into Burke and Pledge, accompanied by a tirade in some form of English Jim could not understand. His accent was so barbarous, the vernacular so odd, all he could comprehend was the man's fury.

Two kicks, three, and Nathaniel Burke jerked awake. He sat up on the floor, cradling his head in both hands, groaning and wheezing. "Who the devil is that? Sweet Christ, Eli – kick me one more time, and I's like to separate you from your breath!"

"Och, so it lives after all," Hobbs sneered. "It's nae dead, though it smells like it oughtta be!" He kicked Joe Pledge again instead, hard enough to physically shove him. "Wake up, ye bloody dobber!"

"I's awake, I's awake, goddamn yer," Pledge howled, though he seemed more than half insensible, eyes shut, arms wrapped around his chest. "Jesus, Mary and friggin' Joseph, where am I?"

It was Willie Tuttle bellowing at him now. "You're in The Raven, where you've been fer bloody days! You're boozed right up to the flamin' eyeballs, you brainless pair of shite-heads."

"Stow your noise, Willie," Burke roared, "before I stow it for you." He was on his knees now, forcing his way up out of the dense fug of a laudanum hangover which could only be vile. He peered blearily at the other two and ran his tongue over parched lips. "What day is this?"

"It's bloody Thursday," Hobbs snarled. "The rain's stopped – and I'll just fuckin' bet ye an' Joe were headed away. Ye'da been gone, vanished, soon as the paths dried up enough fer ye tae *git*."

"Make sense, Eli, or shut your yap," Burke was massaging his skull, trying to get the blood moving in a head Jim knew would be thick as mortar.

"Sense? Aye, it's all about *Captain* Burke," Hobbs sneered. "Ye swindlin' auld swine. Ye was supposed to git the prize an' bring it right back tae the crew – else, send a message."

The mention of the prize seemed to startle Nathaniel Burke back to reality. "The prize," he growled, glaring at Pledge now.

Pledge seemed confused. Sitting on his folded knees, rubbing his temples, he blinked semi-lucidly at Burke. "We found it, did we? You musta found it after I passed out." He hawked and spat. "Christ, me mouth tastes like a rabid rat crawled in an' died – 'ow much did I drink?"

Tuttle swung an open handed blow at the rum bottles, sending them flying. They smashed against the wall as the Mancunian spat, "Too fuckin' much. Which is the *only* reason you bastards is still here, ain't it?"

"Wait!" Burke bellowed. Then, quieter, "Just ... wait, will you? Let me think." He stood swaying, breathing deeply. "Make yourselves useful. Go'n get me a jar of water."

"I'll nae take orders frae the likes of you," Hobbs informed him nastily.

"No?" Burke forced in another breath and turned to face him, startlingly sober by an effort of sheer willpower. "The prize ... is here. Charlie isn't. Charlie's dead."

"Aye, so they told us," Tuttle said acidly.

"They?" Burke echoed.

A pulse drummed in Jim's temple. His voice was low as he said to Toby, "Here we go." He chanced a sidelong glance at him. "You have any idea how to handle these ... gentlemen?"

"I do," Toby whispered. "Stay well out of it, Jim. Don't give them an excuse to drag you into their fracas."

"And you?" Jim would have held him back, but Toby accorded him a blue-eyed wink.

"You forget," he said in a bare undertone, "I sailed with these *gentlemen*."

So he knew exactly who they were, and what – and what they needed to hear, Jim thought as he watched Toby step just inside the tavern's door, making himself visible.

"*Them*. The parson and 'is gammy-legged wee mate," Hobbs was saying. He gestured at Toby. "They come to The Cattlemarket this mornin'."

"Oh, they did?" Burke's face clenched. He cocked his head at Toby. "That was uncommon decent of you, lad. Now, why would you do that?"

Now Jim held his breath, for he had no idea what Toby would say. He kept still, half a step outside the door, and wondered how long it would be before Burke and Pledge realized they were unarmed. Their pistols were in Toby's pockets and Jim's own.

Toby laughed with the balladsinger's skill. The laugh sounded easy, though Jim know it was sham, forced. "Nathaniel! You don't remember, do you? Ha! You don't recall a damn' thing!"

"I recall this much," Burke growled warningly, "if you don't speak straight in the next five seconds, I'll turn you over that bench and give you a taste of my belt that'll flay the hide right off your arse."

With the ease of old, old practice Toby ducked his head and dropped his voice. "I'm sorry, Nathaniel. I just have a lot to celebrate. I thought you'd be glad –"

"If 'e bloody knew what ye was talkin' about," Hobbs barked, "mebbe 'e would be!"

"The – the prize," Toby stammered, talking a calculated step back, away from them. "You don't remember, Nathaniel? Fair enough. We searched this house, top to bottom, while the rain fell … you don't recall how we tore the place to shreds?"

Burke's eyes narrowed. "Upstairs. Aye, I do. I also remember there was nothing to be found."

"Yes." Toby gestured at the smashed rum bottles. "You and Joe were in a fine fury. You sat down to eat … the local ale is a lot stronger than you were expecting. With two tankards inside you, you were shouting for the rum. Master Fairley broke out the best in the house, and – well, you drank a good deal."

"Drank yourselves legless, bastards that ye be," Hobbs muttered.

"And passed out," Toby finished with an expressive shrug. "That was when Master Fairley insisted on knowing what was going on in his house, and I … I told him. What else was I supposed to do? The time for secrets was long past, so I told him everything and he lent me his own hands, worked alongside me to find the prize."

"Is that right, Master Fairley?" Burke angled a hot, dark glance toward Jim. "Now, why would you do such a good deed, lad, for men you despise?"

"Fae a share!" Hobbs roared. "I told ye, Willie, the gammy lad's rowed hisself aboard fae a share – an' it'll nae be comin' outta *my* purse!"

"All he wants," Toby said quietly, "is for the four of you to get out of his house and never show your faces here again."

"So, let the man speak for hisself." Burke cocked his head at Jim. "Well, Master Jim Fairley?"

Jim pushed away from the door jamb. "See this pantomime from my position, Captain. There'll be no peace in my house till you've got what you came for and taken it away with you … and even now I own the foolish notion to keep my skin whole and my head on my shoulders. Of course I helped Toby find this damned prize of yours!"

"They found it," Pledge whispered thickly. "Nathaniel –"

"I heard." Burke hooked both thumbs in his belt. "And, having found it, you took yourselves on an errand to the bawdy house and dragged this pair of bastards out of there."

"Of course we did." Toby kept his voice low and his head half bowed. "You'll forgive me, Nathaniel, if I don't *quite* trust you. I'd a sneaking idea you'd do as Eli and Willie assumed. You'd get hold of the prize and vanish, as soon as the floodwaters went down. Then Eli and Willie would be here in a day or three. They'd never believe a word I said about the divvy-up. We're supposed to play by rules, the old rules *you* made, Nathaniel, but it takes an iron hand at the tiller … your own … to force the likes of Eli and Willie to play fair."

He cast a bleak glance at Hobbs and Tuttle. "Those two would've stolen from me any share you'd given me, before they headed after you – hunting, and doing it on largesse that should have been mine." He dared to lift his chin now, and his voice. "The last half-share is *mine*, Nathaniel. You put your mark on me, and I was loyal. I gave you good service for a long time. You *whistled*, and I went to you, gave you what you wanted, anything you asked for – I gave it freely, without protest or complaint, because I wore your mark and you kept the other bastards off me." He pinned Burke with a glare. "I still wear your mark. You haven't given me any ticket of manumission – not yet. According to the old rules we all lived by, I still belong to you. The best chance I have for a future is for you to do right by me. Keep the scum off me a while longer, give me my small share and my freedom, because I did right by you."

Silence fell on the taproom for several seconds before Pledge said in his thick London voice, "Well, I'll be buggered. The lad's done yer proud, Nathaniel. Yer musta trained 'im good, or been a damn' sight more coddlin' with 'im than I'da been."

"Well, now." Burke seemed not to hear a word Pledge had said. He looked Toby up and down appraisingly. "So this is what you want of me. You want me to take care of Eli and Willie for you, so you don't have to sully your fair hands."

"He ... what?" Hobbs demanded.

"He could've killed the pair of us, Eli," Burke said in a mock-pleasant tone. He gestured at the floor, where he and Pledge had slept for so long. "He could have gutted us like pigs and dumped us in the bay in the dead of night, and no one the wiser. But don't you never forget he was a priest. In some corner of his heart, young Toby still believes the Bible bilge water *just* enough for him to turn up his dainty nose at the red work. He won't kill a man. Never would, never did. You forgotten?"

"Aye, thass right." Hobbs peered rudely at Toby. "Ye coulda been done wi' the pair of 'em, Trelane, if only ye'd 'ad the balls fae it."

Toby's throat bobbed as he swallowed. "Call it weak, craven, if you want. Nathaniel's right. I won't kill a man. I won't have the stain of murder on my soul, not even for a fortune – not when all I have to do is call myself Nathaniel Burke's marked property, still, and hold him to the rules he made himself."

"An' you reckon he's gunna stand by 'em?" Tuttle chuckled acidly.

"I do." Toby frowned levelly at Burke. "They were your rules,

Captain. We all lived by them. I survived by them. Those rules are the only reason any one of is here today. Play out the last hand, and it's over. We walk away, alive and free. All of us."

For some time The Raven was so silent, Jim could hear the sound of pigeons in the thatch above the door. Burke's eyes flayed Toby to the bone and then passed on to fillet Hobbs and Tuttle like trout. At last he said slowly, ruminatingly,

"You's a queer un, Master Trelane. You always were. And you's right. I'll play out the hand. I'll let it be known, you're a free man. If you cross me path in a year or five, I might even buy you a jar of ale." His brow lowered. "Now, I'll thank you to give me what's mine."

The words were like a spark to gunpowder. "*Yours*?" Hobbs roared. "Ye'll nae take ownership o' the treasure we *all* bought wi' our blood!" He was scrambling for a pistol as he spoke, and in the same moment Burke discovered himself unarmed.

Almost faster than Jim could follow what he was doing, Toby whipped the pistol out of his left pocket and tossed it onto the table at Burke's right hand. Burke dove for it, twisting to present a hard target, and while Jim was still blinking, Burke and Hobbs were suddenly eye to eye, two weapons drawn, two hammers cocked, a split second away from blood.

"Jim." Toby's voice was quiet, taut. With a nod, he beckoned Jim away from the scene. They were halfway to the stairs when he said to Burke, "The prize is hidden, Nathaniel, for safety. We'll fetch it."

Burke never took his eyes from Hobbs. "Joe, go with them. Make sure they bring it all."

"Aye." Pledge was patting his pockets, discovering his pistols gone. "I ain't got no cannons."

Careful, surprisingly dextrous, Burke drew a long knife from a sheath at the small of his back, where Toby had missed it when he trussed them. This, he tossed into Pledge's waiting hands. "Tell Master Fairley, Toby," Burke insisted. "Describe Joe's skill with a thing like that. Tell him, at close quarters our Joe's more dangerous with a knife than he is with a pistol in each hand. And then tell your dear Master Fairley to give Joe back his weapons. You bastards disarmed us both, after we passed out – well and good. I'd've done the same. But you think Willie Tuttle's unarmed? Now it'd be your turn to hold by them same rules you're so bloody fond of quoting at me!"

"True," Toby said softly. "Jim?" His eyes flickered to Jim. "You've a pistol in your left pocket, yes?"

"You know I have." Jim licked his lips. In fact, he had a pistol in either pocket, but he clearly heard the note in Toby's voice. *One* pistol, he was saying. One for Burke, one for Pledge, matching the weapons carried by Hobbs and Tuttle and leaving both Toby and Jim himself with one apiece.

"Give Joe back his pistol," Toby said calmly.

Before Jim could respond, Willie Tuttle was a blur. He spun toward Jim, a weapon appearing in his right hand, hammer cocked, so fast, Jim was breathless. "Don't you be tryin' *nuthin'*, Fairley," he growled.

"Just a pistol for Joe," Toby crooned. "Come on, now, Willie ... play the hand out honest and square, like Nathaniel said."

"Like Nathaniel said," Tuttle echoed, mimicking brutally. He spat onto the flags, and held a tight aim on Jim. "Try anythin', Fairley, and I'll put you flat on your bloody back."

Very, very carefully, with only his fingertips Jim lifted the pistol out of his left pocket. Instead of trying to hand it to Pledge, he set it on the corner of the table where the rum bottles had stood till Tuttle slammed them away. With the weapon set down, he lifted both his hands to shoulder height and stepped slowly away, toward Toby.

"Take your cannon, Joe," Burke said, though his eyes did not move from Hobbs by so much as an inch.

And as Pledge set a hand on his pistol, Tuttle turned his back on Jim and covered his old shipmate instead.

Jim forced a chuckle devoid of humor. "You've no love for one another, Captain," he said in Burke's direction. "You'd as soon kill each other as say good morning."

"That we would," Burke agreed, "like any men, anywhere, when there's a king's ransom in the offing. You ain't never seen a crew turn on itself like starved wolves, when they see the glitter of gold and jewels."

"No," Jim said, hushed, "I haven't."

"Get it." Burke's tone was like granite. "Drag it out here, Toby – right *here,* right *now*. And like Willie was sayin' one minute ago, don't you be tryin' anythin'. Not if you've a hankerin' to walk away."

"We're not here to cheat anybody," Toby told him wearily. "My share's coming to me, fair and square – and my freedom. That's good enough for me." He gestured at the stairs. "Joe? After you."

At the bottom of the stairs Willie Tuttle fidgeted, torn between Pledge and the confrontation between Burke and Hobbs till Eli Hobbs snarled, "Well gae up wi' 'em, ye bampot! Ye dinnae trust Pledge nae more an' me!"

"Don't you bloody dare gimme orders," Tuttle barked, but he saw the sense of Hobbs's words and was right behind Jim as Toby led Pledge up.

At the top, Toby turned right and Jim heard the scrape of a chair on the floor, the squeal of the timbers overhead as he cracked open the trapdoor into the loft. He was up on the chair, blinking into the darkness, when Pledge protested,

"Oi, we searched up there afore we went down to eat."

"And Jim and I put the prize here for safekeeping after we dug it out of a wall in the cellar, while you two were snoring in your rum," Toby scoffed. "Here. Catch." Heedless of the pistol, he dropped the solid weight of the bin into Pledge's waiting hands.

Juggling with the weapon, swearing fluently, Pledge caught it. Jim might have expected him to assault Toby at least verbally, but avarice had caught Joe Pledge in its long-taloned fists. He weighed the bin between his hands, felt the roll and give, heard the rattle of the contents, and he was so intent on the prize, Jim could have snatched the pistol away from him and cracked it over his skull.

"Nathaniel!" His voice was a raucous bellow "Nathaniel – I's got it! The bastard were true as 'is word – it's 'ere!"

With that, Pledge dove past the gawping Willie Tuttle and galloped down the stairs like a colt. Tuttle was so intent on the bin, he ignored Jim and Toby utterly and raced after Pledge as if the two were roped together.

For a long moment Jim stayed where he was, leaning against the wall under the trapdoor, and lifted one brow at Toby. "You're sure about this?"

"Oh, I'm positive," Toby said in the same level, soft tone.

"You just gave them the prize!" Jim was aware of trying to roar in a whisper.

Toby nodded slowly. "Yes, I did." He draped both arms over Jim's shoulders, fingertips massaging the back of his neck. "And now, just stay well out of their way." His eyes glittered with an expression that was far indeed from humor. "The fun," he whispered, "is about to begin. You have a pistol?"

"Same as you do." Jim's right hand slipped into his pocket and molded about the hard, unfamiliar shape of the weapon.

"Don't let them see it." Toby drew his lips across Jim's forehead and stepped back. "Don't get between them and the prize. Don't move quickly or make a noise to draw their attention. Don't try to leave the tavern ahead of them."

"All right." Jim pulled both hands over his face and gave Toby a hard look. "I hope to God you know what you're doing."

For the first time, Toby permitted a wry smile. "So do I."

He was gone then, taking the stairs stealthily, slowly, like a stalking cat. Jim followed, and they stopped a few steps up, with a view of the taproom, the table and the four hard men who had squabbled at the head of the mutineer crew. The eight survivors of the *Rose of Gloucester* – Burke and Pledge, Hobbs and Tuttle, the long-dead Charlie Chegwidden and Rufus Bigelow, Barney Bellowes and Toby Trelane himself – were whittled down to these players –

Four men, four drawn pistols; one earthenware bin, which Pledge was opening as Jim watched. He pulled the big cork stopper, uptipped it, and out spilled the incredible fortune for which men had died, and were still dying. Jim was not blind to the irony that so much beauty should be sodden with so much blood. For a surreal moment the four brigands stood gawping at the trove they had dreamed of for eight years, and at last it was Burke who said,

"Willie, Joe, put them pistols away and make yourselves useful."

He was giving orders again, but neither Tuttle nor Pledge seemed to care now. Burke and Hobbs continued to hold each other at gunpoint, but Pledge's pistol clattered down a moment before Tuttle's, and they went for the treasure of Diego Monteras like hawks after hares. Jim's eyes narrowed, watching as the gems cascaded across the worn old timbers of the table surface.

In the late afternoon light from window and door precious stones sparkled, shimmered, winked, as if with a life of their own. Emeralds, diamonds, sapphires, rubies, amethysts, every color, every size, each chosen for its perfection by a man who knew and loved gems; pearls the size of quails' eggs; gold filigree inset with the tiny sparklets of diamonds; ropes of stones set in ancient silver findings. This was the legacy of Diego Monteras, timeless – unchanged since the day he and Fernando had hidden it.

"Holy Saint Hilda," Eli Hobbs whispered, eyes vast, dark. "I cannae believe I'm seein' 'em again."

"Times were," Burke agreed, "I thought I'd never live long enough." With a slow, careful left hand he reached into the inside pocket of his coat and drew out a sheet of parchment, brown with age, much creased and folded. "You remember this, Eli?"

"Och, I recall," Hobbs said darkly. "The manifest."

"The manifest," Burke agreed. He looked at Hobbs and Tuttle.

"Now, will you put them bloody-damn' cannons away and help us match the prize to the manifest?"

"Aye," Hobbs said darkly, "in case auld Charlie were a swindler after all … or Trelane, and the other one over there."

"We took nothing." Toby stepped out and sat on the bottom step. "Nine powder bags is what Charlie hid away. Nine bags is what you've got there. Count them. We packed the hoard just as we found it. Charlie wouldn't cross you, Nathan. Nor would I."

"Not if he wanted to keep on breathin'. Same as you." Burke had unfolded the parchment and was already sorting rubies from emeralds, sapphires from pearls.

With a soft oath, Jim sat on the bottom step, his left thigh pressed to Toby's right. His voice was a bare murmur. "You'd better be right about this. If Charlie took anything for himself, they'll call it swindling – and they might call it our crime, since we're the ones here to answer for it."

"You didn't know Charlie as well as I did. He had a mortal dread of Nathaniel," Toby whispered. "He wanted to live as much as any man does, and Nathaniel scared the wits out of his skull. And even if Charlie did take some small thing out of necessity – perhaps to get himself and the prize home, safe – it'd only be counted as an advance against his share. As the custodian, he was granted the same three shares as the gunners. Eli was a gunner. It's three shares he's trying to protect, and you've seen how much it'll be! Hush now, Jim."

The gems were sorted by color, then by size. Burke lit two lanterns when the afternoon light began to fade as the sun westered, the better to see the manifest. As Jim watched, fascinated, he began to thumb along the lists, matching what he saw to the painstaking tallies which had been made when the treasure was recovered.

Other lists had been made on the same parchment, detailing the shares each man could look forward to, and the lists were labeled with each man's mark. Most of the company could not read or write, so to be fair to all the manifest was made up of colored marks and numbers – Jim saw at a glance how it had been drawn up to make sense even to men who were illiterate. Burke's list bore the same winged 'B' as was branded into Toby's flank; Charlie Chegwidden's mark was two 'C's,' joined like open links of chain. Of them all, only Rufus Bigelow and Toby himself had written their names.

And three of the company were gone. Charlie, Bigelow and Barney Bellowes had no need of their shares, so a great cascade of gems was unclaimed, to be divvied up afresh.

And this was where the squabbling began. Toby growled a humorless laugh beneath his breath. "They're going to fight."

"You knew they would." Jim glanced sidelong at him.

"Oh, yes." Toby was taut, every muscle tensed as if to spring though he was still sitting on the bottom stair. "Watch yourself, Jim."

Deep in his right pocket, Jim's hand curved about the shape of the pistol and his thumb caressed the hammer as Burke bawled,

"*Enough*, Eli Hobbs! One more word, and –"

The staccato snaps of at least two hammers cocking were like needles in Jim's nerve endings, a tenth of a second before Hobbs began to sneer.

"An' ye'll what, ye God-rotted Sassanach? Ye'll shoot me down, will ye? Like ye think I've ever been inclined tae trust ye, Nathaniel high-and-bloody-mighty Burke? To the devil with ye! Ye'd believe Sunday were Friday if it suited ye. Now, ye can think again. Ye can just divvy Charlie's share, and Rufie's, and Barney's, dead even 'twixt the lot of us. Ye'll nae get more than yer due, just fae havin' the spleen to call yerself *Captain*. I never called ye that."

"Nor me." Tuttle was so furious, he was spitting. "You wanna skipper's share of dead men's trove? That's wicked, that is."

"I *am* wicked," Burke said in a voice like gravel. "I'm *evil*. You said it yourself, more than once. You called me the devil hisself – you remember that night?"

"The night in Barbados, on the beach, when you tortured the Portuguee for what he knew about the French carrack." Tuttle's Adam's apple bobbed. "Aye, I said you was wicked as friggin' sin."

"And you may congratulate yourself for bein' right." Burke had not moved in his chair, save to snatch up his pistol in the same instant Tuttle pulled his own weapon from its place in his belt. Burke's aim was unwavering on Tuttle's gut. "You thinkin' I's grown any sweeter in me old age?" He stood now, and kicked the chair back, perhaps with the intention of overwhelming the small, slight Hobbs with his own stature. At his left hand, Pledge climbed carefully to his feet as Burke nailed Tuttle with a glare which might have incinerated him. "You want to follow the Portuguee to hell? Back off, Willie. Sit your arse back down in your chair, and –"

"Yer nae captain o' mine!" Hobbs's voice was shrill with rage he could barely contain – his face was white with it, his hands shaking.

"Nathaniel, watch –" Joe Pledge began, on some blind instinct shoving Burke aside as he saw Hobbs's trembling hands jump.

In the confines of the stone-walled taproom, the pistol shot hurt the eardrums. Jim's ears *pinged* and rang, his heart hammered at his ribs. He was halfway to his feet, but Toby held him back with both hands bruising his arms, and Jim stilled.

Given a solid shove, Burke staggered and almost fell. He caught himself one-handed on the table, but it was Pledge who grunted in shock and pain, and his body gave an odd lurch. Jim had never before seen a man shot, and he caught his breath as Pledge spun around, punched by the impact and flung back into his chair. A spot of crimson blossomed on his shirt, growing as if a flower were opening there.

In less time than it took Pledge to fall, Burke recovered his balance. Hobbs had gone down on one knee, putting the solid width of the table between himself and Burke, and now he was fumbling for powder and shot, desperate to reload. Fury was his enemy. He was shaking too much to control his hands, and gunpowder dribbled over his feet.

The real danger was Willie Tuttle, and both Burke and Pledge knew it. They seemed to fire together – the roar was stunning, making Jim's head spin. His vision dimmed for an instant before he blinked at Tuttle, who had been hurled backward. A great red wound gaped in the middle of his face, obliterating his nose; another darkened in the broadest part of his chest, where heart and lungs and ribs crowded together.

He was dead before he slithered to a halt, jammed into the angle between wall and floor. The body twitched, jerked, but Jim was not fooled. There was no life left in Tuttle. The hazard now came from Hobbs, and Toby's voice was harsh, barking, as he yelled a warning at Burke.

"I's got no powder and shot, lad," Burke bellowed back, "and I can't see the bastard – is he reloaded?"

True enough, Burke's second pistol and all his powder and shot were in the pockets of Jim's coat. Toby had one shot in the pistol he had taken from Pledge and still carried, but Burke's words echoed in Jim's ears: Toby would never shoot a man, never risk taking a human life. Perhaps he had a miserable aim, Jim thought feverishly, and could never be sure of what part of a man he would hit.

But since being just a lad, Jim had shot rabbits, pheasant, pigeons, for the table, and he knew the value of his own aim. Every argument Toby had made about the merits of owning a stainless soul come Judgment Day jabbered at him as he fetched out the pistol. *Don't take a man's life, Jim,* Toby would have begged, and Jim saw no reason to go against the sentiment.

Hobbs had spilled gunpowder on the floor and half a dozen lead balls were rolling like marbles away from his boots, but by some charm the pistol was loaded. He was dragging it up into line with both hands, aiming desperately at the looming figure of Burke. Jim kept both eyes open as he had been taught, sighting along the barrel, and at this distance there was little danger of him being far off target.

The pistol snatched itself out of Hobbs's fingers and he screamed in shock and rage, as if he had been mortally wounded. Bright new blood laved his right hand as he scrambled to his feet, but he was going for his pockets. For a terrible moment Jim was sure he had another pistol, before he saw the wicked flash of lamplight on the slick blade of a knife. Hobbs used it left-handed with more aplomb than most men would have commanded in their right hand.

With a bull-like roar Burke launched himself, half across, half around the table. Jim knew the weight of it, knew what it took to shift it, and swore beneath his breath as the table jerked sideways, tipping a lantern over. Whale oil spilled and flame licked right behind it, leaving a bright lake of fire in the middle of the old wood.

The parchment – the very tally over which these men had fought – caught alight in seconds while rubies, emeralds, sapphires skittered across the timbers. A handful fell and rolled away into the shadows. Others remained in the shallows of the oil lake, flames licking hungrily around them.

Heedless of the fire, Burke crashed into Hobbs with stunning force, sending the pair of them to the floor in a mess of thrashing limbs. Joe Pledge was halfway to his feet, trying to see while both his hands were clasped tight to his middle as if he were trying to hold his insides in place. Jim had no idea how badly Pledge was wounded, but he was not about to offer succor to the man who had threatened to torment Toby.

In fact, Pledge was shouting at Toby now, and Jim forced himself to listen, to disentangle words from sound. "Get him!" Pledge was bellowing. "Get the bastard, Trelane, afore 'e sticks that fuckin' knife in Nathaniel!"

Get him? Jim was intent on the rolling, writhing mass of limbs and for the life of him, he could see no way to get between them. Instead, he gestured with his spent pistol and said to Toby, "Get the fire out while I reload this bloody thing."

"Jim," Toby began.

"Put the fire out!" Jim said, louder, harder. "You won't shoot a man – fair enough. But I can, and I will, if it comes down to it!"

For an instant Toby blinked, and then from somewhere he produced a wide, genuine grin. "Aye, sir." He sketched a salute and dove away toward the kitchen.

The pulses were hammering in Jim's throat and ears as he dumped powder and shot onto the last safe corner of the table and opened both pokes. His eyes were still on Burke and Hobbs, who were struggling for the knife. A matter of scant seconds had passed since they collided, though to Jim time seemed to be passing with bizarre slowness. To his left, Joe Pledge sat slumped in the chair, fish-breathing, nursing his middle as he blinked hazily at the tangle of limbs.

"Get 'im, fer chrissakes get 'im," he moaned at Jim, and Jim heard the threadiness of his voice. Pledge's eyes were wide, dark, filled with shadows and with dread. He was dying, and he knew it.

"I don't dare shoot," Jim muttered. "I could put one square in Burke's heart! He'll have to do Eli Hobbs himself. What, you think he's not big enough or strong enough?"

"Big and strong, aye," Pledge rasped. "But Eli's slippery as a bastard eel. Always were. Don't ... don't trust 'im."

Jim rammed the barrel with wadding and a lead ball, and gave Pledge a hard, sour look. "Trust him? I never trusted any of you, Master Pledge, and I still don't. Now, shut up and let me do what I must."

As he spoke Toby returned, arms filled with the small black cauldron, water slopping over the sides at every step. He cursed and swore under the weight of it, and Jim spared a glance for him as he tipped the whole load over the fire. The flames were out in a moment, and he slammed the cauldron down on the table right by Pledge.

"Trelane," Pledge gasped. "Devil take yer, Trelane, if yer let Eli Hobbs take down Nathaniel."

His voice was weakening, and if Jim was any judge Pledge's vision would already be starting to darken. He doubted the man could see enough to know when Hobbs – slippery as any eel – rolled, feinted, fooled Burke enough to get leverage on one arm, and thrust forward as if with a bayonet.

A scream wrenched out of Burke's throat, hoarse, sharp as much with sock as with pain. Jim never saw the wound struck, but he knew the magnitude of it from the sound of Burke's voice. He had no doubt the knife had found the vitals, and he shot a glance at Toby. Toby's face might have been carved from granite. No hint of expression played across his features as he watched Nathaniel Burke – his old master, old protector, old tormentor.

Fury was a curious force, Jim thought. It could imbue a man's limbs with a power that transcended the simply human or mortal. To be sure, the strength would not last long, but while it did, many a demigod would look on with admiration.

Where Burke found the power, Jim could not know. Burke himself would not have known, but it ripped through him like divine fire. Blood was frothing on his lips and nose as he reared back, got his right hand on the hilt of the knife and tore it out of his chest, all the while keeping Eli Hobbs pinned beneath him with his weight on one elbow and both knees.

Hobbs was badly hurt already. His left arm was useless and one leg refused to move properly. Still, he flailed at Burke, even his teeth snapping as he snarled curses and tried to bite any flesh he could reach. The knife was bright with the cherry-red blood that spelled a creature's very life. Jim had hunted often enough to know the look of such blood, and beside him Toby began to whisper in the old, dead language.

But there was still life in Nathaniel Burke, and strength enough to turn the knife in his right hand, to bat Hobbs's hand out of the way, tuck the point of the blade right in under the jaw bone and thrust up. One hard, uncompromising shove, and it was over for Hobbs with surprising mercy. Death came to him in an instant, like a shadow racing across the hillside ahead of a storm front.

Wheezing, panting, forcing every breath into damaged lungs, Burke clambered to his feet. He stood swaying, trying to get his bearings for a long moment, outlined in the purple murk of late twilight which fell from the open door and window. With one lantern out, the taproom was dim now, and his vision must have been darkening, like Pledge's.

"Joe?" His voice was graveling. "Joe, you still with me?"

And a mere whisper. "Still." Pledge sat slumped in the chair, no longer moving though his eyes were open to slits, shining in the grudging light of the one lantern. Every breath inspired a moan. "It's dark, Nathaniel."

"Aye," Burke wheezed. "Night's comin' on. She's comin' on fast, and she'll be dark as the vaults in hell." He coughed. Blood frothed in his mouth and nose, on his lips, and he spat it out. "You there, Toby, lad?"

Toby took a step forward, closer to the ring of light. "I'm here. I'll light a couple of lanterns, Nathaniel, will I?"

But Burke's head wagged a negative. "Forget 'em." He peered

down at his chest, dragged both hands across his face, smearing it luridly with blood, and gestured at the bin which had contained the dream and the curse of Diego Monteras's legacy. "Pack it. All of it … keep back what you can hold in your own right hand, Toby lad. That'll be your fair share, that and freedom. Aye, time was, you were a good lad, but you done me wrong at the end. You done me sorely wrong and if the strength was left in me, I'd flog you to tatters for it, head to foot, before I called you a free man."

Something in his tone made the hackles prickle on Jim's neck. He was busy with the lanterns, lighting as many as he could lay his hands on, and he glared up at Burke in their odd shadows. "Say what you mean, Captain. Neither of us ever lifted a hand against you."

The dark, hooded eyes were more shadow than iris. Burke seemed not to look at Jim so much as clean through him, as if already he was looking into the next world. The graveyard stare made Jim shiver while Burke searched for his voice, and for words. Toby was doing as he had been bid, raking together the spilled gems, thrusting them into the bin, keeping back a few here, a few there, when size or perfection of form or color caught his eye. Burke's eyes brooded on him as he worked.

"Toby Trelane has never killed a man, Master Fairley, and he'll tell you, he never will. But he has it in him to be a schemin', connivin', underhand, murderous *weasel*. If the lad thinks he'll be judged any more lightly on the day the trumpets call us back out of the ground, and from the bottom of the sea, he's mistaken." Again Burke coughed, and every breath seemed to flute in his throat. Blood dribbled from the corners of his mouth, unheeded, as he thrust out his hand to take the bin. Toby had forced in the stopper a moment before, and gave it to him without comment or protest. Burke tucked it under his arm and stood swaying. "Master Trelane will be judged like the rest of us mortal sinners," he rasped. "Would he wreak death on Eli and Willie in their drunken sleep, back at Polgreen's pox shop? He'd be too good for that, too pious. But he'll bring the buggers here and hand 'em to me, knowin' what'd become of 'em." His eyes blazed accusation at Toby. "Knowin'," he added, "what'd become of *me*."

"That's a lie," Jim began angrily, as confused as he was furious.

"It isn't," Toby said with ominous quiet. He lifted his chin, looking levelly at Jim. "I told you I was bringing the four of them here, face to face, so they could settle their business once and for all, and I'd play no part in it." His brows arched at Jim, and then at Burke. "What force stopped them behaving like decent, civilized men? What prevented them from talking it out, arguing and bickering like siblings if they had to, but thrashing it through and finding a peaceable resolution?" He turned Burke's glare back on him. "I'll tell you what stopped them – Nathaniel already knows, and never mind all his goddamned rhetoric."

"They had blood in their eyes," Jim said bitterly. "All four of them, from the moment I saw them. Murder was written on their faces, plain as the day."

Toby nodded slowly. "That's what they came here for – like Barney. It's *all* they came here for, as if it was a game to be played, with the prize awarded to the winner. Call it, 'last man on his feet with wounds he can be healed of.' They got what they wanted, Jim, when they walked through your door. Nathaniel's only aggrieved because he could never turn me into a murderer. Once, he told me he *could* do it, and he would –"

"I made you the promise," Burke growled, as if he was gargling in blood at every syllable, "while I held you down over a table and gave you what you had comin' to you, little molly-whore that you were."

"If I was," Toby whispered, "it's what you made me. You could have put your mark on me to keep the others off, and then treated me with decency. Only wickedness made you take your sport on me – it was none of my doing, Nathaniel. Don't you dare lay blame on me."

"Threatenin'?" Anger infused Burke with fresh energy. "You's grown the balls to threaten me now?"

"I don't even want to *see* you one minute longer," Toby said with an icy calm. "You've got what you always wanted. You played the game they were all slavering to play – you're the last on his feet, with the prize in your hand. I'm a free man, with the gems I can hold in my right fist – you offered the deal, and I'll claim it now. There's the door, Nathaniel. Take Monteras's bloody legacy and walk away with it. No one's stopping you."

"Aye," Burke growled, coughing, gargling, spitting, "aye, I will, and be damned to you, Trelane. If I see you again, I's like to split you, crotch to gizzard."

He was moving as Joe Pledge struggled up in the chair with the last of his strength. "Nathaniel, don't leave me – fer chrissakes, don't leave me."

For a long moment Burke hovered, peering down at Pledge as if he was already half blind. "You're done for, Joe," he wheezed. "There's more blood out of you than in. I think you'll be in hell a day or two before me ... speak well of me to the master there."

And then he was lurching away from the spill of lantern light. Jim thought he looked closer to shadow than man as he staggered across the doorstep and away into a twilight that had dimmed to steel blue and purple. Pledge would have screamed after him, but the life had ebbed so far from him, barely a croak passed his lips.

"Nathaniel," he panted, "Nathaniel, don't go without me – come back, Christ blight ye! God rot you, devil take ye!"

The stream of curses continued, but Jim stopped listening. He pulled both hands over his face, aware of the sweat on his skin and the chill in his bones. "Do you know where he's going? The man's dead on his feet, Toby. He's not going to make it far. Does he have friends here?"

"Friends?" Toby actually laughed, but Jim heard the edge of something very like hysteria in the sound. "The only *friends* he had in the world just tried to kill him … except for Joe, who took a pistol ball meant for him. And Nathaniel just walked away from him."

"Then, where's he going, damn him?" Jim demanded.

"I don't know." Toby clenched both hands into his hair as if to force his mind to think properly, before he stepped out of the ring of the light. On the threshold he stopped and turned back with a look for Jim that was a hundred years deep.

Then he was gone, and Jim found himself listening to a painful silence. He heard only the soft susurration of the outgoing tide, the labored breathing of Joe Pledge, who clung to life with a tenacity Jim had to admire, and the hammer stroke of his own heart, slowly calming as he found himself alive and with his skin whole.

Moments later, the rasped breathing stopped and when Jim turned back to the chair he saw only glazed, unfocused eyes and a mess of blood which looked slick and black in the lantern light. Pledge was as dead as Hobbs and Tuttle, who were sprawled on the floor, and propped against the wall. The tavern was so full of death, Jim felt suffocated and he dove outside, desperate for fresh air, *any* air.

Chapter Seventeen

He dragged the salt sea wind to the bottom of his lungs while his eyes grew accustomed to the mauve twilight. Of Toby there was already no sign, but he heard barking, sharp and persistent, and he knew that voice. "Boxer," he muttered. "Damnit, Boxer, where are you?"

And where were Bess and Edith Clitheroe? He cast about, following the sound, and swore beneath his breath as it took him to the stable. A crack of candlelight showed under the door, and as he opened it the terrier launched himself into Jim's arms. Jim caught him, held him tight. People who knew dogs always swore they could smell fear, death, fury. Boxer must have been able to smell it for hours now and his small body was trembling with reaction.

But before Jim could call her name, Bess shot past his legs and streaked away into the night. Either her ears or her nose told her where Toby had gone and the last Jim saw of her, she was tearing through the stableyard, headed west toward the path to Exmouth.

"Master Jim, yer alive." The old woman was sitting on a hay bale, and wrapped in a blanket. Two fat tallow candles stood on a barrelhead beside her and her basket was at her feet, still half-full of food and drink. "I 'eard a lot I didn't ken … pistol shots, an' all." She blinked owlishly at him. "Somebody's dead?"

"They're all dead," Jim said bitterly, hardly recognizing his own voice.

"Master Trelane's dead?" She was aghast.

"No … thank gods, he …" Jim swallowed hard. "We brought back two more, a charming pair of cutthroats – be grateful you never made their acquaintance! They fought, as Toby knew they would. Fighting among themselves was the only reason they came here. If Charlie Chegwidden had been alive, he'd have run a mile when he saw the bastards coming, Edith. It's a wonder Toby and I are still alive."

"It's a miracle," she agreed, looking past Jim, out into the yard. "Where is 'e, then? Master Trelane?"

"He went after Nathaniel Burke." Jim shook his head slowly. "Burke was on his feet, but there wasn't much life left in him. He had the prize, but he couldn't have made it far."

"And Master Trelane." Edith worked her way down off the hay bale with an ouch and a wince as old hips and knees protested. "That is, 'e's comin' back, ain't 'e?"

For the first time Jim acknowledged the tiny worm of doubt which had been wriggling through his gut since the moment Toby paused on the doorsill and turned back, face dark with so many shadows and secrets. The handful of gems he had chosen as the very finest still lay on the table, and dozens more had been scattered when the lantern upturned. Burke had taken everything else, though he would not stagger far, Jim thought. With a night's head start, Toby could be twenty miles away – forty, if he bought a horse along the way; and nothing but Jim's word would connect him with The Raven, or with the mutineer crew and his own patchwork history.

"I ..." Jim hesitated, wanting to be honest. In fact, he was far from sure he would see Toby Trelane's handsome face again. Even Bess had raced after him as if afraid she would lose him. For some time He was silent, and at last could not bring himself to speak the truth. He forced a smile and swiped up the basket. "Of course he's coming back. He just went after Burke to make sure of him." To know exactly what became of a dangerous enemy, and secure the treasure of Diego Monteras at the last, keep it out of the hands of some passing stranger, perhaps a yokel from a nearby farm, a fisherman stumbling home with three sheets in the wind, who would be delighted to literally fall over it on the path and claim it as his own. "Come on, Edith," Jim encouraged, "come back to the house. Don't go into the taproom, mind you, but I'll get the kitchen hearth organized. You get a good fire going, and some hot food. It feels like it'll be bloody cold tonight."

She made a face. "It's startin' to stink in there, what wi' the cellar bein' flooded."

"Better than spending the night in the stable, though," he hazarded. "I'll seal the cellar up tight till we can get some men in, get it dry." He set Boxer down and snatched up the blankets. Edith picked up a candle in each hand. "You'll be better in the warm, with a meal inside you," he told her, for want of something to say to cover the sick churning of his insides.

"I will, at that," she admitted. "What 'appened to Bess? I can't see 'er."

"She shot off like a cannonball, after Toby." Jim swallowed the lump in his throat as he steered the woman across the stableyard. He kept talking out of a need to fill the silence where Toby should have been. "Just stay out of the taproom, you hear? I'll wedge the door shut. Then I've got to go over and get Vicar Morley. They were the worst kind of sinners, but they're dead and somebody has to say the right words over them. Then," he said resignedly as they clambered up out of the persistent water, "I ought to ride over to the garrison, report this – to John Hardesty's good friend in person, if he's there. Captain Dixon. If Dixon's not there, his lieutenant will be. And since I'll be riding past Doctor John's door, it'd be damned rude of me not to knock and tell him what happened after he left here yesterday. And remember. Edith – let's keep the story *simple*. Everything that happened, happened *after* Doctor John passed by, you hear? Don't be forgetting, now! It's an innocent tale, but it'll stop a dozen nasty questions before they're even asked."

The backdoor always swelled in the rain. After the flooding it was jammed so tight, it almost seemed to be bolted shut. Jim put his shoulder against it, grunting and swearing as he forced it open. He took a candle from her, lit the three lanterns on the pantry shelf right by the door and set them up where they cast a decent light around the chaos of the kitchen.

The fire basket still stood in the middle of the room; the chairs were shoved into corners, the table thrust against the wall opposite the hearth. Mrs. Clitheroe was right, the reek of must and mildew from the cellar was already like the bilges on a neglected boat, and would only get worse. Muttering vile language, Jim wrestled the big wrought iron basket into place and kicked a chair up beside it. He pulled the table back where it belonged with a squealing of wet wood on filthy floor, and set a lantern by the chair. Edith was hovering, dismayed by the mess, and he urged her into the chair, shushed her.

"I'm just going to bring down enough kindling to get the hearth going," he promised. "We took it all upstairs ... there's nothing to fear now."

Nothing to fear, but still his hackles were prickling as he went through into the taproom and closed the door deliberately behind him. The three bodies seemed to mock him with grotesque shadows as he took a lantern and passed them by, and as he climbed the stairs he thought those shadows plucked at his hair, touched his clothes, with hands he could *almost* feel.

He cursed himself for a fool and swallowed his heart as he shoved his way into the small room, where he and Toby had set the baskets of kindling. Toby had tied it into bundles, and Jim hoisted up two at a time. He slung half a dozen over his shoulder before retrieving the lantern, and took the stairs with exaggerated caution.

The April night was already strikingly cold. The front door and windows were still open, the hearths were out and the floor was still wet, though the water had stopped actually running. It would be the end of summer before the house was fully dried out and smelt right again. Jim sighed as he paused at the bottom of the stairs to ease the kindling on his back. With a glare at the three very dead bodies, he asked himself if he cared enough to stay here and see the work through.

The share of the prize left on the table was more than generous. Toby had picked out the most perfect jewels, even then hedging his bets, covering every eventuality, in case Burke made it away with the rest –

Or had he chosen the very best to leave Jim with a rich gratuity, because he knew he was not coming back? The stones winked and glittered in the lantern light as Jim carried the kindling through to the kitchen. Edith was on her feet again, sweeping, stubbornly pushing and shoving at the piles of muck deposited by the falling water. She knew as many curse words as Jim and she was muttering them all, perhaps too deaf to know he was in the doorway behind her. He dumped a bundle of kindling into the fire basket, and without a word returned to the taproom.

He pulled an old tobacco pouch from the shelves under the bar – it still smelt strongly of tobacco, and the leather was sound. Resigned by now, he gathered his share of the legacy of Diego Monteras into the pouch and shoved it deep into his pocket.

With daylight he would take a broom and sweep the floor, hunt under the tables and into the corners, looking for every last diamond and sapphire. They were his due, he thought – he had earned them, fair and square, even if the balladsinger ran and kept running.

And if he ran, Jim realized he could not find it in himself to blame him. Toby was the last survivor, but he would be called to account for *The Rose of Gloucester*, and he was far from innocent. If the church caught up with him – and it would – his crimes might be dragged into the blue light of day, right back to the time he was caught in carnal embraces with the handsome young verger, and then signed aboard the ship as a man of the cloth when in fact he would already have been dismissed from the priesthood. If Toby should be caught, he might easily pay for his sins at the end of a rope. If he had run tonight, it was out of healthy dread and self-preservation; and Jim could blame him for neither.

Sighing again, he stepped back through into the kitchen and knelt to set the kindling, refire the hearth. The sticks and shavings were dry, and caught in moments. He watched the new fire, blew on it, trimmed it tenderly, before he lifted down one bundle of the firewood that had been stacked along the mantel.

Edith was sorting out the pots and pans, trying to find canisters and jars that had been disordered – looking for tea, coffee, sugar. An assortment of odds and ends gathered on the table as Jim lit a taper from one lantern and used it to light five others.

The fire was stronger, and he held his hands to it. He had not realized how cold he was, and he tried to remember when he had eaten last. Edith had turned up plenty of food which had been kept well out of the water, but just then any bite would have tasted of ash and choked him. He pulled the fire irons closer, poked and moved the wood until the fire blazed up, and then hooked the big hob and pulled it into place. The cauldron clattered onto the black iron plate and he stood back, watching as Edith brimmed it from the tall brown jug.

"Coffee wi' a drop o' rum, an' a good supper," she decided, talking more to herself than to Jim. "Soon as Master Trelane gets back. There's rabbit fer the dogs, an' all."

Cold to the bone, just short of shivering, Jim held his hands to the fire and watched as she hunted for bread, cheese, onions, apples. The smell from the cellar was oppressive and the three dead bodies in the taproom weighed so heavily on his mind, he could not be still.

"I've work to do." He chafed his hands together. "Shout, when the coffee's done. I'm going to wedge the kitchen door tight shut. Just leave it be, Edith, all right?"

She gave him a shrewd look. "I's seen dead men afore. I were just a lass when I seen the bodies they pulled out of a shipwreck."

"But they weren't shot, blood from shoulders to hips, with holes in the middle of their heads where their faces ought to be," he said quietly.

"Mother o' God." She crossed herself. "Aye, then, I'll … I'll be glad to leave it to thee."

And Jim was wishing he could pass the duty to someone else as he hunted under the bar for a piece of sacking. Folded thickly enough, it almost stopped the door swinging. He had to lean all his weight on it to get it closed, and it might take a hammer and chisel to get it back out of there.

The Raven was in a sorry state, filthy, wet, bedchambers gutted, reeking and filled with death. The best he could do was fetch a bundle of old potato sacks from the coach house and cover the bodies where they were. He tugged Pledge straight in the chair before setting a sheet of sackcloth over him, and tried not to look at the mess that had been Willie Tuttle's face as he dropped the potato bag into place. Eli Hobbs's face was blue and bruised after the fight; his eyes were wide open, the whites gone blood red. His own knife was still jammed hilt-deep under the jaw; the blade was in his brain. Jim looked just once at him, and away, and swore lividly as a yard of sacking covered the body. It was a sight that would haunt his dreams, and though every muscle he possessed was shaking with fatigue, he did not relish the thought of sleep.

He straightened in the middle of the room, catching his breath and trying to remember what he was supposed to do next. He had to go somewhere … the vicarage, over in the village. That was it. And then to the doctor, and the garrison. He pressed his face into his hands, willing the images of violent death to let him be and hunting for the strength to do what he must.

"You *will* forget. It takes a little while, but the memories fade away and it'll be months or years before you think of them again."

Toby's voice.

Jim spun toward the sound, perfectly willing to believe he had gone mad and was imagining it, but Toby was on the doorstep, leaning on the jamb with Bess sitting at his feet. The spaniel's tail thumped as he looked down at her, and Jim struggled to find his own voice. "You came back."

"Of course I came back. You thought I'd run out on you? Because of this?" Toby lifted the old oat bin, which was heavy and rattling with the balance of Monteras's dangerous legacy. The pottery was blotched and smeared with Nathaniel Burke's blood. "You thought, once I had the prize in my hands – what, I'd run and not look back?" Toby weighed it between his hands, and held it out for Jim to take it from him.

"I wouldn't have blamed you." Jim just held it for a moment before he set it on the table among the lanterns. He looked Toby up and down, and shook his head over the man. "You look terrible."

"So do you." But Toby came to him, opened his arms, and Jim was glad to grab him in a hug that tested his ribs. "It's *over*," Toby whispered against Jim's hair. "They're all gone now."

"Burke –?"

"Made it a furlong, back towards Exmouth," Toby told him. "I didn't think he'd make it so far, but he was always strong. Stronger than the rest of us, which is how he seized command … last man on his feet, Jim, but not with wounds he could be healed of. I'm sure Eli put the knife into his lung. In the end it was blood he was trying to breathe, not air. I think he drowned in it."

"God." Jim shook himself hard. "Sailing with a mutineer crew, you saw all this before."

"Yes." Toby's arms tightened. "You *do* forget, Jim … you have to be alive to forget." He released Jim, far enough to look into his eyes. "I never meant for any of this to happen."

"I know." Jim touched his face, traced the planes and lines of it, felt the stubble that was almost too fair to show. "You came here looking for Charlie. You tried to search the house without me noticing – you'd have taken the prize back to The Cattlemarket, I imagine, and let the buggers fight it out there."

"Such was my thinking, at the time." Toby ducked his head. "I'd have come right back, though, when it was over. You know by now, they were always going to butcher each other, the only question was where and how. Here, or at the doxie house – in fact, rather here than there! There are too many girls to get in the way at Artie Polgreen's place, and get hurt. And always the chance the buffoon would get his own hands on the prize. If Artie once got one fingertip on it, you know he wouldn't let go." He was trembling as he added, "it's *ours*. I paid for my share of it in sweat and blood and pain. You paid for yours in courage and patience and common decency."

"And there's nobody else," Jim whispered. "You're sure? Nobody to come after them? After us?"

"No one." Toby was certain. The blue eyes closed, squeezed shut. "There were only eight of us at the last, and … it's me, heaven help me. Last man on his feet."

"With a whole skin," Jim added. "Scarred and marked, but whole."

"Marked," Toby said darkly as he and Jim began to relax little by little. "One day I'll drink enough of that laudanum of yours to get up my courage, and I'll let you put an iron in the fire to cancel the brand.

I'll carry Nathaniel's mark to the grave, but I can have it canceled, the way they cancel the brand on a horse when it goes to market."

"I don't want to hurt you," Jim said doubtfully.

"Enough laudanum in me, and you won't." Toby leaned over and pressed a kiss to Jim's forehead. "Do you want to drag the bodies out of here? We could shove them in the stable."

But Jim made negative noises. "I don't want to touch them again. Don't want to even *look* at them again. If you'll take Bess around to the backdoor and watch over Edith, I'll walk over to Budleigh. Fetch the vicar." He cast a bleak glance as the sack-shrouded bodies. "They ought to have something said over them, and I'm sure you don't want to be the one to do it. Not for these three." He lifted a brow at Toby. "Where's Burke?"

Toby made a small gesture into the west. "He collapsed in the bushes at the top of the beach, just off the path. He went down on his back, too weak to get up again, and ... drowned in blood." His voice was tight, odd.

"None of it was your fault," Jim said emphatically. "You only brought them into the same place at the same time, with the innocent well out of the way, and stood back to give them space. The rest was their doing."

"The innocent?" Toby set his palm flat on Jim's breast. "I dragged you into this. I never intended to. You could have been killed."

"It happened the way it had to," Jim said slowly. His hand closed over Toby's. "This was always going to happen, since the day Charlie Chegwidden decided to sell The Raven and my father decided to buy it. And as for me – I'm alive, there's not a bloody scratch anywhere on me, and I've a share in the kind of fortune Blackbeard would have killed for!" He picked up Toby's hand, brought it to his lips and pressed a kiss to the cold, leathery palm. "Better yet, you're here."

"Oh, I'm here," Toby said with a gentle humor which mocked only himself.

"And you'll still be here, won't you," Jim teased, "when I get back with Vicar Morley?" He groaned. "Richard Morley's got a couple of good horses – we'll ride back and then, while he's saying what needs to be said over the dead, I'll ride over to John Hardesty's place. I know he'll want to go on to the garrison with me. The pair of us'll make Captain Dixon, or his lieutenant, privy to the raw details. And *you*," he added, "need to put the prize out of sight till they've all cleared off, and then make yourself scarce. All they need to know is, you're a balladsinger working the taverns between Penzance and Dover. Don't make them ask questions, Toby, and they won't."

"They might talk to Artie Polgreen," Toby mused, "and he could tell them I knew every one of the dead men. He might think it was a great joke to tell Hardesty and Dixon I sailed with them, not just on the mutiny but through their pirate years."

"Damn." Jim knuckled his eyes and forced himself to think. "Then, it's best if you're not seen at all. I'll try not to even mention you ... if Polgreen does, I'll tell John and Dixon you left right after the fight and I don't know where you went." He paused to mull it over. "Mind you, Polgreen's got no call to speak of you, Toby. Anything he says will only connect him and his bawdy house to the likes of Burke and Hobbs – it's the kind of attention that'd be the last thing he'd want." He studied Toby closely, almost able to hear the cogs tick over as the man thought on it. "If I was the bold Captain Dixon, and I'd learned Burke's crew made a beeline for The Cattlemarket first," he went on with chill rationale, "I'd want to know *why*. To be sure, it was all about strong rum and loose women, which they won't get at a modest house like this one. But if Dixon got his curiosity up, he could connect The Raven with The Cattlemarket and *The Rose of Gloucester*. Polgreen might find himself standing in front of a magistrate, and the house he keeps is so disorderly, he'd do anything to avoid that. Yes?"

Toby was with him, thinking it through slowly, soberly, carefully. "Yes. Artie's shrewd. He's got a brain like a bag of monkeys. He's sure to know what'd be going through Dixon's head, and he won't want to answer sticky questions, least of all to a magistrate. It'd be a nightmare come true."

"A nightmare indeed," Jim agreed. "So ... the four of those buggers turned up on this coast, looking for their shipmate – our old Charlie. Would any of them have mentioned the prize to a soul, much less to Polgreen?"

"Not so much as a breath," Toby assured him. "One of the rules Nathaniel set down was utter secrecy, on pain of a very nasty death."

"Then all Polgreen knows is, a company of old shipmates got together in Exmouth and points east and took out ancient grievances on each other." Jim mulled it over, and nodded. "They got stinking drunk – the women at The Cattlemarket can attest to the revels! – old wounds were opened, old arguments were raised. It came to a fight, and they killed each other."

"A fight," Toby echoed. One brow arched. "A fight over what?"

"Honor?" Jim wondered.

"Not among that crew. But *this*, now..." Very deliberately, Toby pulled the cork stopper out of the bin. He burrowed his right hand in and pulled out four big, bright stones. Two emeralds, a ruby, a blue diamond. "Now, *this* they would fight over, and kill for."

Roger Dixon would believe the story in a moment. Jim licked his dry lips and cleared his throat. "Can you bring yourself to push those into Pledge's waistcoat, into the pocket?"

"I can." Toby rolled the stones in his palm. "If John Hardesty's as good a physician as you think he is, he'll want to know what killed Joe, so he'll take a look at the body ... doctors also search pockets, looking for an item to put a name on the dead, so the family can be charged for the burial. He'll find the stones. He and Dixon won't need to know any more."

Jim held his breath as the sackcloth twitched aside, and Toby's long fingers thrust carefully into the mess of blood, hunting for the pocket inside the brown waistcoat. His face twisted as he worked, but it was quickly done and without a word he strode outside, and around the corner to the rain barrel. He scooped out enough water to lave Pledge's blood off his hands.

"Good enough," Jim judged. "The undertaker's wagon's going to be here in the morning. Marcus Stiles should be done and gone by noon ... there's not much more to do than shove the bodies into boxes and load up. You know where to find Burke ... but I'd let Dixon's men find him for themselves. I'll tell them he staggered out of here, and I wasn't about to follow him!"

"All right." Toby laced his fingers at his own nape, massaging his neck there to ease clenched muscles. "The story would convince me. And the prize? Back in the loft?"

"Safest place for it," Jim judged. "If you'll see to it, Toby, then make sure Edith's all right and get yourself something to eat...."

"And you?" Toby lingered in the darkness, one hand on Jim's shoulder.

"The walk over to the vicarage will clear my head. I need the fresh air," Jim told him. "I've got a head full of ghosts and goblins! I need to chase them, Toby. A couple of hours, and I'll be back here with the vicar. You need to be *gone* when we get here."

Some thread of starlight found Toby's face as he smiled. "I know this coast well enough. There's a barn on the slope, not half a mile west of here."

"Belongs to Bert Dowrick, I know it. Don't let him catch you there

– he'll show you the wrong end of a pitchfork, for trying to steal a lamb." He gave Toby his hand. "Just keep one eye on this place ... when you see Stiles pull out, you'll be safe. Dixon won't trouble himself to come back, not when John's found the best reason anyone can think of for bloody murder right there in Joe Pledge's pocket!"

Toby's hand was cold. "I'll watch," he promised. "Will you come around to the kitchen for some coffee and food before you go?"

But Jim could not have forced down a bite. He took the brass dipper from the peg by the barrel and drank the clean, cold rainwater gratefully. "Let me blow the ghosts out of my head with some fresh air. I'll get something later."

"Be sure you do." Toby drew away, back to the door, where a little yellow light spilled out into the night. "I'll get the bin right back up to the loft. And Jim?"

Jim was moving, and turned back to him.

"Be careful," Toby told him. "The path's a mess with driftwood and debris. Mind that leg of yours."

"I will," Jim promised. "The moon's rising, anyway – it's bright enough to see well, once you get away from the lanterns."

"Do you want me to go for the vicar?" Toby offered. "Rest the leg."

"I'm fine," Jim chided. "The night air is just what I need. Better than medicine. Well, that and knowing you'll not be far away."

"Bert Dowrick's barn – dry enough for the night, for Bess and me." Toby managed a soft chuckle. "It won't be the first time we've slept in a barn."

"But it will be the *last*," Jim said with a certain wry humor. "You're a very rich man, Master Trelane."

"Then again, there's two of us, just as well-heeled." Toby's teeth were white in the moonlight as he smiled, and he did not have to force the expression. "Be on your way, then. Mind how you go, and I'll see you tomorrow."

Tomorrow, Jim thought as he picked his way east along a path that was littered with a random clutter of flotsam from the beck as well as the sea. Tomorrow would be a challenge, but with John Hardesty and Roger Dixon satisfied the dead could be laid to rest, and the living ...

The living could begin to *live*, Jim told himself, as they had never been able to before. A hundred paces from The Raven, the ghosts seemed to pare away from him. Two hundred, and he felt as it he were seared clean by the white moonlight and pure, unsullied sea wind. He could already glimpse the lights of the village ahead, and picked up his pace.

Chapter Eighteen

"You're damned lucky to be alive, Jim. You get between brigands and valuables they've set their sights on, and they'll shoot you in your tracks without a second thought. And *these* –" John Hardesty turned his hand to the morning sun to display the gems, which he has washed clean at the rain barrel. "To such cutthroats as murdered each other last night, these stones would be worth the price of twenty lives, not merely yours!"

"I know all this, John, believe me." Jim permitted himself a physical shudder. "I tried to stay well out of it. Certainly out of the firing line." He was leaning on the west wall of the tavern, which caught the sun in the afternoon and grew warm enough to grow beans as early as March.

With slitted eyes he watched the four dragoons who had marched over from Exmouth with Roger Dixon, and did not envy them the job. One of them, a young lad not yet twenty, had spewed up his breakfast already when he made the mistake of looking at Willie Tuttle's face. Dixon, much older, far more wise in the ways of battlefields, firearms and wounds, had barely glanced either at the body or the retching soldier, and continued to ask Jim probing, leading questions.

But the questions were easy to answer. In any case, Dixon was inclined to trust Jim, who had arrived at the garrison in the company of John Hardesty at ten o'clock the previous night, after fetching Vicar Morley to attend to the dead. Hardesty had found the gems almost at once. Pledge's was the first body he had examined in detail, since it was still sitting in the chair and was the easiest to reach.

Dixon was not unlike Hardesty. He was forty, with a growing paunch and hard, capable hands, but his body was muscular, tough, and he had a lifetime of experience with men of all kinds. He cut quite a fine figure in the red uniform coat; his wig was freshly powdered, well dressed, very smart, as befitted a gentleman. His accent had something of the Cornish and a little of the Welsh, and on Hardesty's recommendation, he treated Jim as an honest, intelligent man.

"You say didn't recognize the faces," he was musing as he read through a long list of the names of men wanted in this region for crimes Jim could not even begin to guess.

"Not one of them, Captain." Jim had answered this question before, and it was an honest response. "The most I can tell you is, the bastards came here looking for Chegwidden, who's been dead a long time."

"Whatever their business was," Hardesty speculated, "it was old. It might go back eight or ten years, Roger, long before you arrived in Exmouth, so I doubt you'd have known these scallywags, even if they delivered themselves to your doorstep!"

"Indeed." Dixon's brows rose, creasing his forehead. "What were those names again, Master Fairley?"

Careful, cautious, Jim had told him only that he had overheard the men calling each other by first names. "The one who carried the gems was Joe. The big one – the one your lads fetched back from the path, yonder, was Nathaniel. The one whose face is mostly missing was Willie. The one with the knife thrust from jaw to brains was Eli."

"Such common names," Dixon observed. "I've got at least ten Williams, Wills, Willies, Bills and Billies on this list. Six Nathaniels, Nathans and Nats, a good dozen assorted Josephs, Joes, Joeys, and two sharing the name of Elijah." In frustration, he folded up the list and thrust it back into his jacket.

"You'd do better to ask the local gentry," Hardesty suggested, "who lost those gems, and when. Mark my words, Roger, they were stolen. There's a lord or a lady in these parts who'll know them on sight, and might remember having handed them to a ruffian at pistol point."

"I'll give you long odds on that, old man." Dixon's fingers were busy with a snuffbox. "If the theft were eight or ten years ago, and you'd glimpsed a face in the dark, would *you* remember?"

"Still, worth asking around, surely." Hardesty frowned at the four bodies which had been laid out in a neat row by the path, under the sheets of sacking. They were waiting for the undertaker now. "Mind you, I'd get these bodies buried, Roger, and quickly." He eased his collar, where he was sweating lightly in the morning warmth. "They'll be rank in a day or two, and you *won't* want to be asking milady to try recognizing faces when they're bloated and green. Good God, it could be worth your commission, when milord heard how his delicate little wife fainted dead away at the stink of three-days-rotten corpses!"

"Oh, for heaven's sake, John, what kind of fool d'you take me for?" Dixon chided. "I'd have liked to know who they were, but the cause of all this is lying right there in the palm of your hand! Even if I learned who these men ever were ... even if they'd been the worst criminals on this coast ... what would I do with 'em? Show 'em to a magistrate, and hang 'em. They're already dead!"

Jim pushed away from the wall as the vicar appeared around the corner. Old Richard Morley had a mug in either hand, and proffered one to Jim with a wan little smile. "Mrs. Clitheroe insists, my dear boy. She says you've not eaten in a day."

It was true, and Jim was feeling light headed. He took the coffee with a murmur of thanks while Morley wandered along the path to talk to the undertaker. It was the second time in less than a week that Hardesty and Marcus Stiles had attended The Raven on the account of death here. Morley had buried the Spanish girl whom Barney Bellowes had struck. The vicar was getting along in years now, starting to feel his age. His back was arched even when he was standing straight, and he squinted to see anything past the pages of the big, black Bible which was battered, dog-eared after a lifetime's study. His eyes were fading to a misty, filmy gray, and Jim wondered how much he saw – how much he *cared* to see, when he was asked to pray over men like Nathaniel Burke and Eli Hobbs.

"You could talk to the doxies at The Cattlemarket," Jim said in a deliberately doubtful tone. "Willie and Eli were there for some time after Joe and Nathaniel arrived here. As I told you, the balladsinger and I took the boat along to bring them here." They had made the journey on Burke's orders, he had said, with a shilling in his pocket for his trouble if he complied, and the dead body of Edith Clitheroe at his feet if he refused.

"Doxies," Hardesty grumbled, "*never* remember their clients' names. If they did, they'd have no more clients. Eh, Roger?"

"Very true." Dixon's lip curled at the idea of going there. "I could send a squad over to fetch that corpulent idiot – what's his name? Polgreen – up to the garrison. He damn' well ought to know who was under his roof, drinking his rum, humping his women."

"But he wouldn't tell." Hardesty chuckled. "Artie Polgreen's certainly a buffoon, Roger, but he's not going to name his clients. The Cattlemarket would be so empty it echoed, like *that*." He snapped his fingers. "No, no, you'd be wasting your time there, old boy. It's yours to waste, of course, but … you said it yourself. Even if you learned this Nathaniel character was the villain who put a pistol ball in Lord Cranmer's belly last year, you could only hang him for it. And it's a bit late for that, what?"

"Entirely too late." Dixon held out the little enameled box. "Snuff?"

"Thank you, I will." Hardesty helped himself.

"And this balladsinger," Dixon mused. "He was here for a few days, you said?"

"He was stuck here when we flooded." Jim jerked a thumb over his shoulder, in the direction of the beck. "He was handy, battening the place down, and he helped me row over to The Cattlemarket – which probably saved Edith's life." He slapped his leg. "You know I'm lame. I'm ashamed to confess, I needed the help. I can't row a boat that size on my own. If the balladsinger hadn't been here, I've a dreadful intuition Nathaniel would have made good his threat, and shot the old woman. He assumed she was my grandmother."

"Then, it's just lucky for you the balladsinger was here," Dixon decided. "And he didn't know the bastards, I suppose?"

Jim answered with a shallow shrug. "They treated him like a stranger, and he never mentioned knowing them from anywhere. If he'd seen them before, it would surely have been in taverns like this one. He's very good – sang for his supper, as they say, on a couple of nights, and I did grand business in the middle of the week. I'll tell you this, Captain. If he comes back, I'll be happy to have him stay as long as the rummies who drink here want to listen to him." He cocked his head at Dixon. "I'm afraid he left as soon as Eli and Willie marched into The Raven, and if it hadn't been for this leg of mine, I swear to God, I'd have gone with him. In fact, I told him to get out while he could. At the time, we wondered if he might be able to get through to the garrison and bring back a squad. But the way was still flooded, as you know. He could only have gone east … he could be in Branscombe by now. The truth is, I only stayed at The Raven myself because of this bloody damned leg. If I'd been one whit less lame, you wouldn't have seen hide or hair of me till next week!" Jim mocked himself with a crooked, humorless grin. "If the balladsinger comes back this way, do you want him to come up to the garrison? I'd be glad to tell him."

For a moment Dixon considered it, and then the white-wigged

head shook. "No need, Master Fairley. As I've said already, I could only hang the buggers, no matter who they were, what they'd done, and they've saved me the hangman's wages. If your balladsinger returns one day ... give him my compliments. It was charitable of him to lend a hand when he could, and wise of him to get out when he did. I don't blame him – and wouldn't have blamed you, if you'd been five miles away when the shooting started."

"Thank you, Captain." Jim took a deep breath and began to relax.

"Well, John, I'll leave the rest to you," Dixon decided. "Give the gems to me – I'll see if I can find out where they were stolen, of course, and from whom. After that, death certificates and the parish register are your affair, and Vicar Morley's – and you're welcome to them!" He took the stones, pocketed them and frowned along at the vicar and undertaker, who were talking in whispers by the rank of bodies. "Get the dead properly underground before they start to reek, I've no more need of them."

With that, he accorded Jim a polite half bow and turned away to his men. Jim's shoulders leaned back against the sun-warm plaster of the west wall, and he closed his eyes for a moment in relief.

"Not concerned, were you Jim?" Hardesty asked softly. "Surely you've done nothing to be held accountable for."

"No, but ..." Jim gestured after Dixon. "The law, the dragoons. I've not dealt with them often enough to be comfortable with them."

"Oh, Roger's a decent chap," Hardesty said dismissively. "Any man who does right by his horses and his footmen can be trusted to keep the peace and see the common folk are fairly treated."

"Common folk?" Jim echoed, and indulged himself in a wry chuckle.

"Odd sods like you and me, and old Edith and this balladsinger of yours." Hardesty chuckled. "In fact, I've heard about him – he has the best new songs and stories, so I was told as far away as Exmouth. He tells one particular tale about a hunt for pirate treasure. Just the kind of story I'd like to hear. Would he tell it again?"

Jim disguised a smile behind his mug. "I imagine he'd be glad to tell it, so long as he hears a healthy rattle of coins on the floor. Seriously, John, he had my usual old boozers wrapped around his little finger."

"Then, I hope he wanders back this way." Hardesty dropped a hand on Jim's shoulder. "Let me write up the death notes, so I can let Master Stiles take the bodies. And if you could manage it, find Vicar Morley a bite of breakfast. He's a sweet old duffer, but nowhere near as strong as he thinks he is. He's been here all night?"

"Most of it, bless him." Jim finished the coffee in one swig. "In fact, I'm going to set the best table we can, given the bloody mess we've got in the kitchen. Anybody with half an appetite can sit down and eat his fill. You're invited, John. I'll even open something ..." He gave Hardesty a wink. "Something very French, very rare, and very under the counter,' at least till His Majesty's man has cleared off back to the garrison."

Hardesty slapped him on the back. "Smuggled French brandy? Well now, I don't believe Roger Dixon would refuse a drop. He's quite partial now and then so long as it's, shall we say, *circumspect*."

But the dragoons were already pulling out, and Dixon was up on his tall, cream mare. He paused only to give Hardesty a mock salute with his crop before he led the squad away, west up the sodden, muddy path toward Exmouth. They would be back at the garrison in an hour or so, even at Dixon's leisurely pace. Jim angled a glance at the sun, over the tavern's roof. Morning was old; noon was not so far away, and Toby would soon be getting hungry.

Instinct told Jim he was close. He rounded up the old vicar with a smile and the offer of a sit-down meal, and as he stepped into the house he smelt apple pie, pork pie, roasting potatoes and boiling cabbage.

A glance into the kitchen showed him Edith Clitheroe, dozing in the big leather chair as she waited for the food to finish, with Boxer at her feet and the black cat in her lap. The floor was mopped and half dry by now. The stink of mold and mildew was dissipating with the draft from open doors and windows – and the bucketful of mortar Jim had troweled into the gaps around the trapdoor while Vicar Morley opened his Bible over the dead.

He could chisel the mortar out soon enough, when a gang of laborers came in to bail out the cellar and set the braziers to dry it out, but a voice in the back of his mind asked him, did he want to bother?

For some time he stood in the kitchen doorway, frowning at the big, wet places on the taproom floor where he had scrubbed up the blood. Some of it defied the brush. If the flagstones had been any less than mahogany dark, they would be shadowed with stains. Upstairs, not a bedchamber was habitable. The Raven would be simply a drinking place until he could get new mattresses and linen – yet the story would race along the coast, and customers would come in from far afield to hear it from his own lips.

The thought reminded him of Toby. When the pies came off the wide iron baking hobs he cut a piece of each, swiped the best potato, a ladle full of cabbage, a knob of salt butter, and set aside a plate. Hardesty and Morley were at the long table under the window, where the backgammon tokens often rattled on a winter's evening, and Jim surveyed the taproom with mixed feelings.

He could still see Charlie Chegwidden, sitting at that very window, watching the sea and the path, waiting – as Jim knew now – to see Burke or Hobbs or any of them come sneaking back to The Raven years early. Charlie had fully expected them to try to swindle each other, and only fear had kept that crew honest.

If he narrowed his eyes, he could even glimpse his father standing behind the bar, polishing the best pewter tankards. He smiled at the memory, breathed a sigh and fetched himself back to the present with an act of willpower.

The Raven was rich with memories … filled, he supposed, with ghosts. It had been a sanctuary for a young man as lame as himself, not to mention a healthy young male with a taste for 'the other,' as Toby called it. A sailors' tavern had been magnificently convenient, until Toby Trelane walked up the path, just days ahead of Burke's bastard company. At last, Jim had no need to watch out for handsome sailors who shared his fancies and would respond to a raised brow, a wink, a discreet beckoning into the shadows.

But Fred Bailey's keen old eyes had seen the truth. Lately, the Raven had become as much a prison as it had ever been a haven. The stubborn echo of Fred's voice was in Jim's ears even now, as he ate a slice of pie and listened to Hardesty and Morley talking over parish business. *Your trouble is, you never get out. You never do … stuff. You never see nothin'. You never make the acquaintance of mates and enemies.*

He was right, but knowing it had never made it possible for Jim to 'do stuff,' in the company of those mates and enemies. And now? In the loft was the old oat bin from the kitchen, heavy with the entire treasure of Diego Monteras and the Indian prince who was the love of his life. For Jim Fairley, nothing would ever be the same.

A little before noon, Hardesty permitted himself a comfortable belch and pushed his chair back from the table. "Well, Richard, it's been damn' fine talking to you again, man to man, outside of chapel," he told Morley, "and I'm honestly sorry I have to be on my way. I've got a dozen bally patients who'll be looking for me in half an hour, and it'd behoove me to be on time!" He clasped the vicar's hand, and looked up over the silver head at Jim. "Will I see you for a game of whist and a snifter on Sunday, Jim?"

"Perhaps. If I can be there, I will ... and if I can't, I'll send a lad with a message," Jim told him. "Do you need anything else from me?"

"Regarding the dead, you mean?" Vicar Morley twisted in his chair and peered up at Jim with the faded eyes. "No, no. You've done more than enough, Master Fairley – and it was most decent of you to fetch me to whisper a prayer or two over the likes of them. Lord knows, we're all bound for Judgment one way and another, but I'd like to think those rogues will burn a *lot* longer in Hades than you or I can expect to!" He sighed heavily. "They'll have pine boxes and paupers' graves, and we've no real names ... still, we'll do the best we can, as we did for the poor little Spanish girl."

"Then, it's over," Jim breathed.

"Over and done," Hardesty affirmed. "You heard Roger Dixon. You can't hang a dead man, no matter what he was guilty of. Well, I suppose you *can*, but he's not going to kick very much for your amusement at the end of the rope!"

The humor was black, and Jim gave him a cynical smile. "Thank you, John. I'll be in touch." Hardesty had stepped out when Vicar Morley graced Jim with a benevolent smile. "Take care on the ride home," Jim told the old man. "I'll have the horse I borrowed back in his own stable by evening, my word on it."

"In your own time, my boy." Then Morley shook a long finger at him, mock stern. "I expect to see you in church on Sunday morning, now ... you've a good few prayers of thanks to say. You're alive, against the odds. Call me partial if you will, but I do believe the Almighty was vigilant, Master Fairley, or it'd be *you* being laid to rest tomorrow, right beside your father."

"Amen to that," Jim said softly. "Sunday morning. I'll be there."

With the visitors gone, The Raven was very quiet. Mrs. Clitheroe was singing tunelessly to herself in the kitchen; Boxer sat on the doorstep in the sun while pigeons scratched about in the thatch above; the tomcat had found a patch of warm floor and was rolling luxuriously on it. Everything was so absurdly normal, Jim found himself almost on edge as if he were waiting for *something*, without knowing what it was.

He busied himself, sweeping, bundling wreckage to be taken out and burned, making a list of what was needed to set the tavern to rights, but all the time he was listening. He heard footsteps from the path, and was at the door as the tall, slender figure and the black dog ambled into view.

"All done here?" Toby asked hopefully. By habit his hands were buried in his pockets. His eyes were shadowed, as if he had not slept well, but no lines of dread were etched into his face today. The sea wind played in the long fair hair, tossing it into his eyes, and he raked it back.

"All done," Jim affirmed. "Captain Dixon's happy. The undertaker has carted off the dead, Vicar Morley's putting them in the ground tomorrow. John found the gems on Pledge, as we knew he would. He and Dixon are quite convinced of the motivation for bloodletting ... are you hungry?"

"Starving," Toby confessed. "I'm smelling food."

"I saved you some. Come and eat."

The door closed behind him, and Toby had hung up his coat when Jim seized him bodily, hugged him hard enough to knock the breath out of him, and manhandled him out of sight of the kitchen so they could kiss without Mrs. Clitheroe catching a glimpse of them.

Toby groaned, face buried in the curve of Jim's shoulder. "Eight *years*, I've lived with a bloody cold-sweated fear of these last days, yet how could I not come here? The prize was in the offing and I earned my share. Perhaps I should have stayed away, but ..." He shook himself. "Times, I thought Joe or Eli would kill me, just for the sheer spite of doing it, or maybe even for the fun. The truth is, I used Nathaniel almost as much as he used me."

"Then it was an even trade," Jim judged. "Oh, let it be, Toby. Dame Fortune dealt the hand and they played it out – we all did. For some reason she dealt me into the game, though I never knew it at the time. Damnit – any of those bastards could have walked up to my door, any day of the last six years, and put a pistol to my head. And I wouldn't have known what they were talking about!"

"Fear of Nathaniel, and of each other, kept them more honest than a bench full of judges," Toby said quietly.

"It did." Jim was conscious of the sweat prickling his ribs and scalp as the possibilities began to dawn on him fully. He shook the shadows off with an effort. "The only thing we have to think about now is where we go from here. Sit down, I'll bring your food. Will you have an ale, or a rum?"

"How about both?" Toby pulled a chair up to the table where Hardesty and Morley had sat.

The plate set down before him with a clatter, and Jim fetched a pair of bowls for Bess. Stewed rabbit in one of them, a half pint of brown ale in the other, which she seemed to relish as much as the meat. Toby was eating as he hooked a chair with his foot and drew it closer, and for a time Jim was content to just watch the man until Toby said,

"It's all a question of what you *want* to do now, Jim. You can have anything you care for – we both can."

"What I want?" Jim was only a little overwhelmed. "What I really want is to see some of the world. All the places you've seen and I've only dreamed about after someone like yourself told stories. Places that are just flyspecks on a map to the likes of me."

"Then, we'll buy a ship and outfit it, crew it," Toby suggested. "A merchantman, so she can pay her way with cargo while we see the world."

"And you'll show me Port Royal and Kingston, and the ports of Spain and France." Jim could scarcely believe he was saying these things.

"If that's where you want to go." Satisfied for the moment, Toby sat back and mopped his lips. "First, let me visit a disreputable old dealer I know in Santander. He can turn a handful of gems into gold coin … you can't actually *spend* jewels, you know! If you try, and you don't have the pedigree of a duke or an earl to account for how you came by them, people soon assume you're a thief." He took a long swig of ale. "But there's a clever old merchant with a dark little counting house a few streets back from the docks in Santander. He'll give us half of what the gems are actually worth –"

"Half?" Jim protested.

"And he'll consider himself very clever for cheating us on the little handful of stones," Toby said wryly. "But *half* of their value is still an outrageous fortune, and then all we need is a story people will believe, for where the money came from." His eyes danced as he looked at Jim over the rim of his cup. "I do believe I have a grand uncle in Scotland who's about to pass away and leave me some money … and it seems you bought a treasure map from an old rummy who was so down on his luck, he sold it to you for the price of enough grog to drink himself to death in Portsmouth."

"And we," Jim said slowly, "take this ship of ours and pretend to go hunting for treasure."

Toby spread his hands. "We do, if you want to return to England with a great chest of jewels and a solid explanation for where they came from. It's almost the truth, anyway. That's how the treasure of Diego Monteras was found in the first place. No one ever need know it was found by Nathaniel Burke's crew and lay *here*, unknown for eight years, walled up in your cellar. Perhaps you and I might say we found it right where Hugo and Fernando left it … even if we have to take it back there and find it all over again." He lifted his cup in toast. "Then, if you want to come home, there's no mystery about where the largesse came from. You won't have to hear, and contest, the word 'thief' when you take a ruby or an emerald the size of a pigeon's egg to a dealer in London or Manchester."

"We'll just be rich men," Jim whispered, and groaned, a sound of sheer pleasure. "You and me, Toby. Gentlemen explorers with the whole world to discover."

"Yes." Toby leaned over the table and caught Jim's hand. "But you'll find, Jim, nothing in the world is sweeter than coming home."

"If you've someone to come home to," Jim allowed.

"Or with." Toby took a quick look around to be sure of their privacy, and touched a kiss to Jim's knuckles. "Come with me to Spain. You'll like Santander. It's a port, and like any port it's the crossroads of the very world you're so hungry to explore. You'll see things, hear things, you can't even imagine."

"I don't speak a word of Spanish," Jim protested.

"But I do." Toby was smug. "I learned to speak it well. Where do you think I've been for so long, the law in this country forgot I ever existed! Give it a few weeks, till the excitement dies down. Let's get The Raven back into shape, then we'll take the coach to Plymouth and the first ship we can get to Santander. I'll introduce you to one of life's most charming old rascals, who'll make you laugh, make you like him, even while he's robbing you blind … and you won't care a fig about being robbed."

"And the prize?" Jim wondered. "While we're gone?"

"Right back in the cellar wall," Toby said darkly, "where it was hidden every day you lived here and never suspected a thing. It can stay there while we buy a ship, outfit an expedition. Yes?"

"All right." Jim sat back and rubbed his face, wondering if he might be dreaming and at any moment he would wake and find himself alone, whiling away his days, his years, in the sanctuary that had become a prison. He managed a shaky chuckle. "So, I'm about to buy a treasure map from an old rummy, am I?"

"You could do much worse." Toby echoed his humor.

"And until all this comes to pass we're here at The Raven, putting right the damage." Jim wiped the smile off his face. "The locals already know you as a balladsinger. Even Doctor John's heard of you, and *one* story in particular! You know you'll be singing for your supper, to keep them happy and stop tongues wagging."

"I know enough songs to amuse them for months," Toby said easily. "Supper's not the half of it. There's a few sweet hours to be cherished between supper and breakfast, and no one the wiser if only we're careful."

And a great deal to be explored, discovered, Jim thought, before they took on the world outside, seized it, shook it, made it give them what they wanted. He reached over for the rum bottle and topped off Toby's mug. "To the future," he toasted, holding his cup for Toby to touch his own to it. "To Diego Monteras and Fernando, wherever they are."

"To Jim Fairley and Toby Trelane," Toby added, "wherever they may be in a year, and ten years, or twenty."

"Aye," Jim said readily, "I do believe I'll drink to that."

FORTUNES OF WAR
Mel Keegan

In the spring of 1588 two young men fell in love: an Irish mercenary serving the Spanish ambassador in London, and the son of an English earl. Then Dermot Channon must leave England when the embassy is expelled just prior to the onset of war, and Robin despairs of ever seeing him again. Seven years pass, and when Robin's brother is kidnapped for ransom in Panama in the years following the war between England and Spain, Robin sets sail with a fleet commanded by Francis Drake, hoping to bring home his brother. But soon enough the ship on which Robin is traveling is sunk by privateers — pirates led by none other than Dermot Channon. Reunited by a cruel twist of fate, the two men embark with passion on a series of swashbuckling adventures around the Spanish Main.

Novel length: 150,000 words
Rated: R (18+; sex, violence, language)
ISBN-13: 978-0-9750884-9-4
Publication date: (DreamCraft reissue) August 2005
Publisher: DreamCraft
Price: $9.99 – ebook (also avail. in paper)
Cover: Jade

DANGEROUS MOONLIGHT
Mel Keegan

In the style and spirit of HOME FROM THE SEAS comes this rollicking gay historical set in 1727 ... in the world of highwaymen, of duels fought over honor, fortunes won and lost at the gaming tables, and romance that fairly sizzles Harry Trevellion was well bred and would have been a gentleman if his father's estate had not been lost ... and Nicholas Grey is the favorite son of a wealthy man, who was born 'on the wrong side of the blanket' quite by chance! Nick's brother, Paul, is a wastrel, a scoundrel who is only waiting for their frail old father to pass away. He'll ruin the family ... and he scorns his illegitimate half-brother, though Nicholas is doing difficult, dangerous work for their father.

Nick's job is to courier jewelry safely between manufacturer and client ... and it's only a matter of time before he runs into the irresistible rogue, Harry Trevellion. The two share a stormy relationship until the day Paul Rosewarne has been waiting for arrives: the master of Rosewarne Hall passes on ... and the quirks of an old man's last will and testament put Nicholas behind bars.

It's a world of swords, pistol duels, midnight chases, deceit and sheer sensuality, in a time when fortunes could still be made ... and lost. If you loved Mel's other historicals, including FORTUNES OF WAR and THE DECEIVERS, don't miss this one!

Novel length: 205,000 words
Rated: R (18+; sex, violence, language)
ISBN-13: 978-0-9758080-5-4
Publication date: July 2006
Publisher: DreamCraft
Price: $9.99 – ebook (also avail. in paper)
Cover: Jade

THE DECEIVERS
Mel Keegan

Mel Keegan is back at sea in the days of tall ships and high adventure ...

It's an age when sail and steam are technologies in collision, and the thousand-year tradition of the tall ships is coming to an end. Men like Bill Ryan and Jim Hale are caught in the jaws of change, in a world where survival depends on raw courage, strength and a willingness to take terrible risks

1862, on the east coast of England: the railway is the death knell of the coastal shipping trade, and many small lines like Eastcoast Packet won't survive. Jim Hale is about to inherit Eastcoast and the schooner Spindrift ... if he and Captain Bill Ryan can first survive the explosive violence of the North Sea storms, and the vicious schemes of the shipwrecker, Nathan Kerr. Always a dangerous man, Kerr has a score to settle with Jim – and with Ryan, who has allied himself to Eastcoast. For men who have the courage to be lovers in this time, and this place, the struggle is dire, the rewards astonishing.

Meticulously researched, fabulously detailed, THE DECEIVERS will be treasured by any reader who loved HOME FROM THE SEA and DANGEROUS MOONLIGHT.

Novel length: 125,000 words
Rated: R (18+; sex, violence, language)
ISBN-13: 0-9750884-2-4
Publication date: August 2003
Publisher: DreamCraft
Price: $9.99 – ebook (also avail. in paper)
Cover: Jade

Printed in Great Britain
by Amazon

62524403R00129